Chasin' that Carrot

Chasin' that Carrot

Avril Dalziel Saunders

PNEUMA SPRINGS PUBLISHING UK

First Published 2008
Published by Pneuma Springs Publishing

Chasin' That Carrot

ISBN: 978-1-905809-39-4

This is a work of fiction. All characters portrayed in this book and any resemblances to real people, living or dead, are purely coincidental.

Cover design, editing and typesetting by:
Pneuma Springs Publishing

A Subsidiary of Pneuma Springs Ltd.
7 Groveherst Road, Dartford Kent, DA1 5JD.
E: admin@pneumasprings.co.uk
W: www.pneumasprings.co.uk

A catalogue record for this book is available from the British Library.

I dedicate this book to my grandchildren

If everything in life went according to plan then there would be no need to frown.

Always believe in yourself

One

It was the evening of Saturday 11th October 1969, Linda, closed her eyes and took a deep breath; she felt secure as her new husband James stood behind her and wrapped his strong arms round her. He took the big knife, placed it in her right hand and firmly wrapped his hand over hers then to loud claps and cheers from family and guests, they cut the top tier of their wedding cake. She was brimming over with happiness as she turned her head to look up at James; she thought how tall and handsome he looked with his dark wavy hair and wide smile. It was strange to think that she was no longer a MacGregor but she was proud to be the wife of James Alexander.

The small wedding celebration at her parents', Douglas and Margie MacGregor's house, was going well and being enjoyed by all. Much to the relief of all concerned, James' psycho sister, Iris, didn't attend, which meant that the atmosphere was normal and relaxed. The drinks were flowing; there was lots of laughter with no worry of it turning into a typical 'Iris style' drunken punch-up.

Around ten o'clock, James and Linda decided to make their excuses to leave the party and drive over to their new marital love nest. They ran up the lane towards their wee maroon Ford Anglia with everyone in hot pursuit and were relieved to see that their guests hadn't decorated it with toilet rolls or painted the windows with slogans. They jumped into the car quickly. Linda rolled down her window to shout goodbye to her guests and before anyone had second thoughts or had the chance to add anything to the car, James started up the engine. As they were about to pull away, Linda heard the cry of 'Linda, Linda' being called out over all the shrieks of laughter, she looked through all the faces and could see her mum, Margie, standing looking very alone and emotional in the crowd. With all the excitement Linda had forgot one very important thing, she shouted to James to stop, jumped out of the car and ran through everyone to her mum, giving her a big kiss on the cheek and holding her very tight and warmly. She knew that her mum was worried about her being pregnant and going to live in a pokey wee room and kitchen in Parkhead with an outside toilet in the close. She tried to put her mum at ease, assuring her that it wouldn't be for long and she would be ok. Linda was concerned about Margie now being on her own with Douglas. Although she knew that her mum and dad loved each other dearly, they went everywhere together and couldn't live without each other, Margie had to contend with her husband's black moods, when he drank to obliterate the scars of war embedded at the back of his mind, turning him from a loving, considerate husband into a madman. She told her mother that she would always be there for her and would see her during the week and every weekend. Margie smiled, trying to look brave as James pulled the car away taking her beloved daughter off to a new married life. The noise was deafening, James looked dismayed, 'Oh no!' he said downheartedly to Linda, 'What a time for the car to go wrong!' He jumped out to roars of laughter, "Ye didn't think that ye were gonnie get away that easy, did ye?' shouted Linda's brother Douglas junior. James laughed as he undid all the cans that had been tied and hidden under the back of the car, he left the 'Just Married' sign on the back bumper, then he got back in to the car again to the stifled giggles of their guests and started the engine up. This time there was a clanging noise, he got out once more, by this time everyone was cheering and laughing hysterically. 'Ok', said James, 'I give in, what have you done to my car Alan?' James' lifelong friend and best man Alan was a car mechanic and James knew that this was something that he was responsible for. He searched around looking in the engine and under the car before Alan finally gave in and removed the hubcaps from the wheels to reveal a handful of big copper pennies in each one. James said to him jokingly, 'You realise Alan that your card is stamped, one day I'll get my own back on you, I don't care how long I have to wait!' He started up the engine for a third time and breathed a sigh of relief as it purred over nicely and pulled away quietly. They stuck their hands out of the windows waving to loud cheers from their family and guests and shouts of 'Gaun Yersel',

'Good Luck' and 'Hard Up'.

Within half an hour they were outside their temporary new abode. James worked for his cousin who owned a joinery business in Maryhill. One of their clients, a well off factor who managed property rentals, had promised James a large two room, kitchen with kitchenette and bathroom to rent in the Dennistoun area but it wouldn't be available until nearer Christmas so meantime they would have to make do in this tiny cramped room and kitchen. It was on a main road but they had no problem parking at that time of night. They got out of their car and entered the close. James put the key into the lock then he turned to Linda and said, 'Hang on we mustn't forget tradition.' He scooped Linda up into his arms, she screamed and giggled as he carried her over the threshold, then dropping her down gently he kissed her passionately drowning out her laughter. 'Welcome home Mrs. Alexander, I love you so much, I'm the happiest man on earth,' said James holding her tight in his muscular arms. Linda felt warm and secure, she smiled up at her new husband replying, 'and I love you too James Alexander, you have made me the happiest woman on earth today!'

The next morning Linda woke up with James kissing her on the forehead and singing 'Good morning Starshine'. As she rubbed her eyes she heard loud voices, she sat bolt upright, 'Who's in our house?' she asked James frantically. 'What are you on about Linda?' he replied. 'There're people talking in our kitchen. James listened and he could indeed hear voices coming from the direction of their kitchen. He got out of bed and crept on tip toes towards the bedroom door leading into the kitchen, he peered round the door, took a couple of steps towards the kitchen then burst out laughing, Linda was sitting up in bed with the covers round her, 'What is it James, what's so funny?' she asked him.

'Well Linda, while we live here this is something that you're going to have to get used to.' he told his new wife. 'I don't understand, what do you mean,' she said. James replied. 'The voices you can hear is that of two wives out in the street gossiping and blethering, they are right outside our kitchen window!'

'Oh no!' groaned Linda, 'we can hear every word; they might as well be in the room with us! Let's hope that it won't be too long before we can move into our flat in Dennistoun, I don't think I could live with that outside my window!'

They got washed, dressed and decided to be lazy and stay at

home to enjoy their first day of married life together after the hectic and tiring schedule of their wedding the day before. James promised to take Linda to Edinburgh the following day; she hadn't been there for years and was looking forward to visiting Princes Street and the castle.

It was just after 8am on Monday morning and there was a loud Rat-A-Tat-Tat at their door. 'Who on earth could that be at this time of the morning, we don't know anyone in this neighbourhood?' said Linda. James pulled on his jeans and slowly opened the door to be greeted by a very tall, well built cheery policeman. 'Is this the home of the newly weds?' he asked, laughing heartily. 'Aye, said James, 'what's' wrong?' The policeman replied, 'Well son, what's wrong is that your car is parked outside the close' James answered, 'I know, has something happened to it?' he said in a panic, to which the policeman replied, 'No but if you don't move it now, you'll get a hefty fine son, this is a main road and there's no parking between 8am and 6pm'. James was embarrassed and stammered 'Oh I'm sorry officer, I didn't realise, we've just moved into the area, I'll move it right away.' 'That's alright son, the shopkeeper next door told me that you had just got married and moved in on Saturday so I will allow for the fact that you are on your honeymoon and have other things on your mind, but move it soon and I promise I won't disturb you again!' he told James with a cheeky grin. James pulled on his shirt and shoes and went outside. As he climbed into his car, he could feel eyes on him; he drove round the corner and parked in a quiet side street. The grocer was standing at the door of his shop blethering to a couple of his women customers and as James passed them, the grocer said, 'That wiz a close wan son, luckily we're a' nosey aboot here and ah wiz able tae tell the polis that it wiz your motor and where you lived, ah also thoot that ah wid mention you wir jist merrit. Big Hamish is no' bad fur a polisman, he's goat a hert somewhere, still ye'll know no' tae dae that again, he'll no gie ye a second chance!' James nodded and thanked him before turning quickly into his close, cringing with embarrassment at the thought that they were the talk of the neighbourhood after just one day!

Linda popped into the grocer's shop next door to get some milk and food for their picnic in Edinburgh. The grocer introduced himself as Tony; he was a nice friendly man. He said to Linda, 'Huv ye goet a fridge at hame hen?' when she told him 'No'. Tony replied, 'Well' ah'll tell ye whit ah'll dae fur ye hen. As ye live next door, if ye want, ah'll pit a boattle o' milk in the fridge fur ye every day. It's delivered tae me first thing in the moarnin' and it'll be nice 'n' cool fur ye when ye pick it up. Linda thanked him and said they would really appreciate that. She bought bread, butter and some tomatoes to make sandwiches to take on their trip with them, they didn't have much money left after the wedding and apart from the fact that they couldn't afford much else, Linda had lost her appetite because of her pregnancy and this along with Golden Delicious apples was one of the few things that she could eat and enjoy.

It was a lovely sunny and warm day, Linda and James drove along Princes Street with the car windows down, they found a parking place at the foot of the castle then proceeded to climb up the Royal Mile to the castle forecourt. They had a walk round the castle grounds, then after a while they sat on the wee wall at the top overlooking Princes Street Gardens. It was a beautiful sight to look down at the city from so high up and all the way over to Arthur's Seat. They were tired, hungry and thirsty by this time and munched into their tomato sandwiches, washing it down with tea from their flask. 'Ah James,' said Linda, 'wouldn't it be lovely if we had the money to do this sort of thing all the time and not have to work'. James smiled and answered, 'One Day Linda, One day!'

The next evening James dropped Linda off at her mum's house in Knightswood so that she could have a bath. With no bath at their flat, they could only wash themselves down. This was one luxury that Linda really missed. James went on up to his mother's in Drumchapel to have a bath. Then he stayed a while and had dinner with her. Linda also ate at her parent's house. James picked her up again about 10pm and as the two of them headed out east to Parkhead, back to their wee room and kitchen, James said, 'How do you fancy we go a wee trip to the Border' tomorrow?' 'THE BORDER!' Linda exclaimed in excitement. 'Aye, well, Carlisle' answered James. 'I've never been to ENGLAND, do you think our wee car will make it there?' gushed Linda. 'It's not that far' said James, 'only about 90 miles!' Linda was finding it hard to control her excitement '90 MILES!' that's a long, long way!' she blurted out. 'It's not that far, not even a couple of hours down the A74!' laughed James, 'anyway it's our honeymoon, we should be going to far-away places.' The furthest Linda had ever been was the Isle of Man with James, before that she had only ever been to the Ayrshire coast and Rothesay on the West of Scotland or Edinburgh and Fife on the East of Scotland. To go to England, even though it was just over the border into Carlisle was a dream come true for her. That night she could hardly sleep with excitement. Linda really enjoyed her day in England, she felt like she was a million miles away; they walked round the town, bought some fish and chips and ate it out of the newspaper. 'Ah James, I'm having such a wonderful honeymoon, thanks for taking me to Edinburgh and bringing me to England, what more could a girl ask for?' she said admiringly to James.

They got home from Carlisle just after 10pm that night. As they climbed wearily into bed James said, 'Right Mrs. Alexander, where to tomorrow?' 'Oh we're really living it up, aren't we?' answered Linda. 'Not too far this time, the petrol is running away with our money, what about a wee drive round Loch Lomond to Balmaha? Suggested James, 'Oh, that'll be lovely, for old time's sake' replied Linda as she remembered the many times that they had visited Balmaha when they were courting and had sat at the pier watching the amazing hills and scenery around the Loch.

On Friday Linda caught up with the washing and housework while James sorted out and sharpened his tools ready for going back to work on Monday. Linda's monthly paycheck was due in the bank so in the afternoon they went shopping in the town for some groceries for the weekend and the following week.

It was Saturday and they visited James' mother Molly in the afternoon, she said that she would come over to see them in their wee flat on Thursday evening. Linda invited her to join them for their evening meal after work at 6.30pm. On Saturday night they spent the evening with Linda's parents Margie and Douglas. Linda asked them to join her and James for Sunday lunch the next day; they would be the first guests to have a proper sit-down meal in their wee room and kitchen. That evening when they got home, she soaked the peas, barley and lentils for the Scotch broth and the 'steepy peas' that she was going to make the next day for lunch.

Linda got up bright and early on Sunday morning and boiled the silverside to prepare her stock, it should really have been done the night before but her parents weren't arriving until 4pm. She chopped up all the vegetables and peeled the potatoes. When the meat was cooked, she removed it from the pot and let the stock cool for a couple of hours to allow the fat to float to the top and be scooped off. By the time her parents arrived she had set the table with her new dinner set that one of James' aunts had given them as a wedding present. 'Oh you've done your table lovely enthused Margie; I love your table cloth!' 'That's the one Aunt Betty gave us for an engagement present.' answered Linda. She served the soup up first with bread rolls from the shop next door, 'Well Linda, that soup was delicious, would I be too cheeky to ask for another bowlful?' Douglas asked his daughter 'Of course no problem,' answered Linda, feeling very proud of herself, 'Do you want some more too mum?' she asked Margie. 'Oh no, it was really tasty and I'm very tempted but I know that if I do I will be too full for my next course.' You thought the soup was good, just wait and see the main course!' James told his parents-in-law. Linda dished up sliced silverside, steepy peas, carrots with roast and mashed potatoes. She placed a gravy boat with steaming hot beef gravy in the middle of the table. They all tucked in and Margie and Douglas complimented their daughter on her excellent cooking skills while James was scooping up the last drops of gravy from his empty plate. 'Well if that's a sign of things to come, then I'm not complaining!' said James patting his full stomach. Linda was so excited about cooking for her parents and thrived on everyone's compliments. 'I'm afraid it's just ice cream and fruit for pudding, is that ok?' Linda asked them. 'Oh, I couldn't eat another thing' said Margie, 'maybe later, in an hour or so!' James agreed with Margie, saying that he didn't have any room left for dessert 'Aye well, since you've gone to all that bother Linda, I'll have some of your ice cream and fruit' piped up her dad. Margie laughed and asked him, 'Where on earth do you put it all Douglas?' to which he replied, 'My mother always told me to refuse nothing but a skelp on the erse and I'm sticking to that!' This gave them all a good laugh; there was a nice, happy family atmosphere. Linda was relieved to see her dad back to his nice old self and hoped that this would continue for her mum's sake.

6.30am, Monday morning and it was time to get up for their first day back at work since their wedding. James got washed and dressed first, put the kettle on, then shouted through to Linda in the bedroom, "I'm going into the shop next door to get milk and rolls. Linda got herself dressed, tied her hair up in a neat bun and applied her make up. It was 7.20am by now and she was wondering where on earth he had got to, he had been away at least fifteen minutes. She made herself a cup of coffee, prepared one for James and made some toast for both of them. At last she heard the key in the door; 'You'll never guess who I've just bumped into Linda?' he called out. 'Who?'

answered Linda. 'Danny' James replied, 'Danny who?' she questioned in exasperation. 'Danny that lived next door to my sister Iris and Kevin when they lived in Drumchapel and guess what?' said James, 'What?' said Linda in sheer frustration because the time was getting on now and she didn't want them to be late on their first day back at work. 'He delivers the rolls from the bakery to the shop next door, he said he's always gasping for a cuppa by the time he gets here because he has been out on the road since 4.30am, so I've struck up a deal with him that we'll have a cup of tea ready for him to take with him on the road and he's going to give us half dozen roll every morning, free, gratis!' said James, feeling proud of himself for negotiating the deal. 'Is that why you were so long? Well you'd better get that tea and toast down your throat now because we have to leave in the next five minutes or you'll be late for work!' Linda told James as she quickly made up cheese and tomato rolls for them to take to work with them for their lunch.

Linda and James clambered into their wee Ford Anglia; he didn't go through the city so he dropped her off at the junction of Castle Street and High Street where she caught a bus into town. She got off the bus outside of Strathclyde University; the place was swarming with students making their way to the entrance. She felt a spot of rain and thought to herself, how lucky that she remembered to grab her long walking umbrella just before she left the house. She stopped to open it and just as she raised it over her head, she was showered and completely covered in confetti, the students all started cheering and she was so embarrassed. She got into work early before her clerkess Sally and junior clerkess Beverley.

Sally arrived five minutes later and Linda said in mock anger 'Thank you very much!' Sally looked puzzled, 'For what?' she answered. 'For filling my brolly with confetti!' answered Linda as she told Sally what had happened when she got off the bus. Sally went into fits off laughter; she had tears running down her face as Beverley entered the office. 'What's going on, was the honeymoon that funny?' she said jokingly. Sally told her about Linda, the umbrella and the confetti. Beverley held her stomach as she joined Sally in laughter. 'I'm glad you two think its funny!' said Linda laughing with them. 'That was supposed to happen on your honeymoon; you said you were going to Edinburgh and we figured that it would probably be raining there!' explained Sally. 'I didn't use my brolly on honeymoon because we went everywhere in the car and the weather was good, it has been sitting in my hall for the past week and I just grabbed it this morning before I left for work. I was so embarrassed, I didn't know where to look, I just smiled sweetly at all the students and practically ran all the way to the office.

Linda was 14 weeks pregnant and very sickly; she couldn't stand the smell of cooking and ran past bakers, chip shops and restaurants holding her breath. The only thing that she seemed to really enjoy was Golden Delicious apples and tomatoes; she also started to get a craving for tangerines and 'of all things' PORRIDGE!!! She hated porridge as a child, her dad insisted they have it with salt but when he wasn't around her mum allowed her to have sugar on it and she found it just bearable then. All the way home on the bus from work each evening, she couldn't stop thinking about the porridge that she was going to make for her tea.

She changed to a new doctor in Parkhead; it was a dingy wee shop with the surgery in the back room, nothing like the lovely big new airy surgery with soft music playing in the background that her young 'whiz-kid' doctor in Knightswood had. She didn't like it here nor did she like her new doctor, he was a creepy, stout old man with a Victorian attitude, thinning grey hair, specs halfway down his nose, striped suit with waistcoat and pocket watch. He kept taking his watch out off his pocket to check it, just as if he was timing his consultation with her. He was the only doctor in that area. Every time she had to attend his clinic for a pregnancy check, she gritted her teeth and put up with it telling herself that it wouldn't be for long because hopefully soon they would be moving to Dennistoun.

In the evenings when they were home, they either played records on James' old record player or listened to their wee battery operated radio because they couldn't afford a TV. They soon got into a good routine, every morning, Danny came to the door with 6 freshly baked rolls and handed them his cup from the previous day in return for a cup of coffee to take with him. Linda made up the rolls for their 'work pieces'. On Wednesday evenings, James took Linda up to the self-service launderette at Parkhead Cross with the week's washing then came back and collected her an hour and a half later. On Tuesday's and Thursdays, when James worked late, Linda went to her parent's straight from work and had a bath at their house. James normally went to the public baths round the corner from them in Parkhead after work for a bath but on the nights he worked overtime he had a bath at his mother's house because the public baths were ıat time. He picked Linda up on the way home again just ⌊inda always visited her parents at the weekend so was ıave another bath then.

One week before the end of November, James and Linda got a letter from the factor telling him that the flat in Dennsitoun was theirs. The letter said that the sister and brother-in-law of Miss Burton, the old spinster lady who had lived there would be at the flat clearing out on Saturday and Linda and James were most welcome to go and have a look round the place and make offers for anything they wanted to buy. They had only seen it from the outside but knew that it was the same design inside as the one her brother Douglas Junior and his wife Norma had two streets away in Dennistoun. They were anxious to see inside the flat for themselves, so on Saturday morning, bubbling with excitement they made their way to view what was to be their new place of residence. As they got out of their Ford Anglia car, there was a thud, 'Oi' Shouted James, as a gang of kids grabbed their ball from beneath the car. 'Mind my motor!' he told them. 'Sorry mister, it wiznae me an' it wiznae him either, he's only wan!' replied the one in charge who seemed to be around four years old. Linda and James laughed as they looked down at the wee 'wan year old' that he was referring to. He was standing there looking up at them with his big brown eyes, snot running down his nose that was intermingling with the dummy in his mouth, nappy hanging down from beneath his shorts and dirty face and hands.

They made their way to the close and tentatively they rang the doorbell. A grey haired woman in her sixties answered the door. It looked like she had taken her curlers out and not bothered to comb her hair, She had a frown on her face as she said, 'You've come tae look roon' the flat, huv ye? Her husband a short, fat baldy hen-pecked type stood at the back of her. James and Linda nodded their heads. The lady opened the door wider, tutting and moving her husband out of the way as she did so and invited the young couple into the flat.

Linda was in awe; it was beautiful and tastefully decorated. The lady who had lived there had impeccable taste; sadly she had been in a hospice for the past six months and had died the week before. The hall was massive, it was as big as the living room alone, with all the rooms off it, and the living room was big enough for a three-piece suite, table and chairs. It had a tiled fireplace with an electric fire in front. 'You'll have to buy your own fire, we're taking that one with us!' said the lady quite emotionless. This concerned Linda because the Parkhead flat had a gas fire fitted and she assumed that this flat would be the same. It was going into winter, they would need a fire and she worried where they were going to get the money to buy one from! The main bedroom at the front could easily hold a double bed, wardrobe, dressing table and still leave plenty room for a cot, pram etc. It had a big walk-in shelved out cupboard for storage off of it. The second bedroom could easily hold a double bed, wardrobe and dressing table. There was another big walk in cupboard in the hall, but the bathroom was a dream, it had a big luxurious white bath, the sink was all tiled into a vanity with lots of cupboards around it and under it. Linda was delighted at the thought of having her own bathroom at last! They loved the Venetian blinds and mentioned this to the grey haired lady, 'Ah well, ye cin huv these for £15, they're practically new and oan a' four windaes!' she said trying to convince them that they were getting a good bargain. James said, 'Oh I don't know that's more than we could afford, we could buy them new for that!' The grey haired woman tutted and turned away in disgust with her hen-pecked husband following behind her like a wee dog. As they entered the wee kitchenette Linda said, 'Oh look at the wall cupboards James aren't they gorgeous, so modern, and the cooker? I love the cooker!' she exclaimed. The grey haired lady stood by the door of the kitchenette with her husband shuffling at her back as usual and told them that her deceased sister had taken out HP terms with the Electricity Board for the cooker just before she got ill, so she couldn't sell it to them but she could ask if they could take over the payments. Linda and James agreed to this.

On Monday, Linda and James met up in their lunch breaks and made their way to the factors office to pay the first month's rent on their new flat of £7/19/6d and sign the missive. They were told that the flat was officially theirs from Monday 1st December but as it had all been cleared out and the keys had been handed back then they could move in from the coming Saturday, 29th November.

They had been in their Parkhead room and kitchen for just six weeks, they didn't have very much and had only unpacked their essential wedding presents, so there wasn't really a lot off packing up to do. They asked the man in the shop next door to save them some cardboard boxes and every night after work James called into collect them from him. By Thursday evening they had fourteen boxes full of wedding presents, clothes, linen, towels, crockery, cutlery and nick-knacks ready to be shifted to their new abode.

Friday morning and a letter marked 'OHMS' popped through the letterbox, 'what on earth is this?' Linda questioned. She opened it and was delighted to find a tax rebate cheque for her to the amount of £18 because she was a married woman. 'Oh we can afford an electric fire now!' said James quite relieved.

On Friday evening, James arrived home from work at 4.30pm in his cousins Bedford van, which he had borrowed for the weekend to do their flitting in. He went up to the electric shop and bought a coal effect electric fire that Linda had been admiring for £16/10/-, before going home to cram all the boxes into the van. When Linda returned home, she was delighted with the new electric fire and said, 'That tax rebate was a Godsend, we couldn't have moved into our new place at this time of the year with no heating!' 'Aye! Somebody up there definitely likes us' answered James, then he said to Linda, 'I'm going to take these boxes over to Dennistoun tonight because we are going to have to do quite a few runs back and forth tomorrow, so this will at least get some of it out of the way, Tell you what!' he continued, 'I'll take a change of clothes, some soap and a towel. I'll have a nice bath in our new house because by the time I get back the public baths will be closed! James returned two hours later, raving about the wonderful bath that he had had, this was one thing that Linda was looking forward to, her very own bath, it was something that both of them had had all of their lives but had taken for granted and didn't realise what a necessity it was until it wasn't there, now they felt that it was a luxury!

The next morning, Linda's brother Douglas junior arrived at their door just after 8am to help them with their flitting. They loaded the mattress, settee and electric fire into the van. James took Linda in the van up to their new flat while Douglas junior stayed behind getting the rest of the furniture ready for the next load.

Linda got out of the van very excited, she couldn't wait to see her new place again; she rushed into the hallway held both of her arms out wide and birled around demonstrating how big the area was. There was a loud echo because all the carpets had been removed leaving bare floorboards in every room. From there she peered into the bathroom and felt an uncontrollable smile spreading across her face. She looked at the big bedroom and it looked massive now that all the furniture had been removed from it, but there was something else different, then she twigged what it was. She called out to James,

'The Venetian blinds have been removed,' 'I know' he answered, 'though God knows what good they will be to anyone else because they were made to fit these windows, there's something else…'he continued as Linda gleefully danced through the lounge into the wee kitchenette, she stopped suddenly in her tracks and felt herself become tearful, 'They've taken the wall cabinets, they can't do that, they were fixtures and fitting, how could they?' She asked James as she looked at the big holes in the plaster where the cupboards had been ripped out. James said, 'I didn't know how to tell you that the two things you had admired had been removed, perhaps they were annoyed at us not giving them £15 for the blinds but honest Linda we could have bought new ones for that. If they had said between £5-£7 then we could have considered it. Awe never mind, I will make you much nicer wall cupboards and that will be a priority! Now I must get back to your brother, he'll be waiting for me. Don't overdo it Linda take it easy and if you feel tired just rest on the settee and put your feet up. We'll be back in about an hour or so'.

Linda started to unpack the kitchen stuff, into the base units. There was no room for the cutlery tray and crockery so she placed them in the far corner of the worktop for the meantime until James could get the time to build new wall cupboards. She unpacked the bathroom toiletries and filled the cupboards either side of the vanity sink with fresh folded towels that had been given as wedding presents.

James and Douglas did six more trips, they finally got the Parkhead flat emptied and closed the door for the last time at quarter to five that evening. Their bed was in place along with the wardrobe and chest of drawers in the big bedroom. Two dining chairs sat in the big hall along with the rolled up carpets from the Parkhead flat for James to refit. Their three piece suite sat in the lounge along with the coffee table that Eric and Morag had given them for a wedding present, the gate-leg table sat in the recess with a dining chair either side while the electric fire sat on top of the hearth in front of the tiled fireplace. Douglas junior made sure that there was nothing else for him to do before leaving just after 6 pm.

James and Linda unpacked their clothes into the wardrobe and made their bed up, they decided they had done enough for the day. James had a bath then popped down the road for a pint while Linda soaked in sheer luxury in a bubble bath. Linda was sitting in front of the electric fire in her dressing gown and slippers listening to the radio when about 9.30pm, she heard James' key in they door. He shouted through to her 'There's a great Italian ice-cream shop in Dunchatten Street, they've won all sorts of awards, I've bought us a tub each and some Irn Bru', 'Oh brilliant,' said Linda, 'I just fancy some ice cream and ginger'. They tucked in and made ice cream drinks just like they had done as kids. By 11pm they were shattered and climbed wearily into bed.

James was up bright and early the next morning. Linda came through to the lounge to find him with his tape measure in one hand and writing on a pad with the other. 'What are you doing?' she enquired. 'I'll knock this place into shape in no time!' he confidently told her, 'I can't buy any material today, so I'm going to start taking out that old fashioned tiled fireplace ready for the new wooden surround that I'm going to make. It's a messy job, why don't you jump on a bus and visit your mum and dad for the day?' he suggested to Linda. 'I'd love to, are you sure you don't mind?' she answered, 'No, it's better that you're out of the way, there'll be a lot of dust around, I'll pick you up from your parents house around teatime, then we'll pop up to my mother's for a couple of hours said James. 'Ok then,' agreed Linda, 'but what about your lunch?' 'Don't worry about me, I'll nip out to the shop round the corner and get myself something for a sandwich,' James replied. 'I'll go across now and get something and make sandwiches for you before I go, what do you fancy?' asked Linda. 'Oh, ok then a nice piece of gammon would be lovely,' replied James. Linda pulled on her coat and said, 'I'll call my mum from the phone box while I'm out and tell her that I'm coming to visit them today.'

She went to the phone box first to make sure that her mum and dad would be at home and they were delighted to hear that she was coming to see them. She then went to the shop and bought four rolls, a quarter of the best gammon and two medium sized Scotch tomatoes' She came home and made up two rolls with gammon and tomato and wrapped them up in greaseproof bread paper. 'Ok, it's ten past ten now, I'd better be off now James, don't work too hard, I'll see you later at my parents,' she kissed him before making her way to the door and shouting 'B-Y-E'. 'Bye, sweetheart, go careful now,' answered James.

By the following weekend the old tiled fireplace had gone and James had plastered all the holes in the wall. He used the smaller bedroom as a temporary workshop to make their new wooden surround fireplace. On the Sunday morning they went down to 'The Barras' and bought some lovely modern wallpaper with big blue circles of different shades of blue for the fireplace wall. During that week, James worked well into the evenings painting the ceiling and the three walls white then he papered the fireplace wall with the new wallpaper. He finished putting the last strip of wallpaper up on Friday night. On Saturday morning, Linda went into town to meet her mother, James unrolled the blue carpet that they had brought from their Parkhead flat, they had only bought it just over two months ago. Fortunately their new lounge was the same size and almost the same shape as the Parkhead kitchen. Two hours later and the carpet was laid. James brought in the new wooden fire surround and then placed their new electric coal effect fire in front of it. He brought in the rest of the furniture, the gate-leg table, chairs, black leather three-piece-suite and coffee table. The room was looking grand! James sat down on the settee opposite the fireplace to admire his work; he was proud of himself and couldn't wait for Linda to come home to show off his work to her.

At four o'clock James heard Linda's key in the door, she came into the lounge with her head down and talking, telling James that she had brought some 'spiced beef ham' from Galloway's for that nights tea and that the Pattersons in town had a lovely 17" TV's with screw in legs for £39 and they offered HP terms. 'Do you think we could afford it James, it works out at 17/6d per week?' her voice trailed away as she looked up and couldn't believe her eyes, she sat down on the settee beside James and stared at her beautiful new room and fireplace with its wee wooden shelves for ornaments. She was overwhelmed and hugged James tightly, he beamed with proud delight as she told him 'Oh, you're so clever, this is the nicest room I have ever seen.' Then she said 'Let's stay in tonight and enjoy it, after tea you can nip down for a pint and bring back some of that lovely ice-cream and Irn Bru.'

Later on in the evening, as they tucked into their tubs of ice-cream James said, 'What were you saying about that TV?' Linda repeated what she told him already, then he said, 'I think we can just about manage that, we need a TV, we can't keep playing the same records over and over again on my record player or listening to the radio all the time besides you've been missing out on Coronation Street all this time, you'll need to catch up. Can you pop into Pattersons in your lunch break one day this week and organise it?' Linda was delighted and had no hesitation in replying, 'Consider it done!' That night before they went to bed they stood at the door and admired their lounge and in the morning Linda couldn't wait to get up and see it again.

Linda changed to a new doctor, it was a big modern surgery, in a large old house, so much nicer than the one in Parkhead and her new doctor was a nice understanding caring type in his forties. He arranged for her to have her baby in Duke Street Maternity Hospital and for her to attend her pre-natal classes there too.

A new area manager, Mr. Nightingale, arrived from London at Linda's company. Linda didn't really take to him, he had greasy mousy brown wavy hair and even greasier yellowy skin. There was something that didn't ring true about him and for the first time since she started with the firm as a junior clerkess, Linda found herself dreading going into work. The evil secretary Connie with the skinny legs and massive boobs was very envious of Linda. She had always attempted to cause trouble and make life difficult for her by making up lies and telling tales to the bosses. Previous managers saw through Connie and ignored her shit-stirring, some would have liked to sack her but employment laws tied their hands. This new boss was a sneaky weed. He and Connie were two of a kind. He called Linda into his office to remind her that she would not be allowed to stay in her job after she was six months pregnant. Linda knew this would happen because it was the same everywhere. It wasn't so long ago that firms refused to employ married women, meaning that when a girl got wed she had to give up her job. She decided that she had, had enough and didn't need the agro so she went round some employment agencies in her lunch break and discovered that they didn't discriminate against pregnant ladies. There was plenty of work and the money was really good. She went back and told Mr. Nightingale that she wouldn't wait until the six months was up and would leave at Christmas instead. Temping would suit her much better because she could have time off if needed.

Linda assumed that as her clerkess Sally covered her job while she was on holiday that she would be offered the promotion meaning that the junior clerkess Beverley would be moved up to Sally's job and a new junior clerkess would be employed, but Mr. Nightingale had other ideas! Egged on by Connie, his 'partner in crime', he employed a friend of hers called Yvonne, in her forties, insisting that Sally was too young for such promotion. Linda told him in no uncertain terms that he was talking rubbish because she took the job on when she was Sally's age and Sally was more than capable but he was like a weak greasy puppet on a string controlled by Connie and he disagreed with Linda. There were no prospects or any chances of promotion for Sally or Beverley now and both the girls were extremely upset. Linda was furious and decided to play the nasty boss and his evil secretary at their own game and she went sick on full pay. Sally sung dumb and said she couldn't train Yvonne because she didn't know Linda's job in full and in any case she couldn't neglect her own job. Sally and Beverley both had enough and decided to hand in their notices to leave at Christmas too and go temping. All the girls had always pulled their weight and done more than their fair share but as Mr. Nightingale was showing them no respect, they returned his compliment and only carried out the duties in their job descriptions, which gave them the great satisfaction of watching him and his witch of a secretary attempting to muddle through the sheer mess and chaos.

Linda went to look at prams and cots in the nursery shop in Duke Street; she was very worried that they wouldn't be able to afford either and was beginning to resign herself to the fact that they would probably have to buy second-hand. She fell in love with a beautiful pram, it was very modern, mustard leather and it converted into a pushchair. She took James down one evening half an hour before the shop closed to see it, he told her, 'If that's the one you want then that's the one we get!' They paid a deposit of £3 on it for the shop to hold it until nearer the time, although Linda was still apprehensive as to where the balance of the money was going to come from. James then looked at the cots and studied them, then he said to Linda, 'Don't worry, it's not a problem, I'll make one!' Linda looked at him in disbelief; 'Really!' she said with great relief, 'can you really make a baby's cot?' 'Just you watch me,' answered James. James bought a cot mattress from the foam shop in Duke Street and worked on the cot in the spare room in the evening. Linda popped in now and then to see its progress. After a couple of nights he called Linda into the room and said, 'Right it's finished, come and see what you think,' Linda couldn't belief it, he had made a heart shape headboard and base that rocked to and fro, with the cot bars in between, much nicer than any of the cots in the shop. 'I'll paint it tomorrow night, what colour would you like it?' asked James. 'Oh I think we'd be safer to stick to white' answered Linda. 'Ok, I'll pick up some paint tomorrow; can you buy some transfers to stick on it? It's best you choose them yourself' replied James. When the paint was dry Linda lovingly stuck the nursery rhyme characters on it. James's mother, Molly had given them an old chest of drawers that she no longer needed, James painted it white and Linda stuck some transfers on it too to match the cot. It was a couple of weeks before Christmas and everything was beginning to take shape in preparation for the arrival of their baby in April.

James realised that with his skills, how easy it was for him to make the cot and so decided to put together a prototype dolls cot and see if he could sell it to any of the stallholders at 'The Barras' to make an extra bob or two for Christmas. Early Saturday morning he set off for 'The Barras' and looked around for a toy stall. He approached the fast talking man, with the greased back black hair and fag hanging from his mouth. 'Excuse me, do you sell dolls cots?' asked James. 'Sorry, naw son, ah huvnae goat a supplier for thim' answered the man. 'Well would you be interested in buying one?' asked James in anticipation as he lifted up his dolls cot to show him. The man examined it and said, 'No' bad, no' bad at a', how much dae ye want fur it son?' 'Fifteen shillings' answered James, 'Awe naw son, it wid sell fur seventeen an' a tanner so there widnae be much profit left oot o' that, tell ye whit, call it ten bob 'n' ye've goet a deal! James readily agreed and shook the man's hand as he handed over the cot and accepted a crisp ten-shilling note in exchange. 'Would you be interested in some more?' he asked anxiously. 'Whit! Ye mean there's mer, where ur ye getting' thim fae? Ah hope they're no' knocked aff son! questioned the man looking suspiciously at James. 'No, no, I make them,' answered James. 'Dae ye really, well ah think we could talk business son, cin ye make some mer fur tomorra?' 'Well I'll try!' said James, 'but it won't be too early because I need to wait for the paint to dry' James hurried home stopping to buy some off cuts of wood and dowling, paint and more transfers. He started straight away, he made six heart shaped headboards and six baseboards, he worked on into Saturday evening until he had six beautiful wee dolls cots lined up, he painted two white, two pink and two blue, he gave them a second coat before going to bed. In the morning, Linda stuck the transfers on and wished him luck as he packed them all into his Anglia car and headed for 'The Barras'. The stallholder was delighted, he couldn't belief how quick James had made them, he handed him £3 and asked him 'Cin ye make me mer fur next weekend son? Ah selt that wan yesterday within ten minutes!' James couldn't believe his luck; this extra money was going to come in very handy for Christmas. That week, in the evenings James managed to knock up a dozen more dolls cots, he painted them and Linda stuck the stickers on. When James got there on Saturday morning, his man was delighted that James had a dozen for him and said as he handed him £6 'Oh thank God son, ah wis panickin' incase ye didnae come back, yer dolls cots ur selling like hot cakes, ah've promised the punters that ah wid huv som mer the day, it'll no' take me long tae shift these, we're open on Christmas Eve, wid it be possible tae knock me up fifty? James reeled back in disbelief. 'But this is the 22nd, I couldn't possibly make fifty cots in two days,' Well jist dae me whit ye cin son! We've goet a good wee business goin' here!' James hurried back and started on his cots; he worked flat out and managed to get another ten cots to the man at 'the Barras' by Christmas Eve. 'Sorry mate that's the best I could do at such short notice!' said James. The man was over the moon because he was sold out of dolls cots again. He handed James £5 and said, 'Next year start making them in the summer an' we'll sell thim fae Halloween oanwards son, ok!' 'Aye right said James!' he was glad of the extra money but even more happier that the Christmas rush on the dolls cots was over now meaning he would have more time now to work on the flat.

James built fabulous wall cupboards in the kitchen to replace the ones that had been spitefully torn out by the previous tenant's relatives. The little kitchen looked great with its base and wall units and smart new worktop that James had fitted, he moved the three ringed electric Tricity cooker from its freestanding position to the end of the worktop. They had taken over the HP payments for the cooker from the previous tenant; it was almost new and only £20 in £1 per week installments left to pay so they were very pleased with their bargain. They purchased a fridge on HP and it stood in the space where the cooker once was.

The woman who lived in the house before them had paid for a telephone to be connected, the telephone was still there and all they needed to do was pay a small connection charge. They decided that as Linda was pregnant and their families lived on the other side of the city that this was a necessity, so Linda made a call and by Christmas Eve they had the luxury of a telephone to go with their lovely new television which stood proudly in the corner of the room at the right hand side of the fireplace. Between Christmas and New Year James made a wooden telephone seat in the window recess with a black leather foam filled cushion to match their three-piece-suite. 'Oh the lounge is so cosy, it's becoming more like home every day, I love you so much and I'm so proud of you James Alexander' Linda told her husband. 'I do it all for you, my beautiful wife, I love you too. One day I'll give you the nicest house in the street!' James replied as he pulled her close to him and kissed her tenderly.

It was New Year's Eve, James was working and Linda couldn't get out because James' mother, Molly had popped over in the afternoon for a visit. When James got home at 4.30pm, Linda said to him, 'We don't have any glasses, what if we have anyone first footing us, it'll be awfully embarrassing,' 'Well we're going to your parents after the bells, so I don't think you need to worry,' answered James. 'Yes but even so James, we'll be back tomorrow, if we get visitors, we have to give them a New Years drink and the shops are shut now until 3rd January,' answered a concerned Linda. James was taking his mother home in the car. It was seven o'clock, Molly had to go back to get ready for New Year because James and Linda were picking her up again after the bells to take her to a party at Linda's parents house. Before he left James said to Linda, 'Do you mind if I pop into 'The New Inn' for a Hogmanay pint on the way home?' 'No, I'm going to bed to rest for a couple of hours then I'm going to relax in a nice bubble bath, it's going to be a long night' answered Linda, knowing that the New Year's party wasn't starting until after midnight and would go on until at least breakfast time. She was six months pregnant now, getting bigger, tiring easily, still being sick and feeling uncomfortable. 'Ok, I'll be back in a couple of hours,' James said kissing her on the cheek as he left.

Linda woke up at ten o'clock and James still wasn't home, she assumed that he'd probably met some of his old mates because he was planning to have a drink in the pub that they used to work evenings in before they got married. Just as she was about to start running her bath, James turned up; he looked really annoyed with himself. 'What's up, didn't you have a nice time?' Linda asked him. James answered. 'I got to the pub just before 8 o'clock; it was choc-a-block. Tommy shouted over to me, 'Am I glad to see you? We could really do with another pair of hands in here, how do you fancy doing us a big favour and jumping behind the bar to help us out? It'll only be for an hour and a half, we close at half past nine'. I told him we needed some glasses so I would help him out if he gave me glasses in return and he was more than happy so I got in there and worked flat out until they closed. 'That's great! Well done James, you got us some glasses, where are they?' asked Linda, relieved that they would be properly prepared now for any guests. 'Do you want the good news or the bad news first?' answered James. Linda put her head down and looked up at him questioningly, 'Go on, give me the bad news first,' she said. 'Well Tommy gave me a big box full of assorted glasses for us to keep, I put them on the back seat of the car and drove all the way home, just as I turned the corner into our street a cat ran in front of my car. I swerved to avoid it, the box of glasses fell off the back seat and when I looked into the box everyone of them was smashed to smithereens, I've just put the whole box full of broken glass into the midden, so I worked for nothing,' said James looking disheartened. 'And the good new is?' asked Linda. James looked up in the air, pursed his lips into a forced smile and said 'I didn't spend any money, Tommy let me have two free pints when I finished' Linda laughed and said, 'Well at least you got something out of your hard work! Cheer up it's not the end of the world, there's a whole new year about to start in a couple of hours. I'll go for a bath now then get ready and as soon as the bells go we'll leave to pick up your mother.'

January 1970 and Linda was finding it increasingly difficult to get clothes to fit her. Her mother Margie came to the rescue with her wonderful sewing skills. Linda drew the type of maternity pinafore that she liked, and Margie got some oddments of material and made three for her. A royal blue one, a red one and a Black Watch tartan one. The Black Watch tartan one was Linda's favourite and she donned it to attend her prenatal class at Duke Street Hospital. It was an old hospital and not a patch on the brand, spanking new Queen Mother's Hospital in the west of the city, where Linda really would have loved to have given birth to her first baby but because she now lived in the east side of the city, she didn't qualify. She saw the doctor, who examined her to see that all was well then had some blood taken to be checked. After that she went into prenatal classes for lessons on breathing and what to expect while giving birth. There were nine other pregnant girls in the class. They lay on the floor doing their breathing exercises as the nurse instructed. She walked round them checking that they were carrying out the correct procedure. She stopped at Linda and knelt down by her as she was practicing her panting in preparation for labour. She was leaning over looking into Linda's face, Linda stopped panting, she got worried and asked the nurse, 'What's the matter, is there something wrong?' to which the nurse replied, 'Awe nae, Am jist admiring yer eye liner, it's dead straight, ah wish I could dae it like that, ah always end up looking lik a panda' Linda started to shake with laugher and answered 'Is that all? You had me panicking there!'

One Friday night in January, James' pal Alan and his girlfriend Helen called round to visit. 'We've got some news for you', Helen said. 'You're getting engaged!' Linda excitedly and optimistically guessed. 'No, no'' answered Helen looking awkward. Then the penny dropped and Linda said, 'Oh no you're not, are you?' Helen replied 'Afraid so, I'm almost four months gone', 'FOUR MONTHS?' Linda questioned with surprised astonishment, then she continued, 'You mean you've been keeping it to yourself all this time?' Helen answered 'No, I didn't know I was expecting, my periods are always all over the place and I never felt any different, I only realised last week that something wasn't right and I got it confirmed yesterday'. Alan chipped in with 'We're arranging a quickie wedding, hopefully for next month and I wondered if you would do me the honour of being my best man James?' James face lit up and he replied, 'Of course I am honoured that you have asked me and would be delighted to be your best man'. They opened a couple of cans of beer to celebrate while the two pregnant girls had cups of tea.

It was the middle of January and the agency asked Linda if she fancied a Senior Statistical Clerkess position in the head office of an oil company in the west of the city, the money was much more than she had been earning in the job that she had just left so she decided to give it a bash. She arrived at the offices above a petrol station and was given a warm welcome. Christine the receptionist was just finishing sending a telex. 'Be with you in a minute, just take a seat' she called over to Linda. She was a small cheery faced girl with dark wavy hair and big brown eyes. 'I take it you're our new temp,' said Christine. Linda nodded. 'Oh thank goodness we badly need an extra pair of hands, we're doing a special promotion over the next month and there isn't enough of us to cope, hang on I'll just call Bill our office manager down.' She had a modern switchboard the same type as the one Linda had operated only it was three times bigger. Within five minutes Bill appeared, he had his white shirt sleeves rolled up and had loosened his tie down. 'Hi Linda, we're really glad to see you, come up to our board room and I'll show you what the job involves.' Linda followed him up the one flight of stairs and was shown into the massive executive room with big blue comfy cushioned chairs. 'I'm afraid this will have to be your office for the duration of the job, will that be ok?' he asked Linda. 'Oh I'm not complaining this is lovely' she answered. Bill proceeded to show Linda all the figures that he needed her to work on for the promotion. 'No problem, I'll get started right away' she said. Just before lunchtime Bill popped in to see her and was very impressed to see that she had almost finished the first load of work that he had set out for her. 'Good God Linda, at this rate you will work yourself out of a job; I won't have the next lot of figures ready until tomorrow. You can finish early but that means you won't earn a full days money, that is, unless you can type?' he asked with a cheeky grin. 'Yes, I can type,' she answered. 'Great, I'll bring some lists through to you for typing after lunch, are you sure you don't mind?' said Bill. 'Not at all' answered Linda.

February 21st 1970 and it was Alan and Helen's wedding day, Linda donned her black watch maternity pinafore that her mum had made for her, she was seven and a half months pregnant and feeling very uncomfortable. She and James set out in their wee Ford Anglia car to pick Alan up and take him to the church. Although Helen was now five months pregnant, she decided to squeeze into a long white traditional wedding dress with a long flowing train and veil. She looked stunning and disguised her tiny bump well under the empire line dress. There were fifty guests and Linda sat with Morag and Eric, near to the top table where James was with the main wedding party. James started off his best man's speech by thanking the beautiful bridesmaids, then embarrassing Alan no end telling tales of when they were younger, he finished up by reading out the many telegrams received by well wishers, then sat down relieved that his duties were over and he could now relax and have a drink.

Linda really enjoyed working at the oil company, everyone was so friendly and the atmosphere was very happy and relaxed. It wasn't long until she was exercising all her office skills, including the switchboard and covering staff days off. She was never idle and always found a job to do. The wages clerk was off on a one week's winter holiday and Linda learned his job which apart from preparing all the paper work for all the office staffs monthly salary, also involved going downstairs to the petrol pumps in the garage below at 8.30am every morning to read them at the end of the night shift and before the day shift started, then she checked that the takings in the till tallied with the pump readings. She also made up the garage staff and mechanics weekly cash wages. Shughie, who worked nightshift on the pumps was a nice kindly soul, he was near to retirement age. He told Linda that he had a disabled wife at home and he made jewellery in his spare time to help pay the bills. He always had a warm cup of tea ready for himself and Linda before he finished his nightshift. She felt really sorry for him and used to bring him in a bun or a piece of tea bread every morning. Linda decided to give up work at the end of February, she had made lots of friends at the oil company and was sorry to leave, they were so good to her and even when she had to leave early for clinic appointments, they insisted on paying her the full day's money. They were all sad to see her go too. On her last day they all gathered in the board room and gave her a big card signed by everyone, saying what an asset she had been to the company and how much they were going to miss her. Bill told her that there would always be a job there for her if she decided to come back to work after having the baby then he presented her with a big bouquet of flowers along with chocolates and lots of presents for the baby. Shughie pressed a wee box into her hand and inside it was a beautiful abstract style, gold colour brooch with red stones that he had made himself. Linda felt quite emotional and sad to be leaving, she had only been there six weeks and they had treated her better and shown more respect for her than the company she had worked with for over six years since she left school at the age of fifteen.

The beginning of March and Linda was back at the clinic. The pregnant mothers-to-be were all taken for a tour of the maternity unit and delivery rooms. Linda felt very apprehensive because the wards were big and old fashioned with twenty beds in each. Afterwards they had to see the doctor. She really fancied a bowl of shredded wheat and just wanted to get home. Eventually after about half an hour her name was called. The doctor told her the bad news that her blood count was low and she would have to attend the hospital daily for iron injections for the last six weeks of her pregnancy. Linda dutifully did as she was told although she didn't look forward to it, because it wasn't very pleasant. The doctor kept an eye on her blood count but it still remained a problem.

Linda was standing at the kitchen sink, peeling potatoes for the evening meal when suddenly she felt a flutter on her foot, she looked over her bump and got the fright of her life to see a wee mouse scurrying across the floor and disappearing under the kitchen cupboard. When James came home, she told him and that weekend he went round the kitchen, lounge, hall and bedroom filling any wee holes and putting quadrant round the skirting to keep the mice out. James was tough, he would face up to any big scary animal but he didn't like mice or the way they darted across the floor suddenly disappearing into a hole, they gave him the creeps.

One evening James was sitting in the telephone seat in the window recess, he was talking on the phone to a woman who was asking him if he could possibly make her a wooden fire surround as a private 'homer' job. His mother Molly had told her all about the lovely one that he had made and she wanted similar. James never gave up the opportunity earn an extra penny and was making arrangements to go and see her when suddenly he went white and climbed up on top off the telephone seat while still trying to compose himself to talk to his potential client. Linda was sitting on the settee and wondered what on earth was wrong with him when suddenly she saw this wee mouse at the bottom of the telephone seat, she burst into fits of laughter, the tears were running down her face at the sight of her big, strong husband standing on the seat scared of a wee helpless mouse. James came off the phone and he was in a cold sweat, 'Did you see where it went?' he asked Linda in a panic. 'No, I was too busy laughing at you, ya big fearty!' she answered. 'I'm not scared of mice, I just don't like the way they dart around, you can't catch them and you never know where they'll run next, up your trouser leg or something!' said James. This remark made Linda dissolve into more uncontrollable laughter. 'You can laugh but I'm calling the Sanitary Department in, we can't have mice in the house with a baby on the way!' said James, quite seriously. Linda knew that he was right and so the next morning she called the department to explain the problem.

The following day a wee fat unkempt guy in his mid thirties with a big bag in his hand, his trousers tied up with string and messy long hair arrived at their door. Linda opened the door, 'Am fae the Sanitary Mrs. aboot yer mice!' He announced loudly for all the neighbours to hear. James was at work so Linda quickly ushered him indoors and showed him where they had spotted the mice. She left him to prowl around the flat with his torch. After about fifteen minutes, he shouted her through to the bathroom. He had removed the bath panel, 'Ah've found yer problem Mrs,' he said as she shone a torch under the bath, 'ye'll huvtae watch oot fur rat!' 'RATS!' exclaimed Linda in sheer shock and horror. 'Naw rat' replied the wee sanitary man. 'Are you telling me there're rats below the bath?' asked Linda, who by this time was feeling quite sick at the thought of it. 'NAW MRS!' said the Sanitary man loudly in sheer frustration, 'there's a flair board missing under yer bath an' rats how ra mice ur gettin' in, they're comin' up fae the foundations o' ra building, ye'll huv tae somehow replace that board tae stoap them!' Linda laughed and breathing out a long relieving sigh said 'Oh, you're saying, watch out for that!' 'Aye' replied the man looking at her as if she couldn't understand plain English, then he continued 'anyway ah've pit doon some poison, tell yer man to get that board seen tae as soon as he cin an' yer problems will be o'er'. That evening Linda couldn't tell James for laughing about 'rat' Sanitary man. James replaced the board the next day and that was the end of their wee furry visitors!

James worked hard during March. He painted and decorated the two bedrooms and hallway and built a wardrobe and dressing table unit along the wall in the big main bedroom so that all the mess would be out of the way before the baby arrived. They bought a lovely chocolate & beige colour carpet. The bedroom looked beautiful with the double bed in place and on the opposite wall was the new unit. Beside the wall as you came in the door the cot sat awaiting its new arrival. Linda, Margie, Molly, sister-in-law Norma and both Linda and James' different aunties had been clicking their knitting needles for the past 6 months so the two top drawers of the white painted chest of drawers under the window with it's 'nursery rhyme stickers' was packed full with knitted matinee jackets, mittens, bootees and hats of all sizes and colours. The two bottom drawers were full of baby sleep-suits and vests. On the lower shelf in the walk in cupboard of the bedroom, Linda had two bundles of brand new laundered nappies and some muslin squares, sitting beside them she had a 'Little Red Riding Hood' type basket packed with baby powders, creams, nappy pins, baby oil etc and on the shelf above were two neat piles of cot and pram sheets and baby blankets.

The hallway was almost the same size as the second bedroom. James built a fire surround with an imitation chimney and papered it with stone effect wallpaper. He fitted the red carpet from the bedroom of their Parkhead flat.

The second bedroom looked smart too; they had picked up an oddment of a colourful mix carpet from 'The Barras' and James fitted it. Molly's old wardrobe that had belonged to her mother and that she had given to James and Linda for their Parkhead flat was now painted white and sat in the corner of the room. Douglas and Margie's utility chest of drawers were painted white to match the wardrobe. The plan was that eventually when the baby was around six months old, the cot would be moved in here and this would be the baby's room.

On a shelf in the kitchen stood the Milton sterilising unit ready for the new baby Alexander's bottles. Everything was taking shape now and their wee flat was looking like a palace.

The next-door neighbours in the close were rough and ready but nice with it. They had two wee girls. Senga the mother was in her early thirties, she had a ruddy complexion, always wore a headscarf, slippers with men's socks and had no bottom teeth, Charlie, her husband, was a big stout kind looking man, he needed braces to hold his trousers up and they sagged at the crutch because he wore them below his big beer belly.

One night when James came home from work Charlie stopped him in the close and said, 'Cin a huv a wee word wi' ye James?' 'Sure whit dae ye want tae know Charlie?' answered James. 'Well, see that wee blue Triumph Herald oot in the street, ah goet it fur £35 aff o' a mate,' continued Charlie. 'Aye, ah saw it, good bargain ye got there Charlie!' replied James. 'Well whit a wiz gonnie ask ye is, wid ye gie me some drivin' lessons?' Charlie asked. 'Whit ye mean ye don't drive?' said James. 'Naw an' it gets worse?' said Charlie. 'How dae ye mean?' enquired James, 'Well ah applied fur a cancellation fur a drivin' test an' it's come through fur next week, so ah need tae learn quick!' said Charlie with a desperate look on his face. 'Whit ye mean ye've NEVER EVER had any lessons whatsoever before an' ye've goet yer drivin' test next week? said James trying to stifle his laughter. 'Aye that's right' answered Charlie looking down at the ground sheepishly. 'Oh ah don't think ah cin help ye there Charlie, ah could take ye oot fur some practice but no' until ye've hud some lessons furst!' James told him. 'Ah thooght ye might say that but thanks onyway James,' said Charlie as he turned and went indoors looking a bit embarrassed.

Senga invited Linda in one day for a cup of tea and told her not bother to do her turn of washing the close while she was pregnant and that she would look after it until after the baby was born. Linda enjoyed meeting her neighbours; their house was the same type as theirs only it was a mirror image. She noticed that they had recently put up red and white Venetian blinds on their windows, the same as the ones that had been in her flat. She got up to go and took her cup into the kitchen, where she stopped dead in her tracks; there on the wall were the kitchen units from her house. 'Ye've noticed', said Senga then she went on 'Miss Burrton's sister and brother-in-law gied thim tae us, they said you widnae be needin' thim because yer man wiz a joiner an' could make thim, they gied us the blinds tae because you didnae want them.' Linda nodded in agreement, 'Yes that's right' she said. She was absolutely fuming inside and couldn't wait for James to come home that evening to tell him. 'These nasty spiteful people went to the bother of taking down all the blinds and deliberately ripping out the cupboards to give them to the next-door neighbour, rather than leave them for us AND they left us with the damaged walls to repair! How could they be so horrible? We should have reported them to the factor' said Linda, then she stopped to think and reflected as she hugged James and went on 'Ah but never mind, they've done us a big favour really, we have come out best because we wouldn't have such lovely new wall cupboards if they hadn't done what they did, ours are much nicer!

James' mother Molly was a creature of habit and had visited her son and his new wife every Thursday without fail since they got married. It was April 2nd and Molly arrived as usual at 7pm sharp. James worked late Tuesdays and Thursdays and got in just after 8pm. After James got washed and changed, they all sat down to dinner at 8.30pm Linda served up the meal followed by Molly's favourite blackcurrant jelly and ice cream, which Linda made faithfully for her every week. Molly never ever offered to help serve or clear up before or after the meal, she sat like a lady being waited on. Linda washed and dried all the dishes and cutlery, and as she dried the last pot, she couldn't wait to flop down on her easy chair, her feet were sore and her ankles were swollen It was 9.45 by now, James usually left at 10pm to take his mother home in their car, the round trip usually took one hour. Linda was thinking to herself, *'As soon as they go I'm going to climb into bed and get a good night's sleep!'* She sat on her black leather easy chair and felt uncomfortable, she stood up and looked at the seat, it was wet, she sat down again, feeling embarrassed because she thought that with all the pressure of the baby against her bladder, she had wet herself. She didn't want to get up incase molly saw the wet seat. Molly went to the toilet before her trip home, Linda grabbed James and said, 'quickly get a towel before you're mother comes back, I've wet the seat and I'm so embarrassed!' James was concerned but did as he was told saying, 'are you sure you're ok?' Linda thought for a moment then began to panic inwardly, 'I don't know!' she answered, 'I didn't feel like I needed to go to the toilet, It can't be my waters bursting because it was only a trickle, anyway I've got two weeks to go!' Linda stood up to say Goodbye to Molly and was shocked to see another puddle of water on the seat, she got scared and on the spur of the moment, grabbed her coat and said to James, 'I'm coming with you!' 'Are you sure you feel like the journey Linda?' said Molly, it's getting late and the long bumpy ride might make you feel ill' she continued unsuspectingly. 'No I want to come with you' said Linda determinedly.

Linda sat in the back of the car because Molly always commandeered the front seat. The fact that Linda was very pregnant didn't matter to Molly, she was very possessive of her son and as far as she was concerned it was his car, not Linda's and her place was in the front beside him. Linda just went along with Molly's difficult, contrary beliefs for peace sake, she was very uncomfortable and getting more worried by the minute. Eventually just after 11pm they were back home again, Linda was still leaking trickles of water, James wanted to call the doctor but Linda wouldn't let him, she still convinced herself that it was the pressure of the baby on her bladder. She spent a very uncomfortable night running back and forth to the toilet and eventually just after 7am on Friday morning; James ignored her and insisted on calling their doctor for advice. The doctor told James to call the hospital immediately to arrange for Linda to be admitted. Linda told James that she couldn't go into hospital because it was his sister Maria's twin's third birthday party on Saturday. Then she got upset and tearful, she was concerned that something was wrong but also worried because she realized that this could be the start of labour and in spite of all the pre-natal classes she didn't know what to expect. James called Duke Street Hospital only to be told that there were no beds and they would call him back within half an hour to let him know which hospital to take his wife to. He tried to keep calm for Linda's sake but by this time she was getting her self into a state of panic and asking James to call her mum. James told her that he would call Margie as soon as they knew which hospital they were going to. Although it seemed like hours, twenty minutes later the phone rang to tell James that there was a bed available in Belvedere Hospital in the east side of Glasgow and to take his wife there as soon as possible. Linda felt her stomach churn with nerves, she didn't like this idea, she didn't even know where this hospital was, that part of the city was alien to her.

James called Margie at work just after 9am, she immediately downed her pen, made her excuses to her supervisor and made her way on and off buses and tramcars to the east end of Glasgow where she finally found the hospital. It was an old fashioned series of 'army style' huts, Margie asked at the reception and was directed to the ward that Linda had been admitted to.

It was a nice little ward of six expectant mums, Linda was the only one expecting her first baby and was sitting up in bed quite happy, she didn't have any discomfort only a slight twinge now and then and this trickling of leaking water, The hospital doctor asked James and Margie to sit outside while he examined Linda. He diagnosed that her waters were ruptured and needed to be burst properly. Within twenty minutes she was being wheeled into the operating theatre, where the sister in charge did just that. When she got back to the ward, the sister told James and Margie to say their good-byes and come back in the afternoon at visiting time between 2pm and 3.30pm.

Linda got talking to the other mums-to-be in the ward and said 'Well if this is labour then I don't know what all the fuss is about!' They just laughed and gave each other a look as if to say, 'Poor girl hasn't a clue what she is in for!' The other mums-to-be were talking about the tax rebate that they hoped to get. 'How do you mean?'

asked Linda. 'Well.' replied Jeanette, the small trim immaculate woman in her mid thirties in the next bed, who was amazingly having her 10th child, 'if your baby is born before 5th April then you get the child allowance back in your tax payments for the whole year. 'Really!' said Linda with enthusiasm, 'oh I couldn't be that lucky, I'm not even officially due for another two weeks yet!' 'Oh, you will most likely just make it because your waters have been burst, but the rest of us aren't that far advanced and will probably miss it.' Linda got quite excited at the thought of another tax windfall; it would really come in handy and would solve the problem of paying for the pram.

Friday evening and James brought Linda's mum and dad, Margie and Douglas to visit. The visiting hours were 7.30pm until 8pm.The matron was very strict and only allowed three people per bed at any time. Linda was still being sick but only feeling slight twinges occasionally, excitedly she told James about the tax rebate that they might get if their baby was born before April 5th, then she patted her stomach as if talking to the baby and said, 'C'mon wee one, get a move on, we've got a lovely pram waiting for you!' After visiting was over and everyone had left Linda felt her twinges getting stronger and she felt very sick, she mentioned to Jeanette in the next bed, who called for the nurse. 'Start timing them' the nurse told her as she gave her a steel bowl to be sick in, 'and let me know when they get closer together'. Linda did this but although they were quite powerful, they were all over the place, this continued through the night, there was no definite pattern to her twinges. James rang the hospital at 8am on Saturday morning to be told that there was no real change and not to phone back but come to the hospital at visiting time that afternoon. By 11am Linda's twinges were getting more serious and closer together. James Margie and Douglas arrived at 2pm on the dot. Linda was now on pethadine to ease the labour pains. She was ok between the twinges but bit her bottom lip and grabbed the blankets every time another contraction came on.

After visiting was over the sister pulled the curtains around Linda's bed and the doctor examined her. He told her that it could be some time yet because she wasn't really dilated enough. After they left the room, Jeanette in the next bed said, 'Oh come on girl, get on with it, you've started labour now, don't let it last too long or the taxman will win!' This made Linda laugh, only to be interrupted by another contraction'. Just before 7.30pm and Linda's contractions were very regular and close together but the doctor still wasn't convinced that she was near to the birth. James arrived again with Linda's parents, by this time Linda was doped up on pethadine and in serious labour. She was being sick in between contractions, James was very anxious and went to fetch the matron, who was a tall, lanky stern faced, spinster type with starched white collar and cap, she took one look and said, 'Right Mr. Alexander, this is no place for a man, off you go and don't phone in until 10pm, we might have some idea by then how much longer your wife will be' James didn't want to leave Linda, he hugged her tight and kissed her as she clung to the headboard in pain. Margie and Douglas were very concerned and gave their daughter a hug promising to see her again soon and telling her it won't be long until she'll have her wee bundle in her arms but Linda was oblivious to her visitors. By the time that they walked out to the car park Linda was lifted on to a trolley and whisked into the delivery room. At 8.03pm she gave birth. The sister exclaimed, 'Mrs. Alexander, you have a very handsome son!' then she took the baby away for a few minutes and came back saying, 'he weighs 6lb 7oz, and that's very good considering he is two weeks early!' Linda got a quick peep at her son before the nurse took him into the nursery for the night. Linda was still 'high' on pethadine but felt very proud and just wanted the morning to come so that she could see her baby again and hold him in her arms.

Linda was taken into the postnatal ward. It was in darkness with only a couple of dim nights lights glowing. 'I hope you won't be lonely in here' said the nurse; 'hopefully you'll have company by the morning'. As Linda got used to the dark, she could make out through the haze of her doped up eyes that the five other beds were empty. She was dosing off when a figure appeared, it was James, he couldn't wait until 10pm to ring the hospital and phoned in just before 9pm to be told the good news, he was elated and came back to the hospital straight away. The sister allowed him in to see his wife and son but only for five minutes, he hugged and kissed Linda and thanked her for giving him such a beautiful, healthy son. Linda was floating into a deep sleep and made James laugh by announcing loudly and proudly, 'I've beat the taxman, haven't I?' Douglas and Margie were sitting outside in the car and James asked the sister if they could pop in to see their new grandson. The sister was a nice caring person and replied, 'Oh ok well, the matron has gone home now, don't ever mention this to her or I'll be in serious trouble!' Douglas, Margie and James stood proudly at the nursery window as the sister held up the wee, still unwashed, new addition to the family. Margie had a tear in her eye, Douglas grinned from ear to ear and said, 'Well I've got what I wanted!' while James stood there beaming and mesmerized by the wonder of this new baby son.

James called his sister Maria's house from the hospital public call box. The twins were in bed sleeping after their third birthday celebrations in the afternoon and the adults were partying the night away. James spoke to his mother Molly and said, 'Well you have something else to celebrate now mother, you have another Grandson. 'Oh another boy?' answered Molly half heartedly, at that James could hear a cheer going up and voices shouting and announcing 'It's a boy!' Molly then continued, 'Maybe one day I'll get my granddaughter!'

James dropped Douglas and Margie off at their house. The excitement of becoming a dad for the first time was beginning to kick in. He went to his mum's house then ran along the street to his pal Alan's mother's house and rattled on her door, 'Mrs. Ferguson, Mrs. Ferguson, he shouted in glee, I'm a daddy, I have a son!' Mrs. Ferguson opened the door in her dressing gown and hair rollers, she was a kindly lady, who loved to fuss, she hugged James and welcomed him indoors. Her husband was disabled and in a wheelchair and he said to his wife, 'Get the young man a dram to celebrate Ethel!' James downed the glass of whisky then went knocking on his mother's other neighbour's doors announcing proudly to the world that he was a daddy. Finally he ended up at his sister Maria's house, where the party was in full swing. Everyone congratulated and hugged him. Maria said to James, 'Well done to Linda for having your son on the twin's birthday, that's a hat trick, three grandson's all with the same birthday!' then she shouted out, 'Right has everyone got a drink, we have three good reasons to celebrate now!'

It was 5.30am on Sunday morning Linda was wakened up by the nurse sticking a thermometer in her mouth, then she handed Linda a handful of wee red pills, 'What are these for?' asked Linda. 'To scatter your milk' answered the nurse, breast-feeding was considered old fashioned and the nurse just assumed that Linda would follow the trend and be bottle-feeding her baby. Linda did as she was told and swallowed the pills. There was no going back now and her milk would stop flowing.

She looked around and the ward was full, she realized that all her friends from the prenatal ward were there. As they all slowly came round, Jeanette said, 'Well Linda you certainly started the ball rolling!' 'How do you mean?' asked Linda as Jeanette went on, ' you were whisked along to the delivery room at the end of visiting time, then Carol was next followed by Jean, Ellen, May and lastly myself, I had to make a run for the delivery room because there wasn't a trolley left, the sister didn't know what had hit her, she and the four nurses on night duty delivered six babies within 4 hours, one boy followed by five girls and all before midnight, I just made it at six minutes to twelve, so we will be getting a wee present from the tax man through out letterboxes.' she said laughing.

Linda couldn't wait to see her baby; she was more 'with it' now. One by one the nurses wheeled the brand new wee human beings into the ward in white material cots and put them beside their mother's beds. The third one arrived and was brought to Linda, she peeped into the cot to see, what she thought was, the most beautiful baby ever. He had wonderful smooth skin with not a wrinkle in sight, fair wispy hair, and big eyes exploring his new world. Jeanette came over and said to the others, 'Oh girls come over and see Linda's son, he is so handsome and serene, he'll break a few hearts when he grows up!' Linda felt very proud, especially to hear the words 'Linda's son'. She realized that she was now responsible for this little baby until he grows up to be a man. 'Have you got a name yet for him?' Jeanette asked, 'Yes' replied Linda, 'he's going to be called Stuart MacGregor Alexander'. 'Oh that's a good strong, Scottish, masculine name!' answered Jeanette.

Two days later Linda had her blood checked to see if her blood count had improved, she was feeling very tired but put it down to the experience of giving birth for the first time. Three hours later the sister arrived and told Linda that she would have to go back to bed and be put on a drip to receive some blood because her count was still very low. This upset Linda because she was told that it would take a good few hours meaning that she wouldn't be able to hold, feed or change her son. To crown it all at that point the sister and a nurse came round to give the babies their BCG injections. Linda watched as they picked little Stuart up from his contented sleep and stuck a massive needle in his wee arm, he howled with the shock of it, his little lip quivering, which set Linda off sobbing her heart out because she could do nothing to help him. The sister said caringly to Linda, 'Now Mrs. Alexander, try not to get upset, you'll not help yourself get better, You'll be off the blood transfusion before evening visiting and you'll be able to hold your son again.

After ten days in hospital Linda was fit enough to be discharged and allowed home. James proudly drove up in his wee Anglia car, the nurse carried baby Stuart to the door, Linda handed her a big box of chocolates to share with the staff and thanked her for everything. When they got home to their house, Douglas, Margie and Molly were excitedly waiting. James had collected the new pram and Margie had prepared it with brand new sheets and blankets for baby Stuart. Linda could see that James had been very busy, the house was spotless, he had set the table for dinner for the five of them and had made soup followed by silverside, potatoes and peas, rounded off afterwards with ice-cream.

Linda was new to motherhood and hadn't thought about buying milk for the baby, she assumed that the hospital would give her some for the first few days. Luckily the Indian shop on the corner was open on Sunday's and James was able to buy a box of Cow & Gate from there. Their parents only stayed for a few hours in the afternoon then left to allow Linda to rest between feeds. She was now on her own; there were no nurses to call on. She fed baby Stuart on demand and found that he was quite happily sleeping for five to six hours between feeds. She gave him his last feed for the night at 8pm, changed his nappy and put a fresh sleep-suit on him before tucking him into his new pram. She then said goodnight to James and wheeled the pram through to the bedroom before flopping into bed exhausted. She was out for the count and never heard James come to bed just before midnight. At 2am she was wakened up from her slumber by Stuart crying. She woke James up and said in a panic, 'The baby's crying, what could be the matter with him?' 'He probably needs to be fed and changed' 'WHAT!' exclaimed Linda, 'at this time in the morning, why would he need feeding and changing?' James knew this because his sister Iris' had stayed with the family for the first couple of weeks after her son Jamie was born eight years previously. Nobody told Linda that babies needed feeding and changing every four to six hours, 24 hours a day. She just assumed that when the nurses took the babies through to the nursery at 8pm every night and brought them back at 6am that they had slept through the night. Reality then hit home, this little man depended on her for survival and there was going to be lots of sleepless nights ahead.

Two

Monday morning 7am and James got up for work. Linda only came out of hospital the day before and he hated to leave her and his new baby son. Just less than two hours after James had left for work, Linda heard the key in the door, she got worried, and wondering who on earth it could be when in walked James and his apprentice Davy. They were passing the house on their way to a job and James seized the opportunity to nip in and see his baby son. He was beaming as he picked him up to show him off to Davy. They had a cup of tea then Linda told them that they had better get back to work, she knew how strict his boss, James' cousin, was and that he would be checking up on them. Just as they were leaving, Linda's dad, Douglas MacGregor Senior, walked in. He was a postman and his delivery round was not too far away in the High Street. Linda thought, *'God I'm never going to get anything done this morning between feeds!'* This was to become a habit for Douglas Senior. Every morning just after 9am, he popped in for a cup of tea and to see his wee grandson. He was so proud to be a granddad.

It wasn't long until Linda had a good routine going. Baby Stuart woke up for his bottle around 2am then after he was fed and changed he slept through until 7.00 am. Linda fed and changed him again, he usually slept for two or three hours in the morning and Linda used this time to get washed, dressed and catch up with housework and boiling nappies. She kept baby Stuart immaculate, she had knitted lots of matinee jackets; cardigans, hats, bootees, mittens, cot and pram blankets and so had her mother Margie, James' mother Molly and some of their aunts, so he was a very well dressed baby.

The Friday after Linda came out of hospital, James' two mates came round to visit and see baby Stuart for the first time, Alan with his new (and very pregnant) wife Helen and Eric with his girlfriend Morag. Alan walked in and plonked a Mars Bar, Cadbury's Dairy Milk and a packet of Maltesers on the coffee table. 'These are for the we'an', he said. 'Are you serious?' Linda laughed. Alan cocked his head to the side and looked at her with a questionable frown. 'I tried to tell him, but he wouldn't listen!' said Helen as she breathed out in exasperation and shook her head at him. 'Oh that's alright' said Linda, still giggling, 'they won't go to waste, Stuart's mummy will enjoy them'.

Once a week Linda took Stuart to the Baby Clinic in Bridgeton, she loved to walk out with him in his pram and soon got to know the area well. People's heads turned and they stopped her to admire her modern mustard leather pram. Linda was so proud when they looked in the pram and complimented her saying what a beautiful baby she had.

James and Linda visited her parents Douglas and Margie every weekend, either on a Saturday night or a Sunday afternoon and James' mother Molly every Sunday night. One Sunday morning the weather was so nice that James and Linda set off early to walk to her parent's house, it was ten miles and it took them over two hours. They spent the afternoon and had Sunday lunch with them before walking up to Molly's house. After two hours with Molly they walked to the train station and caught the train from Drumchapel to Belgrove Station in Dennistoun. It had been a long day and they were weary after all their walking.

Sometimes if Margie was off work, Linda caught the train from Belgrove to either Anniesland or Scotstounhill station and spent the day with her mum. James called in to collect her on his way home from work. On other occasions she visited Molly.

Molly had a Victorian attitude; she was a serious church-goer and was shocked that James and Linda hadn't thought about christening Baby Stuart. She nagged them constantly about this and said that she could easily arrange it at her church so Linda told her to go ahead and organise a date for the christening. When Baby Stuart was six weeks old he was christened in Drumchapel Congregational Church. Linda borrowed a christening robe from one of her friends whose baby was six months older than Stuart, Molly knitted a beautiful fine-knit shawl and James' sister Maria loaned them one of her twins silk christening bonnets to wear. Linda's cousin Anne was godmother, Linda and Anne were very close, they had been brought up two streets away from each other and as children were seldom apart, and although they could fight like sisters they wouldn't hear a bad word said about each other from anyone else. When they were little girls, they had promised that they would be each other bridesmaids and godparents to each other's children. Stuart was such a good baby and very well behaved during the ceremony. Outside the church afterwards, the proud godmother Anne, held him in her arms to show him off to all the family and the congregation while a few photos were taken and Anne's dad, Uncle Tom's, cine-camera whirred away to mark the event for posterity. The family and friends all walked round the corner to Molly's house (with Uncle Tom's cine-camera still working over-time), the women all taking it in turn to have a hold and cuddle with the baby. Molly had prepared sandwiches and baked two sponge cakes with jam in the middle and icing on the top, which was thick and drizzling over the edges. Linda and James supplied the booze and a good time was had by all as they celebrated the christening of Baby Stuart.

In June, Helen gave birth to a beautiful baby girl; she started having labour pains one week early. She was very cool, calm and collected as she told Alan, 'I think you had better call an ambulance.' 'What? You mean? I mean? The baby? Right ok, where's the number?' Alan replied in a sheer state of panic. 'For Heaven's sake Alan, pull yourself together, we've gone over this so many times, the number is written on the inside cover of our address book, right beside the phone! Oh, forget it, I'll do it myself' shouted Helen in exasperation. 'Ok, right,' said Alan as he disappeared out the door leaving Helen by herself. 'Now where are you going?' she called in sheer frustration. 'To look for the ambulance,' answered Alan. 'But I haven't even rung for one yet! She yelled then she mumbled under her breath, 'Oh I give up!' as she dialed the number. When the ambulance crew arrived they followed Alan running into the house just in time to see the baby's head appear. Alan was in a cold sweat as Helen told him, 'A fat lot of help you were, leaving me here to get on with things by myself!' Alan replied, 'Well I had to make sure the ambulance men didn't waste time looking for our house!' It was a quick, easy birth, from start to finish, it took no longer than two hours and mother and baby were fine, they called their new daughter Karen.

Linda and James went over the following week on Friday evening to see baby Karen. They parked outside the tenement where Alan and Helen lived, in a wee street just off Maryhill Road, near to Firhill Park, Patrick Thistle FC's ground. They had a one room and kitchen/living room in the close with an inside toilet. As they walked into the living room, they couldn't help but notice Alan's greasy overalls and clothes that he had been wearing that day to work lying in a corner on the floor, 'For goodness sake Alan, pick these up!' said Helen, then she turned to Linda and said, 'it's like having two babies in the house, he just steps out of his clothes and leaves them for me to pick up!' As Alan picked the clothes up from the floor, his underpants fell out. Helen laughed and said, 'Look at the colour of them, they're all black and oily round the fly!' to which Alan replied, 'What do you expect? I'm a car mechanic; I can't take them off by remote control for God sake!' They all had a good laugh at the thought of this.

Linda held Karen in her arms and it made her realize just how much her baby, Stuart, had grown. He was ten weeks old now and so much bigger than one-week old Karen. Linda had knitted a matinee jacket with matching bootees and mittens, she also bought a lovely wee angel top for Karen which Helen was delighted with.

July 1970 and Linda's brother, Douglas Junior's, wife announced that she was pregnant and the baby was due in January. Linda's parents Margie and Douglas were ecstatic at the thought of becoming grandparents for the second time. It seemed to do Douglas good, he was a very caring, loving grandpa', he adored his little grandson Stuart and spent more time with him than he ever spent with Linda or her brother. Linda hoped that the interest of having grandchildren would keep his mind occupied and sway him away from his old pal alcohol, but she still worried about her mother because Margie was a very private person and would never speak about any problems she may be having with her husband. Linda's biggest fear was that her mother was still suffering the consequences of her dad's foul temper and moods through drinking and keeping it to herself.

August 1970 and James came home with some shattering news. Work was thin on the ground and his cousin had no overtime for him. James and Linda relied on his overtime; it took his weekly wage up from £14 to £21. They just about made ends meet on £21. By mid week and after Linda had paid all the bills and shopping for the week, she usually only had £2 left to last them until Friday. There was no way that they could survive on £14 per week. They were sick with worry.

Linda was in the corner shop and heard the Greek owner, Dimitri, saying that his girl who worked from 6pm-8pm three evenings per week was moving to another area and he was going to have to replace her, otherwise it would mean shutting at 6pm on these evenings. When it came to Linda's turn to be served she said to him, 'I couldn't help overhearing, but if you need someone then I can work these evenings. 'Have you any experience?' he asked her. 'Well I ran a sales office' for six years, I'm good at figures and I've had Saturday jobs in shops in retail in the past. 'Can you come in tomorrow at 6pm and we'll see how you get on?' Linda ran home excitedly to tell James that they would have a little bit extra coming in to help. 'Are you sure you're fit enough, you know how tired you get with the baby' asked James worriedly. 'It's not a problem, you get home at 4.30pm every day, so we have plenty time to have dinner, then I can bath and feed Stuart before I go. It's only for a couple of hours, I'll give it a try' she answered.

Linda got on well, she got to know everyone and was soon cutting the meat on the big slicing machine, patting the butter and cutting the cheese to size with the wire. She was paid £1 per evening and the extra £3 came in very handy but they were still struggling financially.

One month later and work still wasn't improving. James said to Linda, 'It's no good, I'm going to have to find another job, we can't go on like this'. Linda knew that he was right, but she worried for him because he had started working for his cousin when he was fourteen, working Saturdays and school holidays. When he left school at fifteen he went to work for him full time and started an apprenticeship. His cousin was a good teacher but he was a mean, dour man with a bad temper. He insisted that James attended evening classes three nights per week to get his City and Guilds passes. James dutifully did this until he was fully qualified. James was very conscientious but his cousin never complimented him, he always found a reason to shout and bully James. However when James qualified and his cousin took on Davy to serve his apprenticeship, he treated him totally different. Davy was allowed one day off work with full pay to attend classes for his City and Guild qualifications, he never bullied Davy. James put it down to the

familiarity; he probably thought it was ok to treat Jan
because he was his cousin.

Linda saw a job vacancy in the Evening Times. A building
Bishopton was advertising for site joiners. He and Linda we
have a look on Saturday morning. The site manager happened to
there. James made enquiries and he was asked to start one week on
Monday.

Monday morning and James handed his notice in, his cousin was taken aback, he couldn't believe that James was leaving the firm. 'I have a wife and baby to keep now and we can't manage on £14 per week' he told his cousin.

The following Monday a very nervous James got ready to leave for his new job, he had never worked on a building site before and was really apprehensive but he knew that he had to go through with this because he had responsibilities. Linda was very concerned and worried about him as she waved him off at 7am and wished him a good first day.

That evening he got home just before 5.30pm, tired but excited, he told Linda all about his day. He was one of the boys! No more bullying from his big cousin, he was doing work that he had never done before and enjoyed learning new skills. He told Linda, 'They have offered me overtime two nights per week and a Saturday but this time the rates are far better than I earned in my last job. Also did you know that they are building brand new houses nearby to Bishopton in Erskine, they are part of the Glasgow overspill and if you work in the area you can qualify for a house.' Linda was relieved to see him so happy and got really excited at the prospect of a brand new council house with a garden.

On Friday James came home with a big grin on his face and handed Linda his unopened wage packet. He only got paid for four days up until the Thursday, but the following week he would get a full wage plus his overtime. Linda looked at the front of the packet, at the bottom and after deductions it read £17/5/-. Linda couldn't believe it, if this was only for four days, what was next week's wage going to be? The following week they felt like millionaires when James came home with £29/7/6d. They hugged each other with relief that their money worries were over.

There were three other men who lived near them and worked on the same building site as James. None of them could drive and travelled by public transport. They were delighted when James suggested that they met him every morning for a lift to work in his car and split the petrol costs. Instead of taking them over an hour to get to work they were all there within 30 minutes.

James and Linda managed to start saving a £1 or two every weekend and bought a baby walker, baby bouncer, a doorway swing and a pushchair for baby Stuart.

One evening per week James dropped Linda off at the self-service laundrette on Duke Street, where she was able to get the weeks washing done and then dried in the big tumble driers. James looked after Stuart then drove back down to pick her up again two hours later. She longed for a washing machine to save her all this bother and disruption of disturbing the baby to take him out in the car at night but they were worried about taking on more debt because they already had a fridge, cooker and TV to pay for every week and both knew that the building site would soon be coming to and end.

James came home from work one night and said to Linda, 'Next time we go to the launderette, make sure that all the washing is out of the car please'. 'How do you mean?' asked Linda. 'Well when I picked the lads up this morning, they jumped in the back of the car to find your black bikini knickers on the back seat, you can imagine the sort of stick that I got all day, the whole site got to know about it!' he laughed, as he threw them over to her. Linda caught them and joined in the laughter, 'they must have fallen out of the plastic bag, well at least they were clean' she answered with a cheeky giggle.

Linda was still working three nights per week in the corner shop and it was all becoming too much to spend another evening per week in the laundrette, she was feeling very tired and said to James, 'we really need to think about getting a washing machine!' Linda was washing the baby's clothes, sheets and nappies by hand every day and hanging them out in the backcourt by her kitchen window. Then she had to go to the laundrette once a week to attend to their clothes and bedding. 'If I had a washing machine, I could get things washed daily, I wouldn't have to stand for ages at the sink every morning and I would have that extra evening at home to relax and catch up on some sleep if nothing else!' James knew that she was right and told her to go into the electricity board in town and choose one on HP terms. Linda did just that and her brand new Servis Twin Tub was delivered the following week. There was no room in her wee kitchenette for it so it was kept in the corner behind the front door in the hallway. Every morning she pushed it through her lounge to the door of her kitchenette. The hose just about reached the sink so she was able to fill the washing machine up and was delighted as it sat in the corner of her lounge by the kitchenette churning away and taking care of that days washing while she attended to her baby and other household chores.

James and Linda both worked hard, when James arrived home from work on Monday, Wednesday and Friday evenings, Linda had baby Stuart bathed and ready for bed then she served up dinner before going off to work in the corner shop until 8pm. On Tuesday and Thursday evenings they dined late because James worked overtime and didn't get home until just after 8pm. James' mother Molly still kept up her visits and every Thursday and dead on 7pm she turned up at the door. It was the same ritual every Thursday, Linda kept Stuart up to see his Nana then after fifteen minutes she put him into his cot in the bedroom and started to make dinner for the three of them. Just after 10pm James took his mother home while Linda cleared up and got all the dishes, pots and pans washed, dried and put away.

It was mid October 1970, Linda was exhausted, baby Stuart was teething and wouldn't settle, when James came in from work to take over, he said to Linda, 'You can't go to work in the shop like that, you are shattered!' Linda replied, 'I have to, I can't let Dimitri down'. When she got back that night James was very pleased to see her, 'I can't do anything with the baby, he's not interested and just keeps yelling,' Linda rubbed some teething gel on Stuart's gums, put him in the pram and walked up and down the hall with him but the baby was having none of it, he screamed louder. 'You'd think he would tire himself out crying and fall off to sleep, wouldn't you? When I take him out for a walk, the fresh air always knocks him out but I can't very well take him outside, it's almost midnight!' exclaimed Linda desperately. 'Who said you can't?' replied James, jumping to his feet, 'get him wrapped up then you sit down and have a rest, I'm taking him for a walk!' Linda looked horrified, 'You can't take a baby out at this time of night?' she answered. 'Can't I, who says so?' said James. Linda was too tired to disagree, she did what James asked and put Stuart's warm all-in-one baby suit on top of his sleep suit, then she put him down in his pram with warm covers. James wheeled the pram out of the close with baby Stuart exercising his lungs to their full potential. Twenty minutes later Linda heard the key going into the lock, she tip-toed towards the door in time to see James gently pushing the wheels of the pram over the threshold, he had his finger to his mouth, gesturing Linda to be as quiet as possible but by the time the pram was fully in the door, baby Stuart woke up and started again. James and Linda looked at each other in desperation, they were both exasperated. 'You had better get to bed James, you've got work in the morning,' said Linda 'What about you? You have a lot to do tomorrow too?' answered James. 'I'll just have to try and cat-nap when I can' replied Linda. Linda finally fell into bed at 2am. They were both woken just after 5am with Stuart started crying again. Linda rubbed her eyes and said as she got up to see to him, 'The poor wee soul he must be in agony, I'll be just as glad as he will when these teeth come through!' When Molly came for her usual Thursday night visit, Stuart was still playing up; Linda decided rather than staying at home while James took his mother home, she and Stuart would go with them for the hour long return journey. The motion of the car always knocked him out, but as soon as they got home and entered the house, he opened his eyes and they were back to square one as they took it in turns to walk the floor trying to calm their screaming baby son.

Early November 1970 and Douglas Junior got the word that he had got a job in a big international company in London. His parents Margie and Douglas were happy for them but devastated that they were moving so far away and they weren't going to have the privilege of seeing their new grandchild grow up. Douglas Junior and Norma decided that he would go down to London and start his new job and she would stay in Scotland until their baby was born before joining him. Norma's parents helped them scrape together the deposit for a house and Douglas Junior spent his weekends searching for a home for his wife and baby. After only two weeks he found the perfect place in a sleepy village on the Surrey/Hampshire border just outside Camberley. It was a two year old, three bedrooms, end of terrace with a nice big back garden laid to lawn, but at £4,450 it was practically double what the same house in Glasgow would have cost. Douglas Junior tried to get up to see his wife every second or third weekend, If he was lucky he managed to get a £5 seat on the late night Royal Mail plane from Heathrow to Glasgow, not everyone knew about this perk so he kept it to himself. Norma couldn't wait to have her baby and join her husband in their new abode.

Fiona Lisa MacGregor was born mid January 1971 by caesarian section, she was a beautiful healthy baby weighing in at 7lb. 2oz. Linda went up to see her in hospital and when she held this brand new little bundle in her arms she immediately felt broody again.

James saw a four year old Vauxhall Victor Estate car for sale in a local showroom for £400. He took Linda down to the showroom to see it. 'The Anglia won't last forever, we should sell it before it gets any older,' he told her, then he continued, 'it'll be perfect for the baby, the pram will fit in the back no bother.' Linda loved it and before they knew it they were discussing HP terms and trading their Anglia in as a deposit.

March 1971 and the Bishopton site came to an end for James, there was no other work in that area which saddened Linda because it put paid to any chance they had of getting a nice brand new Glasgow overspill house in Erskine. Linda and James scoured the job vacancy columns in the local newspapers. James saw one advertised in a site in Bridgeton, when he got there, there was a queue stretching right down the street and round the corner, there must have been over forty men waiting to be interviewed for this one vacancy for a joiner.

Two weeks passed and still there was no sign of work, there were too many tradesmen and not enough jobs to go round. Linda and James' savings were beginning to dwindle. James decided to take the bull by the horns and instead of waiting for vacancies to be advertised, he started driving round the building sites in and around Glasgow. After three days he managed to get a start on a site in Coatbridge. The site foreman told him that he could give him two months work. James was delighted, that was better than nothing. He went home and told Linda who was relieved to hear the good news. 'But what do we do in two months time when the job comes to an end?' she said worriedly. 'Don't worry, we'll cross that bridge when we come to it, I'm a tradesman, I'll always get work, it's not a problem at the moment' answered James. Linda felt secure in James' confidence.

April 1971 and Linda and James were delighted to discover that she was pregnant again; they had planned to have their children close together. Ideally Linda wanted to have three more children before she was thirty, so that she and Douglas could be young with them.

Linda was coping well with her pregnancy; she was healthy and not as sick as she had been when she was expecting Stuart. Everyone was telling her how easy the second one would be and that labour was always quicker and never as long as it is with the first baby.

No-one had seen James' sister Iris for over a month or knew where she was. She had left her son Jamie with her mother while she went away gallivanting , this was nothing new, Iris was famous for taking off whenever she felt fit, she believed that Jamie was as much her mother's responsibility as hers. She only ever turned up when she was in trouble and needed her family, if you didn't hear from her you knew that her life was going well. Molly was upset because she was due to go away with the church for two weeks to Blackpool the following week but if Iris didn't turn up then she would have to cancel. Linda felt sorry for her because she knew how much she had been looking forward to her holiday. On the spur of the moment she said to Molly, 'Don't worry, you go on holiday Jamie can stay with us for two weeks' 'Are you sure, that would solve everything for me?' answered Molly. 'Yes, you go and enjoy yourself!' insisted Linda.

When the weekend came James went to his mothers house and collected his nephew, Jamie jumped out of the car excitedly outside Linda and James' close and shouted 'Aunty Linda, I'm here, I've got my case,' Linda gave him a cuddle and took his wee brown battered case from him. 'Right I've cleared out the wee chest of drawers and put it in the spare room, let's go and put this stuff away. I've borrowed a folding Z-bed from my friend for you while you're here because we haven't got a spare bed.' She might as well have been talking to the wall because wee Jamie wasn't interested. As he was getting older he was becoming quite difficult with moods and tantrums, Linda put it down to his lack of security, he had been so used to moving in and out of friend's houses, he didn't know where he belonged. Linda felt like crying when she looked at his worldly possessions, he had one pair of well worn short trousers, falling apart at the seams, a threadbare pair of jeans, two T shirts, one jumper with holes appearing in the elbows, two pairs of socks with holes in the heels, one pair of washed-out pyjamas and an action man. 'Is this all you've brought with you for two weeks?' Linda asked, 'That's all my mammy gave me when she took me to Nana's' he replied unconcerned, 'can I go out and play now?' he continued.

That evening, Jamie had a bath and changed into his pyjamas,

Linda was gathering up the clothes he had taken off for the wash. She picked up his shoes and was horrified to see that both the shoes he had been wearing had large holes in the soles. 'Haven't you got another pair of shoes? Linda asked Jamie; 'No, my mammy says that they'll have to do me because she can't afford to keep buying me shoes' answered Jamie. After he went to bed, Linda said to James, 'We can't have the wee soul running around with his shoes hanging off his feet, I'll take him out and buy him a new pair tomorrow.' 'Are you sure we can afford that? asked James, 'We'll just have to!' was Linda's swift reply. True to her word, Linda took Jamie out the next morning for new shoes, he choose tan corduroy ones, the same as all the other kids were wearing. 'Can I keep them on Aunty Linda?' he asked with glee 'Of course you can,' she happily answered. The shopkeeper asked, 'Would you like the old shoes in a bag? Linda answered with embarrassment, 'No, can you please chuck them in the bin?' The shopkeeper picked one up in each hand with her index finger and thumbs, screwed her nose up and carried them out to the back shop. Jamie skipped and danced up the road and couldn't wait to show his Uncle James his new shoes.

Two weeks later, Linda packed Jamie's suitcase to take him back to Molly's, 'Can I come back and stay again sometime Aunty Linda?' Jamie asked her. Linda cuddled him and said, 'Of course you can, anytime you want!' Jamie gave a big satisfying sigh and cuddled into Linda. He had behaved impeccably, no moods, no tantrums, made lots of new friends and seemed to have a wonderful time. James and Linda got Jamie and baby Stuart into the back of the car and drove over to Drumchapel. Jamie ran into the house and gave his Nana a big hug, telling her excitedly all about his 'holiday' with Uncle James and Aunty Linda and showing off his new corduroy shoes. 'Have you heard from Iris?' Molly asked James, 'Not a word' answered James. 'I don't know, that girl has no sense of responsibility, she's not fit to be a mother,' Molly said, shaking her head and tutting, then she went on, 'she's not playing fair, I'm getting on and I don't have the same energy any more, I'm finding it hard going looking after an 8 year old. At that the doorbell rang, it was James other sister Maria with her three boys, Adam and Greg (the twins) were now three and a half years old and Darren was almost two. She had her hands full and never got any help from her husband but it never affected her cheery personality, she cracked jokes and loved to embarrass her wee brother James telling 'over exaggerated' stories about when he was little. 'Give it a rest Maria, they've heard it all before, and the stories get a bit added to them every time you tell them!' said James. Maria laughed and said, 'It's all true Linda, right hand up to God, he just doesn't want to admit it!' then she continued, 'Oh mammy did you know that Iris is staying in Dennistoun?' 'SHE'S WHAT?' answered Molly with a questionable stare, 'She's staying in Dennistoun, do you remember Julie who she worked with in the pub in Drumchapel and shared a flat with in Kelvinside, well I met her last week and she told me that they all go to a 'Treble 2 Club there,' said Maria. 'Treble 2 Club in Dennistoun, I've never heard of that, have you Linda?' asked James. Linda pouted her bottom lip and shook her head in agreement. 'Yes! But wait,' said Maria, 'I met her again yesterday and she says that treble 2 is the number in the street in Dennistoun that her new boyfriend lives at, 222 Greenside Street!' 'Her new boyfriend?' answered Molly in complete amazement, she was getting angrier by the minute, 'you mean she has a new boyfriend, she lives near James and Linda in Dennistoun and she has had us all looking after her son while she has been living it up, I have been worried sick wondering where the hell she was, I'll 'new boyfriend' her, just wait until I get my hands on her!' continued Molly shaking with temper.

The following Thursday evening Molly came over to visit James and Linda as usual with wee Jamie in tow, only this time she had Jamie's case with her. 'What's this, are you going somewhere' asked Linda, fully expecting Molly to tell her that she was going away for a few days and ask if her if Jamie could stay again with her and James. 'I've made my mind up, he's going to his mother, that's where he belongs, I am too old to be looking after an 8 year old, it would be different if there was something wrong with her but she's only out partying and boozing it up, leaving me with all the responsibility of her son,' Linda reeled back in amazement and asked, 'How do you mean, he's going back, how are you going to get him back?' Molly answered, 'Well now that we know where she's living when James takes me home tonight we'll stop off and hand Jamie over!' Linda was extremely concerned, poor wee Jamie, he was passed from pillar to post, no wonder he had had moods and tantrums and seemed troubled! James came in from work and Linda beckoned him in to the kitchen to tell him what his mother had planned. 'It's not right, you can't send a child into a house, to someone you know nothing about. What if he has no time for kids and hurts Jamie?' said Linda. 'I appreciate what you are saying Linda but at the same time, my mother is in her mid sixties, she's too old to be looking after a child, she's had her days of bringing up kids, she should be enjoying her life now!' answered James. 'I am very worried and I am not in agreement with this at all, he can stay here,' said Linda. James replied 'We can't have him on a permanent basis, that would be right up Iris' street, I don't mind having him for a couple of weeks here and there, but he is hers and no-one else's responsibility and that is final!'

That evening, baby Stuart was unsettled, so she decided to take him in the car with James, Molly and wee Jamie for the run to Drumchapel. James drove round to Greenside Street; Linda tried to talk Molly and James out of it. 'You can't take him to a strange house at this time of night, what if Iris isn't even there?' But Molly was determined. 'He's going back to his mother, where he belongs!' she insisted. Wee James just sat in the backseat listening to the conversation with his head bowed saying nothing. 'Right there's number 222, stop here' Molly said. Linda felt helpless as she gave wee Jamie a hug. 'Right son c'mon, out you get, here's your case, you're going to stay with your mammy, go and knock on that door' Molly said. Wee Jamie did what he was told and gave Linda a peck on the cheek before climbing out the back of the car. Linda's heart bled as she watched the little fellow walk into the close, with his wee case of worldly goods not worth tuppence. The door opened, Iris looked at her son then looked at the car, staring face to face with Linda, before scowling and grabbing Jamie's shoulder and pulling him indoors. Linda couldn't sleep that night for worrying about wee Jamie and what sort of house they had taken him to; she prayed that he was going to be alright.

The following Sunday they went up to visit Molly as usual. Molly told them that Iris had phoned and said, 'If she sees that bitch Linda in Dennistoun, she will punch her! Molly seemed to take the remark in her stride, she was used to Iris. Linda asked in shock, 'Why does she want to punch me, what have I done other than look after her son for her?' 'Well she blames you for dropping James off at her boyfriend's place!' Linda frowned in anger and said, 'Didn't you tell her that it was nothing to do with me, that I was against it and it was all your idea?' 'No, there was no point, once Iris gets a bee in her bonnet she doesn't listen to anyone!' Molly answered. Linda was really upset that anyone could think she could be so callous as to dump Wee Jamie off at a strange house at 10 o'clock at night but even more upset at the thought of bumping into Iris in Duke Street, Iris was a nutter, she appeared to be envious of Linda. She had given Linda a black eye for nothing at her 21st birthday party and Linda had no doubts that she would have no hesitation in doing it again. Linda was worried about the safety of her unborn baby, what if Iris attacked her from behind, when she was shopping!

Douglas Junior and Norma had asked James and Linda to come down to London for a visit. They decided that the best time to go would be when James' work in Coatbridge came to an end and he would be in-between jobs, Linda didn't want to leave it any longer because she would be too far on in her pregnancy, she had never been to London before and was really looking forward to it, her parents had been to visit Douglas Junior and Norma for Easter and told her all about it, she was really excited.

The day arrived for their trip to London. It was a Friday in the middle of June; James had worked until lunchtime for his last day on the Coatbridge job. Linda could hardly contain herself, she had packed two large suitcases, one for baby Stuart, and one between herself and James, They packed their big estate car to the hilt with Baby Stuart's pram, suitcases, some toys, baby necessities and Linda had filled a big cardboard box with groceries to take with her for Douglas Junior and Norma because she appreciated that they were struggling to pay their mortgage and she didn't expect them to keep James and herself. 'We'd better get on our way, it's almost four o'clock, are you nearly ready Linda?' James asked her. 'Yes, I think that's it now, I hope I haven't forgotten anything!' she answered. At that James disappeared back in to the house and came out a few minutes later carrying his wooden tool box. 'What are you doing?' Linda asked with a puzzled look on her face, as James started rearranging their belongings in the car boot. 'I'm taking my tools, you never know' he answered. Linda looked at him with disbelief then she pouted her lip and cocked her head to the side as if in agreement and said, 'Well it won't do any harm!' They got Stuart settled in the back seat with Linda then James jumped into the driver's seat and off they went for the long drive south.

Douglas Junior had given them directions to drive out of Scotland on the A74 and straight onto the M6. Just after Birmingham they were to look out for the A34 heading towards Banbury, then Oxford,

Reading and finally through the country roads past Eversley heading towards Camberley. They stopped off at the first motorway services on the M6 for a refreshment, toilet break and to call Douglas Junior and Norma to tell them their whereabouts. They had two more stops on the way and at the last one they phoned Douglas Junior and Norma to tell them that they estimated they were about two hours away. It was midnight and they were shattered, they had been travelling for eight hours. Norma told them that she would leave the porch light on so that they could pick out their house from the others in the dark. It was just after 2am and at last they found the village, they had to find the street now. It was pitch black as they drove past the common. Linda had a piece of paper with hand-written directions that her brother had sent to her; she tried to see it in the dark. 'Here, see if this helps' said James as he lit his cigarette lighter and held the naked flame over the paper to allow her to read it. 'That's better,' replied Linda, 'now I think I know where we are! Ok take a right turn here at the top of this road then their road is the second on the right.' James followed her directions, then Linda beamed with delight as she said, 'There's a house with a porch light on, that must be it.' James pulled up outside and got out to see the house number. As he walked back towards the car, he waved and gestured to Linda that this was the right house. Norma had been looking out for them and followed James out to the car to help get their belongings into the house. 'Right, let's get this little boy to bed,' he said as he gently lifted sleeping Stuart in his arms. Norma said, 'Take him straight upstairs, your bedroom is on the immediate left.' James came back down to get the suitcases from the car. 'I'm afraid Douglas couldn't wait up, he needs to go into work tomorrow morning and has to get up at 6.00am to catch the train to London for work, would you like a cup of tea?' Norma asked without stopping to take a breath. 'Oh no, answered Linda, 'thanks very much but there's a little lad that will be waking us up very early in the morning, we really need to catch up on some sleep after that journey if you don't mind.' 'Not at all,' laughed Norma, 'I was only being polite, I am having trouble keeping my eyes open!'

Linda was up early the next morning with baby Stuart and was able see her brother before he set off at 6.30am James came downstairs at 8.15am and said, 'Right! Where are we off to today?' Linda replied, 'Are you sure you feel like driving again after yesterday?' 'No bother,' answered James, he enjoyed driving and couldn't wait to get out and about to see the sights. 'Well I really fancy going into London, just to say that I have seen it,' said Linda with an open eyed questioned expression as if to ask if that would be possible' 'London it is then!' replied James much to Linda's delight, as if he was the Genie in the lamp granting wishes.

They drove as far as Hounslow then decided to park up and get the tube into the city, this was really exciting because they had only ever travelled on the Glasgow Underground Subway before and compared to the London tube that was only like a wee toy train going in a little circle round the town. It was a beautiful sunny June day; they arrived at Trafalgar Square and bought a map from one of the street sellers. They walked down the mall, past St. James' Park, down to Buckingham Palace. They stood there staring in awe at the grandeur of it all, from there they went to see Downing Street, then went back to Trafalgar Square to eat some sandwiches that Linda had prepared before they left that morning. 'Well now you can go back and tell all your pals that you've seen the sights of London!' James said to Linda. 'It's amazing, I can't wait to boast to them all, but we will have to see Piccadilly Circus, and Oxford Street. I've got to tell everyone what the shops are like!' James groaned, he hated shopping and it was Saturday, they couldn't have picked a busier day if they tried, but he appreciated that this was something Linda had to do. 'Right let's get on with it then,' he replied, with a total lack of enthusiasm as he picked up the left-over tin foil from their sandwiches, screwed it up and threw in the bin. Linda put the lid back on their flask, dried out the plastic cups with tissues and placed them along with baby Stuart's bottle of juice and cup in the bag hanging over the handle of their pushchair and off they set for Oxford Street to do some window shopping!

The next morning, Douglas Junior wanted to take them for a walk to see Blackbush airport. After breakfast Norma put the roast in the oven to cook slowly for Sunday lunch then she and Linda prepared the potatoes and vegetables before they all set off to see the small airport from where little private planes flew in and out. They walked through the woods, 'This is like another world,' said Linda as the airport came into view through the trees. James and Douglas Junior were like two schoolboys as they held their babies in their arms pointing to the planes taking off and landing in front of their noses.

Monday morning and Linda called her old friend Katherine, whom she had worked with in her office job in Glasgow. Katherine had lived in London for five years and had married a Londoner called Sam. Linda and Katherine had kept in touch regularly by letter. 'Guess where I am?' Linda announced proudly over the phone. 'Where?' said Katherine, then there was a pause, 'You're never in London?' she shouted down the phone excitedly to Linda. 'Well no…but I'm in Surrey' 'Come over, can you get here today? Sam and I are on holiday from work this week, we're not going anywhere today though, please come and see us, I'd love you to meet Sam,' Katherine blurted out. Linda laughed and said, 'Hang on I'll ask James what his plans are, he's the one who has to do the driving.' She turned to her husband and said 'Katherine wants us to visit her and Sam, they are home from work today,' 'Ok, we've got nothing else planned for today, get directions and we'll go' answered James. Katherine told Linda over the phone how to get to her house in Walthamstow. Linda was a good navigator, but this was London and they got lost a couple of times. Two hours later they arrived at the tower block and parked outside. Katherine and Sam lived on the 18th floor. Linda couldn't wait to see her and practically ran from the lift to find her door. She rattled the letterbox and when Katherine appeared the two pals hugged each other warmly. Katherine picked Stuart up and cuddled him as she said 'What a gorgeous wee son you've got, he's brilliant!' James and Sam got on like a house on fire while Katherine gave Linda a tour of her flat and showed her the view over London from her window. The two women talked non-stop reminiscing about the good times in the past while baby Stuart played happily in the corner with his cars and colouring-in book .The time whizzed by and before they knew it James and Linda were navigating their way through London back towards Surrey.

Tuesday morning and James went out for a drive while Linda helped Norma with the housework and caught up on their washing. 'Is the weather always so hot and sunny down here?' she asked Norma and continued with, 'it's great for drying the clothes!' James returned two hours later, he had a smile on his face from ear to ear. 'What are you so happy about? You look like the cat that has just got the cream!' laughed Linda. 'Well…!' replied James with caution, 'I don't know how you'll feel about this but I have just got a job,' 'WHAT!' answered Linda, not knowing whether to be happy or sad, 'when do you start?' she asked him. 'Tomorrow' answered James as he looked at her with pursed lips waiting for her reaction. 'TOMORROW! But we are only here for two weeks!' Linda answered in shock. 'I can always just work for three days this week then until the end of next week, they are crying out for joiners down here, the money is great, it's three times the wages in Glasgow, it means that I'll be earning instead of spending!' James pleaded. Linda was apprehensive but she agreed for her husband to try it out.

James came back on Wednesday evening and told Linda all about it, 'It's great, because they are really short of chippies......' 'What did you say?' Linda interrupted. 'Chippies it means carpenters, they don't say joiners down here,' explained James. 'God you're learning the lingo already, chippies sounds like a chip shop to me!' replied Linda 'Anyway as I was saying,' said James as he continued, 'because there is a great shortage of chippies in this part of the world, you get treated with great respect, the employers are frightened that you are going to cross the road and work for someone else, and that is exactly how easy it is, there is work on every corner and you can name your price, I earned £8 today on this job, that's £24 I'll collect on Friday for three days work I worked all week in Scotland for £18! If I work all of next week I'll get £40. I worked 5 days plus 2 evenings and a Saturday morning back home to earn three quarters of that!' Linda knew that it made sense and they needed the money, she was glad she got to see London when she did because there wouldn't be any time for sight-seeing now.

After two weeks, James and Linda were due to drive home on Saturday morning. The site foreman was sorry to let James go, he knew a good tradesman when he saw one. When he handed him his wages he gave him the site telephone number and told him that should he change his mind to give him a ring, there was a job waiting for him.

James and Linda were home two days; the job situation in Glasgow was bleak. James said to Linda, 'I don't see that we have any choice, we need an income, I have to go back down south to work!' Linda felt her stomach turn over, she knew that James enjoyed working in Surrey, he was treated with so much more respect, she replied, 'well if that's what you have to do, then do it, if you work down there until nearer the time when the baby is due then we could maybe save up enough for a deposit to buy a house here.' James looked worried, 'yes, but what about you, you're four months pregnant and you have Stuart to look after, I can't leave you to cope on your own in your condition! Can't you come back down with me Linda?' 'But James, where would we stay? You know there are no houses to rent in that part of the country and even if you are lucky enough to find one, they always stipulate 'no children! No, let's just play it by ear, if you think that going back down south to work is the best move for the moment then do it, at least we'll have money coming in, we'll make a final decision nearer to when the baby is due. Don't worry I'm an adult I can cope on my own' answered Linda.

The next day James phoned the site in Surrey and spoke to the foreman. 'When can you start?' was the foreman's swift reply. 'I can drive down tomorrow and start on Thursday morning' answered James. 'See you Thursday morning at 8am' replied the foreman. James told Linda what the foreman had said, she didn't want him to go but she didn't see what else they could do, they needed an income. 'Where are you going to stay? You'll have to call Douglas and Norma and ask them if you can stay with them temporarily until you find digs' James got on the phone and called Douglas Junior, who was very happy for him, 'of course you can stay with us, when can we expect to see you?' 'Tomorrow night' James answered screwing his face up as if to say, *'I know I've got a right cheek!'* 'That's great, not a problem, we look forward to seeing you' answered Douglas Junior. Linda helped James pack his belongings, her heart felt heavy, she was very apprehensive about living on her own but she didn't want James to know this. She went over to the corner shop and told Dimitri that she wouldn't be able to work for him anymore because James was going to London to work and she didn't have anyone to look after Stuart, besides she would have had to pack it up soon anyway because she was four months pregnant and having Stuart to run after, she was tiring easily.

Wednesday morning and James was up and ready to leave for the drive south at 6am. 'Are you sure that you and Stuart are going to be alright Linda, will you cope ok? I mean I won't go if you don't want me to, just say the word' 'Don't be daft, I'll be fine, just go!' answered Linda, trying hard to control her emotions. James put his suitcase and toolbox in the boot of the car, then he came back and picked Stuart up from his cot and held him tight, he carried him out to the street and stood by the car, then he pulled Linda up close, the three of them held on to each other. After a few minutes Linda broke free and said, 'If you're going to go, I think you better go now,' she felt her voice quivering, she didn't want to break down and so much wanted to show James how brave she was. James cuddled Stuart tightly again and gave Linda a warm kiss before handing the baby over to her. He got into the driver's seat and closed the car door. At that his baby son pulled back with outstretched arms, trying to get back to his daddy and crying 'Daddy! Daddy! Daddy!' This was too much and both James and Linda were overcome with emotion. Linda felt her eyes welling up, James was going to get back out of the car but Linda hid her face with her hand and gestured to him to go. She could see a tear running down her husband's cheek and baby Stuart was still crying 'Daddy! Daddy! Daddy!' as the car pulled away. She wiped her baby's tears with her hand then held him close to her with both her arms and sobbed her heart out as she watched the car disappear round the corner. Meanwhile James was having difficulty focusing on the road through his tears, he wondered if he was doing the right thing but he couldn't see any other option, they needed an income and there was nothing for him in Glasgow, there was good money to be earned down south. Every time he thought of his baby son crying after him it started him off again. He reached Carlisle before he was able to control his tears and concentrate on the rest of the journey.

James carried on driving south with a heavy heart, he pushed on with the journey stopping twice on the way to call Linda. He got to Douglas Junior and Norma's house at 2pm that afternoon. Norma was at home, he felt awkward on his own without Linda. That evening over dinner, he promised Douglas Junior and Norma that he would be out from under their feet as soon as he could find digs. He reported for work the following morning at 8am and worked conscientiously day in day out, calling Linda every evening from a public call box on the way home from work. He was very lonely, he missed his wife and baby son so much, he got home from work every evening, and sometimes went for a walk to get out and give Douglas Junior and Norma space and time to themselves, at other times he babysat to allow them to go out for the evening. He worked long hours and found it hard to find time to look for digs or even a place to bring Linda and Stuart down to. Every week he faithfully sent money home to Linda, it was hard because although he was earning good money, he had to live and pay something towards his keep to Douglas Junior and Norma

One month passed and James' work on the site was coming to an end. He called Linda and told her that he would be home at the end of the week. Linda was very excited at the thought of seeing her husband again and holding him in her arms. She was very lonely; she needed her husband more than ever now that she was just over five months pregnant and little Stuart needed his daddy. She found that the days were ok but the nights were very long and lonely. Sometimes she went over to stay at her parents but she appreciated that they had their own life now and as much as they loved their grandson, she felt that she was in their way and upsetting their routine.

James drove home overnight on Friday night and at 6am he pulled his car up outside the flat in Glasgow. Linda could hardly sleep that night for excitement; she kept showing wee Stuart photos of his daddy and telling him that he was coming home. When she heard the car outside she jumped up out of bed and ran to the window, by this time James was walking in through the door, she ran to the door and into his arms, 'Oh I've missed you so much' she said as she flung her arms around her husband, James hugged and held on to her for a few minutes before giving her a long lingering kiss 'Right where's my wee boy? I've brought something for him' said James. 'Oh, go and see him, he'll be awake by now,' answered Linda. James went into the bedroom and picked Stuart up from his cot, the wee boy had just woken up and was looking at his dad as if to say, '*So you've decided to come home, have you?*' James held him close and said 'oh my wee son, I've missed you so much!' Linda put her arms round the both of them and they both cried tears of happiness as they felt the warmth of being together again as a family then James put Stuart down and showed him a big box, the wee boy pointed and said 'Ou Ou At?' which was his way of saying 'What is that?' James tore the box open to reveal a toddler trike. Wee Stuart was delighted as his dad sat him on his new toy, he held onto the handlebars and giggled with joy as his dad pushed him up and down the hallway and tooted the wee horn.

You must be starving!' said Linda to James and she went into the kitchen and made him a full Scottish fry up breakfast of sliced sausage, black pudding, tattie scone, fried dumpling, bacon and egg. Over breakfast she told him about what had been happening at home while he was away. 'Charlie still hasn't passed his test yet and his motor is lying dormant in the street but the best laugh is that he went out one morning and a woman over the road was fast asleep in the back seat, turns out that she had had a big argument with her husband the night before!' James laughed when he heard the story then he turned seriously to Linda and told her that he had found another job to start a week on Monday. Linda had an idea that he was going to come out with something like this and although she was devastated and dreaded him going away again. 'How long is this going to go on for James? I mean I know the money is good and there isn't any work here but we can't go on living like this, the baby is due in just over three months and I am finding it hard-going on my own now with wee Stuart!' James said, 'Well this new job is in a cinema in Farnham, we are converting it into a cinema/bingo hall and I will be in charge of all the carpentry labour, the money is even better than the last job. If we can't find anywhere to live down south nearer to the time of the birth then I will come home, the baby will be born here, I will find some sort of work locally and that will be the end of it, but I will do my very best to get a place for us to live and be a family again, our new addition could well be a wee English person!' Linda always trusted James' judgement and had faith in him that everything would work out ok in the end.

'I've found a room in a house in Camberley for when I go back next week' said James. Linda laughed as he told her, 'the landlady seems very weird and old fashioned, she emphasized that she didn't like being disturbed then went on to show me how to close the door quietly and even how to flush the toilet, but it was better than nothing, I had to find something quick because your mum and dad are going down next week and there will be no room for me at your brothers' place!' Linda said, 'I've an idea, my mum and dad were going to get the London bus all the way because it's the cheapest way to go, then they have to make their way with their cases to Waterloo station to catch a train to Camberley, it will be an awful long journey for them. As you are going back next weekend you could take them with you James!' 'No Bother, it would be daft for them to get a bus when I'm going there anyway, besides it will be good company for me,' said James. 'I'll give them a ring this morning and tell them before they go and buy tickets!' said Linda.

The following Saturday morning James went over at 7am to collect Linda's parents, they were so excited and looking forward to their drive down south but at the same time, Margie was very worried at leaving Linda, although her daughter was married, had a toddler and another baby on the way, she was still only twenty three and the whole family were going down south for two weeks and leaving her on her own, over and above this, Linda had agreed to look after their dog Chienne while her parents were away. Margie was concerned that it would all be too much for her but Linda put on a brave face and told them all not to be so daft and to go and enjoy themselves. As they all piled into the car Linda felt very lonely standing on the pavement watching them, she would have liked nothing better than to have jumped into the car as well but her brother and his wife didn't have the room. Besides she knew it wasn't fair to take advantage of their hospitality. James hugged and kissed Stuart and her before getting into the driver's seat, Margie opened the back window and said to Linda with concern, 'I really don't like leaving you, are you sure you're going to be alright? 'YES! Now just go' said Linda not wanting to prolong the agony. She watched the car disappear round the corner and she felt her heart sink, she didn't really want them to go. She felt all alone, her husband, mum, dad, brother and his wife were all going to be over four hundred miles away. She stood there holding wee Stuart's hand with her right hand and Chienne's leash in her left hand. She looked at wee Stuart as he happily patted the dog, it seemed to take his mind off of everyone going in the car and leaving him. Slowly she turned and walked into the close wondering how much longer they could survive this way of life and what the future held for her, James, Stuart and their unborn child.

Three hours later Linda got a call from James to tell her that there were horrendous traffic jams on the M6 and they weren't moving very fast. 'I'll keep you posted and call you at our next stop' he promised. Five hours went by and they hadn't even reached the junction for the Manchester turn off, this was going to be a long trek. James was worried because the fussy landlady he was due to go to had told him to be there by 6pm. Finally at 9.35pm they pulled up outside Douglas Junior and Norma's house. James helped them in with their suitcases then made a dash for his new digs. He rang the doorbell, 'The sour faced landlady with bleached blonde hair like straw hanging out of a midden and her arms folded over her big bosoms came to the door. 'Oh it's you, you're LATE!' She emphasized. 'I know, I got caught up in terrible traffic jams on the motorway' stammered James, he was very tired and just wanted to get into his room for a good night's sleep. 'Well I'm afraid your room is no longer available, I've let it to someone else who came along tonight after 6pm, I did warn you to be here by that time!' said the mean landlady. James couldn't believe what he was hearing, 'You're surely not serious, I have just driven all the way from Scotland, I left this morning, I couldn't help the traffic on the road, it's 10pm and I have nowhere else to go. The hard face landlady wasn't moved, she stood there with her bottom lip pouting, shrugged her shoulders and said unsympathetically, 'Well, you should have got here sooner, shouldn't you?' James turned and walked away, he couldn't believe that anyone could be so nasty. He didn't want to worry Linda, so he got back into his car and went back to her brother's house. When he told Douglas Junior what had happened, he offered James the settee in the lounge to sleep on for as long as he needed, this wasn't ideal, it wasn't fair on them and James felt that he was pushing everyone off to bed so that he could get some sleep.

James got up early the next morning and went to start his new job. It was very involved; he was to be a working carpenter in charge of all the chippies. The site manager had every faith in James and ran through the plans with him to explain exactly what was happening. By lunchtime James was into the swing of things and enjoying his 'new found' promotion. That evening on the way home, he picked up the local paper to look for digs, he saw one advertised in Aldershot and stopped at the first telephone box to give them a ring. A strong Irish accent answered the phone and told James that the room was still available, 'Can I come over now to see it please?' James politely asked. 'Sure, that'll be fine, we'll be here waiting for you,' replied the Irishman. James felt quite proud of himself; he felt he had overstayed his welcome at Douglas Junior and Norma's. He found the street; the house was middle terrace in what looked like council houses. As he walked up the path a young English woman about 25 answered the door to him. 'Oh have I got the right address? I spoke to an Irishman earlier on the phone about a room to let' enquired James. 'Yes, that was my husband, come in and I'll show you the room'. James entered the house and stepped over a large mongrel lying in the hallway. At that two little children came running out of the kitchen followed by a cat and a woman in her fifties clutching a cup of tea with both hands, 'Oh hello, have you come about the room?' she asked. 'Yes, I'm just showing it to him, by the way this is my mother, she lives with us,' said the young woman turning to James. The room looked ok it was basic with a single bed, chest of drawers and a small wardrobe but it was clean and James just needed a place to put his heads down at night. 'It's £7 per week, one week in advance and you can use our bathroom and kitchen, oh and no friends please, it's only a room for one person!' said the young woman 'That's great, can I move in tomorrow?' asked James. 'Absolutely no problem, what time can we expect to see you?' answered his new landlady. 'After work, about 6pm, is that ok?' James asked. 'That'll be fine, oh and by the way my name is Sharon?' James shook her hand and thanked her. As he went downstairs her husband appeared at the lounge door with a can of Guinness in his hand. 'Paddy, meet our new lodger James!' said Sharon as she introduced the two men, 'he's moving in tomorrow' she continued. 'Ah that's grand, we'll look forward to welcoming ye into the fold' said Paddy with a slur, the can of Guinness obviously wasn't his first drink of the day. James felt a bit more confident, the job seemed to be going well, he had a roof over his head and he couldn't wait to call Linda and tell her all about it.

James worked a 12 hour days at the site, he was a very good lodger, out in the morning by 7am and he didn't return until 9pm after he had eaten and called Linda. By that time the bathroom was free for him to have a bath and then he went to his room and lay down on his bed to read until he fell asleep. He didn't really enjoy lodging with Paddy and Sharon, almost every night he could hear them arguing. It was hell, Paddy was drunk and Sharon was screaming, James felt uncomfortable, he was sure that Paddy was hitting Sharon but they were always so nice to his face and he didn't like to intervene. On Friday nights Paddy and Sharon left her old mum babysitting and they went to the pub. When James got home at 9pm Sharon's mum said to him, 'You can come into the lounge and watch TV if you like, it must be awful boring in that small room!' James had a bath, changed his clothes and then went downstairs to the lounge, it wasn't home but it was better than looking at four walls. 'Here have a beer, Paddy won't miss one!' said Sharon's mum as she handed James a can of Guinness.

It was the end of August 1971, James had been in his digs for a month and Paddy and Sharon's fights and arguing was getting him down. Linda was just over six months pregnant and feeling the strain of coping on her own with the pregnancy and her lively 17 months old toddler son Stuart. James called her every night. He was working long hours and earning great money but one evening Linda told him enough was enough, she and baby Stuart needed him, she didn't care any more about the money she just wanted her husband back living with them so that they could be a family again. James told the foreman who was absolutely gutted by the news that James was intending to go back to Scotland. 'Hang on,' he said, 'my parents are going to Canada for three weeks, I am house-sitting their house for them, so you can bring your Mrs. and the little 'un down here to live in my house in Woking, that will give her a chance to find a place to live while you are working!' James called Linda who was delighted that she would be able to spend three whole weeks with her husband. He told Paddy and Sharon that he would be moving out the following week, they weren't very happy that they had to find a new lodger but understood that James was missing family life and needed to be with his wife and son.

Margie was worried about Linda being pregnant and travelling on the train to London on her own with Stuart to look after too, she couldn't get time off from work to accompany her so Linda asked Molly if she fancied a three week break down south. Molly readily agreed and they set off from Glasgow Central station. Margie and Douglas were on the platform to see them off, Margie had a hint of sadness about her because she knew her daughter was going down south to look for a place to live and be with her husband, she couldn't bear the thought of her son, daughter and grandchildren living so far away. They came on the train and sat with them, talking to wee Stuart and making him giggle. Suddenly they heard the slamming of the doors as the guard was preparing the carriages for the journey south. 'Oh we'd better get off the train now Douglas,' said Margie, 'unless we want to end up in London too! They hugged and kissed their wee grandson and Linda, and quickly climbed down out of the carriage. The guard sounded his whistle and Margie looked very sad, she waved and blew kisses to them as the train pulled away from the platform. Linda could see that her mother had a tear in her eye as her dad cuddled her, Linda felt a tug at her heart strings, she mouthed 'I love you to her parents' and blew them kisses back. Margie and Douglas stood on the platform until the train disappeared out of sight then turned to walk back feeling very lonely indeed.

James was waiting at London Euston for the train to arrive. It pulled in ten minutes early. As Linda got off she spotted James and said to Stuart 'Look there's daddy.' James came running over and scooped Stuart into his arms, hugged Linda and gave her a long lingering kiss. 'You wait to see this house, you will love it Linda' I know it's only temporary accommodation but it will give you a chance to look around for a place for us to live and I can continue to work down here. They got to the house; it was an immaculate semi-detached Victorian three bedroom Villa with a small front garden and a beautiful mature back garden stretching to about 60 feet. It was great to have her husband back and living like a family again.

On Monday morning Linda decided to go out and look for a place for them to rent but every Estate Agent that she went into took one look at her 'pregnancy bump' and wee Stuart then said, 'Sorry no kids!' A week passed and Linda was beginning to feel dejected, she saw no option but for them all to go back to Scotland, which she knew wouldn't be fair on James because he was a grafter and more than earned his money but there was no work in Scotland and he would probably end up on the dole. The following week. Linda noticed that there were lovely new council houses being built along the road from where they were living in Woking so she thought that she would try her luck at the council housing offices to see if they could help them. Linda sat in the waiting room for what seemed like an eternity then finally her name was called. The lady took her into a side room then said, 'Right fill this form in, I'll be back in ten minutes,' Linda completed all the questions to the best of her ability. 'So you're actually living in someone's house while they are away?' said the council lady 'Yes' answered Linda', 'And where are you going to go when they get back then?' asked the lady. 'I don't know what we'll do, I can't find anything, everyone says no children!' replied Linda almost in tears. 'Right, let's see if we can help' said the lady as she looked through Linda's completed form. Linda began to get her hopes up then the lady said, 'I see that you have a place in Glasgow? 'Yes' said Linda, 'but it's only rented' 'Then I suggest that you go back there Mrs. Alexander' answered the lady. Linda couldn't believe what she was hearing and said 'but my husband has a job down here, there's no work in Glasgow and I have been living there with my wee son on my own, I came here to try and find a place so that we could be a family again, I am due to have another baby in November, I can't go on living on my own all that distance away from my husband and he can't come back to Glasgow because he can't get a job, we have always worked and paid our taxes and so have our parents before us, why can't you help us?' pleaded Linda. 'Sorry, you have an address, so there's nothing I can do!' answered the council lady. 'But what good is an address if you can't earn the money to pay the rent, we know that we could pay the rent in this part of the world because my husband is a tradesman, his skills are in demand!' said Linda, trying her hardest to get the council lady to melt her hard exterior. 'Sorry' said the lady and left the room, Linda was devastated. That evening she said to James, 'there's just no way that we are ever going to find a place to live, you are going to have to give up working here and come home to Glasgow!' That weekend Linda couldn't believe what she read in the Woking local paper, President Amin had kicked the Asians out of Uganda and the council was re-housing them in new council houses being built, including the ones along the road. Linda was very hurt, she said to James, 'It's all making sense now why they wouldn't entertain me at the council housing offices, no harm to these poor people, I feel really sorry for them but we have been born and bred in Britain, our fathers fought a war for this country and we have been turned down, what's even worse, there are local people here who desperately need housing, it doesn't seem fair that they are being pushed aside for foreigners, fair enough if there was an overflow of council houses but there isn't, surely the people on the council house waiting list should get first priority and then if there is anything left, offer them to the refugees!'

The three weeks were up and they hadn't found anywhere to live. James resigned himself to the fact that he would have to go back to Scotland. The foreman said, 'Look James can't you please just come back to see the job out, there's only another three weeks to go,' 'but I don't have anywhere to live,' answered James. 'That's not a problem, you can come to stay with me, my wife won't mind,' answered the foreman.

James took Friday off work and drove his mother, Linda and Stuart all the way home to Glasgow, by Sunday night he was at the foreman's house ready to start work again on Monday morning.

James got friendly with Eddie, one of the chippies; he was around ten years older than him and a bit of a lad. James could tell that Eddie wasn't really a time-served carpenter, but he was conscientious and listened and learned as James taught him some tricks of the trade. In return Eddie wanted to help James find a place to live. One Saturday morning he said to James 'Right we're finishing early today to find a home for you and your family if it kills us!' Eddie dragged him round all the estate agents that he knew of from Farnham to Weybridge with no luck, then at last, just as they were about to concede defeat, they called into an estate agent in Weybridge who told them about a two bed roomed flat in New Haw.

James asked 'Can I go and see it now?' The estate agent replied, 'Oh it's a bit late in the day but just hang on, I will give the lady a ring,' James listened intently to the conversation and felt sheer relief when the estate agent said that the lady was happy to meet them there in fifteen minutes.

James and Eddie got back in the car and drove towards New Haw. The flat looked lovely from the outside; it was above shops and didn't look more than three years old. A smiling lady came walking towards them, 'Hi! you must be Mr. Alexander, my name is Noreen,' she said in a lovely Irish lilt as she led them up the stairs at the back of the shops to the flat. She opened the door and James couldn't believe his eyes, straight ahead was a very modern fully fitted kitchen, to the left was an extremely large lounge/dining room in the region of 20ft by 15ft. As they walked through the lounge James noticed that there was a serving hatch from the kitchen through to the dining area. The door from the dining area led to a small hallway with two bedrooms and a bathroom off it. James was completely blown away, this is absolutely perfect, my wife will love it. Noreen seemed happy for him and said, 'Oh and the second garage from the left goes with the flat too! When were you thinking about moving in?' 'As soon as I can get my wife down here!' answered James excitedly as he continued, 'she's almost seven months pregnant so I can't leave her up in Scotland any longer on her own!' 'She's pregnant? Ah that's grand, is this your first?' asked Noreen, James calmed his excitement down and remembering how they hadn't been able to get anywhere to rent before because they had children, he answered with caution, 'Er, no we have a little son, he's eighteen months old.' 'Two little ones? This place will be perfect for you then!' said Noreen. 'You mean it's ours?' James said as he felt a wide smile spread across his face. 'It's yours if you want it, I know only too well how difficult it is to get a place to rent when you have children, I am one of the few landladies who are more than happy to rent to families, It's furnished, £60 per month, paid two weekly, that'll be £30 every second Thursday, will that be ok?' Said Noreen. 'Great, no problem,' answered James, as he gulped, this was a big jump from the £7.96 per month that they were paying in Glasgow but this was Surrey, the work was here and the rents were high, then he went on 'but can we bring any furniture of our own?' 'What items were you thinking about?' asked Noreen. 'Well, my mother-in-law bought us our bed as a wedding present, plus we have our little boy's cot, a fridge and a washing machine!' said James hoping that she would agree. 'Oh that'll be fine, I have just bought a three bedroom house and I could do with another bed, you can hang on to mine until you get yours down from Scotland, but I have to leave the single bed in the small room because by law a rented furnished accommodation must have a bed and a table and chairs!'

As they left the flat, Eddie said to James, 'Cor, £60 per month is a bit steep ain't it? Our mortgage is only £40!' James answered, 'Yes, but to get a mortgage, you have to have a deposit of a few hundred pounds and that's something we don't have, but I'm sure if I can keep earning the sort of wages that I am at the moment, then it won't be long until we save that sort of cash and buy a place of our own. At this moment in time I am just happy to get back to normal living and have my wife and son beside me!' Eddie thought for a minute then said, 'I'll see what Jean can come up with, meanwhile keep thinking positive, once you're down here and settled with a bank account it will be easier!' Eddie's wife Jean worked as a secretary for a local estate agent in Kingston Upon Thames. 'Oh and by the way!' continued Eddie, 'did I tell you that I called into a site in Kingston Upon Thames, they are desperate for chippies and are offering £8 per day, I am thinking about starting there the week after next, are you interested? James turned his bottom lip down and nodded in approval as he replied, '£8 per day eh? Yes, put me down for that!'

James got on the phone to Linda straight away, when she answered he said, 'What are you doing next week?' 'Next week? answered Linda wondering what on earth he was on about, then she went on 'probably the same as this week!' 'No you're not! You're coming down here; I have found a flat for us!' 'Really, where is it? Is it on a permanent basis? How much is it?' Linda could hardly contain herself as she fired question after question at her husband. 'It's ok, I think you'll like it, the only problem is that it is furnished and we won't be able to bring our furniture, only the bed, Stuart's cot, the washing machine and the fridge, I will break up the wardrobes that I built, the wood will come in handy for something else, my mum can have her table and chairs back and you'll have to try to sell the three piece suite!' said James. 'Oh that won't be a problem, when I told the insurance man that we might be moving down south he asked me to give him first refusal if we were thinking about selling it, so that's sorted' answered Linda. 'Well what are you waiting for then? Get packing and get down here!' said James, he didn't want to tell her too much about the flat, he preferred to keep it a big surprise, he knew that she would love it, then he went on, 'Did I tell you that the job I am on finishes soon?' There was a silence, then Linda said, 'How are we going to pay the rent of our new flat?' 'Don't worry, there's plenty work to chose from down here, I have a job to start the week after next in Kingston Upon Thames,' laughed James. Linda was relieved, she hadn't clue where Kingston Upon Thames was but for the first time in a long while she felt secure again.

Linda was ecstatic and called her parents to tell them the news. Margie was happy for her but very sad at the thought of her daughter and grandson moving so far away and she felt very upset and lonely at the prospect of it all. She came off the phone and went to tell Linda's dad but she couldn't help herself and broke down in tears. 'What's up? What's happened?' asked Douglas. He was devastated by the news; he was very attached to his wee grandson. Having wee Stuart made Douglas realize what he had been missing out on for years and he had cut down on his drinking to enjoy the privilege of being a granddad. 'I know they are young and they have to consider what's best for their future, but what is life going to be like with both our children and our grandchildren so far away, there won't be anything to look forward to, we won't see our grandchildren grow up, they won't even know us' sobbed Margie.

Meanwhile Linda was busy packing, she had one week to get everything organized. James had told her to pack up what she could and once she was settled down south he would hire a van and come up for their belongings. They didn't have very much really; the insurance man happily bought their black leather three piece suit. There were still six months of payments left on the electric cooker, so Linda arranged for the electricity board to come and take it back. She gave her two chests of drawers to another young mother in the next close. She spent the week collecting boxes from the shops and wrapping up crockery, ornaments, pictures, lamps and cutlery. She packed two cases for herself and Stuart and the rest of the clothes belonging to the three of them she packed in boxes ready for James to pick up. By the end of the week the flat looked very bare and everything was boxed, even the carpets were rolled up! Linda's baby was due in seven weeks time, she didn't know where she had got the energy from to prepare to move house in one week, and she put it down to an adrenaline rush caused by all the excitement.

James had instructed her to fly down because he didn't want her to have to sit on a long train journey in her advanced state of pregnancy. This was something she was really looking forward to because she had never flown in an aeroplane before. The money from the sale of the three piece suite came in handy, Linda used some of it to purchase the ticket for her flight from Glasgow to London Heathrow for Saturday 9th October which was two days before their second wedding anniversary then she withdrew all their savings of £32.78p and closed their account in 'The Glasgow Savings Bank'.

James was working round the clock to meet the deadline for the new bingo hall and cinema to open. The site was a lot more comfortable, the electricians had come down from a firm in Yorkshire and they had brought sleeping bags to sleep on the premises. The bosses were happy because it meant they worked longer hours and the electricians were happy because they pocketed the accommodation money that their firm paid them. James decided to do the same for the last week before Linda came down and he moved out of his foreman's house, his wife had been very nice, she always had a delicious home cooked meal ready for them when they got home at night but James felt that he was encroaching on their family. The cinema and bingo hall were due to open on Friday that week. James worked all day and through the night for four days cat napping in between. By the time the cinema and bingo hall was ready for the grand opening at 5pm on Friday, James was shattered. The manager told him that he was welcome to watch the movie 'Soldier Blue'. James was looking forward to it, he had heard so much about it but first of all he nipped out to collect the keys for their new flat, it was theirs from today onwards, he got some basic shopping and put it in the boot of his car before going back to the cinema and sitting in the back row of the stalls.......and that's the last he remembered, he woke up just as the last few patrons were exiting, he had his feet over the seats in front and sniggered at the thought that he was possibly snoring all the way through the film.

James got home to his new flat just before midnight. He soaked in a lovely hot bath, and then made himself some supper. He was enjoying the luxury and privacy of having his own place at last and not lodging in someone's back room.

Saturday morning came, Margie and Douglas accompanied Linda and Stuart to the airport, Linda had butterflies in her stomach at the thought of going up in an aeroplane while Margie was worried sick about her daughter, how was she going to cope so far away with two children? She was so young. Margie tried to be happy for Linda but her heart was heavy and sad. Linda cuddled her mum and dad before going through to the departure lounge, then she stopped and said, 'Mum if anything should happen to me will you look after Stuart?' Margie felt her eyes filling up, 'What an awful thing to say Linda, don't be silly, nothing's going to happen but of course I will always be here for Stuart!' answered Margie. Linda hugged her mum and dad tightly and said 'Bye mum and dad.' At that Margie could no longer control her feelings and her tears flowed. Linda felt terrible, she was so excited and looking forward to her new life, she hadn't stopped to think about how all this was affecting her parents, 'Oh mum, don't, you'll start me off' said Linda as she held her mother tightly in her arms, 'But I'm going to miss you so much and my grandchildren won't know me,' Margie blurted out. By this time Linda was crying also, she tried to console her mum as she replied, 'I'm really going to miss you too mum, and the kids WILL know you because you can come down any time you want and stay with us, we'll come up and stay with you and we'll talk all the time on the phone.' Margie smiled through her tears and said, 'you'll call me when you get there and tell me all about your new house, won't you?' Of course I will, and you get prepared to come down within the next six weeks, I'll need you to look after Stuart when I go into hospital to have the baby,' said Linda. 'There, that's something to look forward to Pet, isn't it?' said Douglas as he cuddled his wife. This seemed to buck Margie up a bit as she told Linda, 'Yes....yes, I will be more than happy to do that, now you better go Linda or you'll be missing out on your very first experience of flying.' Linda had Stuart in her arms and the four of them hung on to each other for a long hug before Margie and Douglas kissed Linda and Stuart farewell. Linda walked through into the departure lounge and stopped over and over again to look back at her parents standing there looking very lonely and waving sadly.

Within half an hour she was nervously boarding the plane for London Heathrow. She put her seat belt on as instructed then sat Stuart on her lap. Linda held on tight to her baby as the 'plane sped along the runway, then she looked down and watched in amazement as the land and houses below got smaller and smaller, she tried explaining what was happening to Stuart but he was too young to understand and was fast asleep by the time the 'plane went through the clouds into the sunshine above. The Stewardess' were very pleasant and helpful, they could see that Linda was heavily pregnant and told her that she could lay Stuart down on the empty seat beside her because the plane wasn't very busy.

Linda couldn't wait to see her husband, they were leaving their roots behind to start a new life in Surrey, she looked at her gorgeous wee son fast asleep and wondered what the future would hold for him and his unborn sibling. Would her children be going to school in Surrey and have English accents or would James and her only stay for a short while and come home again to Scotland? She had no idea what lay ahead, all she really cared about at the present time was that they would be resuming a normal family life and her husband would be coming home to her every night instead of calling her from a phone box over four hundred miles away.

Three

Linda looked down over London in wonderment, the aeroplane seemed to follow the River Thames and from her window seat, she could pick out Big Ben, The Houses of Parliament, Tower Bridge and all the other bridges over the river. As the plane descended and skimmed over roof tops on its way to land at Heathrow airport, Linda took a deep breath, she held her stomach as if to protect her unborn child and cuddled into her toddler son Stuart, who lay fast asleep on the next seat, with her other arm. She felt her ears go deaf and people's voices seemed to be in the distance. At last the plane touched down with a gentle bump as the wheels made contact with the tarmac of the runway. Linda woke her sleeping son up and said excitedly to him, 'We're going to see daddy now!' The sleepy wee boy smiled and cuddled into his mummy as she put his jacket on.

Linda followed the other passengers to baggage reclaim; this was all a very new experience for her. By this time her arms were aching with carrying Stuart and she was feeling very uncomfortable with the weight of him added to her eight month pregnancy bump. As she was concentrating on getting on to the escalator beside the staircase to go down to the next level where the cases were, she lifted her head, her heart skipped a beat as she saw her husband James' proud smile beaming back at her from the bottom of the stairs. James whisked Stuart out of his wife's arms and the three of them ecstatically huddled together hugging and kissing in sheer delight. 'Oh, my wee wife, it's so good to have you and my son back with me, you don't know just how much I have missed you both,' said James as his son pushed back in his daddy's arms then looked at him and

Linda as if to say, *'What's going on?'* Linda replied to James, 'It'll be wonderful to have my husband back again, it hasn't been easy living and coping on my own over the past four months, apart from Stuart keeping me busy and not being able to have a rest it has been very lonely on my own, especially in the evenings with no adult company.

They made their way to the car park where James had parked their Vauxhall 101 Estate on the first floor. 'I hope you like your new flat, it's nothing special, it's all that I could find but at least it means we will all be together!' James exclaimed to Linda as he helped her in to the car, 'I'm sure I will love it!' Linda answered but deep down she was very apprehensive, she had given the factor notice to quit her home in Scotland by the end of the month, moved down to Surrey with her eighteen month old son and she was due to have another baby in six weeks time, £32 was all the savings they had in the world. She was so worried that she had done the right thing and thought to herself *'What if the new flat is awful and I don't like it? What if the neighbours are awful? What if we can't afford it? What if........?* 'Penny for them' interrupted James. Linda gave him a nervous smile as she said, 'Oh I was just wondering what our new home was like, I can't wait to see it! After half an hour James pulled up at the back of a parade of shops, 'What have you stopped for?' Linda asked him. James laughed, 'We're home, this is it, we're in New Haw!' Linda looked up at all the doors on the open balcony of the flats above the shops, the parade of shops and the flats all looked pretty new 'Which one is ours then?' she asked James anxiously. It's the second from the end; the stairs are in the middle. The garage second from the end is ours too, it's nice and clean and dry so you can keep the pram in it to save you from bumping it up and down the stairs. James scooped Stuart into his arms and took his wife's hand as he led her up the stairs. They arrived at the door and James put the key in the lock and turned it. Linda stepped into the hall then stopped and gazed in excited amazement at the fabulous kitchen, full of mod cons, she couldn't contain herself, 'Oh James it's out of this world, I can't believe it!' she gushed. 'You ain't seen nothin' yet! mocked James as he led her in to the lounge. Linda's mouth fell open as she took in the size of it, 'Gosh this room must be about twenty five feet long!' she gasped. 'Not quite,' said James, 'it's twenty feet by fifteen feet!' Linda was more relaxed by now, she really liked what she saw and enthused, 'I love the circular dining table and matching long john sideboard, oh and the Indian rugs are great, very posh.' She made her way to the other end of the lounge where there was a door into another hallway. 'this is our room,' said James as he led her into a big airy double bedroom, the bed is only here temporarily until we bring ours down from Scotland, C'mon I'll show you Stuarts bedroom!' He led her back out into the hallway into another room with a neat little single bed in it. 'This bed has to stay because by law a landlord has to provide a bed in a furnished flat,' he told Linda who by this time was in awe as James led her into the big modern bathroom. 'Oh James this is just so wonderful, it's a dream, what a difference from living in a tenement in Glasgow, I will love to bring my children up in a lovely place like this, but are you sure we can afford it?' Linda asked him cautiously. ? 'It won't be a problem, they are crying out for skilled tradesmen in this part of the country, there are so many jobs going and I'm not afraid of hard work!' he answered confidently.

Linda went down to the phone box to call her mum and tell her all about her fantastic new home, Margie was happy for her but upset within that her daughter and only grandchild were so far away. Mum you have to come and see this place it is unbelievable, I feel so lucky,' Linda blurted down the phone. 'I will…I am arranging time off of work for when you have the baby, I can't wait to see you all again, I miss you so much!' answered Margie. Linda was too excited to notice how upset her mum sounded. She went back to the flat and unpacked her and Stuart's clothes into the wardrobe and chest of drawers. 'It been such a hectic and exciting day, let's just get fish and chips from the shop below for dinner' said James. 'Ok, that's fine by me!' Linda readily agreed. She laid the table while James nipped downstairs. Five minutes later he appeared with a bag full of steaming hot fish and chips wrapped in newspaper. Linda unwrapped the newspaper and was splitting the food between three plates when she heard a key in the door. 'Who's that coming in to our flat?' she asked James worriedly, 'It can't be, it's our place now!' he answered. Linda stopped what she was doing, grabbed Stuart and stood behind James as the lounge door swung open. 'Hi, you must be Linda, I'm Noreen, I've been dying to meet you!' this strange lady announced in a southern Irish accent. 'Oh Linda, this is our landlady' said James relieved. Linda came forward and shook Noreen's hand. 'Nice to meet you, we were just about to eat, it's only fish and chips but you're welcome to join us' she said. 'Oh No, I've just finished working in my shop below, I just thought I would pop up and say hello before I go home and feed my brood, I won't delay you any longer, I'll drop in again tomorrow to make sure all is well. I've told the local doctor about you and they are expecting you to call in and register, I'll take you there when you are ready' said Noreen as she made her way back to the door and she was gone as quick as she had arrived. 'She seems a nice lady but I hope she's not going to make a habit of letting herself in and surprising us like that, we are going to be paying her a lot of money for this flat and she must respect our privacy' said Linda to James with a concerned look. 'Oh I'm sure this was just a 'one off', she was probably checking to make sure that we had arrived ok' answered James. 'I hope so, I really hope so' replied Linda.

Sunday morning and they woke up with the sun streaming through their bedroom window. 'Let's make use of today, I'll take you and Stuart for a run in the car through the Surrey countryside so that you know your bearings and find out more about the new area you live in'! 'Oh, I'd like that James, I'll make us all a quick breakfast then I'll get Stuart and myself washed and dressed.' Linda loved the feeling of being a family again and couldn't wait to go out with her husband and son.

They drove through West Byfleet, Woking, Guildford, Chobham then out to Camberley where they popped in briefly to see Linda's brother Douglas junior and his wife Norma. Linda felt so happy, not only was she living in the beautiful, healthy, countryside but she was also near her brother whom she adored.

Monday and it was a wonderful bright autumnal morning, James left at 7am for his job in Kingston Upon Thames, Linda was out pushing Stuart in his pram and ready to explore her new area on foot by 9.30am. The sun shone high in the sky as she walked down Scotland Bridge Road (a name that made her feel welcome) towards West Byfleet. She came to West Byfleet train station and walked through the underpass to be met by a wonderful little village with a variety of shops, including Woolworths', a small supermarket, bookshop, jewellers, bank, restaurant, newsagent and a library. She felt very content within that her son Stuart and unborn child were going to get a very good start in life, and everything was about to get better for them all because they were living in such a beautiful part of Surrey in a lovely flat and James was in demand for his expert skills, so wouldn't be short of work.

Later on that same afternoon, Linda was preparing dinner when she heard the key in the lock, 'Oh is that daddy?' she asked Stuart who ran excitedly to the door. He stopped in his tracks when in breezed Noreen. 'Oh Hello Stuart, are you being a good boy for mummy, how do you like your new home?' asked Noreen kindly, then she turned to Linda, 'are you settling in Ok? I just popped in to tell you that I have made an appointment for you tomorrow at the anti-natal clinic in our local surgery at 10am. You can register yourself, James and Stuart with the GP while you're there, I'll take you there but don't worry if it's not convenient, I'll change it to another time!' she poured out without taking a breath in her southern Irish lilt. 'Ye-es…Yes thank you that'll be ok, thank you very much' answered Linda completely taken aback, she was glad of Noreen's concern, that she had gone to the trouble of booking her into the anti-natal clinic and helping her register with her GP but at the same time she didn't like the way she entered their house whenever she liked without being asked, she decided that she would have to work on this and let Noreen know without appearing ungrateful that she and James would like their privacy respected. James arrived home just as Noreen was leaving and she told him about her and Linda's appointment at the doctors' the following day. 'That's very nice of you Noreen, It's good that you two are getting to know each other!' answered James. After she closed the door Linda told James that Noreen had let herself into the flat again without warning, 'We'll have to let her know subtly that she's going to have to knock and be invited into our home, she might walk in on me when I'm in the bath or worse still when you're in the bath' Linda laughed.

Linda went along with Noreen the next day to register Stuart, James and herself with her new GP. She had a thorough check and blood taken at her new anti-natal clinic, she had only five weeks to go until the birth of her second child, so the doctor instructed the nurse to arrange for Linda to have an appointment at St. Peter's Maternity Hospital for as soon as possible in order to make sure that she would be booked in there for the birth.

The following week Linda was on her way to St. Peter's for an anti-natal check. She got Stuart into his foldable pushchair and stood outside the post office in Woodham Lane waiting for the bus in to Addlestone, after about 15 minutes the bus turned up. Linda struggled to fold the pushchair with one arm and carrying Stuart in the other, the conductor took the pushchair from her as she climbed onto the platform at the back of the double decker bus. They got off the bus at the National Westminster on the corner of Brighton Road and Church Road and the conductor handed her the folded up pushchair. She got Stuart settled then walked round the corner to the library in Church Road to catch a bus to St. Peter's Hospital; she waited 20minutes then had to repeat all the rigmarole again of struggling with folding the pushchair while carrying a toddler. She eventually got to the hospital, the whole journey would have taken just 10 minutes in a car but for Linda it was two bus journeys and just over an hour travelling. By the time she was called for her check-up and then repeated the same procedure to get home again by two buses, she was shattered. It was almost 4.45pm, it had taken the whole afternoon for just one hospital appointment, this was a big difference to where Linda lived in Glasgow, there she just walked to Duke Street Hospital five minutes away at the bottom of her street.

Two weeks later, James hired a van to drive up to Glasgow to pick up the rest of their belongings. He left on the Friday night after work, there was a fog coming down, Linda was very frightened for James. She felt very lonely; she didn't know anyone in her new area, had no phone or television and had only four weeks to go until the birth of her new baby. She didn't sleep well that night, apart for the fact that she was very uncomfortable in the last weeks of her pregnancy she was scared of her and Stuart being alone in a strange land with no way of contacting her husband. She was up at 6am on Saturday morning, got all her housework and washing done before making breakfast for Stuart and her. By 9.30am she was out with Stuart and went to the public telephone box to call James' mother Molly to see if she had heard from him. She was relieved when Molly told her that James phoned her just under two hours ago from Carlisle so he should be due at her house anytime, he told his mother that he had to stop driving last night because of the fog and heavy traffic, he decided to pull into a lay-by for a kip until it lifted and woke up about 2am to find himself parked in someone's front garden. He quickly got on his way before the occupants of the house noticed. He told his mother that the traffic was running well on the M1 and M6 during the night, so he had a good journey to Carlisle. Linda told Molly that she would pop into the local shops to get some groceries and call back in half an hour to speak to James.

Linda wandered round the shops, nervously looking at her watch every two minutes or so and exactly half an hour later she went back to the phone box to call Molly. She heaved a sigh of relief when

James answered the phone. 'Oh thank God you're ok, I was worried sick,' she told him. James laughed and said, 'there was nothing to worry about, you know me, I'll always find a way! Anyway', he continued, 'my Ma's just making me something to eat and then we're heading down to our flat to load the van up and clear the place out, I have to get it all done today because I need to be back on the road home tomorrow, I promised my governor that I would be back at work as usual on Monday morning' 'Ok, I won't hold you back then, I just needed to know that you were ok. Bye then James, we're missing you, I love you!' replied Linda. 'I love you too Linda and I can't wait to get back to you tomorrow night, this'll be the last time we'll be apart. Bye darling, look after yourself and Stuart, and give him a big hug and kiss from his daddy, see you soon honey' answered James as he blew a kiss into the phone before replacing the receiver.

It was 4pm on Sunday afternoon, Linda had called James at his mother's house just after 9am and he told her that he was just finishing his breakfast and would be ready to leave by about 10am. There was no way that they could communicate so she just had to wait in hope that there would be no traffic hold-ups on the journey and he would be home within the next couple of hours. Six o'clock passed and still there was no sign of James, Linda's stomach was churning, she couldn't sit still for a minute and paced up and down the living room stopping every now and then to peer out of the window to see if James' hired van was there. At ten minutes to seven that evening Linda heard the noise of a vehicle stopping outside, she made her way to the window to see James backing the van in to his parking place. She grabbed wee Stuart and scooped him up into her arms as she made her way to the door telling him excitedly, 'Daddy's here, c'mon let's go and meet him'. James ran up the stairs three at a time and gave Linda a big lingering kiss and hug before sweeping Stuart out of her arms and hugging him close, 'Oh my wee son, I've missed you and your mummy so much!' They made their way back to the flat and Linda asked James, 'Are you hungry, do you want something to eat?' 'No I've eaten on the drive down, just a quick cup of tea then I'll unload the van, I'll just put most things into the garage and I'll sort it all out during the week after work,' he answered. Linda bathed Stuart while James went down to the van to get Stuart's cot, he put it together and placed it in the corner of their bedroom.

Linda put Stuart down in his cot then she went to start unpacking the boxes of crockery and cutlery that James was bringing up from the van. He placed their black and white TV in the corner of the lounge by the window then he brought up some toys and boxes of bedding and clothes. James screwed the legs onto the TV, plugged the aerial in and tuned in the set in to the stations, 'Right Mrs. Alexander, that's enough for tonight, I'm going to soak in a nice hot bath then we'll relax and watch a bit of TV before bedtime, you can unpack the clothes and crockery boxes while I'm at work tomorrow' Linda gave James a big hug and said, 'Oh it's beginning to look like home now with our own possessions here,' then she cuddled into him and continued 'Oh I've missed you so much, it was so lonely here without you, knowing no-one and with no means of communication, even nosey Noreen didn't poke her nose in,' she laughed.

Rosie the Baker's wife invited Linda along to a 'baby shower' party that Noreen was organizing at Rosie's house. Noreen was displaying goods and baby clothes from her baby shop. Linda was delighted to meet all her shop-keeper neighbours, they were all extremely friendly they told her all about the area, the clinic, schools and made her very welcome. Linda bought a lovely little aqua-marine baby dungarees and hooded baby jacket to match, that would suit either a boy or a girl.

It was the end of November and the time was drawing near for the birth of Linda and James' second baby. Linda was hoping that it would follow the same pattern as her first pregnancy and be early. Her mum and dad were up in Scotland waiting for the call to pack their bags and come down. They only had two weeks holiday each left from work and were intending to come down as soon as things started to happen so that they could look after Stuart while Linda was in hospital and spend some time with her afterwards. The expected birth date passed and Linda didn't feel any signs of her baby emerging into the world. During the night she was so uncomfortable and couldn't sleep so she stood at the window of their wee flat, looking down at the shops and with all their Christmas trees twinkling in preparation for Christmas. The Saturday after the expected due date for the new arrival had passed, Douglas and Margie decided to wait no longer and caught the London train from Glasgow Central Station complete with Chienne their dog, to be with their daughter for the birth. Linda was delighted to see them because by this time she was exasperated and very tired. James couldn't afford time off from work to be with her and help with wee Stuart because he needed to work every day to pay the rent.

By the Monday afternoon, the first fall of snow of the winter flickered down; Linda was at the end of her tether wondering when this baby was going to arrive. She had heard the stories of the olden days when women whose births were overdue took castor oil to start their labour off, 'Right that's it!' she thought and without telling anyone she went out to the shops and bought some. When she got home she swallowed down two big tablespoonfuls. That evening, she was soaking in a bath just after 10pm when she started getting uncomfortable pains in her tummy and said to James 'I think things are beginning to happen!'. Margie was relieved for her daughter; she saw how shattered she looked, 'Oh at last! Hopefully you'll soon have your wee bundle in your arms!' she answered her encouragingly. Then Linda confessed, 'Mum I took some castor oil earlier on,' 'What, how much did you take?' replied Margie. 'Two tablespoonfuls' answered Linda as she doubled over with a contraction. 'Oh Linda, why did you do that' said Margie, 'I just want this baby to be born, I am so tired and uncomfortable waddling around, I can't sit, I can't lie down, I am awake all night!' Linda told her mum, hesitating as if she regretted taking the castor oil. Meanwhile James called the hospital who told him to bring Linda straight in.

It was just after midnight as Linda, in her dressing gown, climbed into the passenger seat of their Vauxhall 101 estate car as James put her case into the boot. By this time the snow was lying thick on the ground. The car had been giving James problems starting. He turned the key and nothing happened, he tried again still nothing, they looked at each other scared and frightened as he tried again for a third time and sheer relief spread over their faces as the engine coughed and spluttered into action. James drove through the little snowbound country lanes. They arrived at the hospital within twenty minutes. The contractions were getting closer together, Linda felt very lonely, she was about to give birth in a part of the country that was alien to her, she was scared. She was shown into a private room in the labour ward, a large plump Jamaican nurse with a big smiling face said to her, 'Don't worry dear, you'll be ok, just get into bed, I'll look after you!" Linda did as she was told. Her labour pains came and went and came and went and by 6am on Tuesday morning they went. Linda couldn't believe it, *'When is this baby going to decide to make it's entry into the world?'* she thought. The doctor called in to see her just after 8am, 'Don't worry, this can happen' he told Linda. 'Hopefully you'll start up again soon and your baby will be born sometime today which would be very appropriate for you being St. Andrews Day. The fact that it was the patron Saint of Scotland's day had totally slipped Linda's mind!

James stayed with Linda the whole time to reassure her. At midday the twinges started again, they got stronger and stronger; the sister examined Linda but informed her that the birth was not imminent because she wasn't dilated enough. The pains were getting unbearable and Linda was given pethidine injections. The staff changed over at 8pm and Linda was in great pain with severe contractions but no further on with the birth. The plump Jamaican nurse came back on for night duty. 'Are you still here lady, my goodness, that baby is taking its time' she said with a big wide smile. Linda was in too much pain to respond. By 10pm she couldn't take the pain anymore and asked for more pain killers, James was very worried and concerned as he went to fetch the nurse. He spoke to her outside the room and asked, 'Is my wife ok? She never had anything like this with our first baby!' 'Don't worry, she'll be ok, we'll look after her' answered the nurse completely unperturbed. 'I'll get her some gas and air, that should help her with the pain!' James went back into the room, 'The nurse is going to get you something to help the pain' he reassured his wife as he kissed her forehead and rubbed her back as she writhed in pain. Five minutes later the Jamaican nurse appeared with the gas and air and handed Linda the mask to inhale and relieve the pain. 'There lady, you'll be ok, don't worry, I'll look after you,' she said. Linda was getting annoyed by now, that seemed to be all this nurse ever said, she didn't seem to be making any effort to help this baby to be born!

It was just after 1am and the Jamaican nurse came in to Linda's room and announced to James and her that she had spoken to the doctor and he had instructed her to take Linda along to the theatre. Linda was in severe pain and 'high' on gas and air and pethidine, she really didn't care but when the nurse took the gas and air away from her, Linda screamed, 'don't take it away please, I need it and won't make it to the theatre without it!' The nurse apologised and told Linda that she had to leave it behind!

Linda was lying in the operating theatre, through her pain, she was aware that there was at least six people standing with their backs to her discussing what they were going to do, it flashed through Linda's mind that they were considering performing a caesarian section on her. Linda felt an urge to push and let out a yell, the sister turned round, then she shouted out... 'A head, it's a head, quick!' At that the team quickly surrounded her and before she knew it she was at last giving birth after a severe labour lasting almost 28 hours. As the baby emerged Linda got scared when she caught sight of the little blue body that seemed lifeless, at last the baby let out a yell, then the nurse took it away. Linda cried with relief and asked the doctor if she had a boy or a girl, 'Oh I'm not sure,' replied the doctor, 'I think it was a boy, but I'm busy sorting you out at the minute, we'll ask the nurse when she comes back. 'Oh a boy, well he'll be a wee pal for his big brother,' answered Linda. Although Linda's head was still very woozy and she felt weak, she began to feel anxious, why weren't they telling her anything, where was her baby and was there something wrong? At last the nurse came back and placed the baby in a little glass cot in the theatre near Linda. 'Ah here's your baby now, he's a fine little lad' said the doctor. 'A lad?' questioned the nurse, 'what are you talking about doctor? Mrs. Alexander has a beautiful bouncing baby daughter, weighing in at 8lb 2oz!' Linda was so happy, 'Oh my husband and my little boy will be delighted and both mine and my husband's mum will be over they moon when they hear that I've had a wee girl,' said Linda as she looked across at the little bundle. She had a headful of lovely dark hair; she was opening her eyes and turning her little head towards the theatre lights inquisitively as if to say 'Well hello world, I'm here now!' 'She's been here before that one,' the sister laughed. Then as her wee daughter turned her head, Linda looked and stared in fear, 'What's wrong with her head?' she asked the sister in tears. 'Now don't you worry my dear' it's just the pressure of birth that has given her a big bump on her head, we've checked it out, it'll go down in its own time!' At that the nurse came in and said to Linda, 'here's your husband, he wants to see his new little daughter.' James came in dressed in a green gown white paper mop cap and white paper covers on his shoes; he had obviously fallen asleep in the waiting room because his eyes were half closed. Linda was very tired and drowsy but she couldn't help but laugh when she saw him, James cuddled her and said, 'I've been so worried about you, thank goodness it's over!' Then he went over to the cot to admire his new daughter. 'She's got a big bump on her head, but the nurse said it's nothing to worry about, something about the pressure of the birth!' your mum will be pleased, I've done something right at last and given her a granddaughter after five grandsons!' Linda said proudly. After twenty minutes the nurse told James that they would have to get Linda into the ward and asked him to say his goodbyes. It was 3.40am by this time, the nurse and porter transferred Linda on to a trolley then the porter pushed Linda while the nurse wheeled the baby in her wee glass cot. They went into the lift, Linda was able to get a good look at her baby as the cot was alongside her bed. The wee mite's eyes were still wide open as she twisted her head round to examine the lights on the roof of the lift. 'Look at her, she doesn't want to miss a trick, I've never seen a new born baby so alert!' the nurse said admiringly. Once they got to the ward the nurse took Linda's baby daughter into the nursery, then she and the porter transferred Linda into a bed in a six-bed ward. 'Right you get a good rest now, don't worry about your baby, we'll look after her' she said as she tucked Linda in.

Meanwhile James was driving home; he stopped at a telephone box in a dark country road just after 4am to telephone his mother. His mother picked up the phone, 'Hello is that you James,' she answered. Then the reality hit him 'Yes mother, we have a wee daughter, you have a granddaughter at last!' he blurted out emotionally through floods of tears! 'Oh well done! Are Linda and the baby ok' she asked. 'Yes ma, she had a really tough time, thank God it's over now, I've got to get back now and tell Linda's mum and dad, I'll call you back tomorrow after I've had some sleep, love you, bye' he said as he replaced the receiver.

Ten minutes later he was home. Margie couldn't sleep for worrying about her daughter and jumped up when she heard James' key go in the door. 'How is Linda, has she had the baby yet?' she asked impatiently. 'Yes, it's all over,' his eyes filled up, he couldn't control his emotions as he told Margie that she had a new wee granddaughter, you'll be able to go and see her tomorrow, she's beautiful, 8lb 2oz with a whole head of dark hair just like her mum!' James beamed proudly as he wiped away his tears. At that Douglas appeared at the lounge door, 'What's happening? Is Linda ok?' he asked. 'Yes Douglas we have a new wee granddaughter, she's a big baby, 8lb 2oz,' Margie told him, as she reached for a tissue to wipe away her tears. 'And Linda, how is Linda?' Margie asked James with concern, 'She had a hard time, they were going to do a caesarian when the baby started to arrive naturally, poor Linda, I was so worried and felt helpless she was in so much pain.' Thank goodness she's had the baby; she's now having a well earned rest!'

The following day Linda awoke just after 9am. 'Ah you're back in the land of the living!' said the nurse as she stuck a thermometer in Linda's mouth. 'We thought we'd let you sleep on as you had such an adventurous night! Right I'll go and get your baby; I bet you can't wait to see her!' Linda was still feeling very drowsy and would love to have slept on, obviously effects of the pethidine and gas and air were still in her system. The nurse came back, put the cot alongside Linda's bed and plonked a baby's bottle on the bedside cabinet, 'Right, she'll be ready for this soon mother, so when you're ready!' she said as she removed the thermometer from Linda's mouth, checked it, cleaned it and put it back in its container. As soon as she went Linda rolled over and went back to sleep. An hour later the nurse came back and woke Linda up. 'Mother, haven't you fed your baby her bottle?' she demanded. 'No-o, she didn't want it.' Linda answered, it was the first thing that came to her mind, she was so tired and her baby hadn't made a sound so she seemed happy to sleep too! The nurse picked Linda's daughter up and teased her with the teat of the bottle; the baby soon latched on and was sucking for all she was worth. 'Poor little mite is starving!' laughed the nurse. Linda felt awful but she was so tired. The nurse looked at the baby and said,' I suppose we can forgive your mother; you gave her quite a time of it last night didn't you? But then you didn't have an easy time of it making your entry into the world either, did you darling? She cradled the baby in her arms then said to Linda, 'would you like to hold your daughter?' Linda reached out, this was the first time that she had held her baby because they had whisked her away straight after her birth to examine the bump on her head. Linda looked down at her helpless little bundle, who was totally reliant on her and felt an overwhelming feeling of love come over her for her beautiful wee daughter, and she said 'I'm sorry darling, mummy's here now for you, I was just so tired,' The nurse smiled and said, 'you will feel tired for a day or two because you had a very high doze of pethidine, it can affect the baby too, so that's probably why she didn't wake up for a feed!'

Linda was delighted when her mum walked into the ward at the afternoon visiting time. 'Where's Stuart and dad?' she asked her mum disappointingly. They wouldn't let Stuart in but if you go over to the window you'll see them, dad's waiting with Stuart to wave to you. Linda went over and sure enough there on the road, across the grass in the distance, was her dad with Stuart in his arms and they were both waving to her. Linda felt really upset, she missed her little boy and wanted so much to hold him in her arms and cuddle him. She turned round and her mum was looking adoringly at her new granddaughter, 'Oh Linda, she's beautiful and so big, 8lb 2oz, she's the biggest baby in the family so far, you were only 5lb, look at her lovely dark hair, can I pick her up for a cuddle?' cooed Margie, then she continued 'Have you got a name for her yet?' 'Well,' answered Linda as she picked up her baby daughter and placed her into her mum's arms 'I chose Stuart's name and James has said all along if it was a girl he wanted to call her Gabrielle but we haven't really discussed it properly yet' 'Oh she doesn't really look like a Gabrielle, what about something more girlie like Mandy, that's a lovely name? said Margie as she studied her little granddaughter. 'I don't know, we'll see,' answered Linda, then she went on, 'I'm really worried about the bump on her head, the doctors said that it was caused by the pressure of birth and the struggle she had during the birth, they say that it will go down in about a month, what if it doesn't? What if they keep her in hospital?' The tears welled up in Linda's eyes as if she was asking her mum to make everything ok. Margie comforted her daughter and told her, 'the doctors know what they're talking about, don't worry, they would know by this time if there was a problem!' Linda felt reassured by her mother's words then she continued, 'I'm arranging to come home on Friday, if you've got children at home then you don't have to stay in for the whole week and they allow you to go home 48 hours after the birth. I miss Stuart so much, I couldn't stand being away from him for a whole week, just wait until he sees his wee sister, he'll love her!' 'Oh are you sure Linda? You know that you don't have to worry about Stuart he'll be alright with us, besides you need all the rest you can get because when we go back to Glasgow you'll have a toddler and a baby to look after by yourself while James is at work all day! Anyway, I'll say bye-bye now and let your dad pop in, he can't wait to see his new wee granddaughter!' replied Margie. Linda hugged her mum and waited for her dad to arrive. She was still feeling drowsy and tired. Her dad was delighted to see his wee dark haired granddaughter, 'She looks just like my wee mammy, your granny, Linda!' he exclaimed proudly, as he cradled her in his arms. After ten minutes

Douglas said, 'it's time that I was going now, there's a bus due in twenty minutes and it'll take us that long to get back to the bus stop. James is coming up tonight and we'll see you again tomorrow' He gave his daughter a big warm cuddle and lovingly patted his wee granddaughter before leaving. Linda climbed back into bed to rest before her baby woke up for her next feed.

Just before 6am on Thursday morning and Linda was woken up by the nurse sticking a thermometer in her mouth Linda, 'sorry to disturb you' the nurse whispered, 'but we'll be bringing your baby through to you shortly.' Linda couldn't wait to see her baby again, As soon as the nurse brought her through, Linda went straight to her and picked her up, she was anxious to see if the bump on her head had decreased in size at all, but it hadn't! Linda lovingly fed and changed her baby; she chatted to the other mums in the ward and relayed her fears that the doctors might not let her go home because of the bump on her baby daughter's head. The doctors came into the ward to do their rounds and Linda reminded her doctor that she would like to go home the next day. He studied her notes and said, 'That shouldn't be a problem.' Then he turned to the ward sister and said 'Sister, can you arrange this please?' The sister informed Linda that she would be taken home in an ambulance and she would have to travel home in her dressing gown. This was the conditions of early discharge after having a baby. Linda had no option but to agree to this.

That afternoon when Margie came to visit, Linda asked her mum if her dad was bringing Stuart to the window to wave again. 'They'll be there any minute!' Margie laughed and at that moment Linda spotted them, she waved and blew kisses to her wee boy, she was longing to give him a big warm cuddle. Her dad waved back and gestured that he was taking Stuart inside because it was cold. Linda excitedly told her mum that she would be coming home the following morning. She couldn't help but notice that one by one the visitors came over to look at her baby, smiled sweetly and said something in the line of, 'Oh she's beautiful'. Linda didn't know if she was imagining it but she felt that they were coming over specially to look at the bump on her baby's head so when she noticed a woman visitor approaching to have a look, she quickly picked her baby up and placed her back in the cot, lying on the side her bump was on, so that it wasn't prominent. Linda was close to tears and asked her mum 'Why do they keep coming to look mum? Margie consoled her and said, 'Linda you're still not 100% from the birth, they're only coming over to admire your wee daughter, nothing else! You are definitely imagining things; after all, I've done the same and had a peep at all the other babies in the ward'. Linda dried her tears but she wasn't convinced.

James came up to see Linda and his new daughter in the evening. 'You know we'll have to decide on a name soon' Linda told James. 'Well my mind's made up, I've always liked Gabrielle and you chose Stuart's name so I think it's only fair that I choose our daughter's!' Linda's mind was still fuzzy, she wasn't sure, so she decided to drop the subject until she felt more like her normal self again.

Friday morning and Linda was wakened up as usual with the nurse sticking a thermometer in her mouth, it was 6am. As she pulled herself up and rubbed her eyes she suddenly felt very happy, she remembered that she would be seeing her wee son Stuart today, she hadn't seen him since Monday and she was missing him so much. Linda waited in anticipation as the nurses wheeled the babies through from the nursery. The fourth one to come through was her baby daughter. Linda looked down at her wee girl, she seemed so content laying there it was a shame to wake her up to feed her. Linda carefully picked up her wee daughter and looked lovingly and admiringly at her then she said, 'Well today your going to meet your big brother, I wonder what the future will hold for you, will you and your brother like each other?' As Linda was feeding her baby, the sister came through and said to her, 'The ambulance will be here for you at about 11am, providing there's no emergency, if there is that will come first and you will have to wait! You're not allowed to dress yourself. You must go home in your dressing gown and slippers!' Linda couldn't understand the logic in this, why should it matter if she got dressed? But she was anxious to get home to normal life with her family again so she complied and said nothing. Linda finished feeding her baby daughter then she changed her nappy and put on a little white sleep-suit that she had bought in a baby shop in Duke Street, Glasgow. She dug out the matinee jacket and bonnet that she had knitted and left them over the end of the cot along with the shawl that James' mother had crotched ready to put on her baby when they left the hospital. The wee baby girl looked so pretty, much nicer than the washed-out hospital baby nightgowns. Linda had cereal for breakfast then she went through to the bathroom for a bath. Half an hour later she was sitting waiting for the ambulance to arrive and praying that there wouldn't be an emergency, when the sister arrived to give her, her discharge notes to leave the hospital. The sister picked up the baby to give her a cuddle, then looking at the bump on her head she said to Linda, 'Has the doctor said that it would be ok for the baby to go home with you? Linda felt panic rising in her body as she answered, 'I assume so, no-one's said otherwise!' At that the sister took the baby and said, 'I'll be back shortly!' Linda felt her heart sink at the thought of them not allowing her baby to come home with her. After what seemed like an eternity but was in fact no longer than fifteen minutes the sister re-appeared and told Linda, 'The doctor says your baby can go home but you will have to be very careful with that bump, it's fluid caused by the pressure of birth, it will take about a month to go down so don't let your other little one near it!' Linda heaved a sigh of relief. It was just coming up for 11am and still no sign of an ambulance when a petite woman walked into the ward, very smart in a green tweed skirt and brownie/green cape coat, she was wearing a wee dark green Robin Hood style hat cocked to the side of her head and carrying a brown, well worn brief case. 'Hello' she announced to the ward, 'I'm the registrar, does anyone wish to register their baby now? It'll save you the bother of coming into the office in Chertsey!' She made straight for Linda, 'What about you? What is your baby's name?' she asked. Linda didn't know why she said what she did, she was still feeling very tired and from all the gas and air and pethidine that had been pumped into her over the period of twenty four hours two days previously, 'O-o-h-h! she's called Gabrielle,' she found herself saying. 'Well why don't you register her with me now and that'll be the job over and done with' said the registrar. Linda agreed and within five minutes her new baby had a name, she was Gabrielle Alexander. Just as she was handing the pen back to the registrar after signing the form, the sister came in and said, 'Right Mrs. Alexander, get your baby ready, you're going home!' Linda was elated; at last she was going to see her wee son. She put the matinee jacket and the wee bonnet that she had knitted on baby Gabrielle, her lovely head of dark hair curled out from beneath the hat, Linda cuddled her wee daughter lovingly in her arms and admired her, she was so proud that she had produced a daughter, she now had the perfect family, a boy and a girl!

The ambulance wound its way through the country roads as Linda sat in the back cuddling her new daughter. As it approached the parade of shops where Linda lived she looked out and saw her mum running with wee Stuart in the pushchair, keeping up with the ambulance as it maneuvered it's way round to the back of the shops, where the flight of stairs led up to Linda's flat. One ambulance man held baby Gabrielle in his arms while the other one helped Linda out of the ambulance. Linda was elated to see her mum standing there with wee Stuart. She bent down and kissed wee Stuart on his forehead then cuddled her mum. The ambulance man carried the baby upstairs to the flat for Linda while the other one turned the ambulance round. Margie got the keys out and opened the door for them. The big bouncy cream leather pram that Linda had bought from another young mother in Camberley was sitting by the window waiting for its new occupant. 'Oh mum, it's beautiful!' exclaimed Linda as she admired the new white Broidery Anglaise pram quilt and pillow set that Margie had prepared the pram with. Linda laid Gabrielle in her pram then turned and grabbed Stuart, she held him close and cried her eyes out uncontrollably telling him how much she missed him and that she'd never leave him again. Margie's eyes welled up and she joined in cuddling the both of them. The two woman laughed and cried as their tears were tripping them, then Linda said to Stuart, Do you want to see your new wee sister?' as she held him up to look in the pram. His wee face beamed with a broad smile, he looked at Linda, his Gran and then his wee sister and put his hands out to the baby. 'This is Gabrielle; do you want to give her a kiss?' Linda asked him as she held him down close to Gabrielle. Stuart gently kissed his new wee sister on the cheek and smiled. 'I bet you could really murder a cup of tea Linda?' said Margie as Linda put Stuart back down on the floor, 'Oh mum that would be real treat, would you mind?' replied Linda. 'Not at all, I came down here to help you; you need a good rest after what you have been through. Dad's just popped down to the post office at West Byfleet to get some money then he's picking up some shopping on the way back. Did I hear you say that the baby's name was Gabrielle?' Margie asked Linda all in one breath. 'Yes' answered Linda. 'Well it's not definite yet is it? Well not until you've registered her name anyway' Margie replied. 'I've registered her as Gabrielle, the registrar came round the hospital before I left this morning, so I decided to do it there and then to save me going all the way up to Chertsey again.' Linda sensed the disappointment in her mum's voice; she knew that Margie wasn't too keen on the name. 'Oh well I suppose we'll all get used to it,' said Margie in an unconvincing manner.

Half an hour after Linda arrived home, she heard a key go into in the front door lock. 'Who can that be?' asked Margie inquisitively, 'can't be dad because I've got our set of keys!' she continued. Linda was wondering the same thing because it was too early for James to be arriving home from work, then she said, 'Oh no, don't tell me, it can't be!' just at that in walked Noreen their landlady with a beautiful little dress for the baby from her shop, followed by the baker's wife with a cake, the supermarket manager's wife with a little bag full of baby cream, baby talc, nappy pins and a baby bottle, the shoe shop assistant manager with a discount voucher for shoes at her shop below, the greengrocer with a basket of fruit, the sweet shop owner's wife with a big box of chocolates, one of the girl bank clerks from the bank in the parade of shops below with a postal order for £10 and last but not least the chip shop owner's wife with a portion of fish and chips. All of them brought a baby greeting card too. 'We were all dying to see the baby so I thought we'd get it all over and done with together,' beamed Noreen as she picked the baby up out of her pram, then passed her round everyone to have a cuddle. They all stayed for about half an hour before returning to work... Linda was overwhelmed and delighted at everyone's generosity but after the last person left Linda said to her mum, 'I realise that Noreen means well but I just wish that she wouldn't be such a control freak and would learn to respect our privacy. If she'd asked me, I would have told her to leave the neighbours visit for a couple of days or so until I was feeling more up to it. Margie had to agree and told Linda that Noreen had been entering the house uninvited periodically over the time Linda was in hospital to enquire how Linda was. 'I know what you mean Linda', said Margie, 'but you're going to have to nip it in the bud, you're paying rent for this flat and it isn't cheap either, she's going to have to respect your privacy and realize that it's not her home any longer, although she owns it she should knock on the door like anyone else and not make a nuisance of herself by continually visiting you! It makes you wonder if she misses the place and doesn't really want to let go!

Linda was still feeling the after effects of the difficult birth, she felt a bit exhausted after the neighbour's visit so she went for a lay down while Margie looked after the children. As she lay in the quietness of her bedroom she began having doubts as to whether she had done the right thing in registering her baby so quickly without discussing it with James first.

When James got home from work that evening she told him what she had done and he looked at her in shock, 'Why did you do that?' he gently questioned her. Linda was still very sensitive after the birth and burst into tears as she told James 'Well you had made your mind up, it was the name that you wanted.' James cuddled her and explained, 'But there was plenty time, you didn't have to rush into it!' 'I'm sorry, I'm just so tired and mixed up at the moment, I thought that you would be happy,' answered Linda.

After dinner when the children were sleeping, they all started to discuss baby Gabrielle's name again. 'I don't think it will be too late to change it' said Linda. 'Yes but what to?' answered James. 'I don't know we never really got round to discussing a name because you were down here and I was up in Scotland and anytime I asked you about it on the phone, you answered if it's a girl I want to call her Gabrielle, you wouldn't listen to any of my suggestions!' said Linda. 'We could call her Andrea after St. Andrew Day!' suggested Linda.' 'Yes but she was born the day after St Andrews Day so that's not really appropriate,' answered James, After going through every girl's name that they could think of in the alphabet from Ann to Zoe, they couldn't agree. At that Margie piped up, 'I still like Mandy or Amanda. 'Amanda? Now that's a nice name!' exclaimed James' 'Yes' I quite like that name too' replied Linda then she turned to her dad and asked him, 'What do you think of Amanda for the baby's name?' 'Aye that sounds lovely!' exclaimed Douglas. 'Right I'm just going to the phone box to call my mother, I'll ask her what she thinks of the name.' said James. Twenty minutes later he was back. 'Yes my mother likes Amanda too,' shall we all agree to Amanda, it looks like it's unanimous!' said James. Right said Linda, 'I'll go to the registry office first thing on Monday morning. Dad, will you come with me, mum would you mind looking after the kids for a couple of hours please?' 'Yes I'll be here to see to the kids while you and dad sort out the name' answered Margie.

The baby was sleeping well, so on Friday night James told Linda to go to bed at 10pm and said he would wait until she wakes up then give her a bottle and change her and wheel her through to the room in her little carrycot pram. Linda was exhausted by this time and very grateful for James' offer as she was expecting to be wakened up again between 2 and 3am to feed her baby daughter. She fell asleep as soon as her head hit the pillow and didn't remember James coming to bed.

The next thing she knew, the morning light was penetrating through a little space in the curtain. Linda went to roll over then she caught sight of the alarm clock, it was saying 9.05am. Suddenly she sat bolt upright and shouted in despair, 'The baby!' James opened his eyes immediately and shouted back in the confusion, 'What? What is it?' 'The baby hasn't wakened up all night, there's something wrong! A four day old baby doesn't sleep all through the night!' cried Linda. She couldn't bring herself to look. James jumped out of bed and went over to the carrycot. He stroked his wee daughter's face at that her wee mouth opened just like a wee bird waiting for its mother to feed it. James smiled with relief as he picked his daughter up and cradled her in his arms, 'There's nothing wrong with her, she's just a wee sleepy head, she'd rather sleep than eat!' he said as he kissed her and passed her to Linda to be fed. Linda had a feeling of sheer relief as the panic of the situation defused. 'C'm'ere my wee Rip Van Winkle, don't' ever give your mammy and daddy a fright like that again,' she said as she held her baby close and kissed her.

Monday morning and Linda got up early to wash, dress and feed her two children. 'What time do you plan to leave?' asked her dad. 'Oh we can go after I've given the baby her 10am feed, it shouldn't take too long, I have to be back for 2pm because the health visitor is calling to see the baby. It's nice outside and mum can take them both out for a walk. The lady that sold me the pram threw in a toddler seat that sits on the top. I'll get the pram ready at the bottom of the stairs for mum.' Answered Linda. Just before 11am, Linda and her dad waved good bye to Margie who was across the road with the baby in the pram and Stuart sitting quite content on top in his seat as if this was a new adventure for him. Linda and her dad caught the bus into Addlestone, then got off at the National Westminster Bank in Brighton Road. They walked up Church Road towards the bus stop at the Library to catch the bus to the registrar's office opposite St. Peter's Hospital. The bus arrived within fifteen minutes, after just under ten minutes Linda and Douglas got off the bus at the hospital and crossed the road. They followed the signs for the registry office down a long country lane. At last they reached the big old building and rang the bell on the big old fashioned door. A man answered the door and Linda told him what they were there for. He said they were lucky because the register was in the office on Mondays, he showed them into a big room to sit and wait. Five minutes later the same lady who had come into the hospital and registered Linda's daughter appeared at the door and asked them if they'd like to come into her room. Linda and Douglas followed her into a massive room with a high ceiling; the registrar smiled and told them to take a seat at her desk. They sat down in the big antique wooden chairs while the registrar made her way round the big desk to a big comfortable executive chair. Linda thought that the registrar looked like a wee elf sitting there; she seemed so small and out of proportion sitting in the big chair behind the big desk.

'Now then what can I do for you today?' asked the registrar. 'Well, um, I was wondering um.....'Linda stumbled over her words, she was exhausted and still feeling the effects of the traumatic birth. Douglas chimed in, 'What it is, is my daughter wasn't really feeling 100% when you came into the hospital and she registered her daughter as Gabrielle. Her husband is not very happy, so as the baby was only registered on Friday we wondered if we could change the name to Amanda. The registrar bit her bottom lip and looked quite concerned, she got out the big thick registry book and held it open at the page in question showing it to Linda and Douglas as she said , 'I'm afraid, this has all been registered in the main book now and this goes off to Somerset House. You would have to change the name by deed poll now and that could be costly. Linda looked at her dad in dismay, she was worried that she had given her baby a name that she would grow up not liking, if only the registrar hadn't come into the hospital on Friday morning, they wouldn't now have this dilemma. She felt her eyes filling up as the registrar said, 'There is one way round it, there's just enough space for me to squeeze Amanda in, in front of Gabrielle. 'Would that be ok, can you do that?' asked Linda quite relieved. 'Yes, there's room, but I've got to say, I like your first choice of Gabrielle better!' The registrar put Amanda in front of Gabrielle, and re-wrote the birth certificate. 'Right, your daughter is now officially named Amanda Gabrielle' she said smiling as she handed Linda the new birth certificate. 'Oh well; now she can choose which name she prefers' said Linda as she gratefully took possession of her daughter's official birth certificate.

Linda and her dad got off the bus in Woodham Lane near Scotland Bridge Road, they had been away just over an hour and spotted Margie coming towards them, she had taken a walk into the shops at West Byfleet and had some shopping in the basket under the pram. 'Well, how did you get on?' Margie asked as she approached them. 'Linda smiled and waved the new birth certificate in the air, 'It's all done!' she happily told her mum. 'Oh thank goodness for that, that's a load off your shoulders!' answered Margie.

At 2pm on the dot the health visitor arrived, she was a thin spinster type lady with tightly permed salt and pepper coloured hair and little glasses resting on her nose. She wore a navy blue trench-style nurse's coat. She asked Linda to strip the baby then she scooped the little bundle up in one hand and put her into a little net then she hung it on a small scale, 'mmmm...., she's doing well, maintaining her weight, that's good!' said the health visitor. Linda told her about the baby sleeping all night and how she had given them a fright. The health visitor reassured her and told her that, it can take a while for the pethidine to get out of the baby's system, she's only got a little body and she's taken in all that pethidine that was administered to you, she'll be a little bit sleepy until it all wears off, so don't worry!'

Friday morning and Margie and Douglas complete with Chienne the dog had to leave because they were due to start back at work on Monday. Wee Stuart was looking confused as he watched his gran and grandpa packing their cases, he was wondering what was going on. They were very sad too; they loved spending time with their grandchildren. Douglas was a different man and seemed to be re-living the life he should have lived with his own children through his grandchildren, he had controlled his drinking and was a much better husband and dad for it. Douglas and Margie worried how Linda was going to cope on her own; they wished that they weren't so far away from each other. Linda had a heavy heart as her dad brought the suitcases to the door; she was going to miss them so much and wished they could have stayed longer. Noreen had offered to drive them to West Byfleet train station, although she was very over-powering, she had a heart of gold. As Margie and Douglas made their way along the balcony to the stairs, wee Stuart tried to run after them, Linda grabbed him and whisked him up in to her arms. He stretched his arms out to his gran and grandpa crying after them. Margie couldn't take it any longer and ran back to give him a big cuddle, by this time both Margie and Linda were in tears as the wee boy clung on to his gran's neck. Douglas came back and put his arms round them all, his eyes welled up as he gently led Margie away from Linda and their grandson and they made their way to the car below where Noreen was waiting. Linda leaned over the balcony railing waving, as Douglas and Margie waved back. Noreen said to Margie and Douglas, 'Don't worry, I'll look after Linda and the children for you, they'll be ok!' Douglas and Margie waved their arms out of the car windows then the car turned the corner and was gone. Linda cuddled Stuart and sobbed her heart out, she loved her mum and knew that her mum and dad were heartbroken that she and James had moved so far away, meaning that they wouldn't get to see their grandchildren as often as they would have liked. Linda didn't like it either, although she realised that they had to stay where the work was in order to give their children the best chances in life.

Linda went back into the lounge, Stuart looked at his mother's tear-stained face and gave her a big cuddle and kiss, Linda's heart melted as she cuddled him back and she said, 'We're going to have to be strong, it's just you, me, your dad and your baby sister now! This won't be forever though, just until we can save up enough and get on our feet, then we'll go back to Scotland and buy a nice family house near to gran and grandpa and we'll all be together again.

Four

It was early afternoon on Christmas Eve and Linda and James didn't have much cash to spend, James had been working hard but the money was being swallowed up in the rent and household bills and with Linda recently giving birth, she hadn't had much time to think about Christmas. They had £10 in money presents giving to baby Amanda from family and Linda decided that she would buy her wee daughter a silver bangle with the money so they decided to go into West Byfleet to look for a jeweller's and a toy shop to buy wee Stuart a toy peddle car. Linda's mum had said that it would be cruel not to get him one because he was car-mad, everything was a steering wheel from plates, to upside down chairs!

James brought his 101 Vauxhall Victor Estate to the bottom of the stairs at the back of the shops where they lived and Linda climbed in the back with Stuart sitting beside her and baby Amanda on her lap. They pulled out into the Broadway at New Haw heading for the shops in West Byfleet. They had driven about 30 feet and James was travelling at around 15mph when just as they were about to pass the pub on the corner another estate car came screaming out of the pub car park filled with young men obviously out having a drink for Christmas. Their brown car almost spun on two wheels as it skidded out onto the road in front of them, all the men were laughing and shouting, James slammed his brakes on and wee Stuart flew off of the back seat and hit his face on the back of the driver's seat, his front teeth went through his lip, there was blood everywhere and he was crying in pain. James was furious that his wee son had been hurt, he pulled the car up and jumped out shouting and swearing at the brown car but the drunken driver and passengers in the brown car were totally oblivious that they had hurt a child as their car sped off down the road. Linda was distraught that such a thing could happen to wee Stuart, especially on Christmas Eve. They cleaned Stuart up and the cut wasn't too bad but the poor wee soul had a fat lip. James was still very angry that his wee son had been hurt and swearing at the men said to Linda, 'drunken idiots, they shouldn't be driving in that state, I wish we'd seen their number plate, they could have killed us all if it had happened a second earlier.'

When they got to West Byfleet, they parked the car and went into the big department store on the corner, then made their way to the toy department. There on the floor was a wee red plastic toy peddle car, wee Stuart's eyes lit up. Douglas sat him in it. His wee face beamed as he looked at his mummy for approval then he started twisting and turning the steering wheel. A posh-looking gentleman came walking towards them, he was dressed in a smart black suit, white shirt and Paisley patterned tie. 'Oh you like that car, don't you?' he said smiling at wee Stuart. 'How much is it?' enquired Linda. '£7 madam,' answered the kindly salesman. 'Oh it's a bit more than we can afford,' said Linda to James, 'but what can we do? He loves it and Christmas is tomorrow!' she exclaimed. The salesman seemed to feel sorry for them and whispered, 'If you come back at 4.30pm the toys on display, including the car are going for half price' Linda and James were very grateful to the salesman for his honesty, it was 2.15pm, they decided to go to the jeweller's next door where Linda picked out a lovely shiny bangle for her baby daughter then they had a walk round the shops to kill time.

At twenty past four they went back to the department store, it didn't seem too busy and they were excited at the thought of buying their wee boy the peddle car that they knew he would love. They arrived at the toy department in time to see a salesman pick up the peddle car and make his way to the till followed by a young man. 'Oh no!' cried Linda, 'It's been sold! What do we do now? We haven't got anything for Stuart's Christmas, we should just have skint ourselves and bought it earlier when we saw it!' continued Linda, almost close to tears. At that the salesman that they originally spoke to appeared from behind, he seemed to have overheard Linda. 'Oh, you just weren't quick enough,' he said in a genuinely sympathetic voice. 'But you said 4.30pm, it's not quite 4.30pm and it's been sold, where can we buy a peddle car for our wee boy now, most of the shops are closed now until after Christmas! said Linda, in a tearful quivering voice. The salesman looked at his watch and said, 'You're right, he was a bit quick of the mark, just wait there a moment'. Linda and James looked at each other; they were very disappointed and concerned that they were wasting more time standing there when they could be out searching for any toy shops that were still opened. Five minutes later the salesman returned with a smile on his face and carrying a big box, 'We can't see your son without a present on Christmas morning, can we now?' he grinned, then he said 'There you go, a brand new peddle car, all boxed up for you,' as he opened it to let them inspect it. 'So does that mean that it is £7 because I understood that it was just display toys that were half price?' Linda asked the salesman. 'No, £3.50 to you as we agreed' he replied. 'But will that be ok? We're not getting you into any trouble, are we?' Linda asked him with concern. 'You let me worry about that!' answered the kindly salesman, 'I talked you into coming back at 4.30pm and promised that you'd get the car for half price and I don't break a promise!' he smiled.

That night Linda went off to bed at 10pm as usual and James waited up to feed his baby daughter at midnight. This was a special bonding time for father and daughter every night. Baby Amanda gazed up into her daddy's eyes as he talked to her, telling her how beautiful she was, that he was going to work hard to give her everything and one day she would marry a Scottish carpenter just like her daddy!

Christmas morning, Linda got up at 6am as usual to feed and change baby Amanda. At 8am James appeared at the lounge door holding Stuart's hand and asked, 'Has he been yet? Wee Stuarts's face lit up as he tore the box open to reveal a peddle car. He climbed into it looking at his mummy and daddy for approval and said 'Ou-Ou-At?' which was Stuart's version of 'What's that?' James showed him how use the pedals to make the car go but Stuart was happy pushing it along with his feet. James was only having Christmas day off, he was going back to work on Boxing Day, he would be working on his own because nobody else would be on the building site but they needed the money to pay their rent! Linda's brother Douglas and wife Norma invited them over for Christmas dinner, so they put the peddle car in the back of their estate car and set off for Camberley.

Friday was 31st December, James' contract came to an end and he finished early, he had a new job to start on Tuesday. He came home to find Linda in tears. 'What's wrong?' he asked her concernedly. Linda sobbed, 'Well it was bad enough not seeing my mum at Christmas but I can't bear the thought of not being with my family to bring in the New Year!' James thought for a minute then looked at his watch, it was 3pm. 'Right how long will it take you to pack a case?' Linda stopped and looked at him in disbelief; she wiped a tear away and answered, 'What you mean drive up to Glasgow…NOW?' James laughed and nodded as he said, 'I don't see why not, we can drive up tonight, I don't start my new job until Tuesday, so we can drive back on Monday.' 'But we don't have any money' said Linda. 'I can scrape up enough for petrol, what more do we need? Our families will be delighted to see us and especially the kids!' answered James. Linda jumped up and hugged him, 'It won't take me long to throw a few thing into a case' she said with a grateful and excited smile.

Linda prepared the baby's bottle feeds up for the journey, along with a couple of flasks of hot water, one to heat the baby's bottle up in and another for tea. She packed everything she needed for the children while James put the back seats down in their estate car and put the 2 carry cots from the prams and the wheels for the big pram in the back for the children to sleep in. She then made up some sandwiches and by 6pm they were all in the car ready for their long journey north. As they were pulling away, their landlady Noreen appeared, Linda wound her window down and told her that they were going to Glasgow for the weekend, so not to worry if she didn't see them around. Noreen wished them a pleasant journey and waved them off. 'She won't know what to do with herself with us being away, she won't be able to drop in unannounced whenever she feels like it, at least I hope she won't! God James you don't think that she'll be prowling around the flat when we're not there, do you? We came away in such a rush and I've left the file with our bank business and other private matters on top of the sideboard! Linda said to James worriedly. 'I know nosey Noreen can be a pain, constantly letting herself into our flat whenever she likes but I think even she wouldn't stoop to the level of entering our home when we were on holiday' answered James. 'It's a shame, because I really love the flat and I would like to think I will stay there a long time, but she is driving me crazy the way she keeps walking into our house whenever she feels fit, she doesn't seem to grasp that we are paying her £60 per month and it's our private home, I know she's the landlady and entitled to have a key but you'd think that she would back off and give us our privacy. I wonder how she would like it if we kept walking in on her without being invited, I don't think she would be too happy, do you!' Linda asked James. 'I don't suppose so,' replied James.

The roads were fairly busy on the way to the M6 but once they got on to the motorway, the traffic was flowing smoothly. They stopped a couple of times en route at motorway service stations to have a cup of tea, eat their sandwiches, feed and change the children and use the toilets. As they got further up north they could see the snow on the mountains. By the time they reached the Pennines the snow was pretty thick all around. They pushed on regardless and Linda was getting really excited, every now and then she turned to look at her two babies fast asleep in their wee carry cots. She stroked their heads and whispered, 'You'll be in Bonny Scotland soon and you'll see your Gran and Grandpa'.

It was just after midnight and they were getting near to the border. 'Not long now, only another couple of hours and we'll be there!' said James. 'Oh I can't wait, my mum will be delighted. I can't wait to surprise her.' replied Linda. 'Don't you think that we should have warned them we were coming?' James asked Linda. 'No, they never leave the house at New Year, Betty, Duncan, Mary and David will probably have first footed them and us turning up on the doorstep will be the best new year present ever for them!' said Linda.

Linda couldn't help the big satisfied grin that came across her face as they crossed the border in to Scotland. It was just before 1am and Linda commented on the depth of the snow at the side of the motorway when there was a loud clunk and the car lost its power. Luckily there wasn't another car on the A74 and James expertly guided the car into a very convenient lay-by. 'What's wrong James?' Linda asked him, trying not to panic. 'I don't know, but it didn't sound good' answered James, as he opened the glove compartment and took out a torch before getting out of the car into the snow to look under the car bonnet. Linda sat inside the car, she had a horrible feeling at the pit of her stomach as James came back and said, 'it's no good, it's too dark, I can't see what the problem is. If only this had happened an hour ago, we'd have been in England on the motorway and got help, what chance have we got here, just over the border into Scotland on 1st January at 1am, nobody will be working, they'll all be celebrating! We'll just have to stay here until daylight then I'll go and find a phone for help, try not to worry, it'll be alright!' James gave Linda a big hug. She couldn't believe what was happening. They had been travelling for seven hours and were only one hour away from her parents home, who didn't even know that they were on there way to see them. It was pitch black outside, the snow lit up the bleak fields that surrounded them. Linda put a tartan travel rug over the two carry cots to keep the children warm, then she and James lay back on their seats and tried to sleep. They dozed in and out of a light sleep, then just after 2.30 am baby Amanda wakened up for a feed. Linda got the flask out and warmed up her bottle and fed and changed her. By the time she put her down in her carry cot again it was 3.20am. She and James snatched a couple more hours of sleep then just after 5am James decided he would walk to find a telephone to call for help. Linda was worried sick about him walking along by the side of the A74 in the heavy snow, they didn't know how far he'd have to walk also she didn't relish the idea of her and the kids being alone in the car in the middle of nowhere.

Linda checked the flask and found that the water had gone cold, she panicked, the baby would be wakening up for a feed soon, how was she going to warm her bottle? Linda was so relieved when she looked back and saw James in the distance walking towards the car, the snow was covering his ankles,' When he finally got back to the car his shoes, socks and feet were soaking and he was blue with the cold. 'Did you manage to find a phone?' Linda asked him anxiously. 'Yes, I got through to the local police, but don't hold your breath, they said that are very busy with breakdowns on the A74 and will get to us when they can!' answered James. 'I hope it's soon because the baby will be wanting fed and the water in the flask has gone cold,' said Linda worriedly.

It was 7.45am, Linda turned round and touched her children's cheeks, 'Oh James, how long do you think they'll be? The kids faces are freezing, we can't stay here much longer!' Linda exclaimed, she was scared that no-one was interested in helping them, when a police van pulled up alongside. A young policeman jumped out, 'What's the problem then?' he asked James as he bent down to the drivers window. 'I don't know, the car just conked out on us?' 'Right I'll call a garage, though goodness knows how long it'll be before they get to you because we have nine other people in cars in the same predicament as yourselves, you'll have to pay for the assistance,' said the young constable as he rattled off without stopping for a breath.

Linda burst into tears, 'I'm sorry love, it's the best I can do' he said. Linda sobbed ' I have two babies in the back, my daughter is only four weeks old, I only have one bottle left for her and I don't have any hot water to warm it up, my little son will be wakening up soon and I have nothing for him to eat. My babies will die in this cold, they are freezing.' The young constable immediately looked in the back window to see the two wee tots fast asleep. 'Right, that's a different matter, just a minute,' he said. He went into his van and got on to the radio. A few minutes later he came back and said, 'Right let's get you all out of here; you're coming in the van with me. He proceeded, to lift the carrycots with the sleeping children and all of their possessions out of the car into the van assisted by James. 'I'm taking you into the Police Station at Carlisle, you'll get warm water for your baby and be able to call your family for help.' Linda felt relieved but she didn't know how she was going to tell her mum or how her parents would be able to help. There was no transport on 1st January so they couldn't even get a train or a bus to Glasgow. They got to the station and the big cheery sergeant at the desk welcomed them, 'Well PC Blake what have these folk been up to then?' he joked 'Our car broke down' Linda answered. 'Yes, I know all about you my dear, follow me,' he said. 'I hope you'll be comfortable here until you can arrange transport, make yourselves at home, do you have anyone who can pick you up? said the kindly sergeant as he opened a cell door with two bunk beds in it. 'Not really' answered Linda. 'Oh never mind about that at the moment, once PC Blake and your husband gets all your things out of the van and into the cell, come through to the desk and I'll show you where the kitchen is and you can sort out your baby's bottle,' said the sergeant.

Linda got a bottle, baby powder, baby cream and clean nappies for Stuart and Amanda out of the bag. There was a sink in the cell so she was able to wash Stuart and change his nappy. Then she changed the baby's nappy and left her with James while she took Stuart through to find the kitchen. The desk sergeant said, 'Hello again young man, do you want to be a policeman when you grow up?' Stuart smiled shyly at him then the sergeant said, 'here come here and we'll see if this fits you!' He plunked a police helmet on Stuart's head. It wobbled around on his head but Stuart was delighted and the other policemen were laughing at this wee toddler running around with the big policeman's helmet. The sergeant turned to another young PC and said to him. 'Right PC Edmonds, show the young lady where the kitchen is. PC Edmonds smiled and said to Linda, 'follow me, the kitchen's just down this corridor, feel free to make yourselves some tea, there's a toaster and some bread and butter too if you fancy some toast.' Linda was very grateful, she couldn't believe how lovely, helpful and understanding all the policemen were. She made up baby Amanda's bottle and took it through for James to feed her, then she went back to make them tea and toast. On the way back she asked the desk sergeant if she could make a phone call to her mum. 'Certainly, sit yourself down here, you can dial straight out from that 'phone,' he said as he gestured for Linda to sit at a desk at the back. Linda dialed her parents telephone number and waited with butterflies in her stomach for them to answer, it was 9.15am so there was every chance that they would be in their bed after a late night partying. Eventually the phone was picked up, 'Hello', said the man's voice at the other end, 'Hello' answered Linda. 'Hello, who's that?' said the man, 'It's me, Linda, Who's that?' she replied. 'Oh Linda, Happy New Year pet, it's Uncle David here, how are you?' he said. 'Well I've got a bit of a problem, can I speak to my mum please, Uncle David?' she asked. 'Certainly pet, hang on I'll get her, she's making us all breakfast!' he laughed. Linda could hear the commotion in the back as Margie asked Douglas to watch the sausages under the grill while she spoke to Linda, 'But I want to wish Linda and James Happy New Year too,' she heard her dad say. 'I'll speak to her first then I'll take over cooking the breakfast while you speak to her,' she heard her mum answer. Eventually she heard her mum walk towards the phone and pick it up. 'Linda, Happy New Year my wee pet! Mary, David, Betty and Duncan are still here, we've had lots of visitors and neighbours popping in, Uncle David was our first foot, we've been up all night and had a rerr wee party, I'm just making them breakfast before they go. We missed you, what did you do last night?' said Margie practically all in one go without stopping for breath. 'Well we almost made it to your party' said Linda 'How do you mean?' enquired Margie. Linda went on to tell her mum the predicament that they were in and how they didn't know what they were going to do because they had no car and there was no public transport but more importantly they had no money, they were only coming home for the weekend because Linda was desperately homesick. Douglas and the others heard the commotion when Margie gasped 'Oh No!' then she blurted out quickly to them what had happened. 'Right I'm on my way, tell them to be ready in a couple of hours!' said Uncle David, he had matured and mellowed over the years from his young bombastic self and would now help anyone if he thought it was possible. Margie said, 'Are you sure David? But you've been drinking!' 'I haven't had a drink in the last four hours and you're forgetting that I dozed off on the chair for an hour or so!' answered David then he told Mary to call their son to come and pick Betty, Duncan and her up when they were ready. As he grabbed his jacket Margie said 'here David, take these couple of rolls with you, one on ham and one on sausage, hang on the kettles just boiled, I'll fill a flask of tea for you for the journey'. David took the bag with rolls and the flask, grabbed his jacket and shouted cheerio to everyone.

Linda came off the phone and told the desk sergeant that her uncle was on his way to pick them up, she was so relieved. There just wasn't any other way that they were going to get to Glasgow that day. She took the tea and toast through to James and told him the good news. 'You mean Uncle David is going to drive all the way from Glasgow? How can we ever repay him? That's an awful lot to ask of him at any time, never mind the 1st January!' said James still finding it hard to believe.

At 11.55am PC Blake came through and told James and Linda that their Uncle had arrived to pick them up, 'Oh and your car has been towed away, here is the details of the garage, so that you can arrange for repairs,' said the young PC as he handed James a slip of paper. James felt his heart sink, he had temporarily put it out of his mind but he knew that he would have to find the money from somewhere to pay for his car to be fixed.

They came out to the front desk to be greeted by Uncle David's smiling face, Linda felt sheer relief when she saw him and gave him a big hug. Linda wheeled out the big pram with baby Amanda fast asleep in it, while Uncle David took the case and a smaller bag and James carried out the carry cot from the wee pram and held onto Stuart's hand.

Just over two hours later they were pulling up outside Linda's parent's house. Margie and Douglas came running out to meet them and gave them all hugs and kisses. Douglas scooped wee Stuart up into his arms and said 'C'mere ma wee son and tell me a' whit happened!' Linda passed the baby to Margie and they walked towards the house. James and Uncle David got the wee carry cot, the big pram, the case and the wee bag out of the car and carried them into the house. They all collapsed on the settee. 'Right I'll make you some breakfast, what would you like?' asked Margie. 'Oh we need a good night's sleep, we have only cat napped, we're both shattered,' answered Linda. Uncle David said his good-bye's after being told many times how grateful they all were to him. Linda had a sausage sandwich and James had a ham roll, then they went upstairs to catch up with their sleep while Margie and Douglas took over and looked after the children. They thoroughly enjoyed having their grandchildren to themselves and took them down to the park, where wee Stuart had a play on the swings and fed the ducks at the boating pond.

Later that evening, reality was kicking in. How were they going to get back to Surrey?

They had no money and no car, they didn't know how much the repairs were going to come to and had no idea how they could possibly pay for them. The mechanics at the garage where their car had been towed to weren't due to start work again until Wednesday 5th January, as were most businesses in Scotland and this was only 1st January. They still had over two years HP outstanding on the car and they were struggling to pay it so there was no way that they would be able to buy another one. James needed a car for work to carry all his tools and materials. Linda's dad, Douglas, told them both to relax and that between them all they would find a way round their problems. 'Yes, but I have to return to Surrey by Monday night at the latest to start a new job on Tuesday morning, I have to get back because we need the money to pay the rent,' said James worriedly. Linda was close to tears as she chimed in with 'And how are we to get the two carrycots and all the kids stuff back?' 'I think you'll have to resign yourself to the fact that you won't be going anywhere until at least Wednesday, you can call the bus station then and see if you can get seats on the London bus, mum and I will pay your fares so don't worry until you have something to worry about.' answered Douglas, then he continued, 'Just relax now, it's Saturday night, it's New Year, have a wee drink, would you like a beer James?' 'That's another thing, I feel awful being here at New Year and I haven't even been able to buy a carry out!' said James. 'Forget it! You have more things to spend your money on at the moment other than beer. Mum and I are just delighted to see Linda, yourself and the kids. We're relieved that you are safe and well' replied Douglas.

Sunday morning and James called his mate Eddie and told him to tell the supervisor on the new job, that they were due to start on Tuesday, what had happened and that he hoped to start before the end of the week. Then he and Linda set off with baby Amanda in the big pram with Stuart on his toddler seat on top, for the half hour walk to see his mother in Drumchapel. Molly was delighted to see them, she had shortbread, and currant bun out on the coffee table waiting for them. She poured them a glass of her home-made ginger wine each and they all wished each other a Happy New Year. 'Shall we pop down to see Maria because I'm not sure that I'll get another chance to see her before we go home?' James said to his mother.

Within half an hour they all set off for the walk to Maria and her husband Pete's house. James didn't like Pete, he was selfish, self-centered, mean and didn't treat his sister Maria very well. James knew that Maria put on a brave face and lived a life of pretence, almost believing that Pete looked after her well and cared for her. Maria wouldn't hear a word against her husband, probably because she didn't want to admit to everyone how unhappy she really was. Molly couldn't stand Pete, she always thought that Maria could have done a lot better for herself, but then Molly wasn't an easy woman to get on with, she openly admitted in the past that she would have been happy for her two daughter's and James to have stayed at home with her and not to have got married. She had made life very difficult for Linda in the past when she and James were courting, she had her favourite Grandchildren and she made it clear who they were. She only had time for one of Maria's twins, she loved Stuart because he looked like James when he was a toddler. She wasn't keen on baby Amanda, even though she had been on and on about wanting a granddaughter because she had five grandsons but when Linda produced the first granddaughter, Molly appeared to show signs of jealousy. Linda concluded that this was because it was another female in her son's life. It knocked her further down the line of importance. Linda felt that Molly would have preferred for one of her daughter's to having given birth to her first granddaughter.

When they got to Maria's, she welcomed them and made straight for baby Amanda for a cuddle. Maria talked ten to the dozen asking question after question about her new wee niece and life in England. Meanwhile Pete sat with a sarcastic smirk on his face as he poured himself a whisky. 'Pete, pour James a wee half for the New Year, I've got some sherry Linda, would you like some, what about you mammy? Maria asked as she made her way to the cabinet to get the sherry bottle and some glasses. She brought out three stemmed glasses for Linda, her mother and herself and gave Pete a whisky glass for James. She poured the sherry, then turned to Pete and said, 'Are you pouring one for James? 'Don't see why ah should share ma boattle wi' him, heez no' even brought a carry oot wi' him!' answered Pete. There was a stunned silence and Maria was really embarrassed. Linda was worried because she knew that James was already depressed about the situation and he didn't need Pete's arrogant remarks. 'Don't worry, I'm not bothered' said James but Maria continued in a pleading manner to her husband 'Come on Pete, James and Linda have been through a rough time, they don't have any money at the moment, please pour James a drink to wish him a Happy New Year,' to which Pete answered 'Bugger off, they've goet a cheek visiting folk at this time o' the year without a boatle an' tryin' tae scrounge a drink, they shouldnae huv come if they couldnae afford it!' Maria didn't know where to look and offered James a sherry, James refused out of principle, there was plenty he could have said about the times at different family parties when Pete drank them dry guzzling everyone else's drinks. He was an uncouth, rude, greedy person but James decided to say nothing because he was on a sticky wicket, he knew when he left that his sister would suffer for it and there was nothing he could do because Maria tried to hide her husband's cruelty and bullying and got very upset if anyone tried to intervene. Molly piped up with, 'For goodness sake, families are supposed to help each other, one day it might be you that's down on your luck, you're a mean bugger Pete, you wouldn't give anyone daylight in a dark corner!' Pete just ignored his mother-in-laws remarks, he scowled at Maria as if to say '*You wait!*', then sneered at James as he poured himself another whisky and downed it in one.

Molly said, 'C'mon, I'm not staying here any longer to be insulted'. James hugged Maria in the hallway and whispered to her, 'Are you going to be ok?' Maria answered, 'Don't be daft, I'm just sorry you're going, Pete's just overtired, he's not thinking right, he hasn't had much sleep!' As they were walking out the close, James said to Linda, 'Why does Maria keep covering up for him, it's obvious that she hasn't much of a life! I'll never forget the words of that ignorant sod! What does she see in him? He's a tight miserable bastard!'

They stayed overnight at Molly's and just before mid-day on

Monday, James and Linda walked back to her parents house, 'we should have been travelling back home today!' James exclaimed with a dejected look then he continued, 'I wish the garage was opened then I could have some idea of the damage to the car and how much it was going to cost for repairs!' Linda tried to console him and said, 'Don't worry, there's a way round everything, we'll be ok!' but deep down she was worried sick about their future and wondered if they had done the right thing moving to the south of England, although the work and money was in that part of the world and she knew that there would be a better future for her children, the housing was expensive, there was no chance of getting a council house because they weren't as plentiful as they were in Glasgow and they would have to make their own way in life.

Margie and Douglas were delighted to see them all again and kept emphasizing to them not to worry about money, they didn't have much themselves but they would help them as best they could. 'Just enjoy your wee holiday, ok it's longer than you anticipated but there's nothing you can do about that at the moment, so just make the best of it!' said Douglas.

Tuesday evening, Aunty Mary and Uncle David came to see Linda, James and the children. 'Are you going home tomorrow?' asked Uncle David. 'Well we hope to, as soon as the bus station opens in the morning, Linda's going to call them to see if there are any seats left on the London bus tomorrow evening, that's our only option, the train is too expensive!' answered James. 'Well let me know if you manage to get tickets for the bus and I will come and drop you off.' said Uncle David. 'Are you sure? That would be a godsend because we have lots of stuff to carry, when we packed the car, we weren't thinking of public transport!' replied Linda. 'We might have to leave some thing's and get them next time Linda, I mean we haven't got the wheels to the wee pram with us so we might have to leave the wee carry cot here until I'm able to drive up again' James intervened. 'Oh no, I need the wee pram because that's the one I keep in the flat for Amanda to sleep in, this is a nightmare' answered Linda. 'Look don't worry, we'll take everything we can in my car and what the bus can't take then I'll drop back here at your parents house', said Uncle David. 'We can put the wee carry cot inside the big one and it should go into the boot of the bus ok!' exclaimed Linda. 'Yes, but we'll have to get the tube from Euston to Waterloo then the train out to West Byfleet, how are we going to manage all this stuff?' Said James, he was feeling very pessimistic about everything by now. 'Well if the wee carry cot goes inside the big pram, we can put the wee bag in the basket below and the case on top, I can carry Amanda while you push the big pram with everything in it and Stuart can take our hands!' answered Linda. James looked impressed, he always admired Linda's organizing skills.

Wednesday morning and Linda phoned the bus station just after 9am to enquire if there were any seats left for the bus to London that night. I've got nothing for tonight, you could come down on chance for a stand-by incase some passengers don't turn up' said the girl on the other end of the phone. 'I've got a five week old baby and a toddler so that wouldn't be possible, are there any seats on the London bus for tomorrow morning or tomorrow night please?' There was a pause then the girl answered, 'No, I'm sorry, we don't have anything until Saturday night!' 'Oh no, we have to get back, our car has broken down and my husband has to get back to work' cried Linda with a quiver in her voice. The sympathetic girl seemed to sense Linda's dismay and said, 'Look if you leave your telephone number with me, I'll put you first on the list for any cancellations and I'll call you if we have any before Saturday, meanwhile would you like to book seats for Saturday over-night bus to London?' Linda breathed a heavy sigh; she thanked the girl and booked two seats for the Saturday night London bus. When she came off the phone she told James the situation, 'I've booked two seats, we'll have to have the kids on our laps for the duration of the journey. My mum and dad are giving us the money for the fare but I intend to pay them back when we can!'

James called the garage to find out what repairs were needed for his car. He came off the phone holding his head in his hands. 'What's up?' asked Linda. 'Well do you want the bad news or do you want the bad news?' replied James. 'How do you mean?' answered Linda. 'Well it's the engine; the car needs a new engine!' 'Is there more bad new?' Linda asked with her face screwed up as if she was waiting for the painful blow. 'It's estimated at £150,' replied James. '£150!!!!' exclaimed Linda in horror, 'where on earth are we going to get that sort of money from?' 'I'll have to think of something, because we still owe a couple of hundred pounds on it so I can't just tell them to forget it and I need a car for work to carry my tools!' answered James as he ran his hands through his hair in a panicking sort of fashion. He sat quietly thinking for about fifteen minutes then he said 'I've got it, it's our only chance!' 'What?' Linda asked eagerly. 'I'm going to call the finance company and explain to them our predicament!' he exclaimed. 'Do you think they'll be interested?' Linda asked him. 'I can only try!' replied James as he shrugged his shoulders. Linda sat crossing her fingers in the living room as she tried to catch snippets of the conversation James was holding with the finance company on the phone in the hall. She heard him say, 'Yes, but I'm in Scotland, I live in England, I need the car for work and if you don't agree to it, I'm left paying for something I don't have!'. Five minutes later she heard him hang up the phone. 'Well?' said Linda, 'what did they say?' 'They're going to make enquiries and call me back' answered James 'Oh God, that's two calls we're biting our nails waiting for now!' said Linda.

Just over an hour later the phone rang Margie was in the kitchen she ran through to the living room excitedly and shouted, 'James, Linda, quick this could be one of the calls you're waiting for!' James picked up the phone as Linda stood beside him trying to listen, a big smile spread across his face then Linda heard him say, 'Thank you very much for that I really appreciate your help, thank you he repeated again'. He hung up the phone, grabbed Linda and gave her kiss and a hug, 'the finance company is going to pay for the repairs' he announced to everyone with relief. 'Well that's a load off your minds!' said Douglas with a big smile. 'Yes it'll mean the monthly payments will go up but we'll manage somehow!' said James confidently. Just then the phone rang again. Linda picked it up, 'What tonight? That's great! Yes please reserve them for me'. She came off the phone and jumped into James' arms and said, 'that was the bus station, we can start packing they have had two cancellations for the over-night bus tonight, we have to get there to confirm by 5.30pm at the latest because there is a waiting list for standby's. The bus leaves at 6.30pm. Everything is falling into place now!' 'See behind every cloud there's a silver lining' piped up Linda's mum. 'Right I'll call David and ask him if he'll pick you up at half past four, you don't want to be late! said Linda's dad.

James called the garage and told them to go ahead with the repairs to his car and asked them when the car would be ready. They told him that they would have to order the new engine and parts, so it could take at least two weeks.

They were all packed and ready by the time Uncle David arrived with Aunt Mary and their two and a half year old daughter Lisa. They took all their cases prams and luggage out to the pavement and packed them into the boot of Uncle David's car. Margie and Douglas were very sad to see them go. Margie carried baby Amanda in her arms, she fought back tears as she handed her over to Linda. She gave Linda a big hug and said, 'Now you take care of yourself, do you hear? And remember, there's always a place here for you all if you need it, I mean it!' Douglas and Margie gave wee Stuart a big tight hug, then Douglas kissed his daughter on the cheek as he gave her a warm hug and said, 'You two look after yourselves and our wee grandchildren and remember what your mammy said, 'There's always a place here for you all if you need it!' James hugged Margie and kissed her on the cheek then shook Douglas' hand as he thanked them both for all their help and understanding. Margie and Douglas stood on the pavement looking very lonely as they watched the car with their daughter, son-in-law and grandchildren inside, drive into the distance. They dreamed one day that Linda and James would get the 'London Bug' out of their system and return to Glasgow with their young family.

James sat in the front with Uncle David while Linda got in the back with Aunt Mary, she had baby Amanda on her lap and the two toddlers sat between them. 'When do you intend to come up to Carlisle for your car? Uncle David asked James. 'Hopefully it should be ready in two weeks I'll probably get the bus up and drive back on my own', answered James. 'How do you like living in London?' Aunt Mary asked Linda, 'Well I love our flat, it's so big and spacious and New Haw is a lovely, leafy part of Surrey.

There's lots of opportunities and our kids will have a much better start in life than they would ever have in Glasgow.' 'Oh you're lucky, I would love to be going to London, I haven't been there since the war when I was in the Wrens!' said Aunt Mary. They were nearing Buchanan Street Bus Station. 'Right Mrs. Alexander, I hope you're ready for this long haul journey in front of you!' said James to his young wife. Linda groaned at the thought of it. They could see the queues of people standing at the bus station waiting to catch buses to different destinations. 'Gosh it's busy, I have to get to the office and confirm that we're using these seats by 5.30pm, what time is it now?' asked Linda. 'It's only ten past five, you've got plenty time. We'll get parked up and you can go straight to the office while we help James get all your belongings out,' answered Aunt Mary. Uncle David drove past the bus station, 'Where are you going to park David?' Aunt Mary asked her husband. Uncle David didn't answer and carried on driving. 'David, are you listening to me, you've driven past the bus station, where are you going to park?' Uncle David gave one of his cheeky grins and answered, 'We're going to London, that's what you want isn't it?' 'What do you mean? We don't have a change of clothes, I've got nothing for Lisa and no toiletries, toothbrushes or pyjamas!' laughed Aunt Mary. 'We'll get by, don't worry, we'll stop off at a motorway shop and buy toothbrushes,' replied Uncle David, he loved being daring and impulsive and made it quite clear they were not going back! Meanwhile James and Linda were gasping in disbelief and asking Uncle David what he was doing. He again replied with a big-hearted smile 'We're going to London!' They all fell about laughing, 'I don't believe you're doing this Uncle David, are you sure you want to drive all the way? It's a long journey!' Linda asked him. 'Oh, I won't be driving all the way, James will do his fair share at the wheel, my insurance covers any driver with my permission', answered Uncle David. It was pointless trying to change Uncle David's mind, once he got a bee in his bonnet, that was that!

They drove down the M6, and had a couple of stops while Uncle David and James changed over and took turns at driving. Eventually just after midnight they were on the M4 heading towards Reading and London. Aunt Mary, Lisa and Stuart were fast asleep, Linda was dozing in and out of sleep, she looked up and said, 'What is that bridge ahead, I've never seen that?' 'I don't know, neither have I!' answered James. Uncle David went quiet as if he was studying the situation, the motorway was empty, suddenly Uncle David applied the brakes and did a U-turn onto the opposite carriageway, 'What are you doing Uncle David?' asked Linda. 'What's Up' said James. Uncle David was quite unperturbed as he answered, 'We were going the wrong way, I just realised that the bridge ahead was the Severn, we were almost in Wales,' he emphasized laughing. 'WALES! I've never been to Wales' cried Linda, '…and you won't be going there tonight either!' exclaimed Uncle David.

Eventually they reached the six cross-roads at Woking. It was 2.15am and they were driving down Woodham Lane on the very last leg of their journey. They were five minutes from home. 'I wonder if Nosey Noreen will be in the flat waiting for us with a welcoming cup of tea' laughed Linda. 'Nosey Noreen? Who's that' asked Aunt Mary sleepily as she wakened up rubbing her eyes. 'Oh you're back in the land of the living now!' joked Uncle David who was sitting in the front passenger seat while James drove the last leg home. 'She's our landlady and she keeps letting herself into our flat, with her own key, unannounced,' explained Linda. 'What? I wouldn't put up with that, you pay her rent she should respect your privacy,' answered Aunt Mary. 'I know! It's a difficult one, we're going to have to sort it out!' replied Linda as James pulled the car up in front of his garage at the back of the shops. 'Are we here then?' asked Uncle David, 'Yes, home, sweet home! Do you want to come in for a cup of tea or would you prefer to get back up the road home?' James jokingly asked Uncle David. 'I'll have a cup of tea before I hit the road,' replied Uncle David as he pretended to punch James.

Once indoors, Linda gasped in amazement, 'The curtains have been changed, she's been in while we've been away, that's not on, it's out of order, we'll have to talk to Noreen, look I left our bank statements and private business on the sideboard, I wasn't expecting anyone to come into our home!' Linda said angrily to James. 'I would, she's got a right cheek! Said Aunt Mary as Uncle David nodded in agreement. 'We'll sort it out' replied James.

Linda showed Aunt Mary and Uncle David to James and her bedroom and she looked out a nighty to loan to Aunt Mary. Lisa was fast asleep, Linda gave Aunt Mary a pair of Stuart's pyjamas for her and Lisa didn't stir as Aunt Mary undressed her and put them on her before laying her down on the pillow on the big double bed. 'Do you need the cot for Lisa?' asked Linda. 'Och no, it's a big enough bed, she can sleep with us, you'll need the cot for Stuart. Stuart and Baby Amanda were fast asleep. Fortunately Linda had put their pyjamas on them during the journey. James took the cot into the wee second bedroom and laid Stuart in it, while Linda placed baby Amanda into her carrycot. 'Do you want a cup of tea before you go to bed?' Linda asked Aunt Mary and Uncle David. 'Oh no!' her aunt and uncle echoed together, then Aunt Mary continued, 'We'll just get to bed and catch up with our sleep, see you in the morning, goodnight!' 'Goodnight!' they all said to each other. James pulled down the bed settee in the lounge and he and Linda put fresh bedding onto it. 'I don't know what I'm going to do for dinner tomorrow, I don't have any money', Linda said to James. 'Well I'll ask for a sub to my wages at work but I'll have to wait until Friday when I have at least worked a couple of days to prove myself. I can't very well ask for any money up front after one day!' said James. 'I have to feed Aunt Mary and

Uncle David after what they have done for us! I'll have to collect my 80p family allowance and see what I can get for that!

The next morning Linda had fed and changed baby Amanda by the time she waved James off to work at 7am. She got wee Stuart up and made breakfast for them both. She didn't like to disturb Aunt Mary and Uncle David because they were obviously very tired after the long drive the day before. She had just finished washing and dressing Stuart when Aunt Mary came into the lounge carrying Lisa, 'What time is it? You'll be thinking we're awfully lazy' she said to Linda. Linda laughed as she replied, 'No I don't, it's only just after 8 o'clock'. 'Do you mind if we have showers Linda?' Aunt Mary asked, then she went on 'We were thinking that as we've come all this way, we would go and do a bit of sight-seeing in London, before we head home'. 'Not at all, help yourself, I've got nothing special on today, I'll wait until you've finished showering and using the bedroom before I get ready, there's no rush! You are coming back tonight aren't you?' Linda asked. 'Well we don't want to put you out by giving up your bedroom for us, so we thought that we would drive home after a trip to London,' answered Aunt Mary. 'Don't be silly, you're not putting us out, it's nice to have company. You can't drive home to Scotland after walking round London all day, you'll be shattered, come back here and stay another night, then you can get up nice and refreshed in the morning, I insist!' said Linda quite adamantly. 'Oh ok then, I'll speak to Uncle David and see what he says.' replied Aunt Mary.

By 9.30am Aunt Mary, Uncle David and Lisa were washed and dressed. Uncle David nipped downstairs to the wee shop on the corner and bought some milk and bread then they all sat down to cereal, toast and tea. Linda poured Lisa and Stuart a cup of milk each. 'Will that be ok to stay another night then Linda?' Uncle David asked. 'Of course, you go off and enjoy your day, you can't drive all that way back to Scotland today after a day in London, especially as you only drove down here yesterday!' exclaimed Linda.

Linda saw her Aunt, Uncle and wee cousin off just after 10am, then she fed baby Amanda, got herself and the children washed and dressed and headed off for the shops. She didn't have any money on her; she and James had scraped up the last of their cash that they had left between them for his bus fare into Kingston to work for the next two days. She headed for the post office first to collect the 80p family allowance that she got for baby Amanda, and then she went to the local self-service grocery store. She wandered round the store, looking to see what she could possibly get for 80p to feed four adults and two toddlers. She was in despair; she didn't want her aunt and uncle to know just how desperate things were. Finally she decided to get a large fresh steak and kidney pie and some potatoes, it came to 81p and the grocer kindly told her to hand the 1p in the next time she was passing. Thankfully, she had some tinned peas in her kitchen cupboard, so that would help to fill up the plates.

James got back from work just after 5pm. 'How was your day at your new job sweetheart?' Linda asked him. 'Great, it's a good job, new houses on a place called Kingston Hill., they're desperate for carpenters so I can work Saturdays and Sundays. It's £8.50 a day but the bad news is that the working week goes from Thursday to Wednesday and I get paid on the Thursday!' Linda froze on the spot, 'What are we going to live on until next Thursday?' she asked James, her voice quivering with worry. 'Don't worry, the foreman's a nice guy, I asked him about a sub and he said that as I've agreed to work weekends he'll give me £15 up front tomorrow night, so that should see us through until next week. I should collect the balance of £44.50 next Thursday in time for the rent.' Linda breathed a heavy sigh of relief.

Uncle David and Aunt Mary returned with Lisa just as Linda was setting the table for dinner. 'Can I help you Linda?' asked Aunt Mary. 'Oh no, it's ok, everything's under control, it's nothing special, I've just bought a steak and kidney pie, I switched the oven on to warm up ten minutes ago because I suspected that you would be back soon. I've already peeled the potatoes, I'll just go and put the gas on under them and pop the pie in the oven,' said Linda. 'We've brought in a wee cake for after dinner,' said Aunt Mary. 'Oh that's awful kind of you, thank you very much we'll have that for our dessert, it'll save me making anything!' Linda told her aunt, hoping that she didn't suspect the relief in Linda's voice because really there was nothing for pudding! 'Dinner will be ready in about 25 minutes!' Linda announced as she walked out of the kitchen into the lounge.

They all sat down and tucked into their meal. Linda was relieved as there was just enough for everyone and they seemed to enjoy it. Linda was feeding baby Amanda with her bottle as she ate her meal. After dinner, Aunt Mary did the washing up while Linda got baby Amanda and Stuart bathed and into their pyjamas, then Aunt Mary bathed Lisa and put a pair of Stuart's pyjamas on her. Lisa loved her new pyjamas with wee cars on them and danced around showing them off, she was used to wearing nighties.

The kids were all tucked up and in bed by 8pm. The adults sat down and talked about their day. Aunt Mary and Uncle David talked about all the sights that they had seen. Aunt Mary was delighted as she reminisced about her days in the Wrens when she used to come into London for the dancing during the war. 'When were you last in London then?' Linda asked her? 'Oh it must've been about 1945, that's 26 years ago, Oh my! Where does the time go!' Aunt Mary exclaimed in mock shock. Before they knew it it was almost 10pm. 'Well, I'm off to bed now, I have to be up early to feed the baby' said Linda. 'Yes Mrs. we've got an early start tomorrow, so we better think about getting to bed too!' said Uncle David to Aunt Mary. 'What time do you intend to leave then?' Linda asked him. 'I would like to get away by 5am' replied Uncle David. 'Oh we'll disturb Linda and James if they're in the lounge,' said Aunt Mary. 'No you won't, don't worry, we'll sleep in the wee room tonight, that bed is quite big for a single bed, it's much more comfortable than the bed settee!' Linda laughed. 'Are you sure, we don't like to put you out' said Aunt Mary. 'You're not putting us out, how can we ever thank you for all you've done, between Uncle David saving the day for us and coming all the way to Carlisle to pick us up on New Year's Day, then driving us all the way home to Surrey! We really appreciate your kindness!' said Linda. 'Don't be daft, think nothing of it! If the roles were reversed and we needed help, I know that you would do the same if you were in a position to do it!' replied Uncle David. 'Yes, you're right, we would' answered Linda as she gave her Aunt and Uncle a hug and a goodnight kiss before they headed off to bed. 'James are you sure you're ok to wait up and give Amanda her late night feed, you must be very tired?' Linda asked her husband as she gave him a goodnight kiss. 'YES!' replied James jokingly in exasperation then he continued, 'Now just go to your bed!'

Linda woke up at 6am on Friday morning to feed baby Amanda, she wheeled the carrycot through to the lounge, thinking that she should maybe give her aunt and uncle a shout because they wanted to get away on the road early then she went through to the kitchen to put the kettle on and discovered that it was already hot. She dashed through to the bedroom to see the bed all made up. The nighty and the pyjamas that she had loaned Aunt Mary and Lisa were folded on top of the bed along with a wee note thanking them for everything. Linda felt quite sad at not seeing them leave, she enjoyed having family to stay and felt the house was empty again. The previous Friday afternoon she was excitedly packing the cases to go up and surprise her parents for New Year, she felt a pain deep in her chest when she thought about all that had gone wrong in that first week of 1972 and the debt they had to go into to get their car repaired. Deep down Linda worried whether she and James had done the right thing by uprooting themselves and their children four hundred miles away from their families in Glasgow. The pluses were that the earnings were more than double in London and the surrounding areas, the minuses were that the rent and cost of living was high and Linda felt like they were chasing a carrot. There was also the added factor that work was plentiful in this part of the world, James was a first class carpenter, he wasn't afraid of hard work and was becoming quite well known in the building circuit, he had other contractors offering him more money and trying to poach him and could pick and choose his jobs whereby back in Glasgow, there wasn't any work and even if he did manage to get a job, they would have to struggle by on less than £20 per week basic wage because companies very seldom offered overtime in Glasgow and even if he were lucky enough to get extra hours, he would probably only earn approximately £30 per week top whack whereas James worked 7 days a week and earned £59.50 per week in Surrey, so there was no comparison. Linda felt that her hands were tied, she was trying to come to terms with the fact that their future was down south and she knew that her children would get a much better start in life, but her heart was in Glasgow.

Five

James called the garage in Carlisle regularly for updates on his car, then on Wednesday evening of 12th January he got the message that the car would be ready by Friday night. He told them he would pick it up on Saturday morning. He would have to catch the Glasgow bus at Victoria and get off at Carlisle. Linda decided to travel up with him and take the opportunity to visit her parents again for a couple of days in Glasgow. James would be able to pick the car up and drive straight up to Glasgow to join her. She went down to the travel agents on Thursday morning in West Byfleet and was delighted to be able to buy two tickets for the overnight Glasgow bus leaving Victoria at 9pm on Friday.

Linda made a few sandwiches for the journey and she packed a flask with hot tea along with baby Amanda's bottles. They decided that the easiest way to travel was to pack what they needed in the carrycot and wheel it, then they could carry the children. They caught the train from West Byfleet to Waterloo, then they got on the underground from Waterloo to Victoria. From there they walked to Victoria Coach Station. The carrycot and folded wheeled frame was put in the boot of the bus, then Linda and James climbed aboard the bus and found their designated seats halfway down the passageway. They got comfortable, Stuart was very tired and ready for sleeping on James' lap while baby Amanda was already sound asleep on Linda's lap.

The driver dimmed the lights to allow the passengers to sleep. Linda and James dozed into a light sleep with their babies on their laps. They woke up with the lights on the bus being turned on and the driver announcing that they were stopping for a toilet break. Linda poured them both a cup of tea and they had a sandwich each while the children snoozed away happily. Twenty minutes later they were back on the road again. Just before 4am the driver turned the lights on and announced, 'We're stopping at Carlisle in five minutes!' James got his jumper and jacket on, it was a freezing night, Linda said, 'Carlisle already? What are you going to do at this time in the morning?' She was really worried and concerned, James didn't know Carlisle, everywhere was closed and the garage didn't open until 9am! The coach stopped and the driver shouted to remind James that this was his stop. James made his way up the passage, 'How long do you stop here driver?' he asked. 'Jist long enough fur you tae get aff!' came the swift sharp reply. Linda's heart sank as she looked out and waved to James standing out in the pavement all alone. It was still dark, her heart was tumbling over in somersaults wishing that the time would fly until 9am and he would be safely inside his car and back on his way to join them again. She looked down at wee Stuart fast asleep on what was his daddy's seat, she wondered if other young couples had experienced all the hardships and worries in the first couple of years of their married life.

The bus pulled into Glasgow at 6am and Linda was delighted to see her mum and dad waiting for her, she was feeling very vulnerable and close to tears. She got off the bus and handed baby Amanda to her mother, while her dad picked up wee Stuart, they went to the boot to get the carrycot. 'Where's your case Linda?' asked Douglas. 'I don't have one, I just put everything into the carrycot, we're only here for a couple of days' Linda replied. As they walked towards Sauchiehall Street, Douglas spotted a taxi with its hire sign up, he whistled loudly and Linda was delighted as the taxi pulled into the kerb. The driver came out and helped them fold the carrycot's wheels and he packed it into the luggage rack at the side of him. They all climbed aboard and were in Knightswood by ten minutes to seven. Linda's stomach was churning worrying about James and wondering what he was doing. At twenty past seven the phone rang, Linda ran to answer it, 'Hello!' she shouted anxiously down the phone. 'Hello Linda' said the voice at the other end. 'James, James, are you ok? I've been so worried about you, what did you do? Where did you go? Where are you now?' Linda fired question after question at her husband. 'I'm ok, don't worry, luckily the waiting room at the railway station was opened. I've been here since I got off the bus, the wee kiosk has just opened and I'm having a nice hot cup of tea to warm me up. The garage will be opened in an hour and a half, then I will be able to get in my warm car and drive up to you. I will call you again when I pick up the car, now don't worry, I'm ok, the station is beginning to get busy now' James told his worried wife. Linda told James how much she loved him and to take care, she wished they were home in Glasgow for good; life was certainly setting them some challenges since they moved down south.

At 9.20am Linda got the call she was waiting for. James had collected his car and was leaving Carlisle; he would be with her in a couple of hours. Linda banged the phone down and ran into the living room; she picked wee Stuart up and threw him in the air shouting with glee, 'Daddy will be here soon in his car, whheeee!' Wee Stuart had an infectious giggle that set everyone off. 'Thank goodness this nightmare is over,' said Margie. 'When are you driving back then?' she asked Linda. 'Monday, James has to get back to work as soon as possible; we can't afford to lose money now that we have an extra loan to pay for the car repairs now!' Margie's stomach churned she was worried sick about the cost of living and high rent Linda and James had to face to live in Surrey, never mind the existing loan for the car and this new loan for the car repairs, she worried that they had taken on too much. James was self employed and what Linda hadn't told her mum was that he had to stay fit and work seven days a week to pay the bills, he didn't get paid for sickness and holidays, even one day off left them short. Even though they were just managing to make ends meet and there wasn't any money left over at the end of the day to save, Linda assured her mum that they were coping ok. James got paid on Thursday nights which was a worry in the beginning because the rent was due every second Thursday and they couldn't get it into the bank until Friday but the bank manager in their local Nat West Bank seemed to like James and Linda, he realized that they were a struggling but ambitious young couple and saved the day by making sure the rent was paid directly to Noreen, their landlady every second Thursday even though Linda didn't pay the balance of the money due, into their account until the following day.

Just after 11am James arrived on the doorstep. 'You must be shattered, come in and sit down; do you want to put your feet up? What would you like me to make you to eat?' fussed Margie. James was excited and happy about being mobile again. 'I'm fine, how do you all fancy a wee run out to Loch Lomond?' 'Are you sure you feel up to it James, you haven't had a good night's sleep' said Linda. 'Will you all stop fussing, I'm ok!' laughed James. 'James knows whether he's fine or not, leave him alone you women. He's waiting for an answer, do want to go fur a wee run or not?' Douglas chimed in. 'Well if you're sure you don't mind' said Margie. 'Yes, that would be lovely, I'll get the kids ready and make up a couple of bottles for Amanda' answered Linda. 'It'll do the new engine good and help to run the car in, I can't go over 50mph for the first 500 miles!' said James.

Within half an hour they were in Drymen, then they drove five minutes further down the road to Balmaha, where they stopped at the wee pier to admire the wonderful views over the Loch. After that they went onto Rowardennan and parked up to see the loch and the mountains in their splendor, from a different viewpoint. 'This is breath-taking, isn't it?' said Margie with a satisfying smile, we are so lucky to have all this so near to Glasgow.

Sunday morning, Linda, James and the children went up to see Molly, James' mum. 'Right mother, grab your coat, it's a lovely day, we're going for a wee run in the car' James announced as she opened the door to them. She did as she was told; it wasn't every day she got the chance to go in a car. Linda settled Stuart in the back; Molly had already helped herself to the front passenger seat so Linda climbed in the back with Amanda on her lap.

This time they headed out to Luss on the other side of Loch Lomond, they walked out onto the wee pier, the loch was calm but it was freezing cold. 'All this fresh air is making me hungry, how do you fancy we go to Helensburgh for a fish supper?' said James to Linda and his mother. 'Oh that's a great idea, I could do with that' said Linda. Twenty minutes later they were parking on the seafront in Helensburgh. They went into the wee fish and chip restaurant facing the beach and tucked into fresh Scottish haddock and chips along with tea, bread and butter. 'What have you got planned this week?' James asked his mother as they relaxed after their meal. 'Nothing much, I just while away my time looking round the shops, I'll probably call in to see Maria, but I have to go in the morning because Pete gets home from work just after lunchtime every day and he makes it quite clear that I'm not wanted in his house. He's a lazy bugger, he gets paid for a days work but he's never worked a whole day in his life!' answered Molly. 'If you've got nothing special planned, why don't you come back with us for a wee holiday? We're driving home tomorrow,' suggested Linda. 'That's a good idea, why don't you do that mother?' said James. 'Oh I don't know, you'll be leaving early and I haven't got anything ready!'

'How long will it take you?' asked James as he tutted in mock sarcasm. 'Oh go on what's stopping you?' encouraged Linda. 'Nothing, that's it's settled; we'll go home after this to give you a chance to pack a case and sort out anything you need to see to.' Replied James who made it quite clear that he wasn't taking 'no' for an answer.

Monday morning, James and Linda were up at 6am to get the children ready and prepare for their long journey home. Just after 7am James drove up to collect his mother. By 7.30am Linda and the children were washed, dressed and were just finishing off their breakfast that Douglas had made for them. Margie had made them a mound of sandwiches and packed them into a plastic bag along with two flasks of tea, bananas, tangerines, apples and home made fruit cake. She folded and packed the last of the children's clothes that she had washed and put them into the carrycot.

By 8am, everything was in the car. Margie and Douglas hugged their daughter tightly and cuddled their grandchildren warmly. They were very worried about them driving home after what happened the last time that they were driving up to Scotland on New Years Eve. Stuart hung onto his gran and grandpa; the wee boy had become very attached to them and was upset at leaving. 'C'mon Stuart, it's time to go,' said Linda as she gently took him away from his loving grandparents and put him in the car. 'Now take your time, there's no rush, just get home safely and call us the minute you get back, no matter how late it is, now do you hear!' said Douglas. 'We will, and don't worry we'll be ok!' Linda assured her parents. As the car pulled away, Linda felt overcome with emotion, her eyes welled up as she waved and looked back at her dad cuddling and comforting her mum who was wiping away a tear.

James took it easy; this was going to be long journey because he wasn't allowed to do more than 50mph with the new engine. By the time they were approaching Birmingham, they had already stopped three times to eat their sandwiches and use the toilets. It was 7.35pm and dark. Molly suddenly shouted 'James!' she had turned to look at him and noticed that his eyes were blinking with tiredness. He was fighting to keep his eyes open. 'Right that's it, call in at the next services on the motorway, you will have to rest, you can't drive on like this, we have another 100 miles to go yet!' said Linda. 'I have to get back tonight, we can't afford for me to have another day off work.' answered James. 'Your life, our kids lives and the lives of your mum and I come before work, we'll manage somehow!' Linda told her husband in determination but he wasn't listening he insisted on pushing on. Linda sat on edge in the back seat, talking and singing to her husband to keep him awake. Just after midnight they pulled up at the foot of the stairs leading to their flat at back of the shops in New Haw. Linda carried the baby upstairs; she had put the children's pyjamas on them during the journey. Stuart was sound asleep, James carried him upstairs and put him straight into his cot, then he went back down for the carrycot and his mother's wee case. 'I'll nip into the call box and let your mum and dad know we're home safely, while you settle the kids Linda,' said James. 'Ok' Linda replied. 'How do you like our flat Molly?' asked Linda. 'Aye, it's no' bad,' answered Molly who was never one for showing her enthusiasm. 'I'll show you around the flat and the area properly tomorrow' said Linda as she led Molly through to the wee bedroom. 'I don't believe it, she's done it again, this is getting ridiculous!' said Linda angrily. 'What?' enquired Molly. 'Nosey Noreen has been in and changed the bedroom curtains while we've been away, that's not on, it's not right. Just a minute!' said Linda as she disappeared out of the bedroom door. She was back a few seconds later and said to Molly, 'The cheeky bitch has not only changed the curtains in our room but she has also put a different quilt on our bed, she doesn't seem to get it that she's encroaching on our privacy, we pay her rent for this place, she has no right to walk in here when we're not at home'. Molly shook her head in agreement then said, 'That's terrible, you'll have to tell her you're not happy about it.' Linda was really annoyed as she emphasized to Molly, 'we're really going to have to sort this out, it can't go on like this!' then she calmed down as she said 'Anyway, this is your bedroom, the bathroom is just out in the hall to your left. Do you want a cup of tea before you go to bed? I'm putting the kettle on, I have to make up Amanda's bottle, she's due a feed.' 'Aye that would be nice!' answered Molly. James came back just as the kettle was boiling, 'Looks like I've come in just at the right moment' he said to Linda. He seemed to have taken a second lease of life. 'I'll pour the tea, you see to the baby,' he told Linda. Linda told James about what Nosey Noreen had done and they agreed that they would have to pluck up the courage and have a word with her. They all finally got to bed just after 1am and James was back up and had gone to work by 7.30am. He was excited and happy that he was independent and driving again and didn't have to wait for a bus.

It was a lovely day and Linda took Molly out for a walk down to West Byfleet with the children, she never knew whether Molly was enjoying herself or not because she had a serious 'Victorian' attitude and it wasn't always easy to communicate with her, although Molly was quick to complain and speak her mind if something displeased. Linda tended to treat her with kid gloves, as that was the easy option. She assumed that as nothing was being said, she was happy but Linda found her draining and hard work at times though. No matter how many times Linda told Molly to make herself at home and help herself, she never did. She waited for Linda to make her breakfast, lunch, dinner and even a cup of tea, she never offered to help or even wash a dish. Linda was very tired, it was hard enough looking after two babies under the age of two along with all the housework, shopping, cooking and cleaning never mind looking after her mother-in-law too. She couldn't help but compare the difference when her parents visited. Her mum busied herself helping out with the washing and the dishes while her dad did the polishing and vacuuming. They gave a hand with the cooking too, Linda didn't expect all this from them but they appreciated how tired Linda was and made it their business to help their daughter.

The miners strikes were beginning to affect the people of Britain, they were in dispute over their pay but it was escalating and striking miners were not only picketing their own pits but some, known as 'Flying Pickets; were travelling to other areas to heckle and shout 'scab' at anyone who chose to carry on working for the coal industry. This brought the country to its knees as power was rationed to only a few hours per day. The population of Britain got used to using candles and wrapping up with extra clothes and blankets to keep warm in the freezing January winter.

James came home from work that evening, Linda was in the kitchen preparing the evening meal, he cuddled her tightly and gave her a big smacker of a kiss on the lips, he gave baby Amanda a kiss as she lay in her carry cot under the window, he picked up his wee son and threw him in the air blowing raspberries into the giggling wee boy's belly then pretended to his mother that he was going to pick her up and do the same to her. Molly laughed and shouted 'Stop it James, behave yourself!' Linda couldn't help but notice the difference in Molly when she laughed, she was like a different person, if only she would smile more often but she seemed to hold a deep down grudge against life, somewhere within. Linda perceived that somewhere at some point in Molly's life, something had happened that made her bitter but although she never spoke about it, she allowed it to cloud her very existence in life almost to the point that she became anti-social. Linda was always a firm believer in talking problems over, clearing the air and getting it out of your system but she wouldn't dare even approach Molly with this suggestion because she knew that she would be more or less told that it was none of her business so she left things as they were and just hoped that one day Molly would open up to the world and realize that it wasn't such a bad place after all.

'You're in a good mood, have you had a good day?' Linda asked James as he came back into the kitchen. 'Yes' as a matter of fact I have! I am enjoying this job, the money's great and I have just been thinking to myself today that if I carry on earning like this it won't be long until we'll be able to buy our own house and get away from Nosey Noreen!' answered James. 'Linda's eyes lit up and her mouth fell open in disbelief as she stopped what she was doing, 'You mean, own our own house?' her voice squeaked with delight. 'Yes, I definitely see that as a possibility, most of the blokes that I work with own their own places, they were telling me that council houses are not that available, so I can't see any reason why we won't be able to do that too!' Linda was on cloud nine at the thought of them owning their own home, never in her wildest dreams did she think that this would ever be possible for them!

On Sunday morning at just after half past ten, Linda had just finished feeding and changing baby Amanda when there was a knock on the door. 'Who on earth can that be? At this time on a Sunday morning?' she asked James, who replied as he made his way to the door 'I haven't a clue, but one thing's for sure it's not Nosey Noreen because she wouldn't bother to knock, she'd use her key and let herself in!' James was surprised to see his workmate Eddie and his wife Karen standing there. 'Oh hello, this is a surprise, to what do we owe this visit?' James said cheerfully then he changed his tone 'I hope there's nothing wrong, is there?' he enquired. 'No, No,' answered Eddie laughing, 'Karen has something to tell you that you might be interested in, but first of all I better introduce you all, Linda,

James this is my wife Karen, Karen this is Linda, James and these two little uns are Stuart and Amanda,' They all shook hands, Karen looked admiringly at the children and said in a soft voice to wee Stuart 'Hello, are you helping mummy with your baby sister?' Just at that point Molly came into the living room, 'Oh Eddie, Karen this is my mother, and mother, this is my pal from work, Eddie and his wife' said James introducing them.

'What is it that you've come to tell us then Karen?' asked James. 'Well, I don't know if Eddie told you or not that I work as a secretary for an estate agent but I thought you might be interested in a property that is going in Kingston upon Thames.' 'Oh we're not quite ready to buy yet, we need to save for a deposit!' replied James.' 'Yes, this is why I thought that this one might suit you. The man that owns the house has quite a few properties, our company acts as his agent and we collect the rents for him. He has a bric-a-brac and antique business next door to this house; he clears out houses and has a fleet of vans. He uses this particular house for storage. I had a word with him and told him that it seems such a waste; he could be getting rent for it! He told me that, he would probably be retiring and selling it within the next couple of years, so I thought that if you rented it then, not only would it give you time to save up a deposit but there would be a good chance that you could get the first refusal of buying it and if so, you would probably get a good deal as a sitting tenant. Linda and James listened intently, with excited glints in their eyes. 'Do you really think that he'd be willing to rent to us though? We had terrible trouble in the past getting a place to rent with two kids!' Linda asked Karen with a pessimistic voice. 'Yes, well, this is where the catch is! I won't lie to you both, the house is in a terrible state, bear in mind that it has been used for storage and hasn't been lived in for at least seven years! I'm sure with James' skills, it wouldn't be a problem. I feel quite positive that if you were interested, I could talk him round, especially if he knew that he wouldn't have the problem of bringing the house up to standard or decorating it himself!' replied Karen 'What do you think Linda? I think it's worth a viewing' said James. 'Definitely, it's a step in the right direction' beamed Linda. 'Right I'll start the ball rolling tomorrow and I'll let you know the outcome as soon as possible' answered Karen.

James and Linda were so excited; they didn't like to build their hopes up too much because they knew how easy it was for dreams to be shattered.

Tuesday evening James came home from work, he parked his car, ran up the outside stairs three at a time, threw the front door open. 'The guy has agreed!' he blurted out to Linda, who was in the kitchen. Linda flung her arms around his neck, 'our luck's changing at last!' she exclaimed in excitement then she continued, 'When can we go and see it? 'Saturday morning, Eddie's written the directions down, we have to go to their place first and they'll take us to meet the old man and view the property!'

After baby Amanda's 10am feed on Saturday morning, Linda got the kids ready and sat them in the back of the car. Molly, of course, had already claimed the front seat beside her son!' 'Mother I think it's better if Linda's in the front beside me because she'll have to navigate and find Eddie and Karen's place. Molly looked at her son in disbelief, pursed her lips tightly then got out and went into the back. Linda threw her eyes in the air with a quiet smile then got into the front of the car beside her husband. 'Ok, Linda here is the piece of paper that Eddie has written directions on, I know my way to Kingston because I've been working there but it's a big place, when we get over Kingston Bridge, you'll have to guide me to Eddie and Karen's house.'

It was a nice dry, sunny but chilly January morning. They drove through Weybridge, into Walton then towards Hampton Court. 'Look Molly, that's Hampton Court where Henry VIII lived, we must go there one day!' said Linda, 'Molly peered across and answered with a very disinterested 'Aye'. 'Are you studying these directions Linda because we're nearly at Kingston Bridge?' James asked her. Linda looked at the piece of paper in her hand and answered, 'right according to this, as we go over Kingston Bridge, we will see two tall chimneys to the left!' They crossed the bridge and Linda said 'Look James at all these shops, it's like Sauchiehall Street, I wonder if the house is walking distance from here!' Never mind the shops, tell me where I'm supposed to be going' answered James. 'Ok, there's the chimneys, turn left here and look out for a wee railway bridge on the left. There it is James, bear to the left and go under the railway bridge. That should take us out at Lower Ham Road!' Linda peered to look for the street name, 'Yes, we're on the right track, this is Lower Ham Road,' she said with delight as she read the street sign. 'Ok now we drive past the chimneys and bear right into Lower Kings Road.' she continued. 'There's traffic lights up here Linda, do we turn or go straight on?' James asked her. 'No, we go straight over them into Kings Road then drive all the way up. On the left we should pass a parade of shops then a wee castle-like entrance, Eddie's written that it's the old army barracks! There it is! Now be ready to turn left, we come to a catholic church called St.Agatha's, that's it, that's it!' Linda repeated in excitement, 'now turn left here then right into Wyndham Road.' James followed Linda's instructions. At the top of Wyndham Road, they turned left into Park road then immediate right into Bertram Road which is a T junction. 'There should be a road going across the top called Upper Park Road that's where Eddie and Karen live, their house has black garage doors and is left of the house facing us at the top of Bertram Road.' said Linda. James drove the car slowly up Bertram Road, 'Gosh they're big houses around here aren't they?' gasped Linda, then she went on, 'I can see the house with the black garage doors, look James to the left of the house facing us, just like Eddie said, Oh my God, look at the size of it, you didn't tell me that Eddie and Karen were rich!' 'I've never been here before, I never knew where he lived or that they owned a house this size!' answered James in disbelief.

They all piled out the car; Eddie welcomed them at the gate and led them into the house. 'You're a right dark horse, I never knew I had a rich pal!' exclaimed James. Eddie laughed and said, 'I'm anything but rich!' as he led them into the kitchen where Karen was taking the kettle off the boil. 'Right, would you prefer tea or coffee? I thought you might like a cuppa before we head on down to see your new house,' she chuckled.

As they sat round the big wooden farmhouse style kitchen table, Karen told them that she and Eddie had originally been lodgers in the house. They rented the upstairs big room from an old lady, the old lady died and the family offered the house to them as sitting tenants at the discounted price of £2800. '£2800!' exclaimed Linda then she went on, 'but this is a mansion, you'll pay £4000-£5000 for a wee three bedroom terrace house!' 'Yes but this was five years ago, the house was valued at about £4000 then but it's worth £7500 now, we really can't afford to live here, we have a young couple living upstairs they have the big front room that we used to have and Eddie has converted the small back bedroom into a kitchen for them but we share the bathroom.' 'How many rooms do you have then?' asked Linda. 'Well downstairs, we have the front sitting room, kitchen and dining room in the middle, lounge at the back with a conservatory off of it, then upstairs we have four bedrooms, another kitchen and a bathroom. Eddie and I have the back bedroom, our sons have a room each, c'mon I'll show you round!' Linda followed Karen upstairs in the big house, she was in awe, as she admired the big bedrooms with their high ceilings, ornate cornice and ceiling rose around the main lights. The front sitting room downstairs was very grand with a massive big bay window; they then went through to the back lounge, which was equally as big and on into the conservatory. 'Eddie built the conservatory, we have a wee toilet off it, it was originally outside but Eddie redesigned it and put the door off the conservatory, it's really handy for the kids when they're playing in the garden and it also saves us running up and downstairs all the time!' said Karen. 'Oh my goodness Karen, look at the size of your garden, it's gorgeous, I love all these big mature trees and the lawn in the middle, it must be fabulous in the summer, so secluded! You've got a beautiful house Karen, you're very lucky,' Linda told her. 'Yes I agree, it is and I know that I am lucky, we fell on our feet and I keep pinching myself to belief it! I would really like to get rid of the lodgers though and have some privacy but we can't afford to!' Karen confessed.

Just under an hour later they were getting into their car to view their potential new house.

'Right, follow us, it's only five minutes drive from here and we'll take you in to meet Mr. Halliday, the owner.' said Eddie. Linda was so excited; she could hardly wait as they drove down the road. 'We're going back towards the town, oh I hope this house is walking distance to the shops' she said as she turned to wee Stuart, clapped her hands and said, 'we're going to see our new house, are you excited?' Wee Stuart knew that something good was happening; he clapped his hands too and giggled!

They passed a fish and chip shop on a corner, Linda smiled and said, 'Oh I wonder if this is near the house, we can't get away from fish and chip shops!' Then they passed a pub called The Wych Elm. 'That's perfect, a fish and chip shop and a pub, just like we have in New Haw! The house has got to be around here somewhere!' laughed James.

Eddie and Karen pulled up outside a Victorian detached house and James parked up behind them. 'Surely this can't be it?' Linda said, her eyes opened wide in amazement. 'I don't know, let's get out and see,' answered James. Eddie and Karen walked towards them as they got the children out of the back seat of the car. 'Well, what do you think?' asked Karen. Linda could hardly contain herself as she answered 'You mean this IS it! I mean the house that you were talking about?' Karen laughed as she nodded her head and answered a definite 'y-e-e-s-s-!' 'Oh there's a wee garden at the front, it won't take long to tidy that up!' Linda said positively. 'Just hold your horses, you haven't seen inside yet, you might change your mind!' answered Karen. 'Oh by the way, the rent will be £52 per calendar month,' Karen told them. 'What! That's brilliant, we're paying £30 every two weeks to Nosey Noreen!' replied Linda. 'Yes but you have to pay your own rates and water rates, so it'll probably work out about the same! Oh and Mr. Halliday says that he's not looking for any deposit because you'll have enough to spend if you decide to move in here!' said Karen. 'Oh that's good news because we have £30 deposit to collect from Nosey Noreen when we leave so that'll come in handy!'

Molly decided to stay in the car while the rest made their way inside the bric-a-brac shop next door to the house. 'Hello Mr. Halliday' said Karen as she shook the old man's hand, then she went on, 'this is the young couple I was telling you about, James and Linda'. 'You're interested in renting my house are you?' smiled the old man as he shook their hands. 'Well, yes we are, we would like to have a look around if that's ok Mr. Halliday.' replied James. 'No problem, just follow me,' answered the old man as he went to a cupboard in the wall and took out a big bunch of keys.

'We'll leave you to it now, you have a look around and a good think over the weekend and James can let Eddie know on Monday whether or not you would like to rent the house or not,' said Karen to Linda and James. 'Ok' answered Linda then they both thanked Karen and Eddie for all their help.

They walked up the garden path to the front door, Mr. Halliday put the key into the lock then he turned to James and he said, 'Now before we go in, I have to warn you that this house is not habitable as it stands, it hasn't been lived in for seven years, I've used it for storage but Karen tells me that you are capable of turning it into a comfortable home for your wife and children!' 'Well, yes!' answered James nervously, wondering what on earth was going to meet his eyes when the door was opened!

Intrepidly, James and Linda followed Mr. Halliday in through the front door. It was a tiny hallway, with the front room to the left, the back room to the right and a steep staircase right in front of them.

The place smelled musty and damp, Mr. Halliday led them into the front room, there were big tyres from removal lorries, bits of old beds, odd chairs, chest of drawers with no drawers, and numerous ornaments and old newspapers were littered around the room. James looked at Linda worriedly to see her reaction, she looked concerned. They then went through to the back room; it was in the same condition. 'Well at least the wallpaper is intact, we could give the place a coat of paint to clean and freshen it up until we get around to decorating it properly!' said Linda optimistically. Off the back room was a long kitchen with nothing in it but a stainless steel sink under the window. James looked around and gave an exasperated gasp, 'There's a lot needing to be done in here, a new kitchen for starters!' Mr. Halliday said, 'Don't worry, I've got an nice electric cooker I removed from somebody's house in the week, I'll get my boys to bring it in, the kitchen's already got an electric cooker socket, so there should be no problems there!' 'We've already got a fridge and twin tub washing machine that we brought from Scotland. All we need is a worktop and cupboards!' exclaimed Linda. 'I'll bung in a kitchen cabinet for you' said Mr. Halliday. At the end of the kitchen was a bathroom that had been built on as an extension. Now this was ok because it was fairly new, although it was still to be decorated. It was a big bathroom with a brand new suite and another door off it into the toilet. The bath was filthy; it looked like it had been used for storage too! They went back through to the hallway, then up the narrow, steep staircase. The front bedroom was up one step to the left. It was a nice big room with two windows but again it was musty and needed a good clean. 'I will put a double bed in this room for you,' said Mr. Halliday. 'Oh that's ok, we have our own bed' replied Linda. 'Well, by law, I have to supply you with a bed, table and chairs,' answered Mr. Halliday. 'Why is that?' asked Linda. 'Oh it's something to do with protecting my rights, the estate agent has advised me that to rent this place out furnished that's what I have to supply you with!' said Mr. Halliday as he shrugged his shoulders as if to say *'I'm just doing what I've been told'*. They made their way into the middle bedroom that overlooked Mr. Halliday's yard and all his lorries. 'This is a good sized room, we can put your bed in here, if you don't mind Mr. Halliday, it's a good spare room for our parents and friends when they visit' said Linda. 'Oh alright then, that solves the problem' answered Mr. Halliday. They came out the room and made their way along a narrow long corridor to the small room at the back. 'Oh this would be perfect for Stuart! Do you like this room Stuart? ' Linda asked her toddler son enthusiastically. Stuart made his way to the window and peered out of the window. He excitedly pointed to the lorries down below and was doing his best to tell his parents what he could see. 'You like it here, don't you?' said Linda to the happy, smiling wee toddler. James stood with Amanda in his arms but he wasn't saying much.

They made their way to the front door and shook Mr. Halliday's hand again, thanking him for showing them around and said that they would get back to Karen and let him know by the beginning of the week. 'Well, I'm only renting it out to you because I don't have to do anything to it, otherwise I will keep it for storage until I retire in a couple of years time then I'll sell it,' smiled Mr. Halliday.

They got out to the car and Linda said, 'Tell you what, let's walk into the town to see how far it is from here!' They looked in the car and Molly was fast asleep. 'Mother, we're back, do you feel up to a wee walk?' James asked her as he got the pushchair out of the boot. 'Oh aye, alright, what was the house like, are you going to move here?' Molly asked. 'It's nice, needs a lot of work though! We'll have to have a good think about it!' replied James.

Linda put Stuart in the pushchair and James carried Amanda.

There was a church hall opposite the house and a big old fashioned school, next to that was a swing park and recreation ground. 'Oh look Stuart, do you want to go in for a wee swing?' Linda asked. Wee Stuart's eyes lit up as they made their way into the swing park. Molly made her way to the park bench to have a seat, 'Well, what do you think James?' Linda asked as she pushed wee Stuart on a swing. 'I don't know, to be honest, it needs an awful lot of work doing to it and it's definitely not ready to move in to!' 'Yes but it's a lovely old solid Victorian detached cottage, we can get it cleaned up and habitable first then we can concentrate on decorating it to our taste!' Just think of it, I can go out the front door with the pram without having the palaver of having to carry everything up and down all these stairs! Don't get me wrong, I love where we live but I don't drive and I feel so shut off once you've gone to work, I don't have any family to talk to. I walk with the kids around the shops or up to the fields at the back of New Haw one day, then another day I walk to West Byfleet or I jump on a bus to Addlestone or Chertsey and that's about it. Karen says that Kingston has Marks & Spencers, C&A, Littlewoods, British Home Stores, a big

Sainsbury's as well as a great big store called Bentalls and they're all walking distance!' answered Linda. 'You have made friends in New Haw' said James. 'Yes only a few young mothers who live above the shops like ourselves but I can't put my life on hold for that, friends come and go, I'll soon make new ones besides, there is a spare bedroom for my mum and dad or your mum at this house, we wouldn't have to give up our bedroom every time they or anyone else visits us,' replied Linda. James was biting his bottom lip, then he said, 'it's not a problem for me Linda, I know I can make that place into a palace, I'm just worried about the mess that you and the kids will have to live with while all the work's being done!' 'Well I'm willing to give it a try, I'm under no illusions that it won't be difficult but I'm sure all the hard work will be worth it, especially if we get the chance to buy the place in two or three years time.' answered Linda. 'Are you sure that you will be able to put up with all the inconvenience and cope with the two kids during the renovation while I'm out at work because I will only be able to work evenings and weekends?' asked James. 'I'm positive, as long as we're together as a family,' said Linda as she gave James a kiss and cuddled into him' then she continued laughing, 'Anything to get our privacy and as far away from Nosey Noreen as possible!'

'Looks like you've made your mind up then, doesn't it?' smiled James as he hugged her. 'Yes! What's another challenge, we've come through so many already!' replied Linda.

They went to the end of the street, there was another pub on the corner called 'The Canbury Arms', 'You've twisted my arm, it can't be bad, a pub at each end of the street!' laughed James. They got down to the end of Canbury Park Road and on the corner was another pub, 'The South Western', on the other corner was a cinema and across the road from that a further pub called The Three Fishes. They went under the railway bridge by the station. 'Look at the amenities here, this is a mainline station to London! I can see another cinema over there by the bus station, C&A is next door to it and all this five minutes walk away from the house!' beamed Linda. They crossed over by the station, there was a big hotel on the corner, then they went down Fife Road towards Bentalls store and had a walk around it, it was wonderful, this store sold everything that you could imagine, it reminded Linda of Lewis' in Argyle Street, Glasgow. After that they saw Littlewoods and Marks and Spencers. 'I've got to feed and change Amanda now, can we go somewhere for a cuppa?'

Linda asked James, They walked through Clarence Street, the pavements were very narrow as the traffic whizzed by. They passed C&A and found a Wimpy Bar in London Road where they were able to get a burger and a coffee before making their way back to their car.

Monday morning and James went into work and told Eddie that they were going for it! 'I think you're doing the right thing, you'll soon have it knocked into shape' Eddie told James. James asked Eddie to find out if they could move in, in two weeks time, they had to give Nosey Noreen a minimum of two weeks notice, they intended to tell her when they paid their rent that week, they wanted to avoid paying another rent to her after that.

Tuesday 25th January, Molly was going home to Glasgow the following Tuesday1st February, so James and Linda took advantage of her being there to baby-sit and once they got the kids to bed they drove over to their new home in Kingston for a couple of hours every evening to clean and paint it. 'We better take some candles with us and leave them there incase we get a power cut at any time, these miners chose the right time to go on strike didn't they? Right in the middle of January!' said Linda.

On Thursday, when James got home from work, he and Linda went down to Nosey Noreen's shop. 'Oh hello you two, what are you after?' Noreen asked them. 'Er, can we have a word in private please?' James said to her. Noreen looked puzzled and frowned, 'Yes, yes certainly, come through the back,' she answered as she led them through to the back shop.

'Well what is it that you have to say?' asked Noreen cocking her head to the side. 'Well!' James started cautiously, 'We're moving to Kingston,' 'Kingston, when?' Noreen asked him. 'Two weeks on Friday' answered James. 'What? Two weeks time?' replied Noreen in disbelief. Then Linda continued, 'Well yes, we have the chance of a house and it's near all the amenities which will be so much better for the children, we can't let this chance go because we'll have the chance to buy the house eventually too!' Linda blurted out. 'Well, if that's what you want!' said Noreen coldly, she was obviously not very happy!

That evening they went over to Kingston to the house. They worked very hard but Linda had to get back to feed and change Amanda and there was only so much they could do in two hours. They chose a mustard colour for the front room and on Friday night they went over as usual. They just got the tin of paint opened when they were plunged into darkness, 'Oh no, what are we to do now! We've come all this way for nothing and we're running out of time, we have to get this place habitable before we move in next Saturday' groaned Linda. 'We'll just have to paint by candlelight!' said James quite confidently. They lit candles and put them along the window sill and on the mantelpiece and got to work. By 10pm they were pleased with their efforts, they had managed to paint all four walls, albeit that one wall was where the bay window was so there wasn't much to cover there and another wall was mostly taken up by the fireplace. As they packed up there bits and pieces, James held a candle close to one of the walls to admire their work. 'It's looks good Linda, a nice choice of colour!' he said. 'Yes, I saw it in a magazine, apparently it's the 'in' colour at the moment!' she replied. 'Right have you got everything?' James asked her. 'Yes, I'm ready to go, we better get back before Amanda wakes up for her feed!' James led Linda to the front door by candlelight then he blew the candle out. At that very second the lights came back on. James held his arms out and said 'Well thank you very much! You come on now that we're going home!' 'Sod's law' said Linda giggling as she made her way to the car.

Saturday morning and James said, 'C'mon mother, we'll take you over to Kingston to see all the hard work that Linda and I have been putting in. As they pulled up outside the house, Mr. Halliday was out at the front of his shop and gave them a wave. 'You come over to get more work done?' He said as he saw James taking in tins of paint. 'Yes, we've been busy painting all week, we won't get it all done but at least we will freshen up some of the place! Oh by the way Mr. Halliday, would it be possible for you to clear the place of all the bits and pieces lying around because we would like to start bringing bits and pieces of our own over gradually before we move in, in two weeks time' said James. 'No problem, I'll get the lads in there during the week! answered Mr. Halliday.

Linda had gone on into the house with Molly and the children, by the time James came in he found Linda laughing her head off and Molly chuckling away too. 'What's so funny?' asked James. 'C'mere, through here and see this!' she said as she led James through to the front room. 'What is it?' he asked inquisitively. 'Look!' said Linda as she pointed to the walls...'What the......???' said James, then he too burst out laughing. They had worked so hard the night before and thought that they had done a wonderful job getting all four walls painted by candlelight but now it was daylight they could see that the walls were all smudged with light and dark patches of mustard, it looked awful but at least they could see the funny side of it. 'Never mind, I'll go over it today and smooth it all out' said James.

Molly went home on Tuesday and James decided that as he was working in Kingston, it would be best for him to stay on for another couple of hours after work and continue painting. Over the next couple of weeks, he painted the downstairs back room, the kitchen, the bathroom, the main bedroom and the back bedroom for the kids. He used white paint to freshen all the rooms up. The plan was that after they moved in they would renovate and decorate the house properly.

It was Thursday 10th February, the day before they were due to move out and they hadn't seen hide nor hair of Nosey Noreen since they told her they were moving out. James had taken two days off work to organise everything, he had borrowed a van from one of the sub-contractors at the job to move house with. That day he and Linda cleaned the flat from top to bottom. Linda got down on her hands and knees and scrubbed the floors all the way through from the two bedrooms, living room and to the front door. They washed down paintwork, doors and skirting. James had the gas cooker shining like a new pin inside and out.

Just after 5pm they heard a key in the lock, 'Oh here she comes, I hope she's brought our £30 deposit with her!' said James under his breath. Nosey Noreen walked in; her attitude was cold and dry. 'I've just come round to check everything's ok and there's no damage before you move out!' she said as she rubbed her hand down the door and scanned her eyes around the room. 'You'll find everything in order, we've been very busy today, the place is spotless! Would you like to come through and look at the cooker? James has made a lovely job of it!' said Linda. Nosey Noreen followed her through to the kitchen and she had to admit that the cooker looked as good as new, 'Gosh, he has made a good job of it, it looks better than ever!' she said.

'Well that's it then, I hope you'll be happy in Kingston!' Noreen said as she made her way to the door. 'Noreen, what about our deposit? You have to return £30 to us, that was in the agreement!' said James. 'Oh yes, I forgot! I'll pay your electricity bill when it comes in and that should be us quits! I'll let you know if you owe me anything or I'll send you the balance if it's less than £30' said Noreen as if she was trying to elude the question of the deposit. 'James and Linda looked at each other and found themselves agreeing to this arrangement. 'That money would have been really handy just now.' Said Linda after Noreen had left. 'Ah well, Nosey Noreen's already not very happy about us moving out so there's no point in causing more bad feeling, it just means that it's a bill we don't have to worry about!

Friday and the big day of the move arrived, James had already taken over the washing machine, fridge and big items during the week, so all he had to do now was another couple of runs to get the rest of their belongings over to Kingston. Linda hadn't been at the house for over a week and she looked in dismay as she walked in the door. 'I thought Mr. Halliday was going to clear this place out before we moved in!' she said to James. James came in to see Lorry tyres in the back room, infact it looked like there was more rubbish in there than there was before. 'I thought that there was only going to be a table and chairs in here!' There was furniture, chairs and boxes of knick knacks littering the room. 'I'll pop in and see Mr. Halliday now' said James. He came back ten minutes later and told Linda that Mr. Halliday thought they weren't moving in until Saturday. He had intended to get his men to clear the house that day when they got back from the jobs that they were on. 'Oh no! We can't have all this stuff here when we're trying to move in, he's had two weeks to clear out this place! It's not safe; the way this stuff is piled up, it could fall on top of Stuart!' Linda was fighting back tears but she gathered up her strength and battled on while James went back to New Haw to get more of their belongings.

Just after 4pm Mr. Halliday came to see them. He was cheery and couldn't see what the problem was. 'Don't worry girl, if we can't get anything shifted today then we'll definitely get it done tomorrow!' 'Tomorrow!!' gasped Linda; she couldn't believe what she was hearing! 'Well yes, girl, the lads aren't back yet, they have been on a big job in Reading, the traffic must be bad, they finish at 5 o'clock so it won't be practical starting here now. Linda was gutted, how could she get the place organized with all this junk about?

'I can't get over how laid-back Mr. Halliday is. I wonder if he lives like this in his own home because he can't seem to see the problem!' Linda told James. James put the cot up in the back bedroom for Stuart and Amanda slept in her carrycot. That evening Linda went in to the kitchen to wash and clean the kitchen cabinet that Mr. Halliday had left for them. 'God this cabinet is ancient, it looks like utility furniture from the war!' mumbled Linda to herself as she looked around the bleak excuse for a kitchen. All that was in there was a kitchen sink, their washing machine, their fridge and this ugly old kitchen cabinet. She opened the door to the middle compartment of the cabinet when suddenly she let out a scream. James came running through, 'What's up? What's up?' he repeated again in a panic. 'Look!' said Linda, 'I can't possibly put my dishes in there!' she said. James looked and there were maggots crawling around in side the cabinet. 'Get it out of here please; I can't stand the thought of it being in the house!' Linda said to James screwing her face up in disgust. It was right by the back door into Mr. Halliday's yard, so James opened the back door ready to move it out. 'Linda can you grab the other end to help me lift it over the threshold please?' he said. 'Oh no, do I have to?' replied Linda as she just barely touched it. James had his back to the door as he lifted it out, Linda lifted it towards him when suddenly something darted out from the back and disappeared under the fridge. Linda screamed, 'What was that?' 'What?' said James. 'Something just ran from under the cabinet and went under the fridge' she said. James pulled the fridge out and a wee mouse ran for its life into a wee hole in the skirting. 'It's a mouse!' yelled Linda. 'It looks like I have my work cut out for tomorrow. I'll have to check and replace all the skirting to keep the mice out!' said James. Things seemed to be going from bad to worse! James said to Linda, 'Look I've put the bed together in the upstairs bedroom, why don't you have a nice bath then go to bed and have a good night's sleep? It's been a long day, you'll feel different in the morning. I'll wait up to give Amanda her last feed'. Linda looked at the time it was twenty past ten and she was tired so she gladly agreed and took herself upstairs to bed to find her nightdress, dressing gown and towels, in one of the boxes. She went along to the back bedroom to check on the children first and looked around cautiously to see if there were any holes in the skirting but she couldn't see any.

She came back downstairs to the bathroom and said to James, 'I hope there's no mice in the bathroom, James looked around and said 'No, I doubt it, this has not long been built, the bath panel is secure as is the skirting, there're no holes.

Linda soaked in the bath then took herself off to bed just as Amanda was wakening up. 'Don't worry, you carry on, I'll see to

Amanda!' James told her. Linda was soon tucked up in bed and fast asleep.

She woke up just before 6am and went to see Amanda who was lying gurgling happily in her carrycot. 'Oh you're such a good wee girl!' she said as she picked her baby up and gave her a cuddle. Amanda smiled as her mummy spoke to her. Linda took her through to her bed and fed her the bottle of milk that James had made up for her before he came to bed. Linda didn't even remember James coming to bed the night before, she had been so tired! She fell back to sleep with Amanda in her arms and woke up with wee Stuart climbing in to bed with her. 'Where's daddy gone?' said Linda as she looked at the empty side of the bed where James had been lying. She heard a handsaw being used downstairs and the reality and horror of the night before came flooding back, she began to feel very depressed, she cuddled her children, got up put on her dressing gown, picked up Stuart and Amanda, one in each arm and made her way to the stairs. She looked down and saw 2 big lorry tyres lying in the small hall by the front door. She sat down on the top step, holding her children close to her and broke her heart crying. Just at that moment James walked past the bottom of the stairs. 'Linda, what's wrong, what's happened?' he asked concerned. 'Oh James what have we done? What have we brought our children to? This house is not child friendly it needs more than a coat of paint! We don't even have a place in the kitchen to keep our crockery or food or even a worktop to prepare food on! AND the place is teeming with mice! It's all my fault I talked you in to it! It's a mess, full of junk!' she sobbed. James cuddled his tearful wife and said, 'No you didn't, I wouldn't have moved here if I didn't want to! I tell you what, get the kids ready and after breakfast take them out for a long walk and explore the area. I'm almost finished replacing the skirting in the kitchen so that should sort the mice out! By the time you get back, you'll have a kitchen!' 'What do you mean?' said Linda as she wiped away her tears with the sleeve of her dressing gown. 'Never mind! Just do as I say! answered James.

Linda fed Amanda then she put her into the big pram and sat Stuart on his wee seat on the top. She put a baby bottle of milk into the pram bag for Amanda's next feed, spare nappies and some salmon paste sandwiches for Stuart and herself. She stopped off at the newsagents shop two doors down and bought some crisps and a bottle of lemonade then she walked up past the Wych Elm Pub towards Park Road, she found herself walking up Kingston Hill, past Kingston Hospital on the right, she walked all the way up and came to a pub called Robin Hood on the left. Further down on the left she saw gates into Richmond Park. She walked in and saw a sign pointing left and reading 'Kingston Gate'. She walked in this direction stopping off to sit down on a bench to feed and change Amanda. Wee Stuart loved the freedom of running around in the park, Linda sat him back on his pram seat to eat his sandwiches, crisps and drink his lemonade as they walked along. Then he got down again and ran through the grass. Just then Linda looked up and couldn't believe her eyes, before them stood a big deer with massive antlers, scared that Stuart would run over and try to touch it she grabbed him and sat him back on top of the pram, then they stood and admired it. She said, 'Look Stuart, that's a real deer!' as the wee boy looked on in wonderment. They saw more deer in clusters as they made their way towards Kingston Gate.

It was after four o'clock by the time they got to the park gate at Kingston, they had been out of the house for over seven hours! Stuart was tired and had nodded off to sleep, Linda took him out of his seat and put the seat in the basket under the pram then she laid him down in the pram at the opposite end from Amanda. Linda realised that she hadn't a clue where she was. The phone in the house wasn't connected so there was no way that she could contact James. She turned right when she got out of the park and the next road she came to was Park Road, she recognized that it was near to where Eddie and Karen lived and she knew that she had walked up Elm Road towards Park Road from the house, so she walked along until she found Elm Road, she walked down past the Wych Elm again and past the newsagents shop where she had bought the crisps and lemonade.

Linda's stomach was churning as she walked up the path towards the door of the house, she really was regretting that they had left their lovely flat in New Haw and felt like calling up Nosey Noreen to ask if they could come back again! She put her key in the door and opened it shouting. 'James are you there? It's me, I'm back!' James came to meet her, 'Gosh you've been gone a long time, I was getting worried! I thought you had run off back to Glasgow!' he laughed then he went on, 'but you've timed it nicely, I'm just finishing up, come through and let's see what you think!'

Linda was pleased to see that the lorry tyres had gone, she peered into the front room to see a nice little green cottage-style three-piece-suite and as she walked through the back room all that was in there was a neat little 'beech wood' modern display cabinet and a round table to match with four chairs sitting by the back window. 'I see the men have been in and removed all the junk, that's a relief!' she said as she walked into the kitchen then she stopped in her tracks, her mouth fell open in amazement. 'James did you do all this today?' she gasped, 'Well there's no-one else here, is there?' said James mockingly looking around for another person. 'It's amazing, it's wonderful, I can't believe that you've done all this in a day's work! You are a pure genius, so you are!' she exclaimed in delight as she examined her brand new kitchen, James had built a work-top right along the wall with the washing machine and fridge under it, he also put a large cupboard underneath with two doors. He had built wall cabinets along the wall with shelves inside too. 'It was all the wood that we brought from Glasgow from the wardrobes that I built there, I had it in the garage at New Haw, I knew that it would come in handy one day! I'll paint it all tomorrow, then you should be able to unpack your kitchen boxes on Monday,' said James who was feeling quite proud of his work!

Linda was beginning to see a future now, she had a dream custom-built kitchen and this was only the first day at this address. Perhaps her first instincts were right after all and it was a good idea to take on this run-down house. 'James Alexander, I love you so much, you are my hero!' she said as she gave her husband a big hug and a long lingering kiss. 'So we are staying then?' he joked. 'We're definitely staying!' replied Linda with a new found confidence then she announced happily, 'Things can only get better from now on!'

Six

It was 7am on a crisp Monday morning in March 1972, James had just left for work, Linda brought Amanda downstairs and put her in her pram while she went into the kitchen to get her morning bottle ready. Stuart was upstairs sleeping in the back bedroom in his wee second hand bed that Linda had bought from Mr. Halliday next door. There was no central heating in the house, Linda switched on the fan heater and closed the door in the dining room to keep the heat in. The upstairs was freezing at night; Linda had also bought two second hand convector heaters from Mr. Halliday, one for Stuart's wee back bedroom and one for their bedroom where Amanda's cot was. After tea each evening Linda went upstairs and plugged in the convector heaters to warm up the bedrooms half an hour before the children went to bed.

James acquired some parquet flooring that had been left over from a job and he laid it in the wee hallway by the front door. There was a loud clatter as three letters and a postcard, pushed through the letterbox by the postmen, landed on the wooden floor. Linda went through to the hallway and bent down to pick them up, she recognized the writing on one as her mother's, she missed her mother terribly and looked forward to reading her letters, she didn't recognize the writing on another fat envelope, there was a postcard from Auntie Betty and Uncle Duncan who were having an early holiday in Benidorm, the last one in a brown envelope was from Kingston council. Linda thought she'd get the business correspondence out of the way with first so that she could sit down and enjoy her mammy's letter. She sat down at the bottom of the stairs and opened up the one from the council and it was informing her of the cost of her rates and water rates, she threw her eyes in the air and shoved the statement back in the envelope. She smiled as she read the post card and thought how lucky her aunt and uncle were that they could afford to go as far away as Spain for a holiday. She then opened the fat envelope and another envelope stamped electricity board fell out along with a sheet of paper. Linda picked up the piece of paper, it was from Nosey Noreen, their ex landlady from their old flat in New Haw, Linda couldn't believe what she was reading, Noreen had written that she wasn't going to pay the electricity bill as promised and was forwarding it onto them because the flat had been left so dirty that she had to get professional cleaners in to clean it. Linda slowly opened up the bill, it was for £32.45p. Linda sat down and cried, Nosey Noreen had conned them, she had told them when they left the flat that instead of returning their deposit, she would keep it and settle their electricity bill with it, now she was coming out with a lot of lies, breaking her promise and going back on her word. *'How could she insult us by saying the flat was dirty? She even commented when we left what a good job we had done and how immaculate the flat was and also that the cooker was cleaner than it was when she first handed the flat over to us. What a dirty rotten trick to play, where on earth are we going to get the money from to pay this bill?'* thought Linda as she wiped away her tears.

James was furious when he got home and heard about what Noreen had done. He told Linda to take Noreen's letter to the Citizen's Advice the next day to see if they could help. Linda did this and they gave her the name of lawyer in Richmond who gave legal aid advice one evening a week.

On Wednesday evening Linda and James made their way to the lawyer's office. They told him the story and showed him Noreen's letter. The lawyer seemed sympathetic towards the young respectable couple as they sat with a child on each of their laps. He advised them to write back to Noreen telling her that they had taken legal advice and she had broken her contract by not giving them their deposit back, that she had no right to open the electricity bill because it was addressed to Mr. & Mrs. J. Alexander and finally that they were both witnesses to her verbally complimenting them on the clean state that they had left the flat. But as the same time the lawyer warned them not to hold their breath as it was her word against theirs and it would cost a lot more than £32.45p to take her to court.

'You'll just have to rely on her conscience! You should never have been so trusting as to have left the flat without your deposit in your hand, there are a lot of rogues out there!' he told the young worried couple.

When they got home, Linda tucked the children up in bed and sat down to write the letter to Noreen that the lawyer had roughly drafted out for them. The phone rang in the front room and James went through to answer it, Linda heard him saying 'Hello ma, how are you?' She pushed the dining room door shut to concentrate on the letter that she was writing. Twenty minutes later James came through to the dining room with a shocked expression on his face, 'You'll never guess what my ma's just told me Linda!' 'You look surprised, has she won the pools?' Linda joked. 'No, Iris has just had a baby boy,' James blurted out, his face screwed up as if to question that his mother had her facts right. 'WHAT! IRIS HAS HAD A BABY?' Linda repeated as she slammed down her pen in disbelief, 'But she never even said to anyone that she was pregnant, your mother was out in town with her last week, how could she not have noticed? I can't believe that, your mother must have known she was expecting!' Linda insisted. 'No she didn't, she's in a right state of shock, she can't believe that Iris hid this from her and worse still, Iris never even told anyone, not even her doctor!' said James. 'This is getting more ridiculous by the minute, you're telling me that Iris has carried a baby inside her for nine months and nobody noticed?' questioned Linda. 'Apparently so, that guy she's been staying with for the past year is the father, so I take it they are serious about their relationship. Iris is so unpredictable, you never know what she's going to come up with next,' answered James. 'Are Iris and the baby ok?' Linda asked. 'Yes luckily they're both fine,' James replied. 'What did the baby weigh and has she got a name for him?' Linda enquired. 'Oh how would I know, I still can't take all this in? I can't believe my sister could be so stupid as to do this, how many more times will she hurt my ma, it's not the baby's fault, but why did she not confide in her mother and tell her that she was expecting a baby, that's what girls usually do is it not? My ma keeps forgiving Iris and Iris just keeps on hurting her, I keep telling my ma that she'll never change and to wash her hands of her but my ma is wearing blinkers and hoping for a miracle. Iris can't even look after the son she's got; she's always palming wee Jamie off to my ma and anyone else that will have him. How the hell is she going to cope with a baby? said James with concern. 'I'd better phone my ma back to calm her down; she's in an awful state. I was a bit hard on her but I was so taken aback with the news and angry with Iris!' James told Linda. After half an hour he came through to the back room and told Linda that his mother was a bit calmer now. 'Oh by the way the baby weighed 7lb 2oz and his name is Craig,' said James. 'Right I'll buy a card and wee present and send it to your mum's house for him, I really don't want anything to do with Iris but her baby boy is the innocent one in all this, poor wee soul, what has he been born into?' said Linda worriedly.

The next morning Linda had the children ready and fed by 9am and walked up to the post office to post the letter by recorded delivery as the lawyer had suggested. Weeks past and there was no reply from Nosey Noreen, 'Ah well, what goes around, comes around, she'll get paid back for her deceit one day!' Linda told James quite confidently. Linda and James struggled to pay the electricity bill, they realized that they had been naive and were taken in by Nosey Noreen; they were growing up and learning fast not to trust anyone but each other in this new part of the world hundreds of miles from the safety of their parents.

Linda got talking to a neighbour two doors away called Melanie. Melanie was a very quiet shy young woman, her husband Danny was the opposite very cocky and full of confidence, he seemed to fancy himself, he was never at home and did the rounds of the local pubs and clubs every evening leaving Melanie at home alone with their two young daughters Jane and Jessica aged three and eighteen months. Linda asked Melanie about which local doctor was the best. Melanie recommended her doctor in London Road, so Linda made her way up there and registered the family with them. The health visitor called round to see Linda a few days later and gave her details of the local clinic in Acre Road, where she could take the children to be weighed and for their injections. She also mentioned to Linda that she could get the baby's milk at discount price from the clinic.' How are you settling in to the area Linda?' the health visitor asked. 'Oh ok, but I don't really know anyone, only my neighbour Melanie but she's very quiet, she doesn't know anyone and never goes anywhere' replied Linda. 'Oh why don't you join the mother's club at the clinic on Tuesday mornings from 10am until noon!' coaxed the health visitor. 'What's that about?' answered Linda. 'Well there's a playroom with a qualified nurse and a couple of helpers who look after the children while all the mums chat over a tea or coffee in a different room, most weeks they have different interesting speakers. Go on give it a try Linda, I'm sure you'll enjoy it!' encouraged the health visitor. 'I will give it a try!' said Linda although she felt very nervous about going along and making new friends in a strange area. She went along the following Tuesday and shyly introduced herself, Vivienne, the lady who ran the club welcomed Linda and told her to take Stuart and the baby in her pram into the playroom to meet the other children and the nurse. The nurse was a lovely caring girl with blond hair and a happy, smiling face; she was about 30 years of age. 'Hello and what's your name?' she said to Stuart warmly. Stuart stared up at her and said nothing. 'This is Stuart, I'm afraid he doesn't talk too well,' Linda told her. 'Oh not to worry, you're only next door if we need you and how old is this little one?' she asked as she admired Amanda. 'Oh this is Amanda, she's three and a half months old.' answered Linda. 'Fine, now you go and enjoy yourself, they'll be ok with us,' said the nurse cheerfully. Linda nervously did as she was told. She got on very well with one of the other young mother's; she was called Sharon and had a girl a few months older than Stuart and a boy a few months older than Amanda. Sharon showed Linda the ropes, they had a man come along from a garden centre, he talked to them about different kinds of plants and showed them how to plant a hanging basket; it was a beautiful array of red, white and blue flowers. Linda was admiring it when he told the mums to write their names on a piece of paper and put it in a box and he would raffle it off. Linda couldn't believe her luck when her name came out of the box and he announced that she was the winner, she felt a bit of a cheat, it was only her first week there but the other mum's congratulated her and Sharon smiled as she told her 'Well done, that's a nice bit of beginners luck for you! They were just settling down to a nice cup of tea and a biscuit when the nurse came through asking for Linda. 'What's the matter?' Linda panicked. 'Nothing, it's just that Stuart is trying to tell me something and I can't understand him, could you come through and translate please?' laughed the nurse. When Linda got through to the playroom, the nurse told her that he was pointing to something up high in the toy cupboard but she didn't know what he wanted. 'What is it that you want?' Linda asked Stuart. The wee boy looked exasperated as he pointed to the top of the cupboard and said. 'BOA-A-I-T'. 'This is what he wants smiled Linda as she stretched up and got a plastic blue and white boat down from the shelf. 'Oh you mean a bowt' said the nurse laughing, in her south London accent. Linda realized that this was another hurdle that her children would have to get over when learning to speak, for the folks down in this part of the world pronounced their vowels totally different to the people in Scotland.

Melanie never seemed to go anywhere so Linda took her along with Jane and Jessica to the mother's club the following week but Melanie seemed uneasy and nervous about leaving her girls in another room. The two young girls were extremely shy because they weren't used to company and clung onto their mother. In the end Melanie decided to give up and went back home after half an hour. Linda couldn't understand Melanie, she sat in the house all day, and her daughters never mixed with other children or got any exercise. It was as if she wanted to shut herself and the girls away from the outside world.

Meanwhile Linda and Sharon were becoming firm friends. Sharon told her that she had her daughter Lucy's name down on the waiting list for the Salvation Army playgroup in town. They took children from the age of two and a half to four years old and it was 50p from 9am until noon on Wednesday mornings. The following day Sharon took Linda up to town to register Stuart's name to make sure that he would get in by September. Sharon also told Linda that there was a lovely wee school round in Latchmere Road that had a great reputation but it was very difficult to get the children in because they were just outside the catchment area so it depended on how many children were on the list for their year whether they got in or not. She had managed to get them to accept her daughter's name to start when she was four and advised Linda that if she wanted to get Stuart into this school then she would have to act now but it could be too late. Linda went round and made an appointment with the school secretary to see the headmistress of the infant school on Friday, she had a good look at the school and had to agree with Sharon, it was a lovely wee country-like school with a friendly atmosphere, all on one level and not at all like the big old-fashioned church school on three floors opposite their house. When Linda turned up at the school on Friday the secretary asked her to take a seat in the corridor. After a few minutes a kindly lady in her fifties came out and shook Linda's hand, 'Hello you must be Mrs. Alexander, I'm Mrs. Bowie, the headmistress, come into my office,' she said as she beckoned Linda towards the door with Stuart and Amanda. 'So Mrs. Alexander, what makes you want to send your children to our school?' asked Mrs. Bowie. 'Well I've heard about your wonderful reputation, this is just the type of school I would wish my children to attend, I'm not really very keen on them going to a church school plus I attend the mother's club at the clinic and the little friends that Stuart has made are on the list to attend here so I would like him to come here along with them,' answered Linda in anticipation. 'Well, I have to be honest with you, you are actually outside of our catchment area, so it depends how big the in-take will be for when Stuarts due to start in September 1974. I will take his name and put it on the waiting list at the moment but if we have a sudden big influx of children living within the immediate area for that year then I'm afraid they will come first,' said Mrs. Bowie. 'Oh thank you so much,' replied Linda happily. She went straight round to Sharon's house to tell her. Sharon was delighted and said, 'Oh don't worry, if Mrs. Bowie has taken Stuart's name and put it on the waiting list then he's as good as in there!' then she turned to wee Lucy and told her, 'Hey Stuart's going to be in your class at school isn't that great?'

April 1972 and Linda's parents Douglas and Margie came down for a week to stay with Linda and James. They were very concerned when they realised how much work had to be done in the house. 'Are you really happy down here so far away from home?' Margie asked Linda. 'Well what else can we do? The job vacancies are here, there's none in Scotland, how could we possibly survive in Glasgow? Besides if nothing else we're giving our children a good step up in life by living so close to London,' replied Linda.

The weather was warm in the south east of England compared to Scottish weather for that time of year. Margie and Douglas had to admit that they loved life in Kingston upon Thames. Linda took them up to Richmond Park where she showed them Princess Alexandria and her husband Angus Ogilvy's house which was near to the Kingston gate. They saw lots of deer roaming around. Stuart had great fun kicking his football about with his grandpa while Linda fed baby Amanda. Linda could see a big difference in her dad, she never at any time remembered him spending any time or kicking a ball about with her brother when he was young, the pub was his priority in those days but age had mellowed him and he seemed to be making up for the lost time that he wasted getting paralytic drunk when she and her brother were young, he was now sober and the model grandfather. It made Linda very happy inside to see how much her wee son Stuart loved his grandpa and how her dad in return thought the world of his grandchildren. She had a heavy heart when she thought about the hard and difficult upbringing that she and her brother had due to her dad's alcoholic binges but put it to the back of her mind and was only too happy to see the change in him. She always worried about her mum being so far away and on her own with her dad when he drank too much but now she felt a lot more at ease because she could see that he was making a big effort. Margie spread out a tartan rug and laid out the picnic that she had prepared before leaving the house. 'Right! food's ready now,' Margie called out as she poured hot tea from the flask into three plastic cups. Douglas and Stuart came running over, 'Would you like some milk Stuart?' Margie asked her grandson, 'No, tea,' answered Stuart, his talking wasn't great but Margie understood what he was saying. 'Linda, Stuart wants tea, is that ok?' Margie asked her daughter. 'Yes that is fine, just make it nice and milky; more milk than tea' replied Linda as she laid Amanda back into her pram. They all tucked into a selection of cheese, ham and corned beef sandwiches followed by some cup cakes before making their way back home again.

The following day Linda took her parents down to the River Thames, it was only a fifteen minute walk from their house, and there they got on a boat for Hampton Court. It was a lovely sail; they sat on the upper deck of the boat and watched all the life on the river, from big rowing boats racing each other with lots of young men and a cox sitting at the end while a man on a bike was cycling along the river with a megaphone shouting out instructions to them. There were wee kayaks with youngsters having lessons, wonderful houseboats, one even in the shape of a house with dormer windows, lots of other pleasure boats sailed past and they waved to each other. There were beautiful houses that backed onto the river with their own moorings and streamline cruisers moored alongside. Linda dreamed about how wonderful it would be to be rich with her own a house on the river and a boat. Just over half an hour later they arrived at Hampton Court, they wandered around the magnificent grounds then went inside the palace. They walked along the cold stone-floor corridors and made their way down to the wine cellars and kitchen. It was fascinating seeing how people lived in the 16th century. Afterwards they made their way back to the lawns for a picnic then Margie saw a sign for the maze. 'Oh we can't come all this way and not visit the maze.' She said excitedly. 'Ok, I'm up for it, let's go and find it.' answered Linda. They found it near to the gate opposite Bushy Park. There was a turnstile at the entrance so Linda left Amanda's pushchair there and carried her. Douglas raced ahead with Stuart while Margie walked with Linda. They soon lost Douglas and Stuart although they could hear Douglas laughing and saying loudly, 'Do you think this might be the right turning this time Stuart? Oh no, not another dead end!' Stuart's wee infectious laughter echoed through the maze. Margie and Linda were blethering as they wandered round and weren't really paying attention, then it suddenly dawned on them that every time they turned a corner, they were seeing the same faces. 'Not you again!' Margie laughed as they kept bumping into the same people, by this time everyone was in stitches, shouting through the hedges and asking each other the way out. 'Margie is that you?' shouted Douglas. 'Aye, where are you Douglas?' she answered. 'I'm here, at the other side of this hedge, Stuart and I have found the exit, we're just going out now, you have to make your way to the middle, there's a wee bench and then you'll find your way out, it's a different way from where we came in' he shouted over. 'Oh God at this rate we'll still be in here till midnight,' said Linda. By this time they were in fits of laughter, then suddenly there it was, the bench that Douglas told them about. They were glad of it too, they sat down and had a rest, then they decided to make their way to the exit which wasn't as easy as they thought it might be for they kept ending up back at the bench. 'God Linda, what are we to do? We couldn't find the bench to begin with now we can't get away from it' giggled Margie. The two women were laughing so much that they started everyone else off. They kept bumping into this couple with two children about four and six years old. 'Right let's stop and compare notes, we've been that way, that way and that way and they're all dead ends,' said the man, as he led them in three different directions. 'Ok, we've been this way and the same other ways as you so that just leaves this way,' replied Linda. 'Let's go for it,' said the woman. Finally they heard Douglas and Stuart talking so they knew they were in the perimeter. 'Dad, is that you?' we're almost at the end but we can't find the exit,' shouted Linda. 'Douglas shouted instructions through the hedge to them and finally they were so relieved to see the exit. They all came out laughing and saying 'Never again'. The other family thanked Douglas for his help before they left. 'Oh I can't be bothered walking all the way through the grounds back to the pier for the boat, can we just get the bus, look there's a stop just outside the gate across the road?' Linda said wearily. 'That's a great idea,' answered Douglas. There were numerous buses and they all went through Kingston, within three minutes of getting to the stop they were sitting on a big red London bus, eight minutes later they were in Kingston. 'What a great day that was, we packed so much in!' said Douglas enthusiastically. 'Aye but never ask me to go into that maze again!' replied Margie.

When they got home Margie flopped down on the wee green cottage-style three piece suite in the front room. 'Oh just give me five minutes then I'll go in and prepare dinner for us all. This is so comfortable, these modern suites don't have a patch on the old fashioned ones, I'd swap this one for my big black leather contemporary suite any day,' she told Linda.

The next day Douglas, Margie, Linda, Stuart and baby Amanda caught a bus from Kingston town centre to Windsor. Margie was excited because she had never seen Windsor castle before; she had only had the description in her head that Douglas had told her when he was stationed nearby in Bedfont during the second World War.

When they arrived at Windsor, they made their way to the castle; it stood in all its glory up high in the centre of the town. They watched the changing of the guard and walked around the grounds, then they queued up to view 'Queen Mary's Doll's House'. Afterward they sat on a bench in front of the castle turrets with a magnificent view over the whole of Surrey. Margie opened up the bag to get the sandwiches out; Douglas was taking pictures while Linda got Amanda out of her push chair and sat her on her lap. Douglas told Stuart to stand still while he took his photo but the mischievous two years old ran towards the low turret and before anyone could stop him, he climbed up on it, Linda froze with fear, she knew there was a drop of at least fifty feet over the other side, she was frightened to move towards him incase he moved and fell over. Margie edged alongside him and quickly grabbed his arm, pulling him off the turret. 'Oh my God!' she said out loud as she looked over the side. 'Oh mum, thank goodness, you managed to grab his arm, I was scared stiff that if I moved towards him he would try to get away and fall over, that's really dangerous, it should be closed off to kids!' said Linda who was still in a state of shock.

Margie and Douglas said their farewells after a week and returned to Scotland. Linda got depressed, she missed her mammy so much, she consoled herself by saying to James that they would only live in the south of England for two years and any money they managed to save, they would put towards buying a house back in Scotland. James nodded but never actually committed himself to agree.

June 1972, James was working seven days a week and was kept busy every evening painting, decorating and building shelves, units and wardrobes etc, in the house. Linda and James were gradually settling into their new abode. James was earning very good money, they opened a savings account at the Building Society, every week Linda walked up to the town centre and put a few pounds into their account to go towards a deposit for the day that they would be able to buy their house.

James built pine shelf units along one wall in the dining room and a nice boxed pine unit about 20 inches high along the fireplace wall and round the corner on the next wall up to the kitchen door They bought a wee electric fan heater and sat it on top of the unit in front of the fire breast, the rest of the boxed unit served as toy boxes for Stuart and Amanda's toys, it was beginning to feel a lot more homely but Linda's depression got so bad that she began to lose interest. When James shouted good-bye then closed the door behind him to go to work every morning, Linda sobbed her heart out, she didn't know what was wrong with her, the house was taking shape, James was earning good money but there was something missing. Linda knew that she was homesick and just wanted to be nearer to her mammy.

It was a warm sunny morning just after 10am when the doorbell rang, Linda was feeling depressed, she was having problems with bleeding between periods, everything seemed to be an effort for her. When she opened the door Sharon stood there beaming and said, 'It's such a beautiful morning, I thought I would take the kids for a picnic fancy joining us?' Linda took one look at Sharon and burst into tears. 'What's the matter Linda, what's happened? Sharon asked worriedly. 'That's just it, I don't know, I have everything going for me, but I can't help feeling upset!' she told Sharon.' Are you sure there's nothing wrong?' Sharon said firmly. 'Well, I have been bleeding a lot,' answered Linda. 'Have you spoken to your doctor or told James?' Sharon asked her. 'No' replied Linda as she sobbed her heart out, Stuart was looking up at his mummy with a wee concerned frown. Linda pulled him towards her and gave him a big tight cuddle. 'Linda you have to get to the doctor and talk to him, you have to tell him about this blood you're losing. You have so much going on in your life, you've moved to a new part of the world that is alien to you, you're on your own with your children seven days a week, you're missing your mum plus you have a toddler and a four month old baby to look after and be responsible for. You're under a lot of stress, do you want me to make that appointment for you?' said Sharon very seriously. Linda knew that Sharon was right and answered 'it's ok, I know I need to see a doctor, I'm just scared about where this bleeding is coming from' as she held her hands over her face sobbing uncontrollably.' 'Linda make that appointment now, you're probably worrying about nothing.' Linda did as Sharon told her and got an appointment for that same afternoon. Linda was sitting pouring her heart out to the doctor, he was a nice caring man in his late thirties. He asked Linda questions and he listened intently to her answers. She told him about the bleeding and that she didn't know why she was depressed because her husband worked very hard and they had everything going for them. The doctor was very understanding, he examined Linda and told her that he was making an appointment for her to see a gynecologist consultant at the hospital meanwhile he said that she could come and talk to him anytime. He recognized that Linda needed a bit of TLC, she was trying to put the fact that she wasn't feeling too well to the back of her mind, the worry of this was probably initiating the depression that she was feeling, added to this was the fact that she was with the children all day, every day from morning until night and her husband was working all hours.

That evening Linda told James about her chat with the doctor, James was worried and annoyed that she had been keeping all this to herself. 'Why didn't you tell me,' he asked her. 'Because I thought it was just a symptom after having the baby and that it would go away but it's not,' answered Linda tearfully. James held her close and said, 'Don't worry; you've done the right thing seeing the doctor, I'm sure it's nothing to be concerned about.' Linda felt a sense of relief with James' strong arms around her, she was glad that Sharon had called round that morning and encouraged her to visit the doctor; everything was out in the open now.

Phone calls were cheaper after 6pm and at weekends, Linda looked forward to Saturday mornings because she got up early, got the children, fed washed and dressed then she made her weekly call to her mum where she caught up with all the news from home and told her mum how the children were progressing as well as everything else that was happening in their lives down south but she didn't mention her medical problem because she knew it would only cause her mum to worry.

July 1972, James' mum Molly came down to spend two weeks with them. Linda found it hard going when Molly came to stay. Linda was exhausted by the time James came home from work. Sometimes when Linda was too tired to cook an evening meal, James and her 'made-do' with something quick and easy like beans on toast but when Molly was there Linda felt she had to make an effort at mealtimes. The extra shopping, cooking, setting/clearing the table and washing/drying dishes were taking there toll on Linda's health, she was shattered and couldn't help compare the difference when her mum and dad stayed with them. They came not just to visit but to help, her mum Margie attended to the washing, dishes etc., while her dad, Douglas did the polishing, dusting and vacuuming. They took the kids out to give Linda a break, brought lunch and shopping in and took their turn at cooking the evening meal. Linda enjoyed going out with her mum and dad because they took over with the kids, all in all it was like a holiday for her when her mum and dad came to stay.

Towards the end of the first week tension was beginning to build so James decided that he would take a week off and they would all go away for a break, he had seen an advert in the local newsagent advertising a holiday caravan to let in Brighton. On Thursday evening he told Linda to call and see if it was available. She was dismayed when the lady owner said that it was already booked but then the lady said to Linda, 'hold on a minute dear,' Linda could hear her shouting in the background, ''ere Stan, is Ethel using her caravan next week?' Back came Stan's reply, 'No, she said that it was available if anybody asked' Linda breathed a big sigh of relief when the lady came back and confirmed that they could have Ethel's caravan and they could pay by cheque at the reception desk in the caravan site when they picked up the key.

Saturday morning came, Linda and James had been up washed and dressed since 6am, they packed Amanda's small pram into the boot of their Vauxhall 101 Estate car along with 2 large suitcases, Molly's wee case and Stuart wee three-wheeler peddle cycle. Just after 7am Linda made everyone scrambled egg on toast for breakfast then she washed and dressed the children ready for the journey. By 8am they were ready to leave, just as the postman came to the door with a letter. Linda opened the envelope and inside was an invite for herself, James, Stuart and Amanda to her cousin Anne's wedding at the end of August. 'Oh, do you think we can afford to go up to Glasgow next month James? I would hate to miss Anne's wedding, It's a great opportunity to see all the family!' said Linda. 'We'll make a point of affording it, we can drive up, that'll only cost petrol money! Don't you worry about a thing, you shall go to the ball!' mocked James. Linda was cheered up no end, a visit to Glasgow to see her mum was really something to look forward to. They then set off on the road to Brighton; they had never been there before and were excited at the prospect of their first visit to the south coast.

When they got to the caravan site, they checked in at the reception as they were instructed and handed over a cheque in return for the caravan keys. The caravan site was on a slight slope so their caravan was propped up at one side. James opened the door and Linda went in first with the children, 'Gosh this is terrific, it has everything we need, nice seating area, dining area with a table, kitchen with plenty of cupboards, a cooker and a fridge but where're the beds?' she frowned. James, pulled the seats down in the seating area at one end to reveal two beds, then he went to the other end where the dining area was situated, collapsed the table and pulled out four more beds, 'There you go, it's a six berth caravan, my ma can sleep at the other end and we can sleep at this end with the kids!' he said. 'Linda was looking concerned, 'Where's the toilet?' she asked. James laughed as he led her to the door and said, 'Do you see that wee brick building over there? That's it!' 'What! You mean we have to walk all the way over there, what if we're desperate or it's the middle of the night?' she exclaimed. 'You'll just have to make sure that you're not desperate and if you need to go in the middle of the night, you'll have to pee in the pail' James laughed. 'Yuk, this camping lark's not as glamorous as it's made out to be is it?' replied Linda.

They quickly unpacked and went down to the beach with the children, it was a lovely day and the promenade was thronging with holidaymakers and day trippers. Linda and James took Stuart down to the water's edge while Molly sat on a deckchair keeping her eye on Amanda. They rounded off their day with fish and chips. Later that evening Molly wanted to go to the toilet, 'It's dark now Ma, I'll walk you over there, I saw a torch in this drawer' said James as he pulled the drawer beside the cutlery drawer open. 'I'll go when you get back, Stuart's lucky he can use his wee potty, if I had known I would have bought an adult size gizunder' laughed Linda. James returned with Molly then he guided Linda across the field to the toilets. It became apparent why there was a torch in the caravan, it was pitch black outside! 'What's that squeaking noise?' asked Linda. James laughed as he shone the torch towards a wee caravan on the slopes; it was rocking to and fro. 'They'd better watched out, their caravan's going to fall off its perch if they don't slow down, my ma thought that kids must be jumping on their beds, so I just let her believe that' he said with a giggle.

The following Saturday they were heading home, they got as far as Reigate and were going down the hill when Linda smelt burning, 'What's that smell?' she asked, 'What smell? Oh no the brakes have gone, hold on tight I don't have any brakes' shouted James. Linda was terrified, Molly was screaming in the back, they were holding on tight to the kids. James tooted his horn in an attempt to tell other cars to get out of the way and as if by a miracle the cars in front moved just as James' Vauxhall rolled towards them, there was no-one on the pavement so he was able to guide the car onto the grass verge where it eventually came to a stop. James jumped out and looked under the car, then with a look of horror he shouted, 'Get out quick, the car's on fire!' Linda grabbed the kids and jumped out while James helped his mum out. James then went to grab the pram and suitcases from the boot, other cars stopped, a man jumped out with a fire extinguisher while his wife helped James remove their belongings from the car. This all happened in less than two minutes then they realised the fire was spreading and heading for the petrol tank 'Oh no, the extinguisher is empty; only air is coming out and it's fanning the flames' groaned James. Just then a fire engine pulled up followed swiftly by another. The firemen quickly got to work and the flames were doused in seconds. It turned out that there was a Fire Station just around the corner and someone had run round there and broke the news. James and Linda were never so happy to see a fire engine in their lives, they didn't know who it was who had the presence of mind to alert the fire brigade so they never got to thank them. The Firemen and James pushed the broken-down car round to a garage in a side street and while Linda and Molly stood on the grass verge with the kids and all their belongings just glad that they were safe but not having a clue as to how they were going to get home. James returned and said that the garage were happy to keep the car and prepare an estimate for his insurance company. A pleasant young chap in his mid twenties with dark wavy hair and dressed casually in shirt and jeans approached them and said, 'I can see the predicament that you are all in, have you far to go?' 'To Kingston, but we have so much stuff we'll need two taxis and that's not going to be cheap!' answered James. 'That's not a problem, I'll take you home, I have a Vauxhall 101 estate too, so it won't be any problem getting all your belongings in.' Linda and James couldn't believe it, not only did this very kind 'Knight of the Road' turn up out of nowhere but he had an identical car as well, no other car would have been able to take them and all there luggage plus a pram in one go. The young chap told them that he lived in Reigate and his name was Brian. He took them right to their door and helped them in with their belongings. Linda and James couldn't thank him enough, they tried to give him petrol money but he refused saying that it was a pleasure to help them. They shook his hand and told him how grateful they were to him before waving him off.

James and Linda sat down and thanked their lucky stars as they went over the days events, 'firstly the car goes on fire and there's a fire station round the corner, then there's a garage in the next street lastly someone appears from nowhere and offers us a lift home in an identical car to ours, the only car that was big enough to take all of us and our luggage, I think somebody up there likes us!' said James 'I think you're right but I also think that it's time we got rid of that car, it's been one thing after another and nothing but bad luck to us' Linda told James seriously 'Yes you're right, but it's really going to set us back because we are still paying for it and also for the last lot of repairs after breaking down on new year's morning outside of Carlisle,' answered James. 'We'll get it repaired on the insurance then we'll sell it and pay off everything we owe on it, quite honestly I'll be glad to see the back of it, we'll buy an old jalopy, all we need is something to get you to work!' exclaimed Linda then she continued, 'meanwhile how are we going to get to Anne's wedding?' 'God I forgot about that, we're supposed to be driving up to Scotland in two weeks time! Look Linda let's just hire a car for the trip, better be safe than sorry, I'm not so sure that I want to take the 101 on that journey again after what happened at New Year!' said James quite defiantly as if he wasn't taking no for an answer.

At the beginning of August, James handed Linda a crisp £10 note.

'Put this towards getting yourself and the kids something nice to wear for Anne's wedding!' he beamed. Linda's mouth fell open, 'But where did you get this from?' she asked him with a delighted grin. 'The old army major that I'm working for at the moment was so delighted with the new windows that I made for him that he gave me this for a tip!' answered James with his shoulders rising and his chest protruding proudly 'WHAT £10 TIP! Good God he must be loaded!' exclaimed Linda!' 'He is!' replied James laughing proudly.

Linda went into town and bought Stuart a brown waistcoat and long trouser set with a brown velvet bow tie, she got a lovely red velvet angel top trimmed with white lace and red baby shoes for Amanda. She then went into a dress shop in Clarence Street picked out a black silky satin suit, with a mini skirt, then she saw the most gorgeous coat that would go perfectly with her outfit, it was a black mini-coat and it had a hood trimmed with black and white fur and they had it in her trim size 10, she tried it on and she felt a million dollars but it was £11.99. When James got home from work, she showed him the outfit and said with delight, 'Everything came to just over £12, my black patent platform shoes will go perfectly with this suit.' then she continued with a sigh,' I also saw this gorgeous coat that matched my outfit perfectly but there's no way we could afford it', 'How much was it?' asked James, '£11.99' answered Linda with a groan. 'Go and put a deposit on it tomorrow, it won't hurt to take the money out of our savings,' he said. 'But James that money is for our future to go towards buying the house, we'll be taking the money out of our savings to hire a car and then there's a wedding present to buy too and what about you, you need clothes as well!' said Linda feeling guilty. 'Don't worry Linda; I'll make the money up in no time. I'm Ok! I've got my black suit that I got for our wedding, if you can take it to the cleaners, that's fine for me, it'll give me a chance to wear it again! I want my wee wife to be the 'belle of the ball,' replied James with a satisfied expression as he pulled Linda towards him in a tight hug and gave her a long lingering kiss.

The next day Linda went back up to the dress shop in town and tried the coat on again then she asked the assistant if she could put a deposit on it. 'We can hold it for you for ten days at no cost!' answered the cheery young assistant. 'Really! I'll do that then,' answered Linda with delight.

On the way home from work on the Monday before the wedding, James organized a hired car from a company in Kingston. 'I'm picking the car up after work on Thursday Linda, we've got a brand new Ford Escort, it has seat belts fitted, they come as standard in all new cars because the law is changing soon and all cars will have to have them fitted in the front seats! I arranged for them to put kiddie seats in the back for Stuart and Amanda too, that was £5 extra but worth it to know that the kids will be safely strapped in, you know what Jimmy Saville says in that new advert, *'clunk, click every trip'*. We'll turn up at the wedding like the rich relatives from London!' laughed James. 'Gosh we'll be right toffs won't we?' giggled Linda. 'We have to leave first thing Friday morning, that way we'll get to Glasgow late afternoon/early evening and have a day to settle in before the wedding and as a nice surprise for you, you won't need to take the money from the building society for your coat because I'm doing really well on my price work and I've got a good wage coming on Thursday' James told Linda. 'Oh, but when will I get a chance to collect it then, I mean if you're not getting home until Thursday teatime, the shop shuts at 6pm, it's going to be a mad rush for me,' answered Linda with a worried frown. 'You've tried the coat on and it fits doesn't it?' said James, 'Yes' nodded Linda. 'Well, what's the problem, I'll collect it on my way home from work on Thursday, problem solved!' replied James as he went into the bathroom to wash before tea!

James came home from work on Thursday and presented Linda with a large box with the coat inside, before he about turned and ran up the road to the car hire firm to collect the car for their journey to Scotland. Linda was busy preparing tea but she opened the box to have a quick peak at her classy new coat, she smiled with delight then closed the box again. James returned half a hour later, he came in the door jingling the keys to the hired car in front of Linda's eyes, ' Well does madam want to inspect her carriage for the long trip north tomorrow?' enquired James with a grin. Linda picked Amanda up from her baby swing and she followed James, who was holding Stuarts hand, out to see the car. 'Oh, red leather kiddie seats for Stuart and Amanda, they should be nice and comfortable in those for the journey' then she looked at the car 'nice colour, I love red,' said Linda as she admired the Ford Escort. 'Typical woman! More interested in the colour than the car itself,' laughed James. 'Isn't that the most important thing then?' asked Linda with a giggle. James just shook his head and smiled. As they walked back into the house Linda said to James, 'I've done all the packing, just got the last minute things to go in for the kids and my toiletries, make up etc., but they can go in a separate bag so you can close the cases and get them downstairs after tea. I may as well just leave my new coat in the box, it's all neatly wrapped in tissue and will travel better that way, it can go straight into the car boot along with the cases, Oh and I picked your suit up from the cleaners, it's in a polythene bag, we can hang it in the back'.

Linda and James were up at the crack of dawn; she had made sausage rolls and prepared sandwiches the night before. In the morning she prepared bottles of milk and took jars of Heinz baby food for Amanda, cold drinks for Stuart, James and herself. James got everything out to the car and made up a couple of flasks of tea while Linda washed and dressed her two sleepy babies. By 6.30am they were on their way. Linda always got excited at the prospect of going home to Scotland and seeing her parents. Her only regret was that her brother Douglas junior and his family weren't travelling home for the wedding because he couldn't get time off work.

The following morning they woke up early in Douglas and Margie's house. James looked after Amanda in the bedroom while Linda enjoyed an early bath before Stuart woke up. then she borrowed a dressing gown from her mum and took the children downstairs while James had a bath. Douglas was happily making breakfast and whistling merrily in the kitchen when Linda walked in. 'Mmmmmmm, something smells nice dad, what are you making?' Linda asked. 'Well we have sliced sausage, black pudding, dumpling, tattie scones, ham, eggs and tomatoes, oh and not forgetting toast!' replied Douglas as he demonstrated by waving the fish slice in the air that he was using to turn the sausages with and pointing it at the various items he was cooking as if he was a master chef. 'Gosh you've enough there to feed an army!' exclaimed Linda laughing. 'Why? Don't you want a fry-up?' asked Douglas looking disappointed then he went on, 'I thought that we should all have a good breakfast inside us before going to the wedding, it's going to be a long day you know!' 'Of course I want some, but just one of each and I'll miss out the bacon, I'll give Stuart some of mine after he has his cereal but I know for a fact that James will have double everything and really enjoy every bit of it,' said Linda as she gave her dad a reassuring cuddle. Douglas gave a satisfied grin; he loved cooking for the family when they came to stay.

The night before, Linda had taken her new coat out of the box and hung it up on the back of the bedroom door in its polythene cover to make sure that any creases came out before she wore it to the wedding. After breakfast she got the children bathed and dressed in their posh wedding clothes, Amanda looked beautiful in her red velvet dress and red shoes with white tights. Stuart looked very cute in his long brown trousers, matching waistcoat and brown velvet bow tie. Linda had bought a lucky silver horseshoe for him to present to the bride. James looked very smart in his black suit and bow tie. He took the children back downstairs to allow Linda to get dressed. Linda put her hair up in a neat French roll, applied her make-up then slipped into her black silky suit and white blouse with tiers at the neck then she pulled on her black patent platform shoes, she didn't have many clothes because any spare cash was spent on the children, it was a long time since she had a new outfit, she looked in the full length mirror and felt really good. Linda then walked over to the door and removed the polythene bag from her new black coat, she undid the buttons and tried it on over her outfit, she felt like a million dollars then she noticed something on the sleeve of the coat, she looked closer and was horrified to see a flaw and loose threads. 'Oh No, trust this to happen to me!' she groaned. She went downstairs and was greeted by wolf-whistles from James and her dad, then James said, 'What's wrong?' as he noticed the disappointment on her face. Linda showed him her coat, 'It never occurred to me to check it when I picked it up from the shop, the lady had it all in the box ready with your name on it.' said James. 'Don't worry, it's not your fault, I can't believe they never noticed that it had a flaw on it when they were wrapping it up, what am I going to do James?' said Linda, close to tears. 'Don't worry, we'll take it back to the shop when we get home, you will have to wear it to the wedding today, you don't have any other option!' answered James. Linda knew he was right, she didn't have another coat and she worried about wearing it when she knew that it would be going back to the shop the following week, she certainly didn't feel as good as she intended, it kept niggling her that they had paid all this money for a coat that was no better than a rejected second.

They all got into the posh hired car and headed for the church in Milton, Linda enjoyed the trip through Maryhill, Ruchill and up to the area where she used to live. She used to attend Sunday school in the church but was amazed to see that it no longer was a wee wooden hut, but a beautifully brick built church. Douglas carried

Amanda towards the church and Stuart walked hand in hand with Linda and Margie while James locked up the car. They stood on the steps of the church for photographs before entering. Douglas and Margie were very proud of their grandchildren, none of the relatives had seen eight months old Amanda yet and Douglas and Margie couldn't wait to show her off. 'It's such a shame that Douglas junior and Norma couldn't be here with Fiona too, that would have made our day,' said Linda's dad. They settled down in a seat near the back of the church so that they could make a quick exit should the children become restless. As they sat in the church waiting for the bride to arrive, one by one guests were turning round to see the baby so Douglas lifted Amanda up high to show her off to an echo of 'aaaawww' from admiring relatives.

When they were children Anne and Linda were as close as sisters and had made a pact that when they got married they would be bridesmaids to each other. Linda kept to her word and had Anne as her bridesmaid. The church organ started up with 'Here comes the bride', Linda was still wondering why Anne hadn't kept her side of the bargain and wondered who her bridesmaid was going to be because she had no sisters and there was no other cousins as close to her as Linda was. Linda watched as Anne walked up the aisle on her dad's arm followed by, not one, BUT four bridesmaid's, *'FOUR BRIDESMAIDS'* thought Linda to herself as she took a second take! There was their young cousin Maureen, whom Anne didn't really have much in common with, Anne's cousin on her dad's side who Linda didn't know and was quite sure that Anne hardly knew her either because Anne's parents, Auntie Dot and Uncle Tom didn't really keep up with Uncle Tom's side of the family, the young cousin of her husband-to-be AND Daphne Laidlaw, *'DAPHNE LAIDLAW'* thought Linda, practically stopping herself from shouting the name out loud, *'what the hell was she doing at her cousin's wedding never mind being a bridesmaid!'* Daphne Laidlaw hadn't even attended the same school as Anne, she had been in Linda's class at primary, she was a strange girl and the class bore. Linda wasn't even aware that Anne knew Daphne and if she did it was a certainty that she hadn't known her for long! Linda's feelings were really hurt, she couldn't understand why Anne had cousins that she wasn't even close to for her bridesmaids and had not kept her promise to Linda. Linda could never have done that to Anne, she was a girl who thought long and hard before committing herself and when she did she always kept to her word. Linda held her head high and rose above everything; she never let on how upset she was, she could just about accept the other cousins but not bliddy Daphne Laidlaw!

After the wedding ceremony, Stuart presented the bride with a lucky horseshoe as guests clapped and cheered then while the rest of the wedding photographs were being taken, James got everyone in the car and dropped Douglas, Margie and Stuart off at Partick Burgh Hall while he and Linda drove up to James' mother's house. Amanda was a baby who liked her routine; she was normally tucked up in bed by 6.30pm and wouldn't have taken too kindly to the loud music and noise at the reception. Molly had agreed to look after her granddaughter for the evening. James, Linda and Stuart were going straight to Molly's to stay after the reception. Linda got Amanda washed and ready for bed, then fed her with a jar of Heinz baby food before putting her down in her pram with a bottle, leaving Molly to watch her.

James and Linda got back to the wedding reception just in time for the start of the dinner. Linda got the message that the bride and groom would be leaving for their honeymoon at approximately 9.30pm so she rounded up a couple of her cousins. They found out that Anne and her new husband would be leaving in a white Volkswagen Beetle. They got toilet paper, string, empty beer cans, lipstick, cardboard and went out to the street where they found the car to the right of the Partick Burgh Hall, just round the corner about three car spaces down. They set about tying on the empty beer cans and the cardboard with 'Just Married' written on it to the back bumper then they wrapped the car in toilet paper and wrote slogans all over the car windows in Lipstick, 'Hard Up' and 'Bride & Groom on Honeymoon' etc., etc., etc. By the time they had finished the car looked like a huge toilet roll. They got back into the hall just in time to see the bride and groom make their way to the exit, everyone was cheering as Anne and her new husband walked outside then turned LEFT! 'They're going the wrong way' said Linda quite confidently to the others; she couldn't wait to see their face when they saw their car. But they carried on walking down the street followed by everyone and to Linda's horror there before her was.......A WHITE VOLKSWAGON BEETLE!!!! *'Oh no, we've done up the wrong car!'* said Linda to her young cousins, then they started to giggle uncontrollably. 'What's so funny?' asked Linda's mum, Linda whispered to her and soon Margie was doubled up laughing too joined by everyone else as the word spread. 'I just hope it's no-one at the wedding!' exclaimed Linda.

At the end of the evening, Linda, James, Stuart, Douglas and Margie were amongst the last to leave; Stuart was fast asleep in James' arms. Linda had a look down the street and saw that the White Volkswagen Beetle was still standing there with empty beer cans attached, wrapped in toilet paper and slogans written all over the windows in lipstick. Linda giggled again and said merrily to her mum, dad and James, 'someone's in for a shock when they get back to their car!' They all chuckled as they climbed into their car to head for home and James said, 'Let's just hope it's not a hired car like ours!

Monday morning and it was time for the long drive back down south. Linda packed everything up while James took it out to the car. As usual Douglas cooked them a breakfast fit for a king then Linda washed and dressed the children ready for the journey. Linda hated saying goodbye to her parents, she had an ache in her heart and a dull pain in the pit of her stomach, she didn't want to leave them, they looked so sad and lonely standing there on their own waving, Linda opened the car window, she waved and blew kisses until her mum and dad disappeared into the distance.

The roads were clear and they were making good progress through Glasgow. As they approached the A74, Linda said, 'I think we should try out these seatbelt things before going on to the dual carriageway,' 'Aye Ok, we're going to have to get used to them in the near future because everyone will have to get them fitted in their cars and it will be against the law not to wear them,' answered James as he pulled the seatbelt around him. 'Clunk-click every trip,' Linda laughed as she fastened her seat belt.

The A74 was clear as they approached Stonehouse, James was travelling at a steady 60MPH. Linda was singing to the children to pass the time, she noticed some workmen working underneath a bridge on the south bound carriageway, she was about to say to James, 'what a rotten job' when all hell broke loose, the car spun out of control, throwing them all about like rag dolls as it tumbled and tumbled, it bounced off the road and hit off the upward sloping grass embankment then righted itself back onto it's wheels. Linda and James were screaming over and over, 'Oh my God, the kids…the kids! They couldn't get to the children while the car was spinning as the force glued them to their seats; it all happened in a fraction of a minute but seemed like an eternity until the car stopped. Linda and

James' first reaction was to look at the kids, they were still sitting intact in their wee seats but she noticed that the metal bar going across the front of Stuart's seat had snapped. She tried to open the door to get out and get to her children but it was stuck fast, James couldn't get his door open either, they looked back at the workmen and they were standing looking shocked as if they didn't know what to expect, then as if realization hit them that Linda and James were trapped and trying to get out of the car, one by one they threw down their shovels and raced towards them. Four men grabbed a door each and with a couple of tugs from their big strong arms, the doors were open, The workmen pulled Stuart and Amanda out of their kiddie seats, Linda and James jumped out of the car as fast as they could and grabbed their children to make sure they were ok. Linda and James were both shaking and in shock, the car was wrecked, they couldn't believe that they walked out of it with only cuts and bruises on their hands, arms and legs. Amanda was none the worse for her ordeal but Stuart was very quiet and pale as if he wondered what was going on. James grabbed a tartan rug and Amanda's baby bag with spare nappies bottles and a change of baby clothes in it. He spread the rug on the grass embankment for his wife and kids to sit on. 'What about all our belongings and the pram? The car might go on fire!' said Linda in fear through quivering teeth as she held her kids close. 'Naw, don't worry aboot that hen, the car'll no' go oan fire noo, yer stuff is a' safe! Answered one of the workmen. 'I'll have to call the police, have you any idea where the nearest motorway phone is?' James asked the workmen. 'Aye it's just aboot 50 yards doon the motorway oan this side, ye cin practically see it fae here but you stay here wi' yer misses an' ah'll go,' answered one of the big burley road workers. 'No it's ok, it's best I go incase they ask me any questions,' replied James. The workmen stayed with Linda and the children until James got back. 'Right the police are on their way and they are sending an ambulance too' James informed them as he clambered back up the embankment. Just at that they could hear the sirens coming towards them. The police car arrived followed shortly by an ambulance and fire brigade. The police looked at the wrecked car, it was a write-off, then they looked at Linda, James, Stuart and Amanda. 'You mean you were actually travelling in this car and you have walked out of it in one piece?' said one of the policemen in total amazement. 'Yes' answered James. 'Well you were obviously wearing your seatbelts and all I can say is without them you wouldn't be alive to tell the tale now, there's no doubt that they saved your life, coupled by the fact that it is early morning and there was no other traffic on the road, you're all very lucky, an accident like this usually means a fatality.' Linda and James shivered and froze on the spot at the policeman's words, they counted themselves really lucky that, on this occasion, they had the presence of mind to strap themselves and their children into their car seats and vowed to themselves that in future any car they had would have seats belts fitted. The ambulance men told Linda and James that they wanted to get the four of them to a hospital to be checked over. 'But what about our cases and pram in the car?' Linda reiterated once more. 'Don't worry, we'll have the car towed and locked up safely for examination, call this number when you're ready and we will tell you where your car is so that you can collect your belongings, now just get yourselves to hospital, you and your children are more important at this moment in time,' said a kindly policeman as he handed James a piece of paper with the telephone number of the local police station on it.

Linda and James carried their children into the back of the ambulance, the ambulance man seemed quite concerned about Stuart, he checked his tummy, back, legs, arms, head and eyes, and took his pulse. Stuart still looked pale and was sleepy. 'Don't let him sleep mum' the ambulance man instructed Linda. Within ten minutes they arrived at the casualty department of the local Hospital. They were rushed straight into an examination room, the female doctor looked concerned as she checked Stuart over, then she checked Amanda and smiled as she said to the baby girl 'You're ok after your big ordeal aren't you my little beauty! Then she turned to Linda and James and said, we're keeping your little boy in overnight for observation, he must have got a bang on his head, his fontanel has opened up, it should gradually close again on it's own but we have to keep a close eye on him for the next 24 hours. Linda burst into tears, 'oh don't worry mum, I'm sure he'll be ok, it's just routine that we have to do this,' said a young dark-haired nurse with a soft Highland lilt accent as she comforted Linda. But I can't leave him here on his own; we have to get back to my mum's and its miles from here. 'You can phone in any time, we'll tell you in the morning if and when you can pick him up, don't worry he's in safe hands.' Answered the nurse, 'Yes, I know but he's not used to being in strange places without me, he's only two years old. I know he's going to fret. 'Can you please make sure he has his dummy for comfort? At least that might soothe him,' said Linda. 'Yes, give me his dummy and I'll settle him into a cot in the ward while the doctor checks you and your husband over.' Linda felt her stomach turn over as she kissed and cuddled her son before the nurse took him away, he was pale, sleepy and he looked frightened as he put his arms up crying out 'mummy, mummy'. Linda was finding all this too much to bear, put her head in her hands and cried her eyes out as she sobbed to James 'How much more bad luck can we have with cars? We were lucky to walk out of our car alive last month when it went on fire; we have been stuck overnight in the freezing snow with young children when our car broke down in Carlisle at New Year and now this! We hired a new car this time to play safe and even that turns out to be a danger, someone is trying to tell us something, we can't keep walking away from serious accidents, can we?' 'You're getting paranoid now Linda, they are all just coincidences, the main thing is that we are all ok, Stuart will be fine, you'll see! Somebody up there likes us,' he said as he cuddled his wife and baby daughter. After examining Linda and James, the doctor was satisfied that their injuries were just superficial. 'Ok you can go home now,' said the doctor, 'but what about my son, can I see him before I go?' pleaded Linda. 'Hold on I'll just check what ward he is in?' answered the doctor as she walked into a room closing the door behind her. Linda and James sat in the waiting room, they were worried sick about their wee boy, they just wanted to be with him, Linda knew he would be fretting for her because he didn't like changes. James had Amanda on his lap; Linda was wringing her hands with anxiety in between giving Amanda lots of kisses and cuddles. The door opened and the doctor walked toward them, she smiled and said, 'you can pop up to the ward and say your goodbyes but I'm afraid you won't be able to take the baby up to the children's ward. Linda looked at James; her face was torn with worry and fear. 'It's ok honey, you go, I'll stay here with Amanda and wait for you' said James understandingly'. 'Right I'll get a nurse to show you where he is.' Linda followed the nurse, trying to mentally coax her to walk faster; she was so desperate to hold her wee boy in her arms. As they got to the ward, the nurse spoke to the ward sister and told her who Linda was. The ward sister smiled and whispered as she led them towards the ward that Stuart was in. 'He's settled in fine there's no need to worry, perhaps it would be better if you just peeped in without him seeing you, incase he gets upset, I mean it's up to you but you can see for yourself.' Linda asked the ward sister if she could stay overnight with Stuart, Amanda was safe in the arms of her dad and he could take her home to stay at her parents house but the ward sister told a very disappointed Linda that they didn't have provisions at the hospital for mothers to stay overnight. They stopped outside the ward and looked at her wee boy, he was lying in his cot watching the other children playing, he seemed content enough and although it was very tempting for Linda to go and pick him up she decided that it wouldn't be fair on Stuart for him to see her because she would have the heartbreak of leaving him again so she just blew a kiss towards him and walked away tearfully sobbing her heart out.

They got outside the hospital, right I'd better find out how to get us back to your parent's house but first I'll call the local police station. James crossed the road to a phone box, while Linda sat on a wee wall, with a heavy heart, cuddling Amanda and worrying herself sick about her son. She suddenly realised that her mum and dad knew nothing about this and as James was crossing the road back towards her, she called out 'James we have to tell my mum and dad what's happened!' 'Don't worry, I've just called them, they know what's happened and that we are on our way home.' Linda was relieved that James had called them because she didn't feel strong enough emotionally to talk to them on the phone, she knew that she would have burst into tears and worried them even more than they must be. 'The police gave me the number of the garage where the car is, I have called them and they have assured me that the car is safely locked up with our belongings intact, I told them that we will be back tomorrow for them.' James told Linda. They asked a passer-by for directions to where to catch a bus into Glasgow.

Linda was sitting on the bus reflecting of the day's events, they had set out quiet happily a few hours beforehand and now here they were on their way back to her parent's house minus their wee lovable son. Her stomach was churning; she couldn't think straight and knew she wouldn't feel right until she was holding Stuart in her arms again. Suddenly she realized that she or James didn't have a change of clothes. 'What are we to do?' she asked James. 'It's only one day out of our lives, don't worry we'll get by,' James reassured her.

It took them three hours on and off different buses to get to Margie and Douglas. When they got there Margie and Douglas came running out to meet them, 'Oh Linda what's happened?' Margie asked distraughtly. Linda burst into in tears as she told her mum about their car accident and how wee Stuart was kept in hospital for observation because of his fontanel opening up. Margie tried to be brave but she too couldn't help herself from crying, wee Stuart was the apple of everyone's eye. Linda sobbed as she said, 'Oh mum, I can't bear the thought of him being ill and in hospital in strange place all by himself, he needs me and they wouldn't let me stay!'

James called the hired car company to tell them what had happened, he was furious when they asked him quite coldly, 'Is the car alright? James lost it at that point and shouted down the phone, 'F*** your car, my wee boy is in hospital because of your f****** useless car, have you no compassion?' He was shocked by their callous attitude, they actually told him that he could be responsible for the repair bills because he should have checked the car before collecting it, 'read the small print on the back of your agreement.' said the voice at the end of the phone. James replied with, 'Well your car is a f****** write-off mate, I'll be reporting you for hiring out cars that are not road-worthy, you could have killed my family with that heap of junk AND I am losing money because of you too, I was due back at work tomorrow, God knows when I'll get back now, my family are suffering, so I'll be looking for compensation from you not the other way round you cheeky b*****d!' Linda heard him bang the phone down in the hall then he shouted through to the living room, 'I'm going to call my mate Alan, and ask him if he'll take us to the hospital and garage to get our stuff from the car tomorrow, he's the only one I know with a car, there's no other way we'll be able to collect everything' James told Linda. 'It's just a pity that Uncle David is working abroad at the moment, he would have taken you there, no problem' said Margie.

Linda called the hospital three times during the evening to check on wee Stuart before going to bed but she hardly slept a wink that night, she wished the hours away until morning anxious to be re-united with her son. She called the hospital at 7am and they told her that her son was fine; he would be seeing the doctor around 9am and would hopefully be discharged. Linda hoped and prayed that this would be so. Alan was supposed to be picking them up at 9am but as the clock ticked past the hour there was no sign of Alan. Margie called into her work and booked the day off to look after Amanda. Linda couldn't eat breakfast; her stomach was in too much turmoil.

She watched as the hands of the clock slowly approached ten past nine, she was pacing back and forth from the window. Alan was never the best of time-keepers; Linda was becoming panicky as she said to James 'What if Alan can't get away from work? What if he's forgotten? What if....?' 'He'll be here, don't worry!' James interrupted. Linda called the hospital at 9.15 to be given the wonderful news that the doctor had given permission for Stuart to be discharged. Now Linda just wanted to get there and pick up her son. Just after 9.30am Alan's car drew up at the bottom of the lane. Linda wasted no time; she grabbed her coat and ran towards the car with James. Alan was a very laid back person and didn't understand a mother's concerns or worries for her wee sick two year old son in hospital, he laughed and chatted all the way while Linda sat in the back completely switched off and just thinking about Stuart. Over an hour later they arrived outside the hospital, as soon as the car stopped Linda jumped out and ran all the way to the ward. When she got there she explained to the sister at reception who she was, 'ah yes we have been waiting for you, Stuart's been fine, the fontanel should close again in it's own time, just keep an eye on him and if he seems unnaturally sleepy or sick then take him to your own doctor. I've got the paperwork here somewhere; you'll need to sign it before you can take him home. Linda was exasperated as the sister seemed to take forever finding the paperwork. 'Can't we do that later, I just want to see my son,' pleaded Linda. 'Ah here it is, I've found it, now just sign here and I will take you to Stuart,' said the sister smiling but ignoring Linda's suggestion. As Linda scribbled on the paper, her hand was shaking with excitement, she followed the nurse along the corridors, Stuart had been moved into another ward, as she walked in, she was overcome with emotion, her wee boy was standing up in his cot, he looked so lonely, he was the only child in the ward and he was watching a cleaning lady sweeping the floor. 'Why is he here on his own?' Linda asked the sister. 'because we needed the cot in the other ward and we knew that you were coming to get him this morning, don't worry he's only been in here for ten minutes and he hasn't been on his own, a nurse has been keeping an eye on him ' the sister assured Linda. Linda felt so sorry for her wee boy; she wasn't convinced that the sister was telling her the truth. Stuart didn't smile when he saw his mummy; he looked at her as if to say, '*Where have you been? Why did you leave me here?* Linda picked him up and held him tightly as she said 'I'm taking you home Stuart!' he looked into her eyes with confusion as if to say, *'I don't know whether to believe you or not!'* 'Where's your dummy?' Linda said as she searched around the cot. 'It's here in the bedside cabinet' answered the sister. 'I hope they gave it to him last night' Linda demanded. 'Oh don't worry mother, he had his dummy ok, we just took it off him in the morning,' Linda couldn't understand that, her poor wee boy was on his own and they took away the only wee bit of comfort he had. She got out of there as quick as she could and ran all the way back to Alan's car; she got into the back seat with Stuart. Alan drove to the garage where he and James collected the pram, cases and their belongings from the wrecked car and packed them into the boot and back seat beside Linda. Linda held Stuart close to her all the way back to her mum's house. Margie welcomed them with open arms; at last they were altogether again.

Two days later, they were on the London train on their way back to Kingston Upon Thames. This was another episode in their life that Linda and James weren't going to forget in a hurry. Police in Scotland confirmed that the steering in the car was faulty and had collapsed, the hire company dropped their threat of claiming damages from James because James threatened to sue them instead but in reality James and Linda couldn't afford to sue the company, they were struggling financially because James, lost a few days wages plus they never got their deposit back for the hired car and they were forced to sell their 101 Vauxhall Victor Estate car at a complete loss to cover the cost of repairs to it even though they still had two years HP to pay on it. James needed a car for work so they bought a wee old Ford jalopy from a young chap in the Cambridge estate.

Linda took her coat back to the shop, she told the lady the story of how her husband had collected it, how they had put it intact in it's box without checking it into the car boot and how upset she was when she went to wear it on the day of the wedding only to find that their was a flaw on the sleeve. The assistant called the manager, they were a couple of stuck- up old maids, they proceeded to tell Linda that the coat should have been checked before leaving the shop and no way did a coat leave their shop in that condition. Linda was shocked by their attitude and asked 'are you calling me a liar?' then she went on to say, 'You have sold me a coat that is a second!' 'No we haven't, it looks like it as been scratched by a cat!' insisted the manager with the other old maid nodding in agreement. 'Well if that's the case it must be your cat because I don't even have any animals, never mind a cat!' enraged Linda. The two old dears were having nothing to do with it and made it quite clear that they weren't in any way sympathetic to Linda's pleas. Linda bundled the coat back in to the box telling the two old maids that she would never step foot in their shop again and also that she would be telling everyone she knew how she had been conned by them.

Linda was beginning to wonder when their luck would change when three weeks later a letter arrived; Linda was delighted to find out that it was from the advertising company that did the 'clunk-click' seat belts adverts with Jimmy Saville. They were asking if Linda and James would be interested in taking part in an advertising campaign. The idea was for them to stand beside the written-off car with the children to bring to the attention of the nation the importance of wearing seat belts and that the family of four was saved by them. Linda and James had no hesitation in agreeing, apart from the good that it would do to save lives, the advertising company told them that they would be paid for it. Linda and James felt a sense of relief; this would help them to get out of the financial rut that they were in. Three weeks went by and they heard nothing then two days later another letter arrived saying that the car hire company would not give permission to use the car, the advertising company told Linda and James they could only assume that they were scared of bad publicity should anyone recognize their car. So that was the end of their hopes to warn others of the dangers of not 'belting up' and any chance they had to make up the money that they had lost.

September 1972, Linda called round to Sharon's and they walked up to Salvation Army to take Stuart and Lucy to start their first Wednesday morning at playgroup. They were both very shy and clinging to their mum's hands, eventually Sharon and Linda got their children interested in the toys, as they interacted and played with the other children, the playgroup leader whispered, 'I think it's safe for you both to slip away they seem happy enough'. Sharon and Linda left with Sharon's toddler son and Amanda in their pushchairs and crossed the road to Sainsbury's to get some shopping. They returned an hour later to pick Stuart and Lucy up. Linda got a look from Stuart as if to say *'Where have you been?'* She felt a bit guilty but the playgroup leader assured her that he played well with the toys and other children and didn't even notice her missing. She picked him up and gave him a huge hug and kiss, then handed him a bag of chocolate buttons for being such a good boy.

The following Tuesday, Linda was on her way to the mothers' club when she met Melanie coming back from the newsagent's, 'do you fancy coming along and giving mother's club another try Melanie?' Linda asked trying to persuade her. 'Oh No, it's not for me, anyway I've got a few things to attend to indoors'. Linda smiled and said, 'ok then but why don't you pop in to my house this afternoon with the girls, I'm doing nothing special!' Melanie looked happy as she agreed, Linda had a good idea that Melanie had nothing planned for that morning and was only making excuses, she seemed to prefer a one to one and appeared uncomfortable when in a crowd of people. Linda kept up the Tuesday afternoons with Melanie. Melanie even started returning the compliment by taking her turn at her house every alternate Tuesday. Danny's mum bought her grandchildren swings and a see-saw for the garden and Stuart loved to go in and play on them. Amanda had just started walking, she was ten months and a very bright wee girl, she loved the company of the other children.

October 1972 and Linda got the letter to attend the hospital the following week. She was relieved to discover that there was nothing seriously wrong, the gynecologist diagnosed that it was an ulcer on her womb that was causing the excess bleeding, it was probably the result of Amanda's difficult birth but it would have to be cauterized.

Beginning of December 1972, Linda went into Richmond Hospital on her consultant's advice because the waiting list at Kingston Hospital was too long and this was something that needed attending to as soon as possible. James organized four days off work; this was worrying because it would mean losing four days money. Linda arranged for Melanie to look after Stuart and Amanda for an hour in the evening while James came up to the hospital to visit. Luckily Amanda was a good natured baby, she would go to anyone but Linda worried about leaving Stuart for he wouldn't let Linda or James out of his site. James couldn't take Linda into hospital because he wouldn't have been able to drive the car back on his own with the two children in the back so she called a black taxi. With tears running down her face, she kissed and cuddled the children before hugging James tightly and kissing him then she walked out on her own to the taxi carrying her case. The driver was Jamaican, 'Richmond Hospital Please,' she told him. Linda hadn't a clue where Richmond Hospital was, she relied on the honesty of the driver, hoping that he wouldn't take her round in circles to bump up the fare. The driver was very nice, he seemed to feel sorry for her and when they got to the hospital he stopped outside the front door, then got out and carried her case up the eight stairs from the pavement into the hospital reception, wishing her all the best before returning to his cab. It was an old hospital with painted green and cream corridors and high ceilings. Linda checked in, a wee sturdy nurse about Linda's age, with her fair hair up in a tight bun behind her nurse's cap and who certainly wasn't even 5 feet tall because she hardly reached Linda's shoulders, smiled as she grabbed Linda's case and instructed her to 'Follow me!' Linda walked along long corridors, up in a lift then along another corridor before reaching her destination. The nurse walked into a ward and stopped at the first bed; the ward was painted cream, there were ten beds either side facing each other, a clean disinfectant smell filled the air and everything was spotless, you almost expected Florence Nightingale to appear, 'Right this is your home for the next four days, undress and put this on,' the wee nurse instructed Linda as she threw a hospital gown on the bed and drew the curtains around for privacy. Linda felt her stomach churning, she just wanted to turn and run away, she was already missing James and worrying about her children, how she wished that she lived near to her mum, she would have felt more relaxed about everything if James didn't have to take time off work and her mum was looking after the children but her mum was four hundred miles away and anyway she wouldn't have been able get time off from work.

Linda settled in, her operation was scheduled for first thing the following morning. James came up to visit in the evening. He came in quickly and said to Linda, 'you have to come out into the corridor, I have Stuart with me, children are not allowed in the ward, the matron said that it would be ok but I can't stay for the whole hour.' As Linda got out of the bed she ran into the corridor and picked up Stuart giving him a big cuddle. 'Why didn't you leave him with Melanie?' Linda asked James. 'He wouldn't stay and I didn't want to worry Melanie so I had no option but to bring him with me. Linda was secretly delighted, even though it meant that they weren't allowed to stay for the whole visiting hour, it was worth it to get a cuddle from her son. After half and hour the matron asked James to leave, he gave Linda a big tight kiss and cuddle and wished her all the best for the next morning, telling her that he would be thinking about her. Linda walked James and Stuart out as far as the lift. James picked Stuart up and Linda grabbed the both of them and sobbed; she would have done anything to have gone home with them.

The lady in the next bed was in her forties, she introduced herself to Linda with a big welcoming smile, 'Hi, my name's Sally, what's yours?' she asked Linda. She was a pretty petite little red head with a whacky sense of humour; she made Linda laugh and took away the tenseness of the whole situation. Linda found out that her husband was a policeman, she had two adopted children, a girl aged four and a boy aged seven, she was in hospital because she had a lump in her breast. She told Linda that her operation was scheduled for the next morning too. She became serious and her eyes filled up as she admitted to being scared because she was asked to sign a consent form for the doctors to remove her breast if necessary, then as if she didn't want to discuss it any more Sally started joking and said that she had instructed her husband not to come up tomorrow afternoon to see her because she would be too drowsy and wouldn't have time to put her mascara on but most importantly she wouldn't have her teeth in. Linda couldn't help but laughing as Sally said seriously, 'We have been married for fifteen years and he has never seen me without my mascara or teeth!'

Linda didn't sleep well that night, there was an old lady in her nineties in the bed opposite who screamed and shouted most of the night, giving the nurses a hard time, at one point she threw her bed pan across the ward, it clanged on the floor with pee going everywhere. It was when she started calling out for her mummy that Linda realized that the poor old dear was suffering senile dementia.

The next morning Sally and Linda were both given pre-med injections to relax them although Linda didn't feel she needed it because she was so tired from all the commotion in the ward during the night. The hospital porters came to take Sally to the operating theatre. Linda wished her well, saying, 'Good luck Sally, I'll see you later!' they were both drowsy but Sally managed to lift her hand and give Linda a wave. Fifteen minutes later it was Linda's turn to be taken to the operating theatre. She lay on the trolley as the porters pushed it along the corridors and down in the lift, finally it trundled into a wee room. 'Right this is where we leave you my dear, you'll be back in the ward before you know it!' smiled one of the porters. A man in a green outfit and mask stood at the side of Linda, he felt for a vein on the inside of her elbow on her right arm and told her to count to ten and that was the last Linda remembered. The next thing she woke up back in the ward, she turned her head drowsily towards Sally's bed and saw that she was fast asleep then Linda dozed back into another long sleep. Linda woke up again and looked at her watch, it was quarter past one in the afternoon, visiting was at 2.30pm so she thought she would make an effort and put on some make up. Although she still felt tired, she propped herself up and set her wee mirror up on the tray that went across the bed, then she got out her make up to make a start when she heard a sleepy voice say, 'Look at you Miss World, just out of the operating theatre and painting your face!' Linda turned round to see Sally lying smiling at her, 'Hi, how are you Sally?' Linda asked. 'Sore' replied Sally then she dozed off again and so did Linda. An hour later Linda blinked open her eyes, 'Oh hello again Miss World, maybe now you can finish your make up,' teased Sally. Linda looked in the mirror and had to laugh, one eye was all done up with eye shadow, eyeliner and mascara while the other one wasn't. Linda had underestimated how tired she was and had fallen asleep in the middle of applying her make-up. She did her other eye then put on some lipstick just in time for James arriving, 'I managed to sneak away from Stuart while he was playing on the swings in Melanie's garden,' said James. 'Oh I hope he'll be alright! You didn't have to come up today, I'm worried about him, don't stay long, I'm ok,' replied Linda. 'I had to see you after your operation, how are you feeling?' James asked. 'I'm fine said Linda, just a bit tired, not really any more discomfort than expected, I'm glad it's over and just want to get home to you and the kids to get on with my life!' James stayed for half an hour, Linda told him not to bother coming up that night because she realized how difficult it was with the children and in any case she was still feeling tired so would probably fall asleep early.

After James had gone Linda asked Sally if she knew how her operation went, 'As far as I know everything is ok, they have cut away a lump, I'm all bandaged up but my breast is still there, thank God!' answered Sally. 'Oh that's good news,' said Linda. 'Even better news is, I've got my teeth in now, so I'm looking forward to seeing my hubby this evening!' Laughed Sally as she flashed her teeth and clicked them together.

Two days later James arrived with Stuart to take Linda home, Sally was going home too and her husband walked into the ward about five minutes later. Linda was feeling good in herself and also happy for Sally because she had been given the 'all clear'. The doctors told her that her lump was a non-malignant cyst and nothing to worry about. The two ladies exchanged phone numbers and gave each other a hug before leaving.

The following Friday evening James popped up to the local pub for an hour, when he came back he told Linda that he met Melanie's husband Danny. Danny told James how grateful he was to Linda for befriending Melanie, apparently she won't go anywhere and that's why Danny goes out on his own because she just sits in the house all day and night watching television. He also told James about a wee local social club where they could take the children. He said that he's been trying to get Melanie to go but she seems to panic at the thought of it because she doesn't know anyone, but if we agreed to go tomorrow night then Melanie might be keener. 'Are you up for it? Danny will sign us all in.' coaxed James. 'Oh I don't know Amanda's a bit young for that, you know she likes her routine' replied Linda unsure. 'Oh c'mon you'll be doing Melanie a big favour, she never goes anywhere, she needs to be drawn out of herself!' persuaded James. 'Ok, but only for an hour, I'm only doing it to help Melanie, Amanda's really too young!'

Christmas was approaching and Linda couldn't wait because her mum and dad were coming down to spend it with them. She got a wee imitation Christmas tree from the Monday Market and sat with Stuart and Amanda cutting out the egg shapes from yellow and blue polystyrene egg boxes, she pierced two holes on the top of the egg shapes and laced a fine thread threw it, then she pasted the outside of the cup with paper glue and dipped it in glitter. The result was lovely glittery wee bells to hang on the Christmas tree; the children were delighted, although Amanda was more interested in pulling them off the tree rather than hanging them on it. She also got strips of coloured sticky paper and crepe paper, she showed Stuart how to make the strips into rings and loop them together to make paper chains then she pleated the different colours of long crepe paper strips into long garlands to hang up. She was delighted with their efforts; the front room was looking very festive indeed.

James came home from work one evening and told Linda about a guy who worked with him on the building site, his name was Mark, he had just got married and he and his young wife Tracy had just bought a house nearby to James and Linda. 'They are really struggling because it's an old house and doesn't have a bathroom. They're not from this area and both sets of their parents live too far away, so they have to make do and wash in the sink until they can get their bathroom installed and fitted.' James told Linda. Linda was feeling happy and full of Christmas spirit, 'Oh that's awful, why don't you tell them they can have a bath here?' replied Linda.

The next evening Mark and Tracy came round to meet Linda and tell her how grateful they were to her kind offer. Before Linda knew it she was agreeing to Mark and Tracy coming round on Friday nights for a bath. 'We'll baby-sit and you can go out!' Tracy said as if she wasn't accepting 'no' for an answer. Linda was apprehensive, this wasn't what she had intended but she agreed to the arrangement

A week before Christmas, Linda came downstairs about 3am to go to the bathroom, she heard noises, like scratching coming from the front room. She was half asleep and without thinking she threw the door open and put the main light on just in time to see three wee mice scurrying under the sofa. 'Oh my God!' she screamed and ran out banging the door behind her. On hearing his wife's screams, James woke up abruptly, jumped out of bed and ran down the stairs shouting, 'What's wrong, what's wrong Linda?' Linda grabbed James and blurted out what she had seen, James said, 'we can't have mice, I have filled in every hole, and replaced skirting boards, there's no place for them to get in!' 'Well I'm telling you what I saw!' exclaimed Linda. James and Linda went into the front room. James closed the door behind them; he examined all the skirting and floorboards and said 'There just aren't any signs of mice!' Linda replied, 'Well I'm not lying, they definitely went under the sofa, unless, no, you don't think they could be....' 'What in the settee?' said James, completing her sentence. 'Right it's the middle of the night, we're not going to solve the problem now, let's just close the door and we'll report it to Mr. Halliday in the morning,' said James wearily.

In the morning James went next door to tell Mr. Halliday what Linda had seen and where she thought the mice were. Mr. Halliday laughed and said disbelievingly, 'Mice in the settee, that's a new one!' He came into the house with one of his men. They went into the front room and pulled the settee away from the wall. 'Is that mice dirt?' Linda asked as she noticed wee black droppings on the pale green carpet below where the sofa had been. Mr. Halliday's expression changed to serious, 'There's a little whole in the canvas, look!' said his employee pointing to the bottom of the sofa. Mr. Halliday ripped the whole back off the settee and lo and behold mice ran from everywhere, there was a nest of them inside the sofa! Linda quickly closed the door to make sure they didn't get into the other rooms, Mr. Halliday's man ran next door and got a box, he and Mr. Halliday managed to catch the mice in the box then took them along with the settee out of the house. 'Come and have a look in the shop and see what settee you fancy, I have just cleared a couple of houses.' Linda went in and picked a wee two-seater settee with legs this time; she wasn't taking chances of breeding mice again!

That evening Linda laughed as she recalled the day's events saying to James 'Oh don't breath a word of this to my mum, she loved that settee and always remarked how comfortable it was, remember she said they don't make them like that any more! God she would be mortified if she knew she was sitting on a nest of mice!' chuckled Linda.

Christmas was a wonderful family time; Stuart would be three in three months time and was just beginning to understand Santa Claus and what it was all about. Linda woke up about 7am on Christmas morning with Stuart standing at the side of her bed, 'Oh, do you want to see what Santa has brought you?' she asked him excitedly. The wee boy nodded his head; Linda shook James, 'Wake up! we have to see if he's been yet?' 'Ohhhh, do we have to?' groaned James. 'Yes we have to,' laughed Linda. 'Let's go through and get Amanda and gran and grandpa too. They all went downstairs in their pyjamas; Stuart and Amanda were standing by the front room door followed by Linda, Margie, James and Douglas. 'Right one-two three, open the door' said James. Wee Stuart ran in, he was so excited and didn't know what to look at first. 'Oh look what Santa's brought you both' said Linda as she helped her children open their presents. Amanda was mesmerized by it all and was happier scrunching up the wrapping paper. James and Linda had bought Stuart a big train that he could sit on, and lots of little cars, games, clothes, books and a selection box. They got Amanda her first baby doll, building bricks, a spinning top, jig-saw, clothes, books and a selection box. Margie and Douglas bought Stuart a wee toy battery operated dog that walked and barked. Amanda got a wee pink baby pram from them, they also gave their grandchildren clothes, a selection box each and lots of little stocking fillers. While the kids played with their new toys Linda, James, Margie and Douglas exchanged presents. James and Linda couldn't afford to buy each other anything but they bought Douglas a MacGregor tartan scarf and Margie a pair of black gloves trimmed with fur. Margie and Douglas gave James a nice warm colourful sweater and slippers and Linda got a make up set in a box with a mirror, slippers plus a big box of chocolates from her mum and dad. Douglas sat with his tartan scarf on, Margie tried on her new gloves, James had his new sweater on and Linda had her new slippers on, they laughed at the sight of each other sitting there in their pyjamas wearing their new Christmas presents.

Douglas made the breakfast while Linda went upstairs to get herself dressed. After breakfast Margie cleared away the dishes and Linda took the children through to the bathroom to get them washed and dressed in their new Christmas clothes. They were all going over to Douglas junior and Norma's for Christmas dinner.

They arrived at Linda's brother and his wife's house at mid-day; Douglas and Margie were at their happiest when all their family were together. They fussed over Fiona, who was almost two, they got her lots of stocking fillers, clothes and a wee barking dog too and she squealed with delight as she watched it walk and bark. They gave Douglas junior slippers and a sweater too; Norma got slippers, a nightdress and chocolates. Stuart and Amanda got more toys from Douglas junior and Norma. Linda and James gave Fiona a wee toy carpet sweeper and a selection box. Linda and her brother had decided that they, James and Norma would only buy presents for the children and not for each other as none of them could afford it.

Norma served up delicious home made turkey soup for the first course then she and Douglas junior went into the kitchen and brought out a wonderful massive roasted, stuffed turkey on a platter, along with dishes brimming over with Brussels sprouts, carrots, steepy peas, roast potatoes, gravy and cranberry sauce. They rounded off the meal with traditional Christmas pudding and custard.

As they all sat around the table, after the meal they were full to the brim. Douglas stood up and said, 'I would like to give a wee toast, first of all thank you to my son Douglas and his wife Norma for serving up a Christmas dinner fit for a king, I would also like to say how happy your mum and I are that we are here today, It's not often we get all our family together along with our wonderful grandchildren. Thank you too to Linda and James for all their hospitality and to everyone for all your lovely presents, mum and I really appreciate them. We are very proud of you all. Now let's raise our glasses to the family, may you all have long and happy lives together and although we're far apart you are never far from our minds!'

'To the family!' everyone echoed as they stood up and raised their glasses.

Seven

January 1974 and Mark and Tracy finally had their bathroom completed. They had been coming round to James and Linda's house every Friday evening for just over a year and during that time, James had given Mark a hand and carried out various jobs of carpentry work for them, he never charged them because he felt that he was helping friends. Linda was secretly delighted that she would have her home back to herself again on Friday evenings, it hadn't been easy because she and James couldn't really afford to go out every Friday but felt they were being forced out of their own home to give Mark and Tracy privacy, most times they just sat in the pub because the cinema was too expensive, Linda would make a Babycham last two hours and James did the same with a pint of beer, but the most annoying thing was the fact that Mark and Tracy seemed to be under the impression that it was they who were doing Linda and James a big favour.

February 1974, James came home from work one evening and he was livid, Linda stepped back and frowned as she said, 'Who's upset you then?' 'That f------g Mark, that's who!' answered James. Linda realised it had to be something serious because James never swore in front of her unless he was very wound up. 'He and his precious wife only had a f-----g house-warming party last Friday night, the B------s! All the guys on the site knew about it and he never breathed a word to me, I really feel used after allowing them the freedom of our home, hot water and facilities for over a year plus all the work I did for them in their house for free! I feel like putting his lights out!' Linda was shocked and disappointed in Mark and Tracy; she couldn't believe anyone could be so heartless. 'It must be because we have kids, but even then, they could have given us the chance to refuse, what a sly, mean pair they turned out to be, we put ourselves out for them and this is the thanks we get, we've certainly been used!' exclaimed Linda agreeing with James. 'Never mind James, you live and learn, I think there's a lesson here, we need to toughen up a bit! Where we come from people help each other but this is London, there are all sorts of different people out there and they will take what they can from you and give nothing in return,' said Linda, hugging her husband to help calm him down.

Spring 1974, Linda and James were now members of Danny's social club. They had gone there a couple of times with Danny and Melanie but Melanie didn't enjoy it. Linda couldn't understand Melanie; she never took her kids anywhere and was happy to sit indoors with them day and night watching TV. James usually went up to the club by himself for a couple of hours on a Friday night; it was a nice wee club, the other members made him very welcome.

Early on Saturday evenings, Linda and James took the kids to the club when it opened its doors at 7pm and stayed for an hour. The club was quiet at that time as members didn't start arriving until after 8pm for their Saturday night dance. Stuart was four years old now, he was a very likeable wee lad, he loved to sit and chat with old Stan, the doorman at the club. Old Stan was also the club chairman, he never seemed to smile, he just sat by the door wearing his old black suit, untidy white open-necked shirt and no tie. He asked everyone that entered, whether he knew them or not, if they were members. His 'club foot' stuck out as if he were deliberately trying to trip people up as he insisted members must sign their guests in and pay 50p for each one. He was very strict, he never allowed children to run around and if he saw any wandering about on their own he would growl at them, 'where're your parents?' But he liked well mannered children so Stuart became his 'pal'. Amanda loved to dance, when the band was practicing and tuning up, she would be in the middle of the floor dancing on her own full of confidence. Although she was only two and a half, she was already showing signs of being very independent. From the age of eight months, she could climb out of her cot, so James had to make a gate for the top of the stairs with the lock on the opposite side so that Amanda couldn't figure out how to open it, also by the time she was able to sit up independently in her big pram, she hated wearing reins and always managed to free herself from them, no matter how tight Linda fastened the straps in her pram, Amanda always managed to slip them and stand up earning herself the nickname of 'Houdini'. It was very worrying for Linda because she couldn't leave her daughter for a second incase she fell out of her high pram, she was indeed very advanced for her years, she cut her first tooth at four months, started walking at ten months and had a wonderful vocabulary by the time she was eighteen months.

One Sunday morning during a Bank Holiday weekend when Amanda was only about fifteen months old and James' mother Molly was staying with them for a visit, James took Stuart out to the car, which was parked in the street outside, with him to check the oil and water etc., in preparation to take them all out for a run to the coast. Linda was busy getting all the last minute things done indoors while Molly was to-ing and fro-ing between the house and the car. 'Right, that's me now, I've got, nappies for Amanda, spare clothing for them, swimming costumes, towels, buckets, spades, drinks for the kids, flasks of tea for the adults, sandwiches, fruit and crisps, so let's go,' she said to Molly as she pulled the front door shut. 'Where's Amanda, have you shut her in the house? asked Molly. Linda face went white as she felt a tension in her stomach, 'No she's not indoors, she was here five minutes ago but I thought you had taken her out to the car to see her daddy, are you sure she is not in the car?' 'Oh my God, where is she?' shouted Linda, her hands shaking as she quickly opened the door again to check if she was in the house. By this time James realised what was happening and was running up and down the street calling out 'Amanda' while Linda was doing the same indoors, checking every room, under beds, in cupboards etc. Eventually Linda got back to the front door and with tears streaming down her face, she ran her fingers through her hair in panic as she shouted to James 'She's' not indoors, where is she? Where could she have got to in the space of five minutes? We'll have to call the police!' Then James replied, 'She can't be far, she's only fifteen months old, for God sake, how far could she walk in five minutes?' Linda stared at James with a look of fear and blurted out, 'You don't think......oh James you don't think someone could have taken her?' James tried to comfort Linda and said, 'Can you think of anywhere she liked to go with you that's nearby?' 'There's the sweetie shop a couple of doors down,' answered Linda looking hopeful, 'I've checked the shop,' said Molly.' What about the swing park? But that's across the road, she wouldn't cross the road…would she?' Replied Linda doubtfully, who by this time was very upset. Suddenly she stopped and said, 'Unless?' Then she ran out the garden gate. 'What, what is it Linda? Where are you going?' shouted James as he picked Stuart up and ran after his wife. Linda reached Melanie and Danny's house two doors down. 'Why are you going in there, they won't be able to help, you know that they've gone to Danny's parents for the weekend?' James shouted after her. Linda kicked the heavy wooden door into their back garden open, then she stopped in her tracks and breathed a huge sigh of relief, grinning from ear to ear as she gazed at her wee daughter, who was leaning over the swing in her neighbour's garden, rocking to and fro and totally oblivious to the panic that she had caused! Linda scooped her up in her arms and held her like she would never let her go again. 'How did she know how to get to Danny and Melanie's house and how the hell did she get that big heavy door into the back garden open?' asked James in disbelief. 'Your daughter is one very determined, intelligent young lady. The kids all play together on the swings and see-saw when I go to Melanie's for coffee, but I would never have thought she knew her own way here and I haven't a clue how she managed to open that big door, I'm just relieved to have her in my arms now, I am really going to have to keep a closer eye on her, she's too quick for words!

Linda and James always took their children home before the club started to get busy on Saturday nights. On the way home one Saturday, Linda said to James how much she enjoyed her hour at the club on a Saturday, 'it's a nice wee bar, I wouldn't mind working there a couple evenings a week, it would get me out of the house and also give us a bit extra cash!' 'I think you can forget that, the club is like a family, everyone is related to everyone else and they run the place, from the committee to the bar staff', answered James. 'Ah well, I thought it would be too good to be true' said Linda as she pursed her lips in disappointment. Just at that minute, Stuart said to Linda 'Mum, you know how Stan has a club foot?' Linda paused and said 'Yes' wondering what was coming next. Stuart then asked seriously, 'Is that why he's chairman?' Linda and James couldn't help laughing as the wee boy looked at them wondering what was so funny. Linda explained to Stuart what was wrong with Stan's foot and that although it was called a 'club foot', it was nothing to do with his position in the club. 'Funny how kid's minds work, isn't it?' said Linda to James quietly.

The following Friday, James came home from the club and said to Linda, 'Do you still fancy working in the club bar?' 'Yes, but why?' replied Linda. 'Well, I just thought I would mention to Len, the secretary that you were interested and he said to come into his office when we're up there tomorrow night to talk about it. Linda felt her heart pound with fear as she answered, 'Oh my God James, I've never worked in a bar in England, it's all different drinks to what I used to serve when we worked in the bar in Scotland before we got married, oh I don't know that I could do it!' 'Of course you can, I have every confidence in you!' replied James.

Linda couldn't concentrate all day Saturday, at the back of her mind constantly was the interview with the club secretary plus the worry and fear of stepping behind the club bar to work. As they walked up to the club at quarter to seven in the evening, Linda's stomach was churning. 'Calm down, he's not going to eat you', laughed James as he noticed the seriousness in Linda's face.

Once they got into the club and settled with drinks, Linda said to James, 'Well here goes, look after the kids while I'm in there will you?' 'Of course I will!' answered James still smiling. Linda gingerly knocked on the secretary's office door. 'Come in' she heard him call out. She slowly opened the door, he was sitting behind a desk, there was black leather bench seating all around the small room. 'Sit down and make yourself at home.' don't be nervous,' Len told her in his friendly northern accent. 'I understand from your husband that you're keen to work in the bar.' 'Y-e-s,' answered Linda slowly and shyly. 'Have you worked in a bar before?' asked Len. Linda told Len about the bar she and James had worked in, over and above their day jobs, when they were saving up to get married. 'Well it just so happens we could do with another pair of hands to help out, it can get very busy in here in the evenings. Edna opens up the bar up at weekends then we have Doris who's a hundred and eighty and a bit past it but she's been here for years and enjoys her job, trouble is the members will insist on buying her drinks and she's the worse for wear after the first hour or so. The rest of the bar staff are lads so we could do with a bright young female to bring them into line,' said Len. 'But I'm a bit concerned because the drinks are different in this part of the world!' Linda told Len. He assured her that if she had already worked in a bar she would soon get the hang of the drinks. 'Ok, when can you start?' said Len. 'Oh I would prefer just one night a week at the moment, the children are still young, mid-week would be ideal because James has his night out on Friday and we come up here for an hour with the kids on Saturdays' answered Linda. 'Right what about coming in on Tuesday evening to see how you get on, it will be busy because we have darts and pool matches on!' said Len 'Ok,' Linda found herself agreeing as Len saw her to the door. She walked back towards James and he said 'Well, how did you get on?' 'I start on Tuesday night, just for a trial mind you,' replied Linda. 'Och you'll have no bother, you'll take to it like a duck to water!' James assured her.

Tuesday morning, Linda was shattered, she hadn't slept a wink the night before worrying about starting her new job that evening, she was so nervous, it was almost five years since she had worked in the pub in Scotland. Linda considered phoning in to say that she had changed her mind but that wasn't her style because when she committed herself to do something then she carried it out no matter what, so she took a deep breath and told herself not to be so silly that it was just a job and she was perfectly capable of doing it!

That evening, Linda had the kids fed and bathed before James came home from work; she seemed to be on automatic pilot when James asked her 'Are you all excited about getting back out into the adult world again then?' 'Excited? More like a bag of nerves!' exclaimed Linda as she served up James' dinner. 'Are you not eating, c'mon it's not that bad?' said James. 'No, I ate with the kids, so that I could go and get myself ready while you were eating, everything's done, you've only to wash your own dishes then put the kids to bed at 7.30pm.' answered Linda. 'What time are you leaving?' James asked his wife. 'Well I start at 7pm but I thought I'd get there ten minutes early so that I could run through the drinks and prices etc.,' replied Linda. 'Good idea,' smiled James, he was more than aware that Linda wanted to get it right and set a good example especially on her first night.

At quarter to seven Linda kissed the kids goodbye saying, 'mummy has to go to work, I'll see you in the morning!' James couldn't help admiring his wife, although she was nervous, he could sense that she was proud she would be contributing to the family income.

It was only a five minute walk and Linda arrived at the club at ten to seven, to find the door locked! She hung around not knowing what to do; she didn't know who had the key, who was opening up or who she was working with. A few guys gathered outside with pool cues, waiting to go in but Linda didn't know them and they didn't know her. At that a young good-looking man about nineteen appeared, 'C'mon Simon, where the hell have you been, we want to get in to get some practice before the match tonight?' yelled one of the lads waving his pool cue at him. 'Keep your head on, I'll just go and get the key,' answered Simon as he disappeared again, this time to the side door of one of the houses across the road. He appeared a couple of minutes later holding a big bunch of keys, by this time there was around a dozen men waiting at the door, they were making remarks to Simon about their stomach thinking their throats were cut and telling him to get the bar opened double quick. Linda surmised that she would be working with Simon in the bar, this didn't help her nerves, she still had to introduce herself to him. He opened the door and she stood back as everyone piled in, in front of her. Finally she made her way to the bar, Simon was pulling up the bar shutters and jokingly giving the members as good as he got. Linda shyly said to him, 'Hello, I'm Linda, Len asked me to start in the bar tonight.' 'Oh did he? Nobody ever tells me anything, that's great we have darts and pool on tonight, we could do with an extra pair of hands,' replied Simon with a confident smile. He seemed a nice lad, he put the ice bucket in Linda's hands and said, 'Here, you go into the cellar and get some ice, you'll see the ice making machine directly on your right as you walk in.' There was a door off the bar through to the cellar, it was on the same level. Linda went in and she saw a box freezer sitting on a shelf, she pulled the door down and there were trays of ice cubes inside, she took the trays out one at a time and emptied the ice out of them until the bucket was full. She came out of the cellar and said, 'Where does this go Simon?' 'Oh have you done that already, that was quick, there's another one to be filled for the lounge bar but that's not important yet, you can help me serve some of these guys first,' said Simon. Linda approached the bar and said 'Who's next?' 'Me' echoed a chorus of voices. 'Shove off, I'm next, it makes a change to get served by a bit of glamour in here,' said the big ruddy faced Irishman. 'Ah'll have two pints of Guinness please darlin', Mickey what did you say you wanted, was it Guinness and Mild?' he shouted over to his mate. Linda dutifully poured the two pints of Guinness, that wasn't a problem, but what the hell was a Guinness and Mild? She pretended she understood as she sidled up to Simon and whispered, 'help me please, what's a Guinness and Mild?' 'No problem, it's half a Mild in a pint glass with a bottle of

Guinness,' replied Simon, Linda thanked him, she had never heard of such a drink but she served it up to the Irishman as though she knew exactly what she was doing. Once they got rid of the initial rush at the bar. Simon said, 'Right I'll show you where everything is, don't worry you'll soon know your way round alright!' The two bars were back to back with a gantry in the middle. Linda apologised to Simon for not knowing what a Guinness and Mild was, she confessed that she hadn't worked in a bar for five years and it was in Scotland, she had never worked in a bar in England so that's why she hadn't heard of that particular drink, infact she told him that she hadn't even heard of Mild before never mind mixing draught beer with bottle beer. 'Don't worry, if there's anything you want to know just ask,' Simon reassured her. 'Thanks Simon, right I'll go through to the cellar and get some more ice for the lounge bar,' said Linda 'Oh that's a good idea, I wonder where Nicky is, he usually works Tuesday night? Perhaps Len has given him the night off because you are here,' said Simon. 'Well Len said to me that he could do with another pair of hands so it doesn't sound to me like he would cut down on the staff,' replied Linda as she trotted off to the cellar with an ice bucket in her hand.

As she came back out of the cellar, she bumped into a tall gangly young chap, with long straggly red-hair and a big nose; he was about the same age as Simon. He brushed past her and casually threw his jacket on top of a barrel of beer. Linda said, 'Hi I'm Linda, are you Nicky?' He just looked at her with a miserable glare and nodded. Linda wasn't sure about him she felt bad vibes. She went on to serve a customer waiting at the bar, he was an elderly Welshman, he asked for a pint of mild, Linda poured him a beautiful pint with a nice frothy head, exactly the way she had been trained in Scotland and she proudly put it down in front of him. She was embarrassed when he pushed it back towards her complaining bitterly, 'I don't want a parson's collar!' Linda hadn't a clue what he meant, then Simon whispered, 'he means that he wants it topped up without the frothy head, down in this part of the world they go for quantity rather than quality' he laughed. As Linda topped up the pint of Mild for her customer she noticed Nicky slyly smirking in the corner. 'Ah that's better, you're learning lass!' said the Welshman as he walked away happy. The next customer asked Linda for a light and bitter, she whispered to Nicky, 'What's a light and bitter?' to her embarrassment, Nicky said aloud, in front of everyone, 'What are you doing working in a bar if you haven't a clue what the drinks are?' Linda wished that the ground would open up and swallow her, she was beginning to feel that this bar job wasn't a good idea and contemplated getting her coat and going home, she felt tears welling in her eyes but she was determined not to show her emotions in front of Nicky. To her relief, Simon chimed in with, 'Oh and you never had to learn Nicky? Would you like me to tell Linda about when you started working in the bar, how you couldn't pour a pint to save yourself and that was after a week, at least Linda knows how to handle the pumps! Oh and by the way do you think that you could make the effort to be on time in future, I'm fed up with you strolling in half an hour late every shift leaving me to open up and set up the bar! Just ignore him Linda, he's got a serious attitude problem!' said Simon loudly' The members all cheered in agreement with Simon and told Nicky that they would rather look at Linda than his ugly mug. Linda didn't know where to look, this was her first shift and already there was an argument.' After that Nicky kept his mouth shut while Simon was ready to answer any questions that Linda had. By the end of the evening she was feeling a lot more confident, she practically knew all the drinks, prices and got on well with the members. 'Well, how did you enjoy your first night?' said Len as he approached the bar. 'It was good, I think I've got the hang of it!' replied Linda. 'She was very good, fast and efficient, the guys love her, they were all fighting for her to serve them, they didn't want Nicky or me!' laughed Simon.

James was waiting for Linda when she got home, 'Well how did it go?' he asked her enthusiastically. 'Fine, but I'm glad the first night is over, it's a lot to take in, my heads birling round with all the new drinks and prices I've had to learn!' then she went on to tell James about Nicky. 'He's a strange lad, not very friendly; I'm really relieved that Simon was there because I would never stick to it if I had to work with Nicky on my own!'

Just like James predicted, Linda took to the job 'like a duck to water', she became very popular it didn't take her long to learn who was who and what was what, she poured a perfect pint and was polite, cheery and pleasant but could give the lads as good as she got. Len kept asking her if she could work more nights but she was adamant that one night's work was as much as she could cope with at the moment because it was usually at least 10pm before she finally finished doing the washing, ironing and housework for the day. She opened a building society account and every week she faithfully paid her evenings earnings from the club into it. 'It's going to be a great Christmas, my little bit of earnings will soon mount up and we can get the kids nice presents and new clothes, it's a blessing, I don't know how we would have afforded the extra expense of Christmas otherwise!' she confidently told her husband.

It was a lovely sunny Sunday in June 1974, James had been working in the morning and Linda had arranged that when he finished work they would drive to Windsor, in the second-hand white Rover car that they had purchased on HP the previous week, with the children and meet up with her brother Douglas, his wife Norma and their two daughters, Fiona who was three and a half and Donna who was sixteen months old, by the river for a picnic. Linda was just finishing off packing the picnic with the children when James said to her, 'I'm going to pop out to the car to tune in the radio while I'm waiting for you, oh by the way Linda, what time is the garage coming to collect the car tomorrow?' 'They said they'll be here around 9am', replied Linda. 'That's good, it'll make a big difference when they repair my interior handle, it's a bloody nuisance because I can't open my driver's door from the inside, I have to slide along and climb out of the passenger's door every time, it's a right pain!' answered James before disappearing and closing the front door behind him.

Linda had put the children's coats on and was just about to stretch into the cupboard under the stairs to get her coat off the hook when she heard James' key in the door. He flew in shouting, 'Quick Linda, call an ambulance, there's been a terrible accident!' Linda shouted back, 'What? Where?' James yelled, 'Just call an ambulance quick and bring out some towels!' Linda ran into the front room to where the phone was, she froze on the spot when she peered out the window, there right in front of their house three cars were mangled and steam or smoke was rising from them. It looked like two cars travelling in the opposite direction had collided and crashed into a parked car. As Linda pulled the number 9 on the dial round three times, she looked out her front room window and saw James yank the door off one car and froze as she watched him jump into it *'what on earth is he doing?'* she thought to herself. She gave all the details to the emergency operator, then ran to her cupboard and grabbed a bundle of towels, albeit that it was her best towels that they had received in wedding presents because they didn't really have much.

She ran out and there was a man sitting on a dining chair at the side of her house outside Mr. Halliday's yard, his head was covered in blood, as Linda went to offer him a towel, he adamantly pushed her away, she said, 'the towels are clean, they'll just help to soak up the blood,' but the man was determined that he didn't want to be cleaned up. Linda couldn't help but notice the reek of alcohol coming from him. Mr. Halliday shook his head in despair and told Linda, 'he said he doesn't want any help, he just wants an ambulance! I tell you Linda, your James is a real hero; he should get some sort of recognition for this! I was just about to lock up and go home for the day when I heard this almighty bang. By the time I had run out I saw these two cars had collided, James' had already sprung into action! That car on the left is this man's here, he was on his own, and the other car had four men in it. James jumped in and switched off the engine on this man's car because it was revving and revving and could have started a fire, he got this man out and helped the other three men who are sitting on the wall over there to get out their car, the driver is trapped behind the steering wheel, it looks like he'll need to be cut out but your James is keeping him talking and trying to take the poor man's mind off everything. Just at that a young policeman turned up, followed by two ambulances and two fire brigades. The policeman tried to talk to the man on the chair but he wouldn't respond to the policeman. An ambulance man wrapped some bandages around his head and put him in the ambulance. James came over to Linda and Mr. Halliday and said, 'the leg of that guy in the car is badly trapped, the ambulance man is looking after him while the fire brigade try to cut him free! I've got to say though, every one of them reek of alcohol, it's obvious that the four guys in the car coming down the road were coming from the pub at the top of the street and the guy in the car on his own was coming from the pub at the bottom of the street, look at the time, twenty minutes after Sunday lunch closing time! Bloody idiots they could have killed someone, just as well there was no-one in that parked car, if it had been seconds earlier it could have been me because I was sitting in my car!' Linda shuddered at the thought of what could have happened then said, 'That guy who was sitting here refused my help, he wouldn't accept a towel to clean the blood from his face!' said Linda. 'He's not silly, he knows that if he got cleaned up and his wounds didn't look too bad then the police would have breathalysed him but once he's in an ambulance and under the care of the hospital they can't touch him' replied James. 'Ah so that's why he was so anxious to get into an ambulance!' said Mr. Halliday.

Two more police cars turned up just as the second ambulance pulled away, the young police constable stood there nervously with his note pad and pencil in hand, he looked like a new recruit. Out of the back of the one of the police cars stepped an inspector, he stood at least 6ft 4ins and marched up to the rookie copper, looked down at him and bellowed, 'Right what's going on here and what are you doing about it?' 'I-I'm just trying to work out who or what caused the collision sir,' answered the young constable.' 'AND?' questioned the inspector. 'Well the men in the car that was travelling south said that their car swerved to avoid something!' replied the constable. 'What could that have been then mmm?' asked the inspector with his hands clasped behind his back and rocking back and forward from his toes to his heels. 'Well one of them thought it was a white car,' answered the young constable. 'The inspector looked out from under the skip of his hat and said, 'That's a white car over there, have you looked at it?' 'No sir' replied the constable. 'WELL GET ON WITH IT!' insisted the inspector almost bullying the young constable. The young constable followed the inspector over to James' car then the inspector shouted out, 'Does anyone here own this car?' James looked at Linda and said 'Why are they looking at my car?' then he shouted back 'Yes It belongs to me!' 'Why are you parked here?' the inspector asked James. 'James looked puzzled; 'Because I live here!' he answered. 'Open your door!' instructed the inspector as he stood on the road by the driver's door of James' car. James took his keys out and did as he was told. 'Demonstrate to me how far your door opens?' said the inspector. James did as the inspector requested, he couldn't get the gist of what he was on about. Then the inspector instructed the young constable, 'That's it, charge him, it's obvious he opened his door to get out of his car and caused the accident.' James couldn't believe what he was hearing. 'What! You're not trying to blame me, my car door doesn't even open from the inside' at that the young constable stepped in front of James, he seemed to have a false sense of importance encouraged by his bullying inspector as he cautioned James 'Sir I must warn you that anything you say may be taken down and used in evidence against you.' James reeled back. Linda came running over with the two children followed by Mr. Halliday, 'He didn't do anything wrong, he helped everyone,' pleaded Linda then Mr. Halliday piped up, 'This man deserves a medal for his bravery today not blamed for the accident, it was nothing to do with him, if these guys hadn't been drinking they wouldn't have had an accident, this is outrageous!' 'Sir, I must warn you to not to get involved other wise I will charge you! You are obstructing police in their enquires.' Said the young constable, with his 'new-found' confidence, to Mr. Halliday.

Linda and James went back indoors to reflect on the events of the morning. James tried to be brave but he was clearly hurt and confused that the police had taken the easy option by blaming him for the accident. It was obvious that the two drivers and passengers of each car were sozzled with alcohol. Linda felt herself getting more angry towards the police, as she told James, 'How dare they blame you, you are totally innocent, how many others would do as you did? You showed great initiative and care, you did your best to help five drunken bums who had put everyone else's life in danger by driving their cars while under the influence of alcohol, these men should be made an example of, not the hero who risked his own safety by helping them! I am fuming! The police are being lazy and just looking for a scapegoat! It's a disgrace, what encouragement does this give to law abiding citizens to help out in an emergency!' 'None whatsoever. I, for one, will never stop and assist at the scene of an accident again or ever help the police in any way for fear that I end up getting accused of something I never did,' replied James who by this time was feeling pretty dejected. Linda gave him a big cuddle as she said, 'James it's just another hurdle we have to overcome, we've had so many ups and downs in the past couple of years. Don't worry at least we still have each other, we'll get through this!' she lovingly tried to reassure her worried husband. James answered 'We were going to have a nice family day out today, something very rare because I usually work all day, seven days a week and now these selfish drunken bastards have not only ruined my kids day out but I also have a possible court case hanging over my head, I wish I had worked all day now, I would be miles from here and these arse-holes would still have had their accident, they didn't deserve any help from anyone for getting behind the wheels of their cars in that state, who would the police have blamed then? My car door doesn't even open from the inside, for God's sake! Sod it, I'm not going to let them spoil the kid's fun, right let's get in the car and get the hell out of here, we'll go to Windsor as planned to meet Douglas and Norma.' 'Are you sure you feel up to it after all that has happened today?'

Linda asked. 'I'm more than up to it! I'm not going to let idiots spoil the little time that I am able to enjoy with my children!' replied James determinedly. Forty minutes later they met up with Douglas, Norma and their daughters by the riverside at Windsor, they apologized for being late and related their horrible day's events to them. Douglas and Norma were shocked, especially at the police who, instead of doing a proper enquiry, chose to take the easy option by blaming an innocent and perfectly sober man for causing an accident between two drunken drivers and their equally drunk passengers.

The following evening Daniel came to see James and Linda and told him that one of the drivers, who's face had been splattered with blood and had refused a towel to clean himself up had been overheard telling others in a local pub that he managed to give the police the slip and escaped a breathalyzer by refusing help at the scene of the accident and insisting on going to hospital. Apparently the police were waiting to speak to him at the casualty department but the doctor's wouldn't allow this until he had been examined. Once this had been done and he was cleaned up, he asked if he could go to the toilet and made a quick get-a-way from the hospital. He seemed quite pleased with himself. Daniel also told them that the driver who had to be cut free from the other car was still very ill in hospital; he and his passengers were Irish. Linda and James were very angry that the guy who had been in his car on his own was openly boasting about his drunk-driving escapades while they were worried sick about the consequences of being wrongly accused. 'What if the other driver should die, will they do me for manslaughter?' said a seriously worried James. Linda shivered with fear at the thought of it, 'Don't even go into that? He's not going to die!' she tried to convince James. 'Can you be sure of that?' answered James, nervously wringing his hands.

September 1974 and it was Stuart's first day at school. It was a miserable morning, the rain was pouring down, Linda got Amanda into her pushchair, she pushed the back rest up so that Stuart could sit on the little ledge facing her and back to back with Amanda under the hood to keep dry. He wasn't very keen on the idea of going to school and when they got there Linda reported to Mrs. Peterson in Class 10 as instructed. Stuart looked nervously at his mum as if to say, *'You're not going to leave me here I hope!'* Linda just wanted to scoop him up and take him back home again but she knew this wasn't an option. Meanwhile, while Stuart was determined he wasn't going to leave his mummy's side, Amanda was in the corner of the classroom talking and playing with the other children. 'Oh dear, it looks like you are leaving the wrong one!' laughed Mrs. Peterson. Then she took Stuart by the hand and showed him his peg with his name on it. 'This is where you have to hang your coat every morning, look it says S-T-U-A-R-T,' she said as she pointed to his name and slowly pronounced it.

Mrs. Peterson gave all the mums a pattern for a chair back that they had to make for the children to keep their books in. *'That's a job for gran'* Linda thought to herself, she could just about take up a hem and sew on a button but that was her limit as far as sewing went, not like her mum who was a sheer genius with a needle and a thread.

The following week Amanda was due to start playgroup two mornings per week. The playgroup was at the opposite side of town to the school, it started at 9.30am which didn't leave Linda much time to get there after taking Stuart to school so Linda's friend Sharon agreed to take Stuart to school on these mornings to allow her to drop Amanda off.

The first morning Amanda was really excited about going to playgroup and couldn't wait to get there, she loved going to school with Stuart, Linda had to drag her out of the classroom every morning. As soon as they went in the gate leading to the church hall in Norbiton. Amanda ran on ahead, she couldn't wait to get in there. Linda hurried in the door after her, by which time Amanda was over in the corner sitting on a rocking horse. Linda had a word with the playgroup supervisor, 'I think she'll be ok, she has no trouble mixing and interacting with other kids,' 'I can see that,' answered the supervisor with a smile. At that Linda paid her 50p for the morning's fee, had another quick glance to make sure Amanda was ok and left. It was just going on for quarter to ten, Linda walked in to town with Amanda's empty pushchair to get some shopping, she had to be back to pick Amanda up by mid-day which gave her a couple of hours to get round the shops. When she got back to playgroup, she was delighted to see Amanda happily engrossed and playing in the tub of sand with a couple of other children. Linda went over and asked her if she had enjoyed her morning, Amanda nodded at her mummy without looking up. After a few minutes Linda said, 'Well c'mon then, it's time to go home, say bye-bye to your friends, you'll see them again on Wednesday.' Amanda shook her head, 'I want to stay,' she told her mummy, Linda laughed, 'Well you will be very lonely because everyone's going home,' Amanda reluctantly put her coat on and climbed into her pushchair. Linda could see that her wee girl was sleepy; her morning at playgroup had been great fun but had tired her out.

James got a letter to appear in court on the second Tuesday in November, charged with causing the accident outside their house. He and Linda's stomach's churned at the thought of it, they had always been good citizens, James hadn't done anything wrong but how was he going to prove it against police evidence that wrongfully said he was guilty!

James went to see the citizen's advice bureau and explained his dilemma, telling them that he couldn't afford time off work never mind a solicitor, especially for something that he hadn't done. They told him how to claim legal aid and recommended Miss. Stoppard, a solicitor in Hampton Wick. James made an appointment to see the solicitor the next afternoon; she was a buxom lady, with tight permed dark hair. She was wearing a smart two-piece blue suit; and a white blouse. She appeared to be in her mid to late 40's. She listened to James' story and his version of the events of that dreaded day with interest and said that she would be happy to take on his case.

A couple of days later the solicitor called to say that it wasn't looking good because the police were adamant that James caused the accident by opening his car door but the good news was that the driver who had been very ill had made a good recovery and was out of hospital. James explained to her that, at that time, his car door couldn't open from the inside because the handle was broken. 'Have you any proof of this?' the solicitor asked. 'Only the bill from the garage who repaired it the day after the accident, oh and my wife, she can vouch for it!' replied James. 'Ok, give me the garage bill and we'll have your wife as a witness.'

Linda felt the nerves in her stomach doing somersaults with fear when James told her that she would have to stand in the witness box in court but she was determined to do all she could to get her innocent man cleared of the convictions against him.

The day arrived for James and Linda to attend court; they had to be there for 9am. Linda arranged for her friend Sharon to pick the kids up at 8.30am to take Stuart to school and look after Amanda for the day. Linda and James gave Stuart and Amanda big kisses and hugs and told them they would pick them up at Sharon's later then they set off for the Magistrates Court.

They made their way into the building; they had never been inside a court in their lives before. They were directed downstairs to the basement, it seemed cold with dark wood, and green leather bench seats. Miss Stoppard was waiting for them and greeted both James and Linda warmly. She could see that they were both very nervous and tried to calm them down by telling them that, hopefully, they shouldn't be too long in court. 'You will have to wait here until you're called as a witness Mrs. Alexander,' the solicitor told Linda. Linda held onto James hand so tight that her knuckles were going white. She felt for him so much and didn't want to let him go in there on his own.

Before she got a chance to think about it, James had disappeared into the courtroom with his solicitor. Linda sat outside shaking and worrying about her poor husband, she felt her stomach coming up to her mouth with nerves. After about half an hour she was called to be a witness. Linda nervously made her way into the courtroom and took her place in the witness box. She raised her right hand as she was asked to read the oath to tell the truth. The police prosecutor then went on to try to tie Linda in knots by asking why her husband was out in the car, how long had he been out there, what was she doing at the time, Linda stayed as calm as she possibly could, she looked across the courtroom at the one Englishman and four Irishmen who had been in the two cars involved and as she did so they looked away, she could see that they were all as guilty as hell, she felt her anger build up again at the thought of them attempting to blame her hard-working, clean living husband for their drunken binge that caused their cars to crash. The prospect of them getting off Scot-free and James being made their scape-goat gave her the boost of confidence she needed, she answered the police prosecutor's questions with as much courage as she could muster. Eventually he said 'no more questions' then James solicitor stood in front of Linda and asked her to go through the details of that dreaded day. The solicitor questioned Linda as to where the car was parked and which way it was facing then she asked Linda if there was anything different about the car that the court should know about. 'Yes!' replied Linda as she lifted her head away from the solicitor and stared across at the guilty-looking pathetic excuses for men standing opposite her. 'The lock on the driver's door of our car was broken and could not be opened from the inside, only the outside!' Linda watched as one by one the five guilty men looked at each other and bowed their heads as if in shame of being hit with the truth.

Linda watched as her brave husband stood up to take the oath of truth. She wanted to get up there with him to give him support as the bullying police prosecutor attempted to confuse James into confessing to something he hadn't done. She was glad when James' solicitor took over and was more gentle with him, the true story then came out but would the court believe James or the lying, deceitful drunken bums who were driving their cars that terrible day.

The magistrate announced that there would be a recession while they reached a verdict and instructed that everyone was to leave the courtroom and sit in the corridor outside. The solicitor approached Linda and James and said with a smile 'It's looking good, very seldom does the magistrate have a recession to reach a verdict, he must have doubts about the police evidence, which is most unusual because usually when the police prosecute it's just accepted that they are the ones telling the truth. Just at that the solicitor was called away, she came back to James and Linda five minutes later and fed them the bad news that the police weren't happy that their evidence was in doubt and told the solicitor that if the magistrate was to find James not guilty then they would be taking the case further to a higher court. James and Linda looked at each other in disbelief, 'Why are they doing this to us, we haven't done anything wrong, why don't they prosecute the real culprits' cried Linda. At that moment everyone was called back into the courtroom. They took their places and sat in silence as the magistrate looked over his specs waiting for everyone to settle down, then he announced that after lots of deliberation, he found James Alexander guilty of causing the accident. Linda looked at the magistrate then James in disbelief, James seemed to reel back as the colour drained from his face, she wanted to shout out *'No, he's innocent, he cares about people, he doesn't deserve this, these men in the two cars were all drunk!'* but she composed herself and listened in a blur as the magistrate went on to say that James had to pay a fine of £100 plus costs. Linda was close to tears, life was a struggle as it was, where were they going to get all this money from? The solicitor asked the magistrate for time to pay and was granted six weeks. Linda and James were both shaking as they left the court, Linda couldn't help her tears flowing, she caught sight of these men in the corridor and they sheepishly turned away, one looked at Linda as if to say 'sorry'. Then Linda couldn't help herself as she said in a voice loud enough for them to hear, 'I hope they're satisfied, they know fine well that they have convicted an innocent man, the only ones who will suffer is our kids because they won't have a Christmas this year!'

The next day, Linda went up to the court to arrange to pay the fine by installments. She didn't know where on earth James and she were going to get over £20 per week for the next six weeks from, she wished she had never agreed to come down to England to live, if they had stayed in Scotland, this stupid accident would still have happened and with no-one else to blame, maybe then the drunken culprits in the cars who were responsible for causing the collision would have been brought to justice!

Linda and James sat down that evening and looked at their financial situation, 'You know even though you earned less money in Scotland, the rent was only a fraction of what we pay here, now with the worry of this fine round our necks, we're a lot worse off!' Linda told James. 'I know but what do we do? If we don't pay the fine, I go to jail!' replied James. Linda shuddered at the thought of her honest, law-abiding husband being behind bars. 'Don't worry, it won't come to that, we'll get by, I'll ask Len for more evening shifts at the club, he'll probably be glad of extra help behind the bar in the run up to Christmas!' answered Linda trying to appear confident.

Len was happy to help Linda and James out and Linda found herself working Sunday, Monday, Wednesday and Friday nights at the club. This brought in £16 per week although it wasn't enough to cover the weekly payment towards the fine, it was better than nothing. On the nights that Linda wasn't working, James worked over-time, he was working in an office building and part of the job was putting up partitioning between the offices so it was more convenient to do this after the staff had gone home at 5pm.

Linda found herself borrowing from Peter to pay Paul in order to pay bills, she held some things back and only paid the minimum asked. She and James consoled themselves with the fact this was only a temporary set-back and once the six weeks were up, they could get their finances back to normal. It still left them the problem of Christmas and how they were going to buy their kids presents. Linda went to a Christmas fair at the school; she bought a second-hand doll for Amanda for 25p plus a wee toy cooker with plastic pot and pans for 30p. For Stuart she purchased a second-hand crane for 30p and six wee second-hand dinky cars for 25p. Linda also managed to get a pack of four second-hand board games for 30p. This was all she and James could afford for their kid's Christmas this year. On the nights that Linda wasn't working and after the kids had gone to bed, Linda dug out oddments of wool left over from the baby outfits she knitted when she was pregnant. She knitted two dresses, two jackets and two hats for the second-hand doll that she got for Amanda. She also cleaned up all the second-hand toys to make them look as good as new. Christmas was going to be bleak, Linda felt guilty seeing her kids getting all excited about Christmas and hearing what other kids were expecting to get.

Linda explained to her parents, James' mother and her brother and his wife that they couldn't buy anyone presents this Christmas because of what had happened. The family were all worried for them and were also annoyed that they had suffered this injustice.

Linda and James couldn't afford to buy proper Christmas decorations so Linda bought some crepe paper and some gummed coloured paper strips, she sat with the kids and together they made paper chains to hang in the house for Christmas. When an office, in which James was carrying out carpentry work, bought a new Christmas tree he was lucky enough to save the old silver imitation one from the scrap heap. He asked if he could have it and the office supervisor was only too happy to give it to him. Linda saved her yellow and blue polystyrene egg boxes, she cut out the little egg cup shapes from them and the kids had great fun pasting them with glue and dipping them in glitter, then Linda sewed a piece of thread through them and the children hung them on the Christmas tree. They couldn't afford fancy lights but the tree looked grand with its glittery 'egg-cup' bells hanging on it.

The week before Christmas a parcel arrived for the children, it was from Linda's parents, Douglas and Margie, who sent them two books each, a post office set, a wee carpenter's set, a warm jumper and socks for both the children, toy jewellery, a wee toy double-decker bus and a selection box each. An envelope also arrived, inside were two cards with £1 note each in them for Stuart and Amanda's Christmas from James' mum Molly. Linda used Molly's money to take her children see Santa Claus at Bentalls Department store, Stuart got a 'Magic Card' game and Amanda got a 'Crotchet Set.'

On Christmas Eve, James dug out two of his largest socks that his mother, Molly, had knitted for him, Linda helped Stuart and Amanda write their names on a piece of paper and they hung the socks on the fireplace in the front room. 'What about something for Santa?' Stuart asked his mum and dad as he jumped up and down hardly able to contain himself. 'Oh yes, what about a beer for Santa?' said James. 'N-o-o-o-o', Santa doesn't drink beer, he drinks milk!' laughed Stuart. 'Oh right, we'd better leave him out some milk then,' replied James. Linda went through to the kitchen and as she opened the fridge door, Stuart came running in shouting, 'Don't forget a biscuit for Rudolph, my teacher said that he likes digestive ones!' 'Oh well then if that's what the teacher said then it must be true eh!' Linda answered in mock belief. They left out a glass of milk and two digestive biscuits by the fireplace for Santa and Rudolph then Linda took Stuart and Amanda up to bed and told them a bedtime story. 'Goodnight my precious wee babies, remember, straight to sleep now because Santa won't come down the chimney and leave presents for you if you're still awake' she said as she kissed them gently on their foreheads. Linda smiled as both Stuart and Amanda closed their eyes tightly in determined exaggeration.

Just before 6am on Christmas morning, Stuart and Amanda came running into James' and Linda's bedroom and wakened them up shouting 'Has he been yet?' I don't know, maybe daddy knows? laughed Linda. 'Well there's only one way to find out, lets go downstairs and see' replied James. 'YES!' the kids screamed with delight. Linda pulled on her quilted dressing gown, and then they all made their way to the stairs. The kids stood in front of James and Linda, and then James said 'Right on the count of three, open the front room door.' Stuart and Amanda were ecstatic with excitement, they all counted ONE----TWO---THREEEE....and burst into the room. They put their hand into their stocking's to reveal a ten pence piece, a tangerine, an apple and crayons in each one. Linda had a tear in her eye watching her children laughing and giggling as they played with their new toys, they didn't know that most of them were second-hand and it didn't seem to matter. She was thankful for the kindness of their parents for helping to make, what could have been a disastrous Christmas, so special for the children.

Eight

January 1975, Linda breathed a sigh of relief as the court cashier rubber stamped the final installment of James' fine 'Paid in Full'. The few months since the dreadful day that accident happened outside their house had been a strain and the last six weeks finding the money to settle the unjust fine that James was ordered to pay had been very difficult.

Linda was getting ready to go out to her evening job. James gave her a big bear hug as he said, 'Thank goodness, all that horrible business is behind us. It was like a bad dream, I still can't believe that we actually managed to pay all that money off in six weeks. At the time I thought we'd never do it and I would end up in jail for not paying my fine! Just goes to show what we can do when we put our minds to it but now we can relax and you can give up your extra nights. Thank you so much for standing by me Linda, I don't know how I could have come through this without you!'

'We-ell' replied Linda, 'I was thinking, as we have shown just how much we can save when we put our minds to it, we could turn this negative incident into something positive!' 'How do you mean?' frowned James. Linda answered slowly as if she was making sure James would digest what she meant before jumping to the wrong conclusion,

'I thought that if we carry on like this, I mean, I know it will be hard, but we could raise a deposit and approach Mr. Halliday to see if he will sell this house to us!' James let go his grip around her waist, he looked her in the eye as he pursed his lip and put his head to the side as if in deep thought. 'Yes....yes,' he said slowly nodding his head, 'you might have a very good point there, but it won't be easy!'

For the next few months James and Linda worked all the hours they could between them and by summertime they had saved just over £500. Linda made enquiries with the local council who confirmed that she and James were eligible for a council mortgage. 'I think it's time to approach Mr. Halliday and tell him what's on our minds, shall I pop in and see him tomorrow?' Linda asked James. 'Good idea, we should have just about enough for a deposit now!' agreed James.

The next morning Linda took Stuart to school, then she took Amanda by the hand and went next door to see Mr. Halliday. 'Well hello, to what do I owe this pleasure,' smiled the kindly old gent. Linda was excited but apprehensive as she explained their plans to him. Mr. Halliday listened intently with a serious expression. Linda waited for him to say *'Ok, get your mortgage organized and it's yours.* He looked down, crossed his legs and he reached for is pipe, tapped it a couple of times, before refilling it and lighting it. Linda waited in anticipation, she felt like shouting out *'come on, say you agree!'* Mr. Halliday looked down then looked straight into Linda's eyes with a serious expression. 'I'm afraid, we're not selling the house, you see, over the last few weeks, my wife and I have had in depth conversations about our future. The kids are all grown up, the older ones have moved into their own flats and our youngest is leaving this September when he starts university. Our family house is too big so we've decided that, we'll sell it, sell the business and move into your house for our retirement, I'm sorry if that's not what you wanted to hear.' Linda reeled back, she was devastated, 'Oh it doesn't matter,' she heard herself say, then she thought to herself, *'IT DOES MATTER! If Mr. Halliday and his wife want to move into our house, where does that leave us?'* So she blurted out in a stammer, 'When.....when were you thinking about moving into our house?' 'Well, my wife and I figured that James and yourself wouldn't want to stay there forever paying a rent so we thought that you might be considering leaving within the next year or two, we decided we'd give it two years in order to allow you to give us notice rather than the other way round' replied Mr. Halliday. Linda looked at him with a sad expression and said, 'We love the house, James has done so much to it, we thought that we were going to be living there for a long time. We've got the deposit to buy it. Are you sure you won't change your mind and sell it to us?' she asked Mr. Halliday in a pleading manner. Mr. Halliday sympathized with her and apologised once more as he confirmed that his wife and himself had made up their minds to move into the house. Linda thanked him for putting her in the picture and took wee Amanda by the hand as she made to walk out the door, Mr. Halliday shouted after her. 'No hard feelings Linda?' He was a nice man and Linda could see that he was genuinely upset at having to deliver this bad news to her. She turned her head and as she went out the door she smiled and repeated quietly, 'No hard feelings'.

That evening she sobbed as she told James of Mr. & Mrs. Halliday's plans. 'I honestly think that he's seen how nice this house is since you've done all the work on it and he's had second thoughts about it!' I mean we've even put a new front door on!' James pulled his wife up close and wiped away her tears with his hands as he said, 'Never mind, it's not the end of the world, there'll be other houses! The most important thing is that we're not afraid of hard work and we've proved we can do it! We've saved up the deposit so let's get out there and see what houses are available in our price range.' Linda's lips quivered, 'Yes, but I had my heart set on this house, I was sure that Mr. Halliday would sell it to us because it was a junk heap when we moved into it and he just didn't seem interested in it. We've spent money on it and now he wants it back, I feel like he's used us! I actually imagined that he would give us a discount as sitting tenants, can you believe that?' Linda said blowing her nose and wiping the tears from her eyes.

Monday morning Linda went to the estate agents. Their price range was £10,500. Linda brought home pamphlets with details of houses for sale for James to see. They decided they would look at a house in Chessington; it was detached and similar to the one they lived in. They made arrangements to view it the following Saturday afternoon. It was a lovely house, or at least it could be a lovely house, it stunk of animals! The family that lived in it had four dogs and umpteen cats, the kitchen was thick with grease, the sink was piled high with dirty dishes and pots, there wasn't a clear space anywhere, guinea pigs and white mice were in cages on the kitchen worktop amongst the mess, parrots, canaries and budgies were in cages scattered around the house. Linda had never seen anything like it, dogs and cats were running in front of them and tripping them up as they tried to make their way upstairs to look at the bedrooms which were cluttered. The bathroom was filthy, the sink was cracked, the toilet pan had no seat on it and the bath was piled high with dirty clothes. They thanked the family and walked back to there car. 'God I feel itchy, I'm going to bath the kids as soon as we get home then I'm having a bath after them, that house was bogging. I don't want to risk any of us catching anything,' said Linda. 'Yes, but what do you think about the house itself, forget the dirt and mess?' James asked her. 'I like the house, it has great potential but it would have to be fumigated before we moved in' Linda answered. 'It needs a lot spent on it, I would say at least a grand, I don't think it's worth £10,500, considering the condition it's in I would only be prepared to offer them £9000, we'll need the extra money to spend on refurbishing it!'.

Linda called the estate agent and told them what they were prepared to offer. Within the hour the estate agent called back and told them that the vendor refused their offer, he said that they weren't prepared to drop below £10,000. Linda said, 'Well, I'm sorry but it needs too much spent on it, we have to allow for that, so we can't offer more than £9,000!' 'I know you're right, we've tried to tell the vendor this but they are sitting tight!' answered the estate agent. 'Right then I suppose we'll just have to call it a day then, send me on anything else you have in that price range please will you?' replied Linda firmly as she hung up the phone.

They viewed their next house just over a week later. It was in a side street on the borders of Kingston and Surbiton and was on the market for a bit more than their budget at £11,250. 'It's hard to believe, its mid terrace and not as big as the one in Chessington yet they're asking £750 more for it!' exclaimed Linda. 'Yes, but houses are shooting up in price at a frightening rate at the moment, practically £500 per week! It said in the daily paper that people are so desperate to buy before the houses get out of their price range and gazumping is ripe all over the place!' answered James.

It was an immaculate little house with three bedrooms, an old couple had lived there all their married life and they were moving up north to be near their married daughter. Linda and James liked it and stretched to their limit to offer the vendor £11,000. Happily their offer was accepted so Linda excitedly went to the council to collect the mortgage application forms and get the wheels in motion to buy their first house. She was told that when they submitted the forms they would have to pay £75 for a surveyors report on the property. They never realized all the hidden costs that came with buying a house; however they managed to scrape up the extra money and waited patiently for results.

Two weeks later they got a letter from the council telling them that they were refusing them a mortgage on this house because the survey had shown that the property was subsiding. Linda called the council to ask if there was anyway the council would reconsider. 'Only if the vendor put it right and that won't be cheap! Take our advice and steer clear, it will only end up costing you a fortune! You've already lost the money you forked out for the survey!' Linda took their advice and decided to forget about it.

Linda fingered through some estate agents leaflets 'This isn't going to be easy trying to get on the house ownership bandwagon, it seems pointless looking at these house details, they are being snapped up practically the same day they appear on the market! If you're not in the know, you miss your chance meanwhile the prices just keep rising!' Linda told James with a deflated mood.

Two weeks later, they saw a little end of terrace house in a tiny street off Richmond Road, near the river and about ten minutes walk from the town centre. It was only a small house with two bedrooms, a tiny front room with an even smaller back room and a kitchen that you couldn't turn around in but there was room for extension and Linda knew James capabilities and that he loved a challenge. The problem was that it was up for sale at £11,750. Linda and James had saved a bit more in the last few weeks so they went in at the deep end and offered £11,500. The old man that owned it seemed very nice; he was selling up to move in with a lady friend so there was no chain to worry about. He was delighted with their offer and accepted it immediately. 'Third time lucky then' James said to Linda as they climbed into their car. 'I sincerely hope so,' she sighed in reply. They paid the council £80 for the survey on this property; everything seemed to be going up in price by the minute. They hugged each other in sheer relief when two weeks later the council wrote to say that they were satisfied with the survey and they were now processing their mortgage. They were told that they would be ready to exchange contracts in four weeks.

Linda and James started gradually packing some things. 'I can't believe we've done it! In less than a couple of months we will own our very own house!' Linda exclaimed excitedly to James. 'We were really lucky to get in when we did because there's nothing out there under £12,000 now!' James told her. 'I know it's frightening, if it keeps going at this rate an average house in this area will he £15,000 by the end of the year, how are people meant to afford that? At least we'll be sitting pretty, once we've moved into our new place it won't matter if the price rises!' replied Linda.

Four weeks passed, Linda and James were to pay the deposit and exchange contracts on Friday morning, they could hardly contain themselves. James got home from work just before 5pm on the Thursday evening, 'Well only a few more hours to go and it will be all signed and sealed,' said Linda as she hugged her husband in delight. Just at that the phone rang and James picked it up. 'What? He can't do that! We've waited six weeks for this! Talk to him! He wouldn't do that to us!' Linda heard James voice getting louder and more angry as she said, 'What's wrong? What's happened?' James slammed the phone down and shouted. 'The bastards only gazumped us at the eleventh hour!' 'What? He can't do that?' cried Linda 'Well he just has, that was our solicitor, he's not very happy with him either, apparently the old guy's friend has offered him £12,000 cash sale….friend my arse! It's obvious he's taken a higher offer form another punter, the greedy old bastard!' shouted James in temper. 'How could he do this to us? This means we've lost £80 in surveyors fees and not only that, we have to save up more money now for a deposit because six weeks have passed since we agreed the deal and house prices have shot up in that time, we'll be lucky if we can get anything under £13,000 now! It's useless we'll never be able to afford a house of our own; we just seem to be chasing the carrot all the time! What a mean selfish thing to do and I thought he was a nice old man too!' sobbed Linda. James was overcome with anger on seeing his wife's upset and disappointment. He grabbed his jacket and said, 'I'm going to have a word with the old bastard!' 'No James, don't do anything in temper, it's not your place to discuss it with him, that's what solicitors are for!' pleaded Linda. James put his hands on Linda's shoulders and said, 'Don't worry, I'm not going to do anything silly, I just want to put our case to him and ask him to reconsider,' before Linda could stop him James was in his car and off!

James came back half an hour later, he told Linda, 'The old sod didn't want to know, I asked him nicely if he would reconsider and told him how this will set us back because we will have to foot the bill for surveyors fees with nothing at the end of it. I also reminded him that house prices have risen another grand in the past six weeks so by pulling out so late in the deal he is potentially ruining our chance of getting on the property ladder because we now have to struggle to find money for more surveyors fees for another property plus a steeper deposit and hope that the council will give us a bigger mortgage. I tried appealing to his better nature and mentioned how heartbroken you were and the financial strain he was putting us under. I asked him where his heart was to do a thing like this at the last minute, after six weeks and the night before we were due to exchange contracts! But he didn't care and didn't want to know, he just kept repeating that his friend had offered him £12,000 cash! I said to him to tell the truth, that there was no friend and that it was obvious he was gazumping us at the last minute for more money! He closed the door on me. I'm afraid I lost it, I kicked his door and shouted that he was greedy, selfish old bastard!' Linda cuddled her husband as she said emotionally 'There's nothing else for it, we'll just have to pick up the pieces and start again!'

It was August 1975, Linda decided that she would try to get a full time job back in book-keeping to help save as she was finding going out working four nights a week as well as looking after the house and children a strain. She went into an agency in town to enquire what sort of work was available to her. They informed her that they had a permanent vacancy in a large company in Kingston, the job was in credit control but pretty similar to what Linda had done in the office she worked in, in Glasgow before she had Stuart. Linda then had to think about someone to look after Amanda as well as take Stuart and pick him up again from school. Her friend Sharon told her about a very nice lady in the next street who had an excellent reputation for child-minding, apparently she had a vacancy so the very next day Linda went round with Amanda to see her. Elsie welcomed them both into her house, Amanda seemed to feel at home straight away, she played with the other kids while Linda spoke to Elsie about the hours she intended to work and fees etc. Elsie told Linda that she would have a vacancy at the start of the new school term at the beginning of September as one of the kids she looked after was starting school. She said that she would hold the place for Amanda but asked Linda to confirm it by the end of the week. She also agreed that Linda could drop Stuart off at her house and she would take him and collect him from school. Linda was delighted, she went back to the agency and they arranged for her to attend an interview at the company the next day.

Linda dropped Stuart and Amanda off at her friend Sharon's

house then she nervously walked into town. It had been almost six years since Linda had worked in an office and she was feeling quite apprehensive. Linda went into the reception area and told the girl at the desk that she was here to attend an interview. The girl told Linda to take a seat and someone would be down soon to get her. After almost five minutes a well dressed lady in her 40's walked through the door and introduced herself as Vanessa, she complimented Linda on her smart appearance then told her that she would be conducting the interview. They made their way through a maze of corridors before turning into an office at the end of a corridor. It was very modern with a pine desk, matching units and a big black leather settee. The interview only lasted twenty minutes, Linda felt quite relaxed, she liked the friendly atmosphere of this place and was even more overwhelmed when she heard the wage was £44 per week. Linda couldn't believe it, when she left her office supervisor's job in Glasgow in 1970 she wasn't even earning that a month but this was London and inflation had put everything up in price over the last few years including wages. She felt that she conducted herself well during the interview and gave Vanessa all the correct answers. As they left the office Vanessa then said, 'Let me show you where you will be working!' Linda's heart skipped a beat because this seemed to indicate that the job was hers. Vanessa led Linda into a big open-plan office with rows of desks, there was at least twelve people working there. 'Dawn, this is Linda,' then she turned to Linda and said,' Dawn's the supervisor and you will be working directly under her' said Vanessa as she introduced Linda to the glamorous blond girl in her mid thirties. Linda nervously shook her hand, 'Hello Linda, we work flexi-time here so as long as you do your forty hours per week you can stop and start anytime between 6am and 8pm, it works well because you can build up your hours and have the odd day off here and there!' smiled Dawn. Linda liked the idea of that. After ten minutes looking round the office Vanessa escorted Linda back to the front door and told her she would let the agency know by tomorrow.

Linda made her way back to the agency because they had asked her to drop in and let them know how the interview went. As she walked through the door, Tina, the girl who had arranged Linda's interview called out, 'Congratulations Linda,' 'What for? I haven't got the job yet, I've only attended an interview!' answered Linda. ''Ah that's where you are very much wrong, Vanessa has just called me and she would like to offer you the job!' beamed Tina. 'What! But she said she would let you know tomorrow.' exclaimed Linda in delight. 'Well she was very impressed with you and decided that there was no need to wait any longer. Well done! Because she has already turned down four girls I sent along, you obviously were the person she was looking for…so when can you start?' Linda's heart was beating fast with excitement; she arranged to start her new job in two weeks time at the beginning of September. She couldn't wait to tell James the good news. She handed in her notice at the club. Len told her he was very sorry to let her go and that there was always a job there for her if things didn't work out.

Linda had a serious discussion with James about their housing predicament, 'I am going to be earning good money so I think we should both work hard and save for the next six months. We should have a tidy wee sum put away and…' Linda hesitated then continued 'I would really like you to consider going back to Glasgow to buy a house, we're never going to get one here with all the gazumping that's going on, every time we save enough the prices go up again, we're banging our heads off a brick wall' Linda then waited for James' reaction. 'I don't know, it's all very well getting the deposit together but how do we pay the mortgage if I can't get a job? You know the work situation for joiners in Glasgow is non-existent whereas I have my choice of jobs in this part of the country!' answered James doubtfully. 'We'll get by, I can go back to work!' replied Linda confidently. 'And who's going to look after the kids?' enquired James. 'Amanda will be four at the end of the year and she will be starting school after summer next year so I can get a job between school hours,' answered Linda as if attempting to convince James. 'We'll see! We'll have to look into the work and housing situation in Glasgow before we make any decisions!' answered James. Linda looked disappointed, she missed her mum immensely and she knew that her parents would be overjoyed if they moved back to Glasgow because they loved their grandchildren and felt like they never saw enough of them. Stuart and Amanda thought the world of them; they loved their gran and grandpa to bits and always got excited when they saw them.

On the Sunday night before Linda started her new job, she got the children bathed and off to bed, then she laid out Stuart's school uniform, Amanda's clothes for the next day and a calf length black 'A' line skirt, smart white blouse, black jacket and black court shoes for her first day at work. She prepared mince for the next night's dinner, popped it in the oven and then soaked in a bath as she nervously thought about her return to the big world of business. It had been almost six years since she worked full time in an office and she felt like she was fifteen again and starting her first job but hoped that she would settle in and cope alright.

Monday morning and Linda was up at 6.30am. She got her hair and make up done before getting dressed. She peeled potatoes in preparation for that night's evening meal then she got the children up, washed and dressed before sitting them down to breakfast. Just after 8am Linda left the house with Stuart and Amanda and made her way round to Elsie's house. Stuart had his favourite toy fire engine with him and Amanda had her pull-along 'Snoopy Dog'. Elsie greeted them warmly with a big smile, Amanda went straight into the room where the toys were while Linda checked that Stuart had his sandwiches and everything he needed for school in his satchel before telling him that Elsie would be taking him and collecting him from school from now on. Stuart made his way into the playroom beside Amanda and two other young children, a boy of about four called Jason and a girl about three called Lorraine. Linda felt a sigh of relief as Stuart showed the little boy his toy fire engine, she bent down and gave her two children a big hug and kiss and said, 'be good for Elsie, mummy's off to work now, I'll collect you both at teatime!' but she might as well have been talking to herself because her children seemed more interested in what was in the toy box which put Linda at ease, it would have been terrible if they had cried as she left.

Linda walked down the road towards the town centre; her mind was working over-time, thinking about how her first day at work would go and worrying if she was doing the right thing. She got to her office, Dawn was there and she told her that the first thing she must do is clock in to build up her flexi-time. After doing this Dawn took her to the cloakroom to hang up her coat and then showed her to her desk which was three desks away from hers. Then Dawn got out a load of customer account cards and said to Linda 'There's quite a lot to take in but we'll start with these, don't worry you'll soon pick it up, it looks worse than it is but it's easy really!'

Linda wasn't sure if she liked the atmosphere in this big open-plan office, although everyone was friendly enough, it was a lot different to what she had been used to in previous offices she had worked, she likened it to a strict school classroom, you could hear a pin drop and everyone sat in rows with their heads down. Linda was studying the customers account cards when at one point she looked up from her desk with her pen in her mouth while deep in thought, immediately Dawn looked along and said, 'Is everything ok Linda?' 'Ye-es, yes its fine I was just studying the accounts and making sense of them all in my head' replied Linda. 'Oh just ask, if there's anything you need to know,' answered Dawn as if she was telling Linda not to worry but this was not Linda's style, she knew Dawn meant well but she liked to figure out and understand things for herself and would only ask as a last resort.

At 12 noon, Dawn said right I'm off to lunch now, would you like to come too Linda and I'll show you where the canteen is?' 'Ok,' replied Linda as she downed her pen, she was glad to get a break, her head was swimming with figures. As she walked out the door Dawn said, 'Isn't there something you've forgotten?' Linda looked around 'No, I have my handbag and my cardigan, the canteen's inside the building isn't it so I won't need my coat, will I?' Dawn laughed, 'No, not any of those things, you must clock out when you go for lunch but remember to clock back in again when you return, that is more important for your own benefit!' Linda and Dawn made their way along the long corridor and down a flight of stairs to the canteen. Linda felt quite uncomfortable, she was missing her children but this was only her first day and she realized that she would have to give it time.

On the way home that evening she reflected on her day, she really wasn't sure that she had done the right thing but realized that she would have to stick it out because they needed the money and she couldn't very well hand her notice in after only one day. She hurried up the road towards Elsie's house; she couldn't wait to see Stuart and Amanda. When she got there, she rang the door bell. Elsie's husband was home from work and he answered the door. 'Hello, I'm Ken, come on in,' Linda made her way through to the back room where the kids were playing. 'Well have you two behaved yourselves then?' Linda asked as she bent down and gave them both a cuddle. 'They have been as good as gold, Amanda ate up all her lunch and Stuart went into school no bother, he walked all the way there and back holding onto the other children's hands' answered Elsie.

Linda got home with the children just after 6pm, 'Daddy, daddy,' Stuart and Amanda screamed in delight as they entered the house and saw their daddy, James gave them both a kiss and tight cuddle before turning to Linda, he pulled her close into him and gave her a kiss then said, 'Well how was your first day?' Linda pursed her lips and said, 'we'll talk later, after we've got dinner out of the way and the kids are bathed and in bed.' James raised his eyebrows and nodded as if he realized that something wasn't quite right then he said, 'what did you intend to have for dinner tonight?' Linda replied, 'I prepared mince last night, it's in the fridge and just needs warming up in the oven, the potatoes are all peeled in a pot on top of the cooker, I did that early this morning before I got the kids up.' James answered, 'Right I'll see to everything, you relax and spend some time with Stuart and Amanda.'

After dinner James and Linda bathed their children then Linda tucked them up in bed with a bedtime story, she sang lullabies to them and finished up with their favourite one:

Sleep while thy fond mother sings
And the sweet birds fold their wings,
Now nature's voices are still,
Hushed is the wind on the hill,
See the bright moon in the sky,
Sailing so calmly on by,
Sleep dearest babes do not cry,
Mother will sing lullaby,
Sing lu-u-u-u-la-by
Sing lu-u-u-u-la-by

The children knew that when they heard this song that was the end of their stories and lullabies and they had to go to sleep but Linda always had a wee joke with them during this song and they waited excitedly for her to add a wee extra 'tra-la-la la la' in a silly voice between lines and they would giggle hysterically.

Linda came wearily downstairs; James cuddled her and said 'right now tell me all about your day!' Linda cuddled into her husband and raised her head to look up at him as she said, 'I'm not sure I can go through with this, the company is not like any I've worked for before, the people are ok but it is so regimental and I miss the kids so much, I feel guilty at leaving them,' Linda blurted out as she wiped the tears from her eyes. 'Look Linda you don't have to do this, if you're unhappy then don't go back,' said James consoling her. 'I can't do that, I've only been there one day, I have to give it time and besides the money will come in really handy in helping us to save for a deposit on a house should we return to Scotland,' answered Linda. James closed his eyes and bit his lip as he replied, 'Well it's up to you but don't do it if it's going to make you unhappy,' he really didn't want to return to Scotland because he knew that there wasn't any work there for him and they would be back to square one if they returned. Linda smiled and said, 'I won't but I have to stick it out for at least a month, even until Christmas to help make it a better Christmas for the kids than it was last year.'

November 1975 and James' contract finished on the job he was on. First thing in the morning, he called into a site at the top of their street and asked if they needed any carpenters. 'Sorry mate, we don't need any here but there's a site a couple of streets away you can try.' The site foreman told him. James drove round to the other site and asked for the site foreman. 'Aye mate, whit dae ye want?' asked the Glaswegian in his fifties with the weather-beaten face and bunnet as he walked toward him. 'I was just wondering if you had any vacancies for carpenters?' enquired James. 'Aye man, ye couldnae huv timed it better, ah need a second fixing joiner, can ye dae that?' 'No problem,' answered James, 'Right cin ye start the noo?' 'Aye, I mean yes' replied James.

James settled well into the site, he got on well with Hughie, the site foreman, who appreciated James' skills. Hughie told him that the executive houses on the site were originally built for the private market but a housing association in Manchester had come along and bought the lot, they got a loan from the local council on the condition that they gave 50% of the houses to people on the council house waiting list. 'Lovely houses, but there's no chance that I'll get one because we're not on the council waiting list' said James. 'Then apply to rent one privately' said Hughie. 'WHAT!" you mean the rest are for rent and not for sale?' answered James excitedly. 'That's right son' smiled Hughie with a glint in his eye. 'If yer interested, ah'll introduce ye tae the hoosin' manager, she's comin' doon at the end o' the week tae see the progress'. James couldn't believe what he was hearing, and exclaimed, 'I'm definitely interested!'

That evening he couldn't wait to tell Linda. 'It would be the end to our problems, if we got a nice brand new place at a reasonable rent, we can settle here. I know you were getting excited at the prospect of returning to Scotland but there just isn't the work for me there, besides Stuart is settling in so well at school it would mean that we wouldn't have to uproot him AND who knows we might even get the chance to buy the place eventually!' he told Linda, hoping that she would see the prospects in the same way as him. 'Well, it sounds too good to be true, if you ask me. This sort of luck never comes our way but I suppose it won't do any harm to give it a try' replied Linda. James was delighted and gave her a hug so tight that she was gasping for breath!

The next day he told Hughie that he had talked it over with his wife and they would like to know the procedure to take to apply for a house on the site although he emphasized that he realized there were only 30 houses for private rental so didn't hold out much chance of getting one but it was worth a try. 'Dinnie be so doubtful son, we'll get an application form fur ye tae fill in, as far as ah know nane o' the hooses have been allocated yet', said Hughie. James knew it was wrong to build up his hopes but he couldn't help himself.

On Friday, Hughie introduced James to Rita the housing manager. She was a calm hippy-type that oozed a relaxing atmosphere. 'I believe you would like an application form to rent one of the houses,' she said to James as she opened her brief case and handed him a form. 'Thanks, I mean thank-you!' blurted James nervously then he plucked up courage and asked her, 'What chance do we have of getting one?' 'As much chance as anyone, it depends on your answers, there is a point system. 'Well, we live in a privately rented house, but the landlord wants the house for his own use,' James told her. 'Then you'll be homeless,' answered Rita, 'well, yes' replied James. 'Then you should score enough points to qualify to be considered,' Rita told him. 'Is that right?' James asked her beaming from ear to ear. 'That's right,' smiled Rita, 'I'm around again tomorrow so if you can get your completed form back to me I can take it back to the office with me, Oh by the way, would you be interested in 3, 4 or 5 bedrooms?' Before he had a chance to answer Hughie chipped in with, 'He would like 5 bedrooms!' then he winked at James and whispered, *'there's only one 5 bedroom house ready and it was the original show-house, everything in it is up to first class standard.'*

James and Linda excitedly filled the form in that evening although they both still believed that they couldn't be that lucky.

The next day James handed the form to Rita, 'When can we expect to know anything?' he asked her. 'Well we'll be looking at all the applications over the next month but it will probably be after the

Christmas holidays before we get round to sending out letters to applicants to let them know if they have been successful or not. At a quick glance I would say that you shouldn't have a problem but it's not just down to me, there are others on the panel so I can't give you a definite, just put it out of your mind and enjoy Christmas.' Rita told James. James thanked her and walked away thinking how on earth he and Linda were going to get through the next few weeks with something as big as this on their minds, it wasn't just a house, it was the decider on their future because if this didn't happen James knew that they would be moving back to Scotland.

At the end of November Linda was still working and although Stuart and Amanda had settled in well with Elsie, Linda still felt guilty about leaving them, she missed them terribly. This was most likely contributing to the fact that she hated her job.

Stuart had cut his foot and it had become red and swollen, Linda was worried about it. She took him round to Elsie's and told her not to send him to school because when she got to work she was going to call her doctor to make an afternoon appointment for him. She had spare hours on flexi-time and knew that she could have the afternoon off. As` soon as she settled at her desk, she called the doctor. The snotty receptionist at the other end told her to bring her son along in an hour, Linda politely replied that she was at work and needed an afternoon appointment. To her immense upset the rude receptionist shouted down the phone at her that mothers like her shouldn't have children if they wanted to work and their place was at home with the children, she accused Linda of being uncaring. Linda burst into uncontrollable tears and put the phone down on the outspoken nasty receptionist. 'What's the matter Linda?' asked Dawn as she rushed over to her in genuine concern. When Linda told her Dawn retorted, 'Bloody interfering bitch, it's none of her damn business. If I were you Linda, I would report her and complain to your doctor. Linda was still sobbing when Dawn said, 'Linda why don't you go now, go on, pick up your son and take him to casualty at Kingston Hospital, you are well in credit with your hours, take tomorrow off too and spend time with him to make sure he's ok!' Linda grabbed her coat and left the office. She was still upset on the bus journey back. She jumped off the bus and ran all the way to Elsie's house. Elsie could see that Linda was visibly upset, 'That woman, she did the same to me when my dad was seriously ill; you know she is the senior doctor's wife so you won't get much joy if you complain to him.'

Linda took Stuart to the hospital and told them the story, 'Bloody GP's' said the sister as she sympathetically dressed Stuart's foot and gave Linda a prescription for a course of antibiotics for him.

James was furious when he found out how this woman had upset his wife. Linda was anything but an uncaring mother, she loved and cared for her children, she hated leaving them to go to work but it was to give them a better future that she was persevering with the heartache of leaving them every day. 'Right, get our medical cards looked out, no-one's going to talk to you like that! We're changing our GP but not before I go in and have a word with our doctor!' said James angrily.

They arrived at the surgery and James asked to see their regular doctor only to be told that he was on holiday. The other doctor, whose wife was the busybody receptionist on duty that morning refused to see James. James took his family round the corner to another GP's surgery; he told them that he would like to register his family there and the reason why. The receptionist was kind and understanding, she was astonished at how rude the receptionist at the other surgery had been and told him that they wouldn't have that problem at their surgery, they would never turn away children and respected working mothers.

James said to Linda, 'I think this has made our minds up for us hasn't it? We can't have you upset like that, I know you hate your job and miss the kids! Money isn't everything, hand in your notice, if you really want to work you can always go back and do a couple of evenings in the bar at the club, you enjoyed that and it didn't disrupt the children.' Linda felt a sense of relief, she knew James was right, she wrote out her notice ready to hand in when she returned to work.

The next morning the door bell went, Linda opened it to find the health visitor from her old surgery there, she seemed concerned and said 'I would like to know what happened yesterday, your doctor returned from his holiday and was informed that you had moved to another surgery because of some difference of opinion with the receptionist!' Linda told the health visitor the story and said that she wouldn't be spoken to like that from anyone, let alone the doctor's receptionist. The health visitor understood and told Linda her doctor wasn't happy because she wasn't the first of his patients to move to another surgery because of this interfering receptionist but his hands were tied because she was the senior partner's wife. 'Well he has a problem on his hands then, hasn't he?' answered Linda.

Dawn was disappointed that Linda had decided to leave but she was understanding about the circumstances and said that although she was sorry to let her go she didn't blame her.

Linda worked her last day at her office the Friday before Christmas. She was taken aback by everyone's kindness. After lunch Dawn and Vanessa presented her with flowers, chocolates and a big card signed by everyone in the office saying how much they were going to miss her. Vanessa also gave her an envelope with a lovely typewritten letter inside saying how efficient she had been and that if she ever decided to go back to work in the future then there would always be a job there for her. Linda felt so overwhelmed that at one point she seriously wondered if she was doing the right thing but as soon as she walked out the building, she felt such a sense of freedom that she knew she had made the correct decision and looked forward to spending more time with her children.

James and Linda had saved quite a bit over the last few months that Linda had worked and had a nice healthy bank balance. They had a wonderful Christmas which was in complete contrast to the previous one they had. Amongst lots of other things, Linda bought Stuart a 'ride-on' tractor and trailer. She bought Amanda a foldable doll's pushchair and a large doll to sit in it. Linda had always wanted a doll's pushchair for Christmas as a child but sadly never got it so she was making sure that Amanda got one.

They decided to drive up to Scotland and stay with Linda's parents for New Year to help take their minds off the fact that the decision as to whether they would get a house in the new development or not was imminent but they could hardly contain themselves and couldn't wait to get back to find out if they had been successful.

They arrived back to a stack of mail behind the door, Linda quickly sifted through the letters banging them down on the table one by one, then she came across one that was franked 'MC Housing Association' she tore open the letter as James stood at her side and quickly read through the lines until she came across the part offering them the house with five bedrooms that they wanted in 'Apple Blossom Way', Linda read the letter over and over again nipping herself in disbelief that this wonderful luck had actually come their way. They were both ecstatic as they phoned their parents to tell them the good news; they celebrated that evening with some sherry that they had left over from Christmas. 'Imagine us having a house with FIVE BEDROOMS James? We'll feel like millionaires with all that space! Tell me this is not a dream please!' Linda said as she snuggled contentedly into her husband on the settee.

Nine

James started back at work on the site the second week in January, Hughie greeted him with, 'Huv ye heard anything fae the hoosin' association yet son?' James beamed from ear to ear as he told Hughie that they had been offered the show house. 'Well fancy that?' answered Hughie as he walked past him then he turned round with a cheeky grin and winked. James realized that he owed it all to Hughie; he had put in a good word for him with the housing manager. 'Right c'mon, we'll have a look round this house of yours, ah'll get the keys fae the hut!' said Hughie. James quickly followed him; he hadn't seen inside the house yet because he had been working on the second phase of the site and this house was one of two that were completed in the first phase of twenty dwellings. He couldn't believe what he was seeing, there were five bedrooms over three floors with lots of space, two bathrooms, a utility room, a beautifully fitted kitchen and a massive 22ft x 15ft lounge and as if that wasn't enough there was an attached double garage! James was still nipping himself to believe that he wasn't dreaming. 'Can I bring my wife and kids round to see their new home please?' he nervously asked Hughie, this was all too good to be true and he was still very pessimistic that the housing association would change their minds. 'Nae bother son, whenever ye like!' replied Hughie. 'What about after school today? It's not far from here, they could call in on their way home!' answered James. 'Aye son that'll be fine by me!' 'Use the phone in the shed tae gie her ring!' Hughie told him. James quickly called Linda and made arrangements for her to come and see her new home.

Just after 3.30pm Linda nervously came to the building site gates and asked one of the workmen if he could get James for her. After about five minutes she saw James approaching, Stuart and Amanda kept asking, 'Is this where we're going to live?' They were very excited although it was still a building site at the moment. James wouldn't tell Linda which house was theirs, he wanted to surprise her. They walked up to the site managers shed. Once inside James introduced Linda to Hughie who said to her, 'Ye've got a smashin' hoose hen, it was meant tae be the show hoose before the hoosin' association bought the site, so the workmanship is perfect, not that the other hooses aren't perfect but ye know whit ah mean, it was built tae impress!' Linda giggled as Hughie tied himself in knots trying to explain what he meant. 'Ach it'll be great for the kids, its good tae see a nice young family getting a wee step up the ladder.' Hughie said with a confident and satisfied nod.

'Right follow me,' James told Linda as he swept Amanda up into his arms and grabbed Stuart by the hand. Linda took Stuarts' other hand and excitedly they all walked along the unfinished road. James kept calm as he stopped and walked down a drive, Linda watched with a questionable frown as he entered the porch and put the key in the door. 'Is this it?' she gasped 'This is it!' answered James proudly. Linda stepped back and looked up at the outside of the magnificent brand new building and said 'God, I feel like I've won the pools, I can't believe it!'

Once inside Linda enthused in nervous amazement at the amount of rooms and doors as she said 'Oh my god, it's like a maze, every time you think you've got to the end another surprise pops up! There was a room at the back on the ground floor with French windows in to the garden, 'Oh look James, this'll make a perfect playroom for the kids,' she shouted in sheer excitement. Linda was ecstatic when she saw the fully fitted kitchen and the massive lounge. Stuart and Amanda were in their element running through the lounge into the kitchen, out the other kitchen door into the hallway, back into the lounge, into the kitchen and so on. They all made their way upstairs. 'Right the big bedroom at the front is for dad and I, you two kids go and make your minds up which bedroom you would each like' Linda told Stuart and Amanda, who ran excitedly into the upstairs hall to look at the other rooms. Linda measured the windows for curtains, while James measured the walls to build wardrobes. Less than five minutes later Stuart and Amanda burst into the room and shouted in echo together as they giggled loudly, 'We've decided!', 'I'm having the wee room at the front and Amanda's having the room at the back!' exclaimed Stuart before he and his wee sister ran out of the bedroom to explore their new house further. Just over an hour later Linda and James had all the measurements they needed. 'C'mon kids, it's time to go home,' she shouted. 'But I thought this was our new house?' Stuart questioned. Linda laughed, 'It is but we can't move in yet, we have to move our furniture and belongings in first, you don't have a bed to sleep in or any toys here do you?

Hughie told them that the house would be locked up securely so they could come in, in advance and put curtains up, lay carpet down or leave anything that they want to before their official move-in date. 'Thanks Hughie, that's a big help, I really appreciate your help!' said Linda. 'Nae bother hen, if ever ye want access, just come tae the hut and ah'll gie ye the key.'

Linda popped back and forward before their moving-in date, putting up curtains etc. Three days before they moved in Amanda walked to their new house with her mummy; she took her dollies in their pram to show them their new house. When it was time to go home Amanda said, 'Mummy can I leave my dollies here in the new house?' 'Why, can't you be bothered pushing the pram back?' asked Linda, 'they like it here, I'll see them again tomorrow, won't I mummy?' replied Amanda. 'Yes, we'll be back again tomorrow precious,' answered Linda as she fastened up her wee daughter's warm sheepskin coat.

Moving in day came, Linda and James didn't have enough furniture to fill a house that size, the place looked very empty but they couldn't have been happier. They took delivery of a new three piece suite that they had ordered as soon as they had confirmation of being allocated the house and a wee second hand round dining table and chairs that they had bought from their ex-landlord Mr. Halliday. They split the children's bunk beds into two single beds and put one in each of their rooms.

James and Linda had £640 which they had saved over the last year for a deposit on a house, most of which came from Linda going out to work full time because the biggest part of James' wages were swallowed up paying for rent, rates, household and food bills.

They decided that they would use most of this money to buy carpets for the house.

Hughie came round to see them; He sat on their settee with a big ginger cat at his side. Linda wasn't too happy about him bringing the site cat in with him, especially with it sitting on her brand new settee. 'Right yer the first tae move in, the site's no' finished yet, so we have tae keep the big gates up so ah'll gie ye keys.' He told Linda; 'Oh, it'll be like our own private estate!' laughed Linda. 'Aye but remember, ye cannae get yer phone connected up yet because they huvnae finished laying the cables, oh an' the street lights urnae connected up yet either, so it'll be dark here at night' said Hughie. This all went over the top of Linda's head, she had the house of her dreams and these sort of things were only trivial. 'What's your cat's name?' she asked Hughie. Hughie looked puzzled, he screwed his face up as he replied, 'Ma cat? Ah thought it was your cat hen, ah've never seen it before in ma life!' 'It's not my cat, I thought it was your cat,' Linda said as she jumped up shouting, 'I can't stand cats, get it out of here!' She shooshed it out of the door, then she and Hughie laughed their heads off.

James was working in the second phase of the site over-looking the back garden, he looked out the window and his chest swelled with pride as he watched, Stuart playing with his tractor and trailer and Amanda with her doll's pram in their new back garden, even though it was just hard soil with no grass or flowers.

Linda had arranged for her milkman to deliver her milk at her new house, he told her he would give her £1 for every new customer she got him in the new street. Linda saw this as a nice chance to earn some pocket money and promised him that she would see what she could do.

Meanwhile Linda started working back at the social club two evenings per week, she worked beside a nice gentlemanly Irishman called Gerry, he lived with his wife Colleen, their three year old daughter and new-born daughter in a pokey old flat above the shops by the Fish Market, overlooking the church graveyard. He worked evenings in the club to supplement his income. Linda had been to see the new baby at their flat, they were a lovely couple and she felt sorry for them. He managed the shop below, the flat was tied to his job and there seemed no way out for them, if he changed his job, they would lose their living accommodation. Linda said to Gerry, 'Why don't you apply for one of these houses where we live? I know for a fact that there are still about twenty not allocated yet because they're not finished.' 'What's the point, we wouldn't be that lucky Linda,' replied Gerry. 'Well you'll never know if you don't try! I would never have believed six months ago that we would have a brand new house with five bedrooms! Leave it with me, I'm seeing the housing manager soon, I'll get you an application form' said Linda. Gerry's eyes lit up, 'Do you think it's worth a try then?' he said. 'Definitely!' answered Linda.

The following week Rita, the housing manager, called into the site. Hughie brought her round to see Linda and introduced her. 'I'd like to have a quick word with James and yourself if it's convenient to you,' she told Linda. 'Yes, yes that'll be fine,' replied Linda, feeling apprehensive and wondering what Rita had to say. 'Ah'll go an' tell James ye want him,' said Hughie as he walked out the door.

Ten minutes later James came home and said, 'Hughie said you wanted me!' 'I've just made some tea James, would you like a cup?' Linda asked him. 'I wouldn't say no, oh and what's this? Jam doughnuts, my favourite, I hope there's one for me!'

They sat round the table and Rita said, 'Right, would you be interested in some more work James?' James looked at Linda and said, 'well it depends what it involves?' Rita went on, 'well as you know, we're based in Manchester, it's going to be difficult for us to look after the maintenance on the site, would you be prepared to organise it or do it where you can James?' 'As I said, it depends on what it involves!' he replied. 'Well, if any of the residents needs any repairs doing that are the responsibility of the housing association, can you organise it or, even better, carry the work out yourself? Answered Rita. 'What about payment?' James asked. 'Easy, you just invoice us for materials and your time and if you need to call in other trades they can do the same!' Rita told him. 'Can I think about it?' asked James. 'Of course you can, but tenants start moving in next week so I will need to know within the next couple of days,' said Rita. 'Oh, while we're on the subject of tenants, am I right in saying that the last phase of houses haven't been allocated yet?' Linda asked Rita. 'Yes' replied Rita. 'Do you mean 'yes' they have been allocated or 'yes I'm right that they haven't? enquired Linda with an inquisitive frown. 'No, I mean yes, you're right that they haven't been allocated yet,' laughed Rita. 'Ah then, would it be possible for me to have an application form for very good friends of ours please?' Linda went on to tell Rita about the pokey little unacceptable flat that Gerry and Colleen lived in, in the middle of town, overlooking the grave yard, she laid it on thick as she told her how it wasn't a place to bring kids up because there was nowhere for them to play, how the smell of fish from the market, especially on a hot day, stunk the flat out and most important of all, if Gerry left his job they would be homeless because the house was tied to it, she could see that Rita was sympathizing with Gerry and Colleen's predicament as she went into her brief case and took out an application form, 'Tell them to fill this in and get it back to me as soon as possible, it shouldn't be a problem, they're coming well recommended by you, what did you say their names were?' 'Gerry and Colleen McConnell,' answered Linda as Rita wrote their names in her diary. 'Right!' said James, 'I'll let you know tomorrow about the maintenance job Rita, Linda and I will have a talk about it.' Rita shook their hands and left them to think it over. 'What do you think then Linda?' James asked his wife as he closed the door behind Rita. 'I don't know, it'll be nice to have a bit more money but do you think you'll have time to do more work? I mean you're working six days a week on this site as it is and I would like you to have SOME time off,' emphasized Linda. 'Yes but, I won't always be working here, this site is in its last stages,' said James. 'Well, I suppose it won't hurt to give it a try, if it doesn't work out you can always tell them to get someone else' answered Linda then she went on to say, 'I can't wait to give this application form to Gerry and Colleen, they'll be delighted!' 'They've as good as got a house here, after the sob story you gave Rita, you had her almost in tears,' laughed James. 'Do you think so? I'd love it if they did, it's nice to be able to help others, isn't it?' replied Linda. 'Well put it this way, if they just applied on their own they wouldn't stand a chance! Rita almost as good as told you that there'll be a house for them because you have recommended them, make sure that they fill in their application form right away!'

James drove Linda to work in the club that evening and they took the kids in for an early evening refreshment. Colleen was there with her two wee daughters, Linda gave the form to Gerry and her and told them that they had to get it in as soon as possible because the houses that were left would be getting allocated very soon. James told them that Linda had put in a good word for them; the housing manager knew their name and was waiting for their completed application form. He also mentioned they wouldn't have a snowballs chance in hell of getting one if they applied on their own because 50% were going to tenants on the council waiting list and the rest were going to people working in the police, ambulance, hospitals and fire service. 'Remember, it's not what you know, it's who you know,' winked James.

James called Rita the following day and agreed to take on the maintenance of the site, but only on a trial basis as a side-line. He made it clear to the Housing Association that if it, in any way, interfered in his family or working life then they would have to find someone else. Rita asked James if Linda would be prepared to hold onto the keys of the houses so that prospective tenants could view their new house in advance of moving in. Linda said she'd give it a go because, if nothing else, it would help her to get to know her new neighbours. Rita said she would send details of the prospective tenant's names and house numbers in the post; she also instructed Linda that under no circumstances must she part with the keys because the tenants coming to view at this point will only have been offered the house and won't have signed anything or paid any rent. Linda thought that she might be offered a small fee for helping out the Housing Association but nothing was mentioned. She remembered her milkman offering her £1 for every new customer she could get him and she thought, *'Well, if I can get the majority of the new neighbours to get their milk from him at least I'll get something for putting myself out.'*

The first couple, Mr. & Mrs. Matthews, came to view their new house, Rita had instructed them to knock on James and Linda's door. The woman was in her late twenties, she seemed very sweet and pleasant. She had a natural round, smiling face, sparkling eyes and seemed to ooze personality. Her red hair was very short, neatly trimmed in a bob and combed forward into a fringe at the front. At her side stood her blond, curly-haired 'tom-boy looking' daughter about eight years old, a quiet mousey-haired wee son about four years old and a baby boy around one year old in her arms. Linda introduced herself, 'Hi my name's Linda.' 'Oh I'm Kay and this is Roger, my husband, said the young woman. Her husband was of average build and height, he had straight long dark hair to his shoulders, a big prominent nose with wide nostrils and seemed very good with the children but he was quiet and expressionless. Kay appeared embarrassed by his silence as Linda walked over to the property with them. Linda left them to look around and told them to knock on her door when they were finished and she would go over and lock up. They were back fifteen minutes later, Kay Matthews had a broad smile on her face, 'we're hoping to move in next week,' she told Linda excitedly while her sullen husband stood in the background.

Mr. & Mrs. Summers were the next couple to appear at Linda's door two days later. They were both well dressed and looked as if they were in their early thirties. She had well groomed long fair hair and wore a black mini-skirt with matching black collarless jacket buttoned up to the neck, black patent high heels and a matching shoulder bag. She was around 5ft 8ins, had a figure to die for and great long legs but the illusion was spoilt when she opened her mouth to reveal a common accent as she said loudly to Linda, 'I hope we haven't far to walk, I'm dying for a piss!' She followed her remark with a vulgar laugh. Her husband giggled at her admiringly, he was a nice looking, slightly built man with, a tanned complexion and dark wavy hair. He wore black trousers with a smart open-necked black shirt under a beige casual jacket and highly polished black slip-on, Italian-style shoes. It became obvious that she definitely wore the trousers; she barked orders and her obedient hen-pecked husband immediately jumped to attention. She told Linda her name was Sadie and her husband was Greg. They had two kids, a boy of about four, who had all the mannerisms of a brat, and he seemed to have a sarcastic smirk on his face as if he was challenging his parents. Sadie kept shouting his name, 'OLIVER!' at the top of her voice over and over again, making threats that he obviously knew she would never carry out. His older sister was very quiet, she had long waist-length dark hair and had a tanned complexion like her dad, she looked about ten years old. She rolled her eyes at her brother's naughtiness and her mother's meaningless threats towards him.

They were followed that afternoon by a Welsh couple, Mr. & Mrs. Davies. Linda knew that she was the sister of one of the young mothers from her children's school. The young mother had told Linda that she didn't get on with her sister but found out that she had been offered one of the new houses and said, 'God help the neighbours, my sister Rose is a nightmare, she wants to know everyone's business, she looks down her nose at folk and wonders why they don't like her, she's such a snob, it's not everyone she will talk to and ever since her four-year-old son said the 'F' word she won't allow her children to play or mix with the other kids in the street!' Linda could see that Rose Davies' sister was right. Rose was a small, chubby lady, immaculately dressed with a grey polo neck sweater and a pristinely ironed red open necked blouse on top, grey tweed skirt and sturdy solid 'granny type' low-heeled black shoes. Her eyes stared through you, her teeth protruded and her neat light brown page-boy style hair was combed to one side and resting on her shoulder. She was a right little busybody and wanted to know all about who was who and what her new neighbours would be like. She yattered ten to the dozen as she told Linda that she loved where she lived at the moment but had to move because she had terrible neighbours who were a bad influence on her family. She didn't want her children growing up in that environment and wanted to make sure this wasn't going to happen again. Her husband, Matt, was just as bad although he wasn't as neat and tidy, in fact he looked a bit sloppy compared to Rose, he wore a dark blue creased sweatshirt and jeans with scruffy looking trainers, his mousey brown hair was combed back in an Elvis style' quiff, it looked as if it had been chopped by an amateur, it was straggling unevenly down the back of his neck and looked greasy and unkempt. He nodded in agreement like an old fish wife. Linda never let on to Mrs. Davies that she knew her sister as she replied sympathetically, 'Well I can't help you there, I'm sorry but I only have names, I don't know anyone personally so can't tell you what your new neighbours will be like!'

Linda showed many more people their houses including an odd couple called Mr. & Mrs. Suko. After Linda introduced herself, they told her their names were Tariq and Hannah and they looked like a comedy double act. He was far eastern, about 5ft4ins, chubby and balding with bandy legs. She was over 6ft with dyed platinum/white hair, she had the skinniest legs Linda had ever seen, Linda would have described them as 'lucky legs' (lucky they managed to hold her up!) The stiletto heels on her shoes took her up to about 6ft 4ins. They were both rather posh and spoke as if they had plums in their mouths; he was definitely the boss and treated her inferior, like a dumb blonde.

That evening Linda got the kids to bed then sat down with James and went over the days events, she said 'You know, I never realised there were so many different types of people in the world, you do the same job for them all, some are very cheerful and grateful, others look down their nose at you while there are ones who couldn't give a damn!' 'Don't let people talk down to you Linda, remember you're doing the Housing Association a favour, you're not getting paid for it!' said James. 'I know but I find it interesting meeting all these people, it's not as if I'll have to do it forever and in any case, they've all agreed so far to get their milk delivered by our milkman, so I'll be getting a few pounds at the end of it all,' smiled Linda.

Three weeks later Colleen and Gerry were elated to find out that they had been allocated a house with three bedrooms in Apple Blossom Way. They were a lovely couple and James and Linda were delighted to have helped them. Linda thanked Rita for doing this for them because it was going to make a huge difference to their lives.

Linda and James' new next door neighbours, Mr. and Mrs. Capaldi moved in, they were Italian, there was mum, dad, and eight siblings ranging from the age of twenty-three down to eleven. The mum, Enza, was a large, happy, warm-natured lady in her mid-forties, Linda took to her right away, and within weeks Enza treated Linda like another daughter and Stuart and Amanda like her grandchildren. The dad Giovanni was more serious, he was very strict with his children, he wouldn't allow them any freedom, they didn't go out with friends in the evening, Giovanni had a minibus and they always went out as a family whether it was to visit relatives in the area or to go to the Italian food shop, the eldest daughters, aged twenty-three and twenty-one were not allowed to wear make-up. Enza worked full time as a cleaner and the girls had to come straight home from work or school and help their mum, the boys helped their dad with gardening, decorating and repairing his car etc. On pay day the children who worked had to hand their wages to their dad. Giovanni and Enza had typical Italian temperaments, when they argued, you could hear them two streets away but no-one could understand a word apart from the odd 'Bloody Hell' or 'Bugger off' that would slip in between the flow of Italian dialect. In spite of everything they were a really big happy family, the kids respected and loved their parents. Giovanni and Enza invited Linda, James, Stuart and Amanda in for a meal, the table ran the length of the 22ft lounge in order to seat all fourteen of them, but this wasn't anything unusual, it was just a typical meal in the Capaldi household. Linda soon learned that the Italians all had big appetites, they started off with a very large bowl of pasta each, it was too much for Linda, she couldn't finish it, 'C'mon-a, that's-a only your-a start-a, you have-a your-a main-a meal-a to come-a next-a!' exclaimed Enza 'What! I am full up, that was more than enough!' replied Linda, but no-one was listening. 'I make-a Chicken-a cacciatore for-a you-a' said Enza as she placed another large plate in front of Linda with a quarter chicken, green beans done in oil and what looked like six big chips, but Linda was assured they were not chips but fried potatoes Italian style. Linda then glanced at her children's plates, the portions were almost as big as hers, 'They'll never eat all that, they're probably full up from the pasta, just split one plate between them,' Linda told Enza with a giggle but Enza wouldn't hear of 'No-a, its-a alright-a, we have-a plenty-a-food-a, they don't-a like-a, they take-a home-a!' she insisted shrugging her shoulders. Linda didn't want to offend Enza so she agreed. They finished up with ice-cream and an Italian cake that tasted like it was laced with alcohol. The Italian wine flowed during the meal and they finished up with a delicious Italian aniseed liqueur. By this time they were all merry and Enza started singing in Italian, the kids all joined in, Linda responded by singing an Italian song she remembered from school, 'Santa Lucia'. Then the eldest daughter burst out with, 'When the moon in the sky's like a big pizza pie…….' Before they knew it, all fourteen of them had joined hands and were holding them in the air as they sat round the big table and sang their hearts out. They all collapsed laughing; then the youngest boy Giuseppe said to Linda, 'Do you know 'Catch a falling Star?' 'Yes, I used to sing that with my cousins at family parties when I was young' replied Linda. Giuseppe started it; Linda joined in harmonising and singing the verse a line behind him like Perry Como did. By 8pm it was time to go home because the kids had school the next day. They had the time of their lives; the Capaldis had welcomed them into their big family. Giovanni and Enza had asked Stuart and Amanda to call them uncle and auntie. Amanda was fussed over by the Italian daughters and Stuart had two great pals in the Italian sons, even though they were eleven and sixteen and he was only five. They were wonderful, friendly neighbours, Enza showed Linda how to make Pizza bread, the eldest daughter was a hairdresser and she did Linda and Amanda's hair. James and Linda returned the compliment by inviting them into their home for meals, cooked Scottish style, and drinks. During one of these times Giovanni suggested they knock a hole through the wall in the lounge and make a door to save them going outside, Linda and James laughed, and then they realized that he was deadly serious. They quickly changed the subject because they didn't think that would be a good idea.

Linda's mum and dad, Douglas and Margie came down for the Easter holiday. James drove Linda and the children up to Euston Railway Station to meet them coming off the train. The kids loved it when their gran and grandpa came to stay and Douglas and Margie equally loved spending quality time with their grandchildren. They stood on the platform waiting for the train coming in from Glasgow Central Station. James got a trolley ready for their suitcases then they saw the train approach in the distance. They had walked right up to the end of the platform, Stuart and Amanda watched in anticipation as every carriage passed to see if they could catch a glimpse of their grandparents, then they spotted their grandpa, his nose pressed against the window and a huge grin. The children jumped up and down with glee as they all made their way to the door of the carriage that their grandparents were in. Douglas and Margie came off the train and gave their grandchildren a huge hug and kiss then they turned and did the same to Linda. James hugged Margie and gave her a peck on the cheek then shook hands with Douglas. 'Oh it's great to see you again mammy!' said Linda as she linked arms with her mum. 'It's great to be here, I can't wait to see your new house!' replied Margie. 'Oh it's nothing to rave about,' lied Linda, she hadn't told her mum much about their house in Apple Blossom Way. Forty minutes later James pulled the car up in their drive, Margie looked amazed, 'Are we here? You mean you have your own driveway?' she said breathlessly, then she got out of the car and her face lit up, 'Is this your house?' she gasped. 'Yes, I gather that you like it?' replied Linda proudly. Douglas had a broad smile across his face from ear to ear; he and Margie couldn't wait to see inside! James opened the front door and Linda showed her parents the big room by the door and said, 'This will be your bedroom, hopefully by the next time you visit us, we are going to make it a family room cum office cum spare bedroom. James is going to build wardrobes with a pull-down bed in them, but meantime you can sleep in our bedroom.' 'But what about James and you, where will you sleep?' asked Margie concerned. 'Oh don't worry about us, Amanda has a big room and we have a double airbed in there while you're here.' answered Linda. 'Oh that's very kind of you both, I feel awful about that, we're putting you out aren't we?' said Margie who loved to fuss over everybody but never expected anything in return. 'Don't be daft, we're fine, I just can't tell you how good it is to have you stay with us!' smiled Linda as she hugged her mum again. Douglas and Margie were really impressed with the house, they were extremely happy and proud to see James and Linda get on so well. 'Just wait until I tell everybody back home about your mansion in Surrey!' beamed Douglas with pride.

Three months had past and James and Linda were settled into their new house. James had built wardrobes in the bedrooms and a pine table and bench set for the kitchen. Linda always wanted to have four children but had vowed that as she had her first child at 22, her second at 23, she didn't want to be having babies in her 30's and as she was now 28, time was running out so she was absolutely delighted to discover she was pregnant. Stuart was six and Amanda was four so they were old enough to understand and were really excited about the prospect of having a baby brother or sister.

September 1976, Apple Blossom Way was complete and all the houses were occupied. Amanda was very excited because, at last, she was starting school and she couldn't wait to go there along with Stuart. James got a job on another building site in the next street, opposite his children's school. 'I'll be able to wave to you both in the playground,' James told the excited Stuart and Amanda.

James and Linda didn't bargain for the extra workload involved in the maintenance of Apple Blossom Way. Although they had agreed with the housing manager that James would look after the maintenance for them, they never realized just how demanding and helpless some people could be. The bell on their front door and their telephone seemed to ring endlessly with residents complaining about anything from a central heating problem to a dripping tap.

Linda was taken aback when Rita, the housing manager arrived just before teatime one evening and made herself comfortable in Linda's big room by the door telling her that she had sent out a circular informing residents that if they wanted to talk to her about anything then she would be available at Linda and James' house between 6pm and 7pm that evening. Linda was furious but she bit her tongue, she didn't want her house used as a 'Housing Association Office', especially as she was paying her rent just like all the other residents and not getting compensated in anyway from the housing association for the use of her house and even if they offered to pay her, she would have told them 'no' because this is her family home, not their office!'

The housing association asked the residents to vote to decide if they wanted a 'No Ball Games' sign, the decision was unanimously 'Yes' because, although almost every family had kids and there were about fifty children under the age of ten in Apple Blossom Way, the residents main concern was that it would be very dangerous for children to play in the street because of the amount of vehicles entering and exiting the cul-de-sac daily, there was a large recreation ground round the corner with wide open spaces, swings, roundabouts and slides for the children. It made more sense for the children to play there rather than have them risking their lives on the street. The housing Association asked James to organise the signs and he offered to make them at his own expense. Linda and James' week-ends and evenings were very busy as James attended to the tenant's problems. Sometimes they were sitting round the table eating dinner when the door would go; Linda was infuriated when James left the table to go round to someone's house to mend something. 'I'm sure they could have waited until you finished your dinner, it can't have been that important!' Linda told him on his return as she removed his half-eaten meal from the oven, but this became a regular occurrence and Linda's patience was running out, especially when the blonde Scandinavian divorcee a few doors down kept coming round in the evening, putting on the 'helpless act' and asking James to come to fix something, meanwhile Linda was doing her own household repairs!

When James told Linda that he had agreed with Rita the housing manager that he would cut the grass on the front lawns and weed the flower beds when necessary, Linda decided that enough was enough, she was pregnant and she wasn't getting any quality time with her husband and neither were the children seeing much of their daddy. 'Where on earth are you going to find the time to tend to gardens, as well as work full time and deal with all the maintenance on Apple Blossom Way?' she asked James with concern. 'It won't need doing very often and besides they are supplying a petrol mower and will pay me £5 for every time I cut the grass', '£5, is this per house?' asked Linda. 'No, £5 in total for all the lawns' I just have to invoice them!' James answered trying to convince Linda. 'James, I have been invoicing them since you agreed to take on this maintenance six months ago and they haven't paid us a penny yet! They owe us just over £50 and that's just for materials because you never charge them for your time!' replied Linda then she went on, 'We will have to set some hard and fast rules, the housing association is too far away to manage the site themselves and obviously they are quite happy for you to take the pressure off them by working your backside off for peanuts! They are getting more than their money's worth out of you and are taking the mickey! 'You do too much, you are spoiling the tenants, for heavens sake you even made 'No Ball Games' signs at our expense. It will have to be made clear to the residents that you are NOT a caretaker! I get the impression that they think we are living here rent-free and you are moon-lighting when you go out to work every day! Some of these people expect you to change their light bulbs for them! Every morning when I walk the kids to school with all the other mums, the subject always turns to problems with their floors, doors, water, kitchens and what have you, I don't want to hear that, I want to talk about the light-hearted every-day things that all the other young mums discuss, I find myself avoiding these people in the street now, I am sick of it!' said Linda as her eyes welled up with tears. James enjoyed looking after the maintenance but he never realized just how much of his time was being taken up by it and the pressure that Linda was under, she was almost five months pregnant with her third child and he never seemed to be around anymore to spend time with her or the kids. Linda and James had a good discussion and he had to agree with Linda that it was 'more or less' a voluntary/pocket money hobby, not a job and had to be treated as such. In future his family would have to come before Apple Blossom Way's problems and if that didn't work then the housing association would have to find someone else to attend to their maintenance! Rita, the housing manager was due to visit Apple Blossom Way in two days time so Linda and James invited her to come and have a chat with them. Linda got everything off her chest and cleared the air, she told Rita that they couldn't continue like this because it was interfering with their family life, she didn't want tenants coming into her house because this was their family home, she requested that a letter be sent out from the housing association explaining that James wasn't a caretaker and asking residents to respect their privacy by not calling at their door or ringing them but if they had a complaint or a problem they were to put a note through James and Linda's letterbox and their issue would be dealt with in a reasonable time. Linda also brought up the matter of non-payment of invoices. Rita told them that the housing association preferred to let invoices build up to a decent amount then settle with one cheque. 'Yes, that's fine for you but we're out of pocket, we never catch up, we're buying material for repairs and by the time you pay us, we've spent more!' explained Linda. Rita could see that Linda was at the end of her tether and said to her, 'I'll see what I can do to get a payment out to you!'

November 1976 and James' old pal Eric arrived at the door with his pregnant new wife Becky in tow, he had emigrated to South Africa with his first wife Morag, who had been a good friend of Linda's before they all got married. The marriage didn't last but no-one expected that it would because they had, had an on/off relationship since they were fourteen and were as different as chalk and cheese. Becky was originally from Northern England, she seemed nice although a bit scatty. 'We've come back for good because Becky doesn't want our baby to be born or brought up in South Africa, would you mind if we kipped here until we find a place?' Eric asked James. James turned to Linda who heaved out a big sigh, 'Well we can't see you without a roof over your head, but it can only be a temporary arrangement because, we have quite a houseful as it is, I'm pregnant too and our parent's come to stay often so we need the space.'

It was approaching Christmas and there was still no sign of Eric and Becky moving out, her baby was due in January and Linda's in March. Eric seemed to be too fussy about what job he did, he had bull-shitted his way off the tools to a white-collar job in South Africa but found that it wasn't as easy in the UK. Linda caught a glimpse of his CV on the dining room table. 'Six o-levels! Since when? You left school at fifteen and worked as an electrician's apprentice!' teased Linda then she caught sight of the shocked look on Becky's face and realized that she had spoken out of turn. Eric was always boasting about his lifestyle and women in South Africa, he was such a bighead and as time went on he became an unbearable bore. James and Linda decided that they had to tell Eric and Becky that they had over-stayed their welcome and it was time for them to make the effort and find a place of their own. 'We've made them too comfortable, they are beginning to take over our home, they don't seem to have any intention of moving out and we can't possibly have two new mothers and two new babies under the one roof. Ok they buy some food but Eric's not working and not contributing to the bills, we can't afford to keep them any longer. We're going to have to tell them that we need our own space and besides we have all our parents coming down for Christmas so Eric and Becky will have to go!' said Linda. James agreed that he would take Eric out for a pint that evening and break the news to him. While they were out Becky asked Linda what she meant about Eric not having six 'O' levels. Linda was embarrassed and replied, 'Well maybe I'm wrong, we lost touch for a few years, he probably has got them by now!' 'He's been in South Africa all this time, how could he have 'O' levels since you last saw him? He's lying isn't he? I'm finding out so much about him that I never knew. I thought he was rich but he's been fooling me, he let me believe that he owned his own company in South Africa, he had a flash car and travelled around staying in top class hotels, he used to take me with him sometimes but it turns out that he only worked for the company and he was living on his expense account. We'd only known each other a couple of months when I got pregnant and we got married in haste, now he's admitted that he thought I was loaded and he was trying to impress me but it turns out that we're both as poor as each other and don't have two halfpennies to rub together,' answered Becky with disappointment in her voice. Linda had to secretly smile, she put two and two together and concluded that they were both gold-diggers and had pulled the wool over one another's eyes so they deserved each other. Becky's baby was due early January so Linda was relieved when she and Eric found a place to rent in West Molesey and moved out from under James and Linda's feet the week before Christmas. On January 3rd Becky gave birth to a baby boy, they called him Darren. Linda and James never saw much of them after that and came to the conclusion that they had been used once again. 'When are we ever going to learn? You'd think we would have known better after the way Mark and Tracy treated us!' Linda said to James.

James and Linda had got to know most of the residents pretty well and made lots of new friends. There were a handful of characters who James gave secret 'word-associated' nicknames to. There was Liz and Bill who James called 'Lily and Billy', Liz was expecting her 7th baby but this was her husband Bill's first child. Lily was very secretive and seemed like she was on another planet most of the time, she never spoke about where her other children were, but there were rumours that every one of them had a different father, some were with their respective fathers and others were in care or fostered.

'Alfie the Alky' used to meet his cronies every night in the pub and never got home until well after closing time. He never spent any time with his wife or four children and she was left to raise their children on her own. She met another man who treated her and her children like human beings so the inevitable happened and one day Alfie came home to a note telling him that she'd had enough and met someone else who offered her and the kids a much better life. Alfie was devastated but he still didn't have the common sense to realize where he went wrong, he had the audacity to blame his wife and call her all the whores under the sun for going off with someone else, it never entered his selfish mind for one minute that he was totally to blame for neglecting his wife in the first place by putting his drinking mates before her and their children.

Alfie was now a sad case, at least when his wife was at home he looked presentable but now he was on his own he had let himself go, he never looked clean, he shaved his head to save himself the bother of washing his hair, his weight had soared to 22 stone, his crushed trousers hung around his hips with his bum showing above the belt and the crutch sagging, he wore brewery T-shirts that he got free from the pub, the white ones were only ever white the first time he wore them, after that they were a washed-in dirty grey colour with food spills and stains down the front. Ironically and in spite of his lack of hygiene, he drove the delivery van for the local bakery. He finished his deliveries by early afternoon and was in the pub by 3pm every day. He staggered up the road every evening, shouting and putting the world to rights. He had custody of his four children on Saturday but all they ever saw was the inside of the pub, he was the talk of the place as his six year son, eight year old twin daughters, ten year old son sat in the smoky pub, quite obviously bored out of their skulls every Saturday, while he threw back pint after pint, shouting verbal abuse at the football on the pub television and telling his kids to 'shut-up'. Around mid-afternoon the kids got excited when he gave them money and permission to go to the sweet shop next door, the look of relief on their faces to get out of the pub for five minutes was heart-breaking. Around teatime when Alfie had more than enough to drink, he climbed off the barstool, swaying to and fro, digging into his pocket to give his kids money to get a take-away from the Chinese across the roads for their dinner. Then the poor wee souls had to embarrassedly witness their dad falling against the high hedgerows as they walked home. Regulars in the pub could be heard passing comments, 'He doesn't deserve to have these kids! You'd think that he would take them somewhere nice to spend quality time together, imagine taking your kids to the pub all day Saturday, what a loser!' But the landlord wasn't complaining, Alfie spent a lot of money in the pub!

Richard and Richard lived happily together, they were a friendly gay couple, James nick-named them 'Dicky and Ricky'. Dicky was short and plump, in his 50's, he was the housewife, he could be seen most mornings standing on the corner, shopping bag in hand, blethering with the local women and complaining about the price of sugar. Ricky, who was in his 30's, had bleached blond spiky, shoulder length hair and dressed very modern, with smart trousers, tight brightly coloured tops and cheeky white casual leather shoes. He worked in 'The Royal Crest' which was the local pub, he was very 'over the top' camp with a cheeky sense of humour.

'Rainbow Barbara' was a hippy. She was a big friendly lady, who was always there to help and would never do you a wrong turn. Colour co-ordination didn't matter to her so she looked like a rainbow squashed into her 'tent-like' tops and long bright skirts. She had long straggly auburn hair. She made jewellery, toys, clothes, household items and knew where to get almost anything.

James nicknamed Rose Davies 'Nosey Rosie'. She lived up to her reputation and knew everybody's business; she spent the best part of her days behind the net curtain. If you wanted to know anything about anyone you only had to ask Nosey Rosie.

'Rhona the Moaner' complained about everything, she was the bane of James and Linda's life, she used to come to their door or phone them complaining about everything from the position of her back gate to the noise of her toilet flush. It was a blessing when the Housing Association put a stop to residents pestering James and Linda and instructed residents to put notes through their door with any maintenance issues but Rhona the Moaner lived over the back and there was only a wire fence between their gardens, so every time Linda or James went into their back garden they had to check first that the coast was clear otherwise she kept them there for hours boring them to tears with her moans and groans. One day Linda looked out the back window to see Rhona talking to herself and complaining loudly. It was a hot summer's day, she had her swimming costume on and her sun lounger out, the shadow of the house was cast over most of her back garden and she was trying to follow the sun. Linda couldn't help laughing as she watched Rhona pull her sun lounger onto her son-in-law's vegetable patch, then she laid down on it to sun bathe in between the green beans and potatoes. Half an hour later her down-trodden son-in-law appeared, looking dismayed at where she was lying but he stood there saying nothing as she nagged him saying that his vegetable patch was taking up the sunniest part of the garden.

'Lisa the Teaser' was Scandinavian. She was a sexy 'dyed-blonde' divorcee. She openly flirted with the men in the street and would infuriate the women by cheekily knocking their doors and asking if she could borrow their husbands for a 'little job'.

'Neurotic Nancy' was a dangerous lady, she had a terrible temper. Her husband was a big well-built man but even he backed down when she flew off the handle. She never accepted 'no' for an answer. She gave James a time of it as she insisted in doing things her way. When she came to view the house before she moved in, Linda took her over, opened the door then left her to it telling her to close the door behind her when she was finished, Linda had done this with all the residents but she hadn't reckoned on the cheek of Neurotic Nancy. James used to go round the empty houses to check the heating which he had put on low to avoid burst pipes in the frosty nights. He was speechless when he opened the door of Neurotic Nancy's future residence, it was stacked out with boxes, TV, stereo, coffee table, chairs, he thought, *'How the hell did this stuff get in here?'* and panicked that there might be squatters, he checked the back door and discovered that it was unlocked, he locked the place up securely and called the housing manager in the morning. That evening he had just got in from work when there was an angry rat-a-tat-tat at the door, when he opened it he was confronted by Neurotic Nancy who was red with anger, 'What do you mean by reporting me to the Housing Association?' she yelled. 'Reporting you? I don't know what you're talking about,' answered James. 'You know fine well what I mean, you phoned them up to say that I had moved some of my belongings into my house, if anything's damaged I will be suing you! shouted Neurotic Nancy defiantly. 'Oh is that what you're on about? Well firstly I didn't know it was your belongings, I have been told not to allow any belongings into the house before their official moving-in day and secondly it's not your house, you have only viewed it, you haven't signed an agreement yet! The housing association have told me to make sure the properties are secure incase squatters move in, you deliberately left the back door open so that you could come back in the evening and move stuff in, if unwelcome squatters had taken up residence, you wouldn't only have lost your belongings but your house too and I would have been in big trouble with the housing association, you had no right leaving the back door open, you should be grateful to me!' James told her sharply.

About a month after Neurotic Nancy had moved in, she called James to say that her bath was cracked and she wanted a new one. When James went to inspect the bath, he found that it wasn't the original one that had been fitted. 'Neurotic Nancy' had decided to change the bath, and not only that, she changed the lay-out of the bathroom, and fitted a new wash hand basin and toilet pan too. Her dad had fitted them and obviously cracked the new bath that he was installing; she thought that she had no more to do than get the housing association to replace it. When James told her to claim her household insurance because the housing association would never agree to it because there was nothing wrong with the bath she removed, she flew into a rage, and her language was unladylike to say the least. She tried to claim that the original bath she took out was broken. James knew that she was lying through her teeth because if there had been something wrong with the bath she would have been the first to complain. 'If that was the case then you should have called me over to inspect it, the housing association will never agree to replace this bath, anyway where is the old bath now?' said James. 'My dad dumped it!' she shouted in temper. 'Well, it's pointless then,' said James as he closed his book and walked away to the sound of her yelling verbal abuse in the background.

Sadie Summers nickname was 'Sex-mad Sadie'. She had a naughty sense of humour. When walking back from school in the morning with the other mums after dropping the kids off, she would openly discuss and make fun of her sex-life by demonstrating the positions she and her husband liked. She thought nothing of it and it was as if she was attempting to shock the other mums. She had a girl and a boy and said that after she had her daughter her husband was desperate for a son. She had heard that you had to do it 'doggie-fashion' to conceive a boy, they did this at least four times a night and she fell pregnant with her son within weeks. Sex-mad Sadie loved to talk dirty, she liked to flirt and openly touch-up the men in the pub, they tended to avoid her because she thought nothing of grabbing their crutches. Strangely enough her husband Greg never passed comment on her behaviour. It wasn't the first time that she was told she was a 'cock-teaser'; she seemed to take great pride in this title.

'Ron the Con' was in his early 60's. He was known as being a bit of a scrooge; he always seemed to disappear when it was his turn to buy a round of drinks. He made out he was a caring person who would help anyone out. Some people had the wool pulled over their eyes and actually believed this but those who knew him better were aware that he did nothing for nothing. He picked up old people in his car and took them to their hospital/doctors appointments, collected their prescriptions and shopping for them. Others complimented him for being so caring and he would reply, 'Oh I don't mind helping out the old uns.' What he didn't tell people was that he had a good little earner going, ripping the old buddies off, he did nothing for nothing, he charged £10 a time to run them to the hospital and anywhere else they wanted to go, he even took money from them for collecting their medicines and shopping.

It was the last day of February 1977, Linda woke up that morning at 7am and as she got out of bed her waters burst, she quickly got the children up and ready for school telling them that mummy had to go into hospital and they would soon be getting a new wee brother or sister, maybe even today! Linda had already arranged with Colleen for her to take the children to and from school and look after them until James got home from work while she was in hospital so James took them over to Colleen's house. James drove Linda up to Kingston Hospital. It was the rush hour by this time and he was getting panicky as he sat in heavy traffic in Park Road. They finally got to the hospital and Linda was given a bed, the midwife examined her and said that it could be a good few hours yet. At 2pm nothing had changed much so the doctor decided to put Linda on a drip to induce the birth. By 5pm Linda was in serious labour. James was with her making her comfortable and rubbing her back. The midwife asked Linda's permission for two young trainee midwives to come in and see the birth. Linda nodded her head, by this stage Linda couldn't have cared less who witnessed the birth. Just after 7pm the baby's head started to appear, Linda gripped James' hand tight as he encouraged her to push. After what seemed like an eternity she heard James cry 'it's a girl!' They both hung on tight to each other and sobbed with happiness and relief as the midwife handed Linda their beautiful fair skinned baby girl. 'What are they crying for?' asked one of the trainee mid-wives in a cold, hard-hearted manner. 'Because it's a very emotional experience, you're going to have to get used to that if you want to do this job for a living!' answered the mature midwife firmly putting the thoughtless young trainee in her place. Linda and James' new baby girl weighed 8lb 11oz and she was perfect in every way. Stuart and Amanda were delighted when their daddy told them that they had a new wee sister and couldn't wait to get up to the hospital to see her. The next evening James dressed the children in their best clothes and even managed to put Amanda's hair in bunches. They ran into the ward and gave their mummy a big hug, Linda noticed that Amanda seemed to be holding her breath and looked very serious, Linda pulled Amanda towards her and as she did she felt the tiers on the back of her pretty red dress, they had been pulled and knotted so tight that the wee girl could hardly breath, 'What on earth have you done here James? It's not your working boots that you were doing up, you're not meant to pull these tiers so tight, the poor wee soul must have been in agony all this time!' said Linda as she loosened the tiers then she turned to Amanda and asked, 'Why didn't you tell daddy that he tied your dress too tight pet?' Amanda replied in a whisper, 'I did but he was too busy'. 'Oh c'm'ere precious give me a big cuddle. Right, now let me do your hair properly then we'll get a picture of Stuart and you with your new wee sister.' The children missed their mummy being at home and enjoyed sitting on the hospital bed holding their new baby. 'What's her name mummy?' Amanda asked Linda. 'Oh we haven't quite decided yet, we can't make our minds up' replied Linda. 'Can we call her Andrea?' said Amanda. Linda and James looked at each other, 'that's a nice name, what do you think Stuart?' said James. 'Yes, I like Andrea' replied Stuart enthusiastically. 'Then it looks like Andrea it is,' smiled Linda.

Sam, the woman in the next bed to Linda, had a baby girl a few hours after Linda. She was a character, a big girl with a deep voice and not very feminine at all, Linda was sore with laughing at her stories. Sam said that her baby girl came out so fast and slippery that she almost flew straight out the open window at the end of the bed because the midwife had trouble catching her. Linda giggled as she pictured the scene because the delivery room was tiny, the bed took up most of the space and there was a big sash window at the bottom of it. It was a tight squeeze with the doctor popping in and out,

James, the midwife, nurse and two trainees. Sam told Linda that her husband had been excited at the prospect of being present at the birth but he went to the toilet for five minutes and missed everything. Because of the speed of her delivery Sam had to have stitches, she said she laid back there with her legs straddled high in the air while the young doctor stitched up her bits, 'Can you do me a monogram?' she asked him, 'Sure what's your initials?' he replied.

Linda and Sam were in the nursery breast-feeding their babies. The upper part of the wall between the nursery and the corridor was glass, Linda was sitting below the glass and Sam was sitting opposite it. Sam wasn't one for being discreet and she sat there topless while she fed and changed her baby, she talked continuously but every now and then she stopped for a breath, smiled and nodded towards the glass above Linda's head. 'The nurses must be busy today!' exclaimed Linda 'Why do you say that?' asked Sam, 'because you keep nodding to them in the corridor,' answered Linda. 'No it's not the nurses I'm nodding at, it's a young doctor out there, he must be new because I haven't seen him before' Sam said. Linda turned round and she saw a young man wearing a white coat then she went into fits of hysterical laughter. 'What? What's so funny?' asked Sam. Linda managed to blurt out between gasping for breath and giggles 'That's not a doctor Sam, that's the window cleaner and you have just been giving him the treat of a lifetime!' Sam roared loudly with laughter, she wasn't the sort to get embarrassed. 'Oh well, I hope I've made his day for him, he'll go home a happy boy now' she giggled.

On the day that Linda was due to bring baby Andrea home from hospital, James took the day of work. Stuart and Amanda went to school reluctantly because they wanted to see their mummy and baby sister but James assured them that they would be waiting for them indoors when they got home that day. Linda was discharged from the hospital at lunchtime, she was home by 2pm. James, opened the front door and took Linda's case in first then went back to help his wife. He carefully picked up his new wee daughter and talked to her as he showed her round the house starting with the playroom. Just after 3pm James set off for the school to pick up Stuart and Amanda. Their excitement was immense and they ran all the way home to see their mummy and new baby sister. They stood at the front door impatiently while James fumbled for his keys, as soon as the door unlocked they pushed it open and ran to the lounge, 'mummy, mummy' they shouted in unison as Linda threw her arms around them hugging them emotionally saying, 'oh you don't know how much I have missed you two! Look come and see your baby, she's in the carrycot by the fireplace' The children peered into the carrycot and touched their new baby's hands, 'When can she come out to play with me mummy?' asked Amanda 'Oh not for a wee while yet, she has to learn to walk and talk first!' laughed Linda.

April 1977, the Queen's Silver Jubilee was approaching. 'What do you think about a street party to celebrate?' James asked Linda. 'I think that's a great idea, it would help everyone to get to know one another, but we can't organize it on our own, we do enough gratis jobs in Apple Blossom Way!' exclaimed Linda. 'Yes, you're right, we would need to organize a committee but there's not much time, it's on June 7th!' answered James. Well, I'll type out a short note and you can post one each through everyone's door. Within hours replies came flooding back, almost everyone was up for it, some said they would like to be on the committee, others offered their services and useful items they could get or borrow from work to help out, so with only a few weeks to spare Apple Blossom Way's, Silver Jubilee Street party was underway.

The day of the Silver Jubilee celebrations dawned. There was a wonderful community spirit, everyone in the street had pulled together; all the houses were decorated red, white and blue. The committee had raised money by carrying out two door-to-door raffles every week to help pay for everything. James' mum Molly was staying with them for a visit and had spent the whole week at the sewing machine making bunting to hang from the lampposts. James had arranged for a Jamaican comedy actress who lived in the next street to come and officially open Apple Blossom Way's Street party at 1pm and at 12.45 he set out in his white estate car to collect her. Linda had decorated the car with red, white and blue ribbons. All the residents' children were in fancy dress and they lined both sides of the street waiting for James to return with the celebrity. As the car approached they all started cheering and waving their union jack flags. One of the residents had got a low-loader lorry trailer from work to use as a stage; they decorated it in red, white and blue and parked it across the end of the street. Another resident worked in a caravan sales centre and he borrowed a caravan to use as a dressing room and to store prizes for the children's games. An amateur photographer who lived in the street offered his services and took lots of photos for tenants to buy from him at cost after the event. There were three legged races, egg and spoon races, a fancy dress competition, a prize for the best decorated house, a Punch and Judy show, the table was set the length of the street with all sorts of goodies for the children, and the local press came and took a photo of the children tucking in. Everyone waved and cheered loudly as an airship flew above filming all the street parties from the sky. In the evening the residents enjoyed a disco by a DJ that lived in the street. The atmosphere was electric, it was a warm balmy night, there were tables and chairs set up in front gardens and the booze was flowing. Nosey Rosie and her husband Matt, Rhona the Moaner along with her daughter, son-in-law, Neurotic Nancy, her husband, Ron the Con and his wife were all sitting at the same table, it was the happiest James had seen any of them and later on in the evening they announced to James that they thought Apple Blossom Way needed a Residents Association so they were going to start it up. 'Good idea!' said James thinking to himself, *'God help the housing association if that lot are on the committee!'* People were dancing in the street and everyone was everyone's friend and neighbour, it was a night to remember.

Sure as fate, Nosey Rosie, Matt, Rhona the Moaner along with her daughter, son-in-law, Neurotic Nancy, her husband, Ron the Con and his wife put notes round the doors informing the residents that they had appointed themselves as the Residents Association for Apple Blossom Way. James knew that wasn't democratic because there hadn't been a vote but no-one opposed it because they weren't really interested. Opinions soon changed when this little gang got to work because instead of working for the residents they started behaving like a bunch of 'Little Hitlers' and working against them. Within a week, they were putting letters through resident's doors telling them to tidy up their back gardens, not to walk on the grass at the front, not to park in the lay-by because they decided that was for visitors cars etc, etc, etc. The residents started getting up in arms and complaining to James because they were sick of this little self-appointed mob dictating to them how they should live their lives. Between this and the work attached to the maintenance job, James and Linda were getting fed up having no quality time to themselves. Linda wanted the two of them to enjoy summer with their children and told James she wouldn't be sorry if he decided to pack it up.

James said he would seriously think about it then he went to the garage and got the lawnmower out to make a start on cutting the residents front lawns. Linda despaired that he would never give the job up nor would he ever see that the housing association was using him for cheap labour. That night they were fast asleep when suddenly the phone on their bedside cabinet rang out loudly, Linda woke up with a start and shook James. 'James, the phone's ringing' she said worriedly. James was still asleep as he replied; 'answer it well' then he quickly came round and realized that it was the early hours of the morning. He cautiously picked up the phone, 'Hello' he said then he screwed his face up in a disgusted manner before saying firmly, 'so what would you like me to do?' Linda leaned over to try to hear what was being said. 'What now? This minute?' shouted James then he went on 'I'll come over at MY convenience and don't dare call and disturb my family at this time of the morning, you stupid neurotic bitch!' By this time Linda was throwing her hands in the air and attempting to ask him who it was. James slammed the phone down. 'I don't believe that woman!' he said 'Who?' demanded Linda. 'That nutter across the road....Neurotic Nancy! She's only called to say that I didn't sweep up after myself when I cut her lawn and I left some grass on her drive!' answered James. 'What? At 2am in the morning?' replied Linda. 'That's it, my mind's made up, I'm definitely packing this job in, it's not as if I'm getting anything out of it, I thought it was just going to be a hobby but it's taking up every spare minute I have, I could be spending that time with my family!' said James 'That's what I have been trying to tell you.' answered Linda with relief.

At the end of July 1977, before James had a chance to hand in his notice to the housing association he had a nasty accident when he slipped off a roof at work on a building site; he shattered his heel bones and was told he would have to rest for at least three months. He decided that he would use this time as an excuse to introduce and supervise local building firms to carry out the maintenance required in Apple Blossom Way and instructed them to invoice the housing association for payment. A few residents ignored the plea to put any repairs needing attending to in writing and post it through Linda and James' door and instead they carried on coming to the door and phoning at all times. It was really getting to Linda, as well as looking after the three children and James, some tenants were pestering her with their complaints, some of which were really petty but worst of all was that the housing association hadn't paid James since Christmas for the repairs he had carried out in Apple Blossom Way. Linda had the worry of making ends meet because he wasn't earning. James had bought all the material for the repairs himself so he was well out of pocket. 'This will have to stop, I can't deal with the residents complaints too, especially as we're not being paid for it!' said Linda. James was concerned as he said, 'When I'm back to myself and able to walk again, I'll put it to the housing association that the residents call the local building firm direct for any maintenance jobs, they seem to be coping ok!' 'Brilliant idea, just get these people off our back! He'll soon get fed up though when he realizes how long he has to wait to be paid' answered Linda. 'That won't be our problem!' answered James.

James managed to get about on crutches before the end of August, he was very conscientious and felt guilty about the gardens being overgrown, Linda couldn't understand why because, he was going to pack the job up soon and, as yet, the housing association still hadn't paid any of the invoices he had sent them for cutting the grass. James struggled out to the street on his crutches, holding a trowel and sat on the grass as he weeded the flower beds, he wouldn't get paid for it because the grass had to be cut too before he could invoice them. 'Ron the Con' came out, he seemed genuinely concerned about James and asked if he could help but when James said he wouldn't mind a hand, 'Ron the Con' replied, 'how much will the housing association pay me if I tend to the gardens while you are sick? I am on shift work so I could see to the work during the day.' James was taken aback but bearing in mind that Linda wasn't happy about being tied down with all the extra work and especially as it wasn't bringing in any extra money because the housing association were so far behind in paying their invoices, James found himself saying, 'Why don't you call them Ron, tell them you've spoken to me and I'm happy about it because I am incapacitated,' 'Great, I'll go inside and call them now,' replied 'Ron the Con'. Ten minutes later he was back, with a grin beaming from ear to ear, 'Thanks for that James, they've agreed to pay me £20 for every time I do the gardens, that twenty quid a week will come in really handy,' he said rubbing his hands together. James was stuck for words, '£20, how did you manage to get them to agree to that, they only pay me a fiver?' said James. 'A fiver, you're joking! I told them I wouldn't even look at it for less than £20,' replied 'Ron the Con'. James felt angry with the housing association but he was glad to offload the work and he didn't mention to 'Ron the Con' how long he would have to wait to be paid.

Meanwhile the Residents Association approached James and said that they wanted a new 'No Balls Games' sign because one had disappeared. There was no 'please or thank you'; they just assumed that it was James' place to supply it to them free of charge. Linda was angry that James didn't emphasize that he had made and donated the last signs free of charge. 'How dare they order you to make a new sign! Who do these people think they are?' said Linda angrily.

James was balancing on his crutches over a bench in his garage making the sign, he had just finished it and was waiting for it to dry so he came out to his garden to relax and have a cup of tea when suddenly 'Rhona the Moaner' who was sunbathing on a folding sun bed in her swimming costume on her son-in-laws vegetable patch, shouted over the fence arrogantly, 'Isn't that sign ready yet? We ordered them over a week ago, what's the hold-up?' Now James was very mild mannered, it took a lot to make him lose his temper but he boiled over at that point. As he hobbled back into the garage he was thinking, *'How dare she! Who does she think he is? I am on the sick and I'm doing them a big favour at my own expense!'* He shoved the sign under his arm, calmly hobbled back into the back garden on his crutches, then slung the sign into 'Rhona the Moaners' back garden as he shouted, 'There's your precious f*****g sign, you ungrateful bitch, stick it up your arse!' This behaviour was extremely out-of-character for James, it can only be assumed that as he was normally a very strong, active and independent man, he was frustrated and depressed with his lack of mobility. 'Rhona the Moaner' was taken aback, she wasn't expecting this reaction, she had it in her head that when she spoke, everyone jumped to attention, she was well and truly brought down to size and she didn't like it one little bit. The next thing she pulled her flowery kaftan over her swimming costume and marched out into the street with her nose in the air, straight to Neurotic Nancy's house, obviously to report the event to her little bunch of dictators. This made James decide there and then that he had enough of ungrateful people taking him for granted and that he was going to hand in his notice immediately into the housing association , it was too much agro for too little (or no) money.

Linda and James were well respected by the majority of the residents in Apple Blossom Way who were nice friendly people, they appreciated that James and Linda had their own lives. The residents Association, on the other hand, had made themselves most unpopular amongst their fellow neighbours, people living in the street wanted rid of them and tension was building up. One of the tenants discovered that the residents association was planning to have a meeting and warned James and Linda that apparently the main agenda was to discuss a new caretaker but most importantly they wanted James and Linda's house because they insisted that they wanted a caretaker who lived on site. James was livid, 'Who do these people think they are? I'm not a caretaker, I deal with their maintenance and I am well out of pocket because the housing association are lousy payers, they don't realize how lucky they are!' said James furiously. Linda was happy, she had wanted James to give the job up long ago because they got nothing out of it and it interfered with their personal life too much. On the evening of the committee meeting at Neurotic Nancy's house, James watched from his window as all the little dictators filed in the door, he gave them fifteen minutes then he hobbled over on his crutches to Neurotic 'Nancy's and rang the bell. Neurotic Nancy was taken aback when she opened the door to see James standing there, 'Can I come in?' he asked firmly with pursed lips as he clumsily brushed past Neurotic Nancy on his crutches into the hallway. He threw open the living room door and announced in a loud serious tone, 'If anyone has anything to say about me then say it to my face!' There was a long pause then Nosey Rosie sheepishly started off in a nervous stammer 'W-e-e-e-ll, y-you l-o-ost your temper with Rhona for no reason, you threw the 'No ball Games' sign and missed her by a fraction of an inch, you could have killed her!' said Nosey Rosie. 'Bollocks! Answered James, then he informed them 'I threw the 'No Ball Games' sign in her garden, absolutely nowhere near her, after she nagged me to finish it! I was doing this as a favour for you lot at my own expense, tell me who was going to pay me? Certainly not you nor the housing association! Oh and while we're on the subject, I am NOT a caretaker, I deal with the maintenance as a favour to the housing association, it's not a job, it's more a hobby, they don't pay me for months, half the jobs I don't even invoice them for and when I am fortunate enough to get any money out of them, it is only a mere pittance. I pay my rent just the same as you lot, it's my family home. I won't be giving up my house to a caretaker so you can take that idea right off your agenda NOW!' Demanded James with an authority that none of the little dictators had seen him use before. 'Yes, but you're supposed to do the gardens and Ron has been doing it for you out of the goodness of his heart, otherwise they would be all overgrown!' said Neurotic Nancy with a sly 'know-it- all' smirk. 'What? Do you mean Ron hasn't told the true facts?' Said James calmly as he looked over at Ron whose face was now beetroot red. 'Well Ron, do you want to tell them or shall I? No, I'll put them in the picture. Ron offered to take over the gardens for me because of my injuries but the price had to be right! He's getting £20 every time he tidies up your gardens whereas I only got £5 but he wouldn't do it for that so the housing association hands were tied,' James could hear the gasps, 'Is that right Ron, why didn't you tell us?' asked Rhona the Moaner, 'W..w..well, it's j..j..just a nominal fee?' stammered Ron. 'Some Nominal fee it's four times what I got, quite honestly I'm glad to be rid of this lot, it's been nothing but hassle, I've lost count of the amount of favours I've done for residents (you lot included) and repairs that I have never charged the housing association for. On the occasions I have had to invoice them for materials, I have to wait months for my money. Over and above everything else, myself and Linda have the inconvenience of people like you creating an unnecessary extra workload and giving us GBH in our ear holes at all times of the day and night with petty complaints against the other residents about them not keeping their back gardens up to your pathetic self-made standards or neighbour's radios being played too loud! No, I'm sick of all the stick myself and Linda have had to suffer from people like you, one of you can take the job on, you seem to think you know so much about it?' said James then he turned and looked at them in disgust and added 'You haven't got a clue, none of you!' He left with a feeling of self satisfaction.

The following week, one of James' contacts in the building industry offered him a sub-contracting job which was due to start in November, just in time for him returning to work. He and Linda talked it over, it would mean a lot of responsibility, he would have to find all the carpenters and labourers for the building site in question, this would mean a lot of paperwork for both he and Linda, pricing up the job, accounts, time sheets, making up wages, tax forms etc., etc., etc., but they decided that it was a great opportunity and a chance they had to take. They had nothing to lose, if it didn't work out, he could always go back to working for someone else on the other hand if it did work out this could be a wonderful step up the ladder of prosperity for them.

Ten

Summer 1986 and life was good, James and Linda had taken that gamble nine years previously and things had snowballed. He was now the main subcontractor on sites for large developers in London and the south east of England. At any time James had up to eighty men working for him. He was too busy now to work on the tools himself and spent more time travelling from site to site to check up on the standard of work and make sure his men were working to schedule. Linda now worked part time, three days per week as a book-keeper in the office of a local engineering firm; she also attended to James' company accounts and wages etc. They owned their house now because the housing association in Manchester had struggled on without James as their maintenance representative in Apple Blossom Way for two years but they were finding it too difficult to cope so they offered the residents the chance to buy their houses at discount, this was the best news Linda and James could possibly hope for. They were worried that the offer would be withdrawn again so with the help of a friend who was a mortgage broker they were able to quickly organise their mortgage. All but five of the residents purchased their homes from the housing association, they were very grateful to James and Linda and were only too aware that the only reason they got this wonderful opportunity was because the housing association in Manchester didn't have the means to maintain Apple Blossom Way from so far away and they found it impossible to manage without James' voluntary contribution to the maintenance of their houses. Linda and James house was valued on the market at £38,000. They scraped together the deposit and in the early months of 1980, they were the first residents to purchase their home for the bargain sum of £26,600.

They both worked hard and played hard, James now had three company vans and Linda had an XJ6 Jaguar in British racing green. All the family were well kitted out in excellent quality clothes and apart from their regular visits to see their parents in Scotland, they were able to take the children abroad on holiday which was a far cry from a few years before when all they could afford was camping holidays.

'The Riverside Inn' was a new pub/restaurant that had opened nearby on the banks of the River Thames. James and Linda often frequented it as well as their local 'The Royal Crest' which James had used for years. James was well respected at 'The Royal Crest,' every Christmas Eve he invited all his workers to the pub for a Christmas drink; he packed the place out from lunchtime onwards, paid for food and put £500 over the bar for drinks. Ricky the poof, as he was affectionately known and answered to, still worked in The Royal Crest'. He loved it when James brought all his builders into the pub, he teased them mercilessly and they, in turn, took it all in good fun. Ricky's old boyfriend Dicky had passed away five years previously and Ricky now had a new lover called 'Mickey'.

Linda usually called into the pub around teatime, the lads held her in high regard and they all treated her with great respect. One or two would shout out in mock panic, 'the Governor's missus is here!' and they would then stand to attention and salute. Linda usually ended up doing two or three car runs taking home stragglers who didn't have a lift before she and James finally returned home themselves.

Ricky the Poof invited James and Linda along to the pub to celebrate his 40th Birthday on a Friday evening. It was to go on after hours in order to bring Ricky's birthday in at midnight on the Saturday. Linda arrived wearing a new 'Sherlock Holmes' type leather coat, Ricky and Mickey both gasped in admiration. By 10pm the pub was packed with party revelers, including the local rugby team. When the doors of the pub shut at closing time, there were just approximately twenty invited guests left. Ricky brought out a wonderful buffet for his friends which he had prepared himself. By this time there wasn't a sober person in the house and the rugby team started singing.....'*There was a young man*.........Apparently everyone had to sing a verse and if you couldn't think of one then you had to take an item of clothing off. Linda was mortified, the doors were locked, what was she to do? As the person next to her finished singing, everyone looked at her; Ricky had a cheeky grin as he looked the terrified Linda straight in the eye. Suddenly, without thinking twice, she burst out with........

There was a young fellow called Dirkin,
Who was always jerkin' his gherkin,
His mother said Dirkin, stop jerkin your gherkin,
Your gherkin's for firkin' not jerkin'

The whole place erupted with laughter; Linda remembered it from a Matt McGinn LP called 'The Two-Heided Man' that she and James had. She couldn't believe she had actually sung it in front of all these people but it saved the day for her! The local rugby team thought it was a classic and asked her to write the verse down for them saying that they were going to add it to their official club song. Ricky had a devilish sense of humour and was always teasing James, who made no secret about letting Ricky know in no uncertain terms that he wasn't interested in gays; this became a joke between them. As they were getting ready to go, Ricky put Linda's long leather coat on then he walked up behind James and put his arms around him. James was very drunk and thinking it was Linda, he didn't flinch. As James turned round, Ricky snuggled into him and jokingly went to kiss him, suddenly James became aware of what was going on and shouted at the top of his voice, 'bugger off you poof!' He seemed to sober up immediately while Ricky was laughing uncontrollably as he blurted out in between wiping tears from his eyes, 'I nearly got you that time!'

Ricky had the evening off for his birthday on Saturday so fourteen of them, including Linda and James, booked a table for dinner at 'The Riverside Inn.' Mo and Patsy The landlord and landlady invited them all to stay behind for a celebratory drink after hours and they all got very merry. It was a very hot and balmy August evening, suddenly one of the women, Alison, said, 'I'm going for a swim to cool down, and before anyone could stop her, she had stripped down to her bra, waist petticoat and pants and had jumped into the River Thames. This encouraged the others to do the same and there were a dozen folk swimming around in the dark. James stood at the riverbank and started to take off his top, 'What do you think you're doing?' demanded Linda. 'I'm going for a swim' replied James through a laughing slur. 'Oh no, you're not, you're not in any fit state to walk home never mind swim in the Thames!' answered Linda sharply. James looked at her and put on a drunken petted lip but did as he was told. Alison's husband Jake was swimming out at the middle when suddenly he started shouting, 'Help! Help!' Linda froze on the spot, she knew the river was dangerous with currents and it was foolhardy to go swimming in it at any time never mind in the pitch black and drunk. 'What's up Jake?' shouted Alison, 'I've lost my boxers, they've slipped off,' he replied in a panic. 'Oh is that all, I thought you were in trouble!' Alison shouted back. Jake shouted out, 'Someone help me then!' but no-one did, they all thought it was funny and dared him to come out of the water. Finally as Jake carried on whimpering for help, Allison swam over to him and said, 'Oh for goodness sake Jake, stop whinging, put this on,' she whipped off her white nylon waist petticoat and handed it to him. Jake gratefully fumbled under the water to pull the petticoat on to cover up his embarrassment. As he climbed out of the water, his friend's laughter echoed along the quiet riverbank, the wet nylon petticoat was completely see-through so he might as well not have bothered. They all made their way back into they pub, it was 1am by this time. 'You lot stink, that water's filthy!' exclaimed Linda. They ordered another round of drinks while they dried out. After about half an hour Alison said, 'Where's Jake?' They searched round the pub and toilet and panic set in again as they realized he was nowhere to be seen and neither was the pub's 12 stone Rottweiler. Mo and Patsy always brought their dog down from the living premises into the pub after closing time. Mo dashed to the faraway doors leading to another toilet, he came back in fits of laughter saying 'I wish I had a camera as he led Jake back into the bar area. Jake was white as a sheet and very sober by this time with fright. Mo told everyone he had found Jake standing trapped in a corner outside the toilets at the other side of the pub, he was still wearing only the petticoat, his hands were grasping and protecting his privates and the Rottweiler's nose was pressing against him as it growled and bore his teeth. Of course it wasn't funny and could have been very serious but Jake got absolutely no sympathy from his pals.

Nine years had made a difference to the residents of Apple Blossom Way. 'Lily and Billy' had split up when she gave birth to a black baby, Billy was shocked and disappointed, he had been so looking forward to becoming a daddy but this obviously wasn't his son. Lily already had six children by different dads. Meanwhile Sex-mad Sadie caught Billy on the rebound and they had an affair. Sadie's husband Greg went berserk when he found a golf tee in their bed; he didn't mind her flirting in front of him but made it quite obvious that he wasn't going to stand for any hanky-panky behind his back. In all the years they had been married, Sadie had never seen Greg so angry, he demanded to know who the golf tee belonged to. Sadie couldn't understand how a golf tee had got into their bed; she assumed it must have belonged to Billy and confessed to her affair. Greg marched over to have it out with Billy, meanwhile Sadie picked up the golf tee, only to discover that it was the applicator for Greg's haemorrhoids cream. 'Oh no, the daft b*****d' she said out loud as she realized that she needn't have told Greg anything, she dashed over to Lily and Billy's but it was too late. Greg had threatened Billy. Lily had called the police and Greg ended up in the back of the police van. What a mess their lives were in. Sadie and Billy's affair came to an abrupt end. Greg didn't want her back and collected his belongings as soon as the police freed him. So Sadie ended up on her own, she had different boyfriends but none of them were permanent. Meanwhile, Lily decided that she had enough of men and turned to a lesbian relationship with another woman called Gilly. They were very happy together and this time Lily's relationship seemed to be lasting so it was now 'Lily and Gilly' not 'Lily and Billy', the nick-name was almost the same but the sex was different. They bought their house and Gilly completely renovated it, she was a big, scary, butch woman with a shaved head. The teenagers in the street used to tease Gilly, calling her a man. One day Gilly marched across the road, lifted her top showing her bra-less saggy boobs and bellowed, 'These are tits, men don't have tits, now f**k off!' The kids were struck dumb and stared in amazement but they never bothered Gilly again. In 1984 Lilly and Gilly sold their house and moved to the continent. They made a big profit and were able to buy a villa in Spain and still had a good few thousand pounds left over.

'Rainbow Barbara' sold her house and bought a shop with a flat above in Surbiton. She was in her glory selling her home-made jewellery, toys and clothes etc.

'Nosey Rosie' and her husband Matt took advantage of the deal to buy their house. This gave her more power to be able to move whenever she felt the need. This is exactly what happened, she decided she didn't like her neighbours and moved to another house in a new development a couple of streets away but that only lasted three years and she moved again. Linda and James lost track of her after that.

'Rhona the Moaner's' daughter put her out after her husband threatened either she went or he did. Rhona was now living in a one-bedroom rented flat which brought her right down to earth. Rhona's daughter and her husband decided to make a clean start, they sold their house and moved into a Victorian house at the other side of town. They didn't speak to Rhona because she had made too many enemies for them.

'Lisa the Teaser' now lived in the south of France. Five years after she bought her house she gifted it to her grown-up children after she met and married a millionaire businessman.

'Neurotic Nancy's' husband couldn't take anymore. They sold their house and split the money. He moved into a flat and she bought a smaller house for herself and her young daughter.

'Ron the Con' had bought his house. His son and daughter inherited it when he died at the age of ninety one. They sold the house and were able to buy themselves a flat each from the proceeds. They lived comfortably on all the money he had miserly stashed away over the years.

James and Linda's Irish friends Colleen and Gerry had bought their house months after Linda and James. They went on to have a son and another daughter and now had four children. In the mid 1980's they sold up and were able to by a bungalow and a retail business back home in Southern Ireland with the proceeds.

By the millennium, there were all new people living in Apple Blossom Way; James and Linda were out at work most of the time so hardly knew any of their neighbours anymore. Their children had grown up and moved out to places of their own. James mother Molly and Linda's parents, Douglas and Margie had all passed away a few years previously. They felt that their house was too big for just the two of them. They thought long and hard about which way to turn then made a big decision to retire early and move back to Scotland.

They worked out that they could live comfortably on their private pensions, would have enough equity in their Kingston house to buy a nice place north of the border and there would be plenty money left over for a rainy day. They talked it over with their children who were fine about it because they knew that their parent's hearts were in Scotland, it was only an hour's flight away and that they would still be able to see each other at anytime.

James and Linda didn't rush into anything; they took their time to make sure they had made the right decision and by mid-summer 2002 they were living in a beautiful bungalow on the west coast of Scotland overlooking the River Clyde near Largs.

May 2008, Linda and James' children are all married, they have five grandchildren now and they couldn't be happier. Their family all come to visit them every opportunity they have and James and Linda fly down to London on a regular basis.

'Well we certainly have come the full circle haven't we?' said James as he gave Linda a cuddle. 'Yes, when I think of the chance we took in life, no wonder my mother was worried, we went down to London with a toddler, another baby on the way and only £32 in the bank between us!' replied Linda. 'Yes, but our gamble paid off didn't it?' smiled James. 'It certainly did, what would our parents say now if they knew we owned outright a house worth £400,000 plus a very comfortable bank account? 'Yes who would have thought that our house in Apple Blossom Way would eventually be worth almost half a million, we had some wonderful neighbours there but no-one would believe what went on behind some of the closed doors, it was like Peyton Place at times, you could write a book about it!' laughed Linda then she went on to say, 'Time flies past so quick, it's hard to imagine that our kids are all happily married with children of their own and all have bought their own houses! We have five beautiful grandchildren, what more could we want in life?' said Linda as James chipped in with 'We've had some hard struggles on the way, but we've also had some great times. 'There's one thing I would never change about my life, I was only a boy but it was the biggest and best decision I ever made 39 years ago.' 'Oh and what was that?' enquired Linda with a giggle. 'As if you don't know Mrs. Alexander!' replied James as he pulled Linda towards him and kissed her saying, 'My wee wife Linda Macgregor, you're the best thing that ever happened to me!' Linda wrapped her arms tightly round him and replied 'We are soul mates James Alexander; I could never picture life without you either!' James reminisced, 'We've worked hard together for everything we've got, we also contributed a lot to many lives down south, I could never begin to count the amount of houses in the south east of England that I have built or worked in plus we gave jobs to, trained and employed all these people!' Linda joined in with, 'Don't forget all the people in Apple Blossom Way who were able to buy their house and make better lives for themselves because you forced the housing association into selling!' James replied, 'No Linda that was more your doing, if it had been left to me, I would probably still be working away for nothing and making the housing association rich! You are the person that all these particular people of Apple Blossom Way owe their prosperity to; you gave me the ultimatum to tell the housing association I was finished with working for them. This was the best thing you ever did because after that it was obvious that the housing association couldn't cope and were forced to offer us our homes for sale at discount AND you were the one who gave me the encouragement to take on the sub-contracting job! You gave me the confidence and told me I was perfectly capable of doing the job but at the same time you made it clear that there wouldn't be a problem if it didn't work out and had to return to working on the sites for someone else. You're some woman Linda MacGregor!' said James as he held Linda lovingly in his arms. 'Incase you've forgotten my name is Linda Alexander, it has been for the past 39 years,' laughed Linda. 'Your name might be Alexander by marriage but there's only one Linda MacGregor, yo showed me over the years that life is what you make it,' answere James. Linda snuggled up to her husband and smiled as she replie 'In other words you get nothing for nothing in this life, if you wo hard and 'Chase that Carrot' then 'What's For Ye, Won't Go By 'Precisely' nodded James in agreement.

---THE END---